THE COMPLETE CASES OF PETER KANE

Hugh B. Cave

HUGH B. CAVE

THE COMPLETE CASES OF

PETER KANE™

HUGH B. CAVE

INTRODUCTION BY

BOB BYRNE

ILLUSTRATIONS BY

JOHN FLEMING GOULD

BOSTON • 2018

PUBLISHING HISTORY

"The Late Mr. Smythe" originally appeared in the August 1, 1934 issue of *Dime Detective* magazine. Copyright 1934 by Popular Publications, Inc. Copyright renewed 1961 and assigned to Steeger Properties, LLC. All rights reserved.

"Hell on Hume Street" originally appeared in the November 1, 1934 issue of *Dime Detective* magazine. Copyright 1934 by Popular Publications, Inc. Copyright renewed 1961 and assigned to Steeger Properties, LLC. All rights reserved.

"Bottled in Blonde" originally appeared in the January 1, 1935 issue of *Dime Detective* magazine. Copyright 1935 by Popular Publications, Inc. Copyright renewed 1962 and assigned to Steeger Properties, LLC. All rights reserved.

"The Man Who Looked Sick" originally appeared in the April 1, 1935 issue of *Dime Detective* magazine. Copyright 1935 by Popular Publications, Inc. Copyright renewed 1962 and assigned to Steeger Properties, LLC. All rights reserved.

"The Screaming Phantom" originally appeared in the May 1, 1935 issue of *Dime Detective* magazine. Copyright 1935 by Popular Publications, Inc. Copyright renewed 1962 and assigned to Steeger Properties, LLC. All rights reserved.

"The Brand of Kane" originally appeared in the June 15, 1935 issue of *Dime Detective* magazine. Copyright 1935 by Popular Publications, Inc. Copyright renewed 1962 and assigned to Steeger Properties, LLC. All rights reserved.

"Ding Dong Belle" originally appeared in the August, 1941 issue of *Dime Detective* magazine. Copyright 1941 by Popular Publications, Inc. Copyright renewed 1968 and assigned to Steeger Properties, LLC. All rights reserved.

"The Dead Don't Swim" originally appeared in the November, 1941 issue of *Dime Detective* magazine. Copyright 1941 by Popular Publications, Inc. Copyright renewed 1968 and assigned to Steeger Properties, LLC. All rights reserved.

"No Place to Hide" originally appeared in the February, 1942 issue of *Dime Detective* magazine. Copyright 1942 by Popular Publications, Inc. Copyright renewed 1969 and assigned to Steeger Properties, LLC. All rights reserved.

TABLE OF CONTENTS

INTRODUCTION i

THE LATE MR. SMYTHE 1

HELL ON HUME STREET 41

BOTTLED IN BLONDE 79

THE MAN WHO LOOKED SICK 115

THE SCREAMING PHANTOM 159

THE BRAND OF KANE 201

DING DONG BELLE 243

THE DEAD DON'T SWIM 275

NO PLACE TO HIDE 305

KANE'S OLD MAN 341

INTRODUCTION
BOB BYRNE

HUGH B. CAVE was the last of the great pulp-sters. From hundreds of short stories in the pulp magazines of the thirties, to his final novel in 2004, Cave wrote over a thousand shorts and over three dozen novels. He was also a war reporter and later even owned and managed a coffee plantation in Jamaica.

While H.P. Lovecraft, Clark Ashton Smith, August Derleth and Robert E. Howard are better remembered for weird menace/horror stories, Cave is worthy of standing alongside them. But early in his career, Cave also wrote extensively in the mystery field.

He was one of the few to write for the last three (named) editors of the king of mystery pulps, *Black Mask:* the legendary Joseph 'Cap' Shaw, Fanny Ellsworth and Kenneth S. White.

Black Mask's major competition came in the form of *Dime Detective Magazine,* which touted itself as "twice as good—for half the price" *(Black Mask* cost 20 cents at the time; though the price would shortly drop to 15 cents, in part due to *Dime Detective's* success at the cheaper cost).

Editor Kenneth White was instructed to lure as many writers from *Black Mask* as he could, paying an extra penny a word as enticement. And with a going rate of one to two cents for pulp writers *(Black Mask's* three cents a word was indicative of its standing and quality in the field), the four cent rate made a significant difference to writers. As the prolific Erle Stanley Gardner supposedly replied to observations that he always seemed to use his hero's last bullet to knock off the story's antagonist:

> At three cents a word, every time I say "Bang" in the story I get three cents. If you think I'm going to finish the gun battle while my hero still has fifteen cents worth of unexploded ammunition in his gun, you're nuts.

Writers were forbidden from doing novel serializations and were also instructed to create their own characters, which could not appear elsewhere, for the magazine. The onslaught was successful, with many of the era's most popular writers switching to *Dime Detective*. Carroll John Daly (who brought the iconic Race Williams with him), Erle Stanley Gardner, Frederick Nebel and Norbert Davis (whose humorous stories were frequently rejected by Shaw but who flourished at his new home) were among those lured to *Dime Detective*.

Some authors would publish stories in other magazines but never return to *Black Mask* after moving to *Dime Detective*. Many fans would say that the best of those who switched was Frederick Nebel, Cap Shaw's hand-picked successor to Hammett when Dash left the pulps for more lucrative writing pastures. I'm one of those fans.

Nebel was the creator of *Black Mask* staples MacBride and Kennedy and Tough Dick Donahue, and his Jack Cardigan of the Cosmos Detective Agency dominated the pages of *Dime Detective*.

But for the combination of entertainment value and quality writing, Cave, who was far more than just a weird menace pulpster, might have topped the list with his Peter

Kane stories (though Davis' Max Latin probably has his adherents).

And now that we've finished the *"Dime Detective* Primer" portion of our Introduction, let's turn to the star of this book!

Cave wrote for over a dozen mystery pulps, including *Black Book Detective, Detective Fiction Weekly, Double Detective, Private Detective Stories, Super Detective Stories* and *Spicy Detective Stories* (notice a common theme in naming conventions?). He had largely left the detective genre by the mid-forties, focusing his efforts in other fields—especially the horror/weird menace genre. There would be a story here and there, with brief spurts of activity in the field, but Cave's mystery days were effectively behind him.

Long before Robert B. Parker, William Tapply, Linda Barnes and others made Boston the backdrop for their mysteries, New Englander Cave was already there. From August, 1934 through July, 1935, *Dime Detective* featured six tales of Peter Kane, the biggest and best detective at Boston's Beacon Agency. The private eye would return in August and November of 1941, with a final appearance in February of 1942.

Kane was a Drunk. Note the capital "D." He didn't have hangovers because he was always too drunk to enter hangover mode (that's a slight exaggeration, but not by much). Yet, somehow, he functioned while constantly inebriated to varying degrees.

The picture is painted pretty clearly in the first paragraph of the debut story, "The Late Mr. Smythe:"

> The room was beginning to go round and round, faster and faster, like a monstrous revolving barrel in a beach-resort playhouse. Peter Kane heaved himself off the bed and stood swaying.

He had flopped into bed drunk. Now, after sleeping five hours and lying awake for another hour, staring at an unsteady ceiling, he was drunker. And sick.

Here's our initial view of him in the following tale, "Hell on Hume Street:"

> Peter Kane… was drunk. Kane had been drunk more or less, mostly more, for a period running into its third liquid week. He knew he was drunk and he liked to be drunk.

It would be easy to dismiss Kane as just a caricature: A stereotype of the drunken, ex-cop P.I. But Cave is too good of a writer to let that happen. Anne, Kane's former girlfriend, now married to police captain Moe Finch, enters after that description and we read, "Kane put both hands on the table and pushed himself to his feet, wishing suddenly that he were not drunk, at least not so drunk that it showed…. Then he wanted to be very drunk, because there was something in the woman's dark eyes, something accusing and—and pitying—that made him feel really rotten down inside."

Then we learn about Kane's past relationship with Anne, how and why it ended, and the role that Moroni, Kane's rival on the force, played in it all. The groundwork is in place for the rest of the series. And it is all deftly handled by Cave.

Cave excels in describing Kane's drunken movements and moments: "…his top-heavy body rocked from side to side…," and "Steering an unsteady course…." And that's just on page one of the first story.

> On a job like this, with Large Mouth Moroni and a lot of heaving green ocean all over the place, the only thing to do was to get thoroughly plastered and remain that way.

In the hands of a lesser writer, the final confrontation in "Hell on Hume Street" would read like a farce. But there's nothing funny the way Cave tells it. Hugh B. Cave was a Writer with a capital 'W.'

There are two regulars in the series: Captain Moe Finch, Kane's former boss on the force, and Lieutenant Moroni. Both appear in eight of the nine stories, in very different roles.

Kane despises Moroni. When he finds a mechanical cockroach, he names it Moroni. Throughout the series, the cop is tagged with sneering nicknames such as "The Wise One," "Know It all" and "The Great Brain."

We learn early on that when Kane was going off the rails with drink, Moroni helped ensure that Kane (a better detective than he was) was booted from the force. And a drunk with no job was a bad bet for a young woman—so even though Anne loved Kane, she married Moe Finch. Anne is presented as noble and good, though there's certainly another angle one could take on that.

Moroni yells and bullies, though it doesn't appear that he beats confessions out of suspects. His deductions aren't terrible, but he's always wrong—and Kane's always (eventually) right. It's certainly not beyond Kane to let Moroni think that the policeman is on the right track: and then expose him at the finish. And in front of the press when suitable.

Moroni wants Finch's job. He constantly arranges matters so that he gets the credit when things go well, and mildly explains that he was just following Finch's directions when they don't. He grows more ambitious, snarling at Kane "I had my fill of you when Moe Finch was in his prime, Kane. I've got more to say now, and I'm tough!"

Kane never responds in kind to Moroni's volume and anger. Throughout the series, he replies softly, but clearly in a dismissive manner: "Dear, dear," "Wouldn't I, though?" "I'm all ears," " 'In case you hadn't noticed, he's dead,' Kane said, shaking his head in mock pity."

Moroni hates Kane at least as much as Kane hates him, so their enmity is a constant. It's almost jarring when they sort of, kind of work together in "The Man Who Looked Sick."

The other regular is police captain Moe Finch, who comes across as a weak sister. He mostly whines to Kane about needing his help, occasionally shifting to resignedly complaining that Moroni is undermining him. Finch is, frankly, tiresome:

> The voice took on a plaintive wine. "I thought you was gonna help me out Kane. I thought you were gonna stay sober long enough to be a pal. Here I am in a jam, and you were gonna...."
>
> ...and for an hour (Finch) moaned his troubles into Kane's unwilling ears.... "I'm in a spot. I need help. Even from a drunken, no-good private shamus like you, I need help.... Be a pal."
>
> "I been hoping you'd show up. So help me, I'm frantic... You're a pal, Kane; so help me, you are. I figured you'd be out drinking somewhere...Where you going?" Finch wailed.
>
> "I thought you were going to be a pal and help me out. Now look! Plastered to the gills!"
>
> Moe Finch looked small and worried behind his desk.

Finch never actually steps up even once, though Cave does paint him as a devoted husband and noble cop who doesn't have time to cater to the press and play the political game in the latter part of the series. But it doesn't really salvage Finch, who seems to exist primarily so somebody "good" wins when Kane beats Moroni. It's a rather unsatisfying role.

Of the nine stories, "The Screaming Phantom" is notable for a couple of reasons. First and foremost, it's a weird menace story, and that's the genre in which Cave is regarded as one of the best. Kane, drunk as usual, and thus hours late for an out-of-town assignment, finds himself driving past a closed amusement park in the dead of night (and the dead of winter). He witnesses (he thinks) a screaming, naked girl riding in a roller coaster car that is guaranteed to go flying off of the icy tracks. There's more spookiness, murder and rough stuff for Kane as the story goes on. Because of the weird menace overtones, it's one of my favorites.

Normally, Kane sums up the case at police headquarters, explaining things to a grateful Finch and an angry Moroni. That's not gonna work in this story. So, we find Kane, sitting at his desk at the Beacon Detective Agency, drinking from the bottle he keeps in a drawer and explaining things to the "competent blonde" who works in the office. Kane had stopped at his desk in one earlier story, grabbing some mail and leaving. This gumshoe drinks and goes places. He actually does his thinking in a bar called Limpy's. His office is not an important part of the series, but it's where this story ends.

The first couple stories involve typical city settings. "The Screaming Phantom" put Kane in a more distinctive locale; a closed-down amusement park. The next story, "The Brand of Kane," forced the drunken detective to work aboard a grounded steamship. "The Dead Don't Swim" is out of town and the final tale, "No Place to Hide," takes place in a country rest home. So, Cave expanded his terrain in the later stories—possibly to keep his interest in the character.

Kane brings to mind Carroll John Daly's Race Williams, who came before, and Mickey Spillane's Mike Hammer, who came after. Simply put, Cave was a better writer than Daly. And it's hard to put a finger on it, but Kane has more depth (though a lot less sex!) than the ultra-hard-boiled Hammer. Cave's plotting is relatively straight-forward compared to the labyrinthine mazes created by Raymond Chandler. But they're not simple and they allow Kane and Moroni to go down separate mean streets before coming back together for the finale. And that is a key element of the series.

You hold in your hands perhaps the best of the hard drinking, two fisted pulp private eyes. Kane is not well-remembered in the field, and the stories are not routinely listed among Cave's best works. But the Boston detective can stand up to Philip Marlowe, Jack Cardigan, Sam Spade and the others; though he might wobble a little and have trouble focusing on them!

Bob Byrne blogs for the World Fantasy Award-winning site, BlackGate. com and has contributed to several volumes of the MX Book of New Sherlock Holmes Stories. *He is a leading expert on August Derleth's Solar Pons (www.SolarPons.com) and has been nominated multiple times for The Robert E. Howard Foundation Awards. He is a periodic contributor to* Black Mask Magazine.

THE LATE MR. SMYTHE

ALIVE, SMYTHE HAD BEEN JUST
AS MUCH OF A PHONY AS THE "Y"
IN HIS NAME. AND WHEN HE GOT
BUMPED OFF IN HIS KITCHENETTE
EVERYONE WAS PLEASED—
INCLUDING THE COPS. BUT EVEN
PHONIES, WHEN THEY ARE
MURDERED, MUST BE AVENGED.
THOUGH IT TAKE THE WHOLE
DETECTIVE FORCE AND A VERY
DRUNK SHAMUS TO BOOT.

CHAPTER ONE
CURTAINS FOR TWO

THE ROOM was beginning to go round and round, faster and faster, like a monstrous revolving barrel in a beach-resort playhouse. Kane heaved himself off the bed and stood up, stood swaying. He had flopped into bed drunk; now, after sleeping five hours and lying awake another hour staring at an unsteady ceiling, he was drunker—and sick.

He was a big man, the biggest on the Beacon Agency payroll, and when he walked very slowly out of the bedroom, down the apartment hallway into the sitting room, his top-heavy body rocked from side to side like something on the deck of a wallowing ship. He had bloodshot eyes and dry gray hair, and his thin lips curled inward as if holding a dangling cigarette. He stood swaying over a smoke stand, aimed a cigarette at his mouth, turned a slow half-circle and listened to the phone ringing.

He steered an unsteady course to the table, let his hand flop down on the instrument, picked the thing up and said into it, with his head rolling: "Yeah? Wha's trouble?"

A masculine voice with a growl in it said: "And how is little Peter Kane *this* morning?"

"Lousy, Finch. Lousy."

"You had one swell time last night. I heard all about it."

"I'm having one right now."

"Listen." The voice took on a plaintive whine. "I thought you were gonna help me out. I thought you were gonna stay sober long enough to be a pal of mine. Here I am in a jam, and you were gonna be a swell guy and—"

"All right, all right." Kane scowled down at himself, made a face, He had socks on, a pajama jacket, a pair of blue serge pants covered with lint from the bed-sheets. "I'll be down. Don't get excited so early in the morning." He forked the phone and pressed cold palms against his temples. "Finch," he snorted. "Always Finch when I feel lousy."

HE WENT back to the bedroom and got dressed, thinking about Smiley Smythe. Smiley was a wop and his real name was Cusellero. He was small and neat and had dark keen eyes in a sallow face—a combination the women seemed to go for in large helpings. He spelled his name with a "y" to make them fall harder, and dressed like something out of a Commonwealth Avenue Easter parade; but that hadn't kept him from being rubbed out night before last and left in the kitchenette of his hundred-dollar-a-month apartment, with the back of his head blown out and most of his brains decorating the gas stove.

Moe Finch, down at headquarters, had grinned from mule-ear to mule-ear, leaned over the desk and said glee-fully to a line-up of city dicks: "Now ain't that nice? For six months we try to get something on that blackmailin' rat, and now someone else blows his brains out and saves us time and trouble. But listen"—and Finch's grin had become a growl—"that don't mean you mugs are gonna lay down. Go find out who done it and why, and also when.

For a minute the kid's attention wandered.

"Smiley had a gun in his fist and there was one shot fired out of it. That means there was gunplay, and Smiley was right in his element. The fact that the slug from his gun didn't land in no wall or floor or ceiling or anywheres around the apartment is positive proof he hit what he aimed at. See? And the bullet is right now lodged somewheres in the framework of the guy that killed him. So you got somethin' to work on, anyhow.

"And get this," Finch had said to the city dicks. "This here is a horrible, atrocious murder and the guilty party must be delivered into the hands of justice right away quick. If you don't believe me, look in the papers."

Later, Moe Finch had bumped into Peter Kane in an all-night restaurant and, for an hour, moaned his troubles into Kane's unwilling ears. "I'll probably lose my job, Kane;

that's all it means. Get fired off the department. Because why? Because there ain't a dick on the entire city payroll with enough brains to break this thing down. I'm in a spot; I need help. Even from a drunken, no-good private shamus like you, I need help. You knew Smiley—and all his angles. Be a pal, Kane. When you used to work for the city I was good as hell to you. Be a pal."

Moe Finch had said all that. Standing with one foot on a radiator while he tied knots in a shoelace, Kane remembered Finch's words distinctly. Finch was an optimist. Finding out who had blown Smiley Smythe's block off and spattered those brains all over the gas range would be like finding out who won the war. And the answer was the same to both problems—who cared?

KANE MOPED out of his apartment, ran himself down in the elevator and took a cab to Limpy's on Stuart Street. He asked the driver what time it was; the driver said ten fifteen, took a good look at him and added, "A.M., Tuesday," and grinned. Traffic milled along Huntington Avenue; sunlight ricochetted from fast-moving windshields, stabbed Kane's bloodshot eyes and gave him a headache. He sat on a bar-stool in Limpy's and Limpy squinted at him, mixed him a pick-up of vermouth, rye and Fernet Branca without asking what he wanted. Kane pawed the glass, murmured, "Boy, is my life an open book!" and downed the drink without batting an eye.

Limpy said: "I guess you were on a time last night." He was a small man with a head too big for his shoulders; he had a game leg that dragged when he walked. He'd been a cop, pickpocket, nigger-pooler, night-club operator, and now ran one of the best dine-but-don't-dance places in town. He knew Kane well.

Kane said: "Yeah, I was plastered," and rolled his empty glass around on the bar, making wet circles. The place was empty this early; Limpy's assistant was polishing taps at the far end of the bar. The door opened and a customer came in. The customer glanced at Kane, sat down five stools away and said: " 'Lo, Limpy."

"I hear your pal was bumped off," Limpy said.

"Yeah."

"You'll miss him, huh?"

"Yeah. I'll weep."

The customer was a medium-tall Italian, well dressed in chalky gray; he had a dark, smooth face and even across a distance of five stools Kane caught a sweetish stink of brilliantine from his jet hair. He looked at Kane, smiled with thin lips slightly parted and teeth gleaming white.

"Greetings, gumshoe."

"I been meaning to talk to you," Kane said.

"I'm popular since Smiley went," the Italian said. "But then, I was always popular." That was true; as Smiley's pal, Joe DiVina had always been popular, with con-men and fast ladies. "Already I've had visits from most all of Moe Finch's dumb-head dicks. Scotch, Limpy."

Limpy put Scotch on the bar and did things with a damp rag. DiVina downed the drink, pushed his hat off his eyes, turned slowly on his stool as someone else came in. Kane turned too, grinned, said sarcastically: "Don't tell me you serve muggs like Hoban, Limpy."

"Save it," said the newcomer. He was a moon-faced H.Q. dick and a good guy in spite of his protruding stomach. "I see you're drunk yet. It's a good thing you don't have to work for a living, like me."

He walked toward DiVina and put a hand on DiVina's shoulder. "Moe Finch wants to talk to you, down at headquarters."

The Italian's black dots of eyes narrowed. He climbed off the stool, stared. "Say, listen—"

"Don't be startin' a fuss now. You'll only make me angry. Come along quiet."

DiVina stood very stiff; then he went limp, shrugged, laughed softly. "Don't kid me, Hoban. You ain't got nothin'."

Hoban steered him to the door. Kane, scowling, said: "What is this?"

"Accordin' to Finch, it was this guy spattered Smiley Smythe's brains all over that nice clean gas stove."

THE DOOR closed and Kane sat on his stool, staring at it with big eyes. He cocked his feet up, hooked both heels on the iron half-moon midway up the stool-stem, put his elbows on his knees and made a low whistling sound that stuck on his whiskey-thick tongue.

"Well, who'd've thought it? Imagine Hoban taking time out from his beer drinking to do a thing like that. Can you imagine it, Limpy?"

"I ain't a dick like you. I ain't got enough capacity; I pass out too quick."

"Imagine a guy like DiVina blowing Smiley Smythe's brains out."

"DiVina ain't so soft."

"We should have a drink to Hoban. Have a drink with me to Hoban, Limpy. He's a great guy, even if he does labor for Moe Finch."

Limpy said, "Sure, he's a great guy," and poured rye out of a pint bottle. He pushed the cork back in the bottle and stood suddenly stiff, one hand clutching the neck of the bottle and the other hand poised over the counter. From the street outside came a sound like a typewriter rattle amplified through deep, heavy megaphones. When it stopped, a woman was screaming in a shrill, high-flung voice and people were running past the door, yelling incoherently.

Kane said, "What the hell!" and climbed off his stool; his elbow slapped the glass of rye on the bar and the rye spilled over Limpy's apron. Kane put his feet under him, walked a quick straight line to the door, clawed the door open and stood staring on the sill. Twenty yards distant, in front of a secondhand book store, a knot of excited people milled around something on the sidewalk; the proprietor of the book store was standing wide-legged in his doorway, yelling at a uniformed cop running diagonally across Stuart Street. The window of the book store was perforated by a shoulder-high line of bullet holes that looked like cut-glass flowers.

Kane sucked a deep breath through tight lips and ploughed along the sidewalk, elbowed into the crowd, stood swaying and made large eyes at the thing in the sacred inner circle. Things! He said thickly: "God!" A middle-aged woman with bundles in her arms was croaking: "I seen it happen! The two men was walking along and a car slowed up to the curbing and the men inside the car started shooting with a machine gun even before the car stopped! I seen the whole thing!"

One of the men on the sidewalk was lying face up with his legs buckled; he had sat down first and then tipped over. Blood was bubbling out of his torn vest; a look of panic was on his face; his eyes were bulging and his mouth was wide open. Kane stared down, made a sobbing sound, said gutturally: "Hoban, you poor—damned—"The other man, sprawled face down about four long strides distant, was the Italian Hoban had hauled out of Limpy's. He tried to run for it, had been cut down in flight. He had slid on his face and chest before stopping.

The cop in uniform shoved a hand against Kane's shoulder. "One side, you. One side."

"Take them in Limpy's," Kane mumbled. "Both of them."

"Huh? Say—"

"In Limpy's. And bust up this crowd of buzzards."

The cop gaped. "Oh, it's you. Geez, is this a mess!" He waved his nightstick and made growling sounds. He and Kane and the proprietor of the second-hand book store took Hoban into Limpy's, laid him on a booth table in the back room. The cop and the bookstore man went out again, brought in DiVina and laid him face up on the floor. The cop went to a phone. Kane stood over DiVina and DiVina would have died again if looks could kill.

Limpy said: "They didn't want Hoban; they wanted the wop. DiVina rubbed out Smiley Smythe and they went out to get him."

Kane stooped, emptied DiVina's pockets, dropped the stuff on a table and pawed through it. There were enveloped letters, rubber-banded together, cigarettes, a lighter, matches and a bill-fold. One of the machine-gun slugs had ripped through the bill-fold, chewed a jagged hole through greenbacks, driver's license, registration certificate.

The letters, all addressed in the same feminine handwriting, were two years old by their postmarks, and addressed to Mr. Conrad Smythe. Conrad Smythe, Kane remembered, was Smiley Smythe's Sunday-go-to-meeting label.

He peered around to be sure the cop was not looking, then stuffed the letters in his own pocket, nodded to Limpy, and walked out. Afterward he was not sure just why he had been in such a hurry.

CHAPTER TWO
THE GIRL AT 113

MORONI, THE WISE ONE, stared at Kane leeringly, and Moe Finch, chewing an unlighted cigar, glared across the desk at headquarters into Kane's face. Finch was big, square-jowled, had slate-gray hair in small quantities and a lot of face to wash. He had rings around his eyes and he looked pathetic.

"Always you're drunk. Always when I need a pal the worst way, you're on a toot."

"I'm sober enough," Kane scowled. "Hoban was a friend of mine."

Finch rocked back in his chair, made a helpless gesture. Moroni stood with hands hipped and stomach protruding, and said: "Listen. Where you fit in this case, I don't know; but it's open and shut. DiVina rubbed out Smiley Smythe and Smiley's friends got even, that's all. All we gotta do is find out which ones did it. He had a lot of 'em."

"And what about the letters?" Finch demanded.

"Letters," said Kane, "don't mean a thing to Moroni. He's illiterate."

Moroni said "Yeah?" from deep inside his lobster-red neck and hiked to the door. He turned, glaring; "Well, I get paid for working here, and you don't. Think that over. And I'm gonna look up Smiley's pals. If you want to be a sap and read love letters, go ahead."

He went out, slammed the door. Moe Finch sighed, relaxed, peered sadly at Kane. "With him a dope and you drunk, I'm nuts. Here," he pushed forward the letters that had come from DiVina's pocket—"you said you wanted these for something. Take 'em and stop bothering me; and don't lose them or I'll get hell. You and Moroni are both crazy. I'm gonna call in some boy scout and tell him to find out who had a grudge against Hoban. You never thought of that, did you?"

"No," Kane said, "I never did. I'm just dumb."

He jammed the letters into his pocket and went out. Outside, he caught a cab, climbed in, sprawled on the seat and dragged the letters out again. A return address on some of the envelopes said *113 Bligh Street.*

To the driver Kane said: "One-one-three Bligh Street, buddy."

Bligh Street was a short, narrow lane off Mt. Vernon, on Beacon Hill, lined with small elms and large brownstone houses. One-one-three was the second house from the corner. Kane climbed the steps, peered at the name *Lang* on a gleaming brass door-plate, put a thumb against the bell. A maid opened the door, looked at him questioningly.

"Miss Barbara in?" Kane grunted.

"Who is calling, please?"

"Friend of Smiley Smythe."

"Of—whom?"

"The name is Conrad. Mr. Conrad Smythe. With a 'y.'"

The maid retreated, returned in a moment and said: "Miss Lang will see you." A slender, severely dressed young woman came up behind her, stared into Kane's face, said quietly: "It's all right, Helen," and regarded Kane with unblinking dark eyes until the maid had vanished again.

"What do you want?"

"Did you ever," Kane said casually, "hear of a guy named DiVina?"

Barbara Lang had evidently heard of a guy named DiVina. She took just enough of a sharp, deep breath to cause a sudden contraction of her throat muscles. She said stiffly: "What do you mean?"

Kane turned the lapel of his coat, showed a police badge that did not belong to him. "Maybe you wouldn't understand. Anyhow, I'd like a talk with you."

THE GIRL stared, exhaled slowly and stepped backward. She acted like she wanted to slam the door in his face, but she turned, led him silently into an expensively furnished living room and stood with both hands gripping a table-edge behind her while he slumped into a chair.

"Do you mind telling me why you came here?"

"Snooping's a habit of mine."

"Then I assure you," she said coldly, "I have no desire to entertain drunkards!" She made thin crescents of her eyes and curled her lips angrily. She was an unusually attractive girl, Kane decided, but too stuffed with the highbrow creed that money could handle anything.

He rocked in his chair, leaned forward. The room was warm and the heat made his tongue thick. "Listen, sister. Not so long ago, somebody smeared Mr. Conrad Smythe's brains all over a nice clean gas stove. Understand? It seems DiVina did the job, and the idea, if I do say so, was pretty swell."

"May I ask how this concerns me?"

"Then"—the interruption affected Kane not at all—"someone else got messy and rubbed DiVina all over a sidewalk, and killed an officer of the law at the same time. And killing a cop isn't a swell idea at all. And we just happened to find some letters in DiVina's pocket." He narrowed his eyes and stared at the girl intently. "They were nice gooey mash notes, and you wrote 'em. You wrote 'em two years ago to Conrad Smythe. And judging from the way you used the sugar, I'd say you were completely nuts about the guy."

He rocked back again, pushed his feet out in front of him and rolled a dry tongue around the inside of his cheek. Talking was an effort. "That sort of puts you in a spot, sister."

Barbara Lang had a lot of self-control. "Are all detectives as—as vicious as you?"

"The cop who got killed," Kane growled, "was my pal."

"Oh."

"He was a good guy. Smythe and DiVina, they were scum; they don't interest me. Besides, I'm not a regular dick; I play hunches and I don't tell all I know."

The girl raised one shoulder half an inch above the other; the gesture was supposed to be a polite shrug. "There's nothing I can tell you. I did write letters to Conrad Smythe. That was two years ago. I thought I loved him."

"You haven't seen him since?"

"No."

"Or DiVina either?"

"I hardly knew DiVina, except as one of Conrad's many friends."

"Yeah. He had a lot of friends." Kane stood up, stood swaying. "Nice ones. Usually, when guys like that get a clutch on letters like yours, they try to sell 'em back to the lady for all she's got." He steered an uneven course to the door, turned on one foot and was in danger of falling.

"Anytime you feel a little more talkative, buzz headquarters. Until then, I'm holding the letters."

He stopped at the foot of the steps, said aloud, "My God, you're lit!" and paraded down Bligh Street to Mt. Vernon.

In a drug store on the corner of Mt. Vernon and Charles he used a booth phone, called Moe Finch, worked his thick tongue to lubricate it and said: "Greetings. I have news for Mr. Moroni. The young lady who wrote those letters says she hasn't seen Smiley Smythe—pardon me, I mean Conrad—in two years. That's what *she* says."

"Where you now?" Finch whined. "I thought you were gonna be a pal and—"

"I'm parked in a drug store, padre, about to have coffee and a sandwich. Tell Moroni about the lady."

"I'll tell him. Only make sure it's coffee you have. Never in my life did I have a pal like I need one now, and—"

KANE HAD coffee and a sandwich at the counter, bought cigarettes and hiked across Charles Street to a cab stand. He gave the address of Mr. Conrad Smythe's apartment house on Audubon Road. The apartment house was a five-story red-brick building with a spacious hallway, a run-it-yourself elevator, and a janitor in the basement. The front buzz-door was open.

Kane prowled downstairs, navigated a concrete ramp between massive oil burners, and rapped on the door of the janitor's apartment.

A large, Swedish-looking woman opened the door and pushed a red melon of a face toward him. A sticky-mouthed youngster came and clung to her hand, swung there grinning.

"Talk to you about Mr. Smythe," Kane said. "I'm a detective."

The woman scowled. "Can't you come some other time? I'm busy."

"I won't keep you long."

He pushed inside, leaned against the doorjamb, "You keep a pretty close check on things that go on around here, don't you Mrs.—"

"Groler. Anna Groler's my name. Not unless I get complaints, I don't."

"The night Smiley Smythe was killed did he have any visitors you know of?"

"No. I don't know nothin' about what he was doin' that night."

"He had a lot of visitors other nights?"

"Well, yes."

"Women, mostly?"

"Well, yes. Mostly."

"Any one in particular?"

"Say, I don't want to be gettin' in any trouble. Me and my man, we just work here, that's all. We ain't supposed to know—"

"This is confidential," Kane said. "What's this special lady-friend of his look like?"

"Well, she was a nice-lookin' girl, but snooty. She was kind of thin and serious-lookin', and she was always dressed elegant. I guess she had lots of money."

"Know her name?"

"Well, I wouldn't remember. I heard him call her by it one night in the hall, but I wouldn't remember it off-hand."

"Barbara, was it?"

"Well yes, I guess it was."

"Was she here the night he got killed?"

"I told you I don't know nothin' about that night. I don't want to get in any trouble."

Kane put a hand in his pocket, brought out a five-dollar bill and pushed it against the woman's palm. "Was she here?"

"Yes, she was. She come in about nine o'clock. I didn't see either of them go out. It was just by accident I seen her come in. I was late pickin' up the garbage and—"

"You ever meet a friend of Smiley's named DiVina?"

"Yes. I used to get whisky for both him and Smiley."

"He was here that night?"

"If he was, I didn't see him come in or go out."

"O.K." Kane straightened, swayed unsteadily. "Sister, you wouldn't have a shot of that whisky around the house, would you?"

"You mean you want a drink?"

"Me? My God, no. I hate the stuff. But the doctor said—"

Mrs. Groler brought a pint bottle and a thick jelly glass. She said: "Listen. Don't be tellin' my husband about me givin' you any information. He's been calmed down for a good long while now and I don't want him all boiled up again."

"Oh-oh. Meaning what?"

"Well, he didn't like me bringin' liquor up there to Mr. Smythe. He figured I done more than bring the booze." The woman put a crooked grin on her face. "What I done up in Smiley's apartment is my business."

Kane poured four fingers into the jelly glass, downed the stuff and gagged. "Where's your husband now?"

"He ain't here. He's downtown." She leaned against the door jamb. "Why?"

"Nix, sister, nix." Kane downed another four fingers, handed back the bottle. "Listen, if a flat-foot by the name of Moroni comes around asking insulting questions, throw him out; don't tell him a thing."

He turned away, stopped after taking three steps. "And if that girl-friend of Smiley's should show up, ring head-quarters quick as hell and ask for Kane. That's me—Kane. I don't live there but they can generally get in touch with me real quick."

He went out and took a cab back to headquarters.

A SMALL man with tight, pale features and slept-in clothes was sitting in a chair in Moe Finch's office, fumbling with a dirty felt hat and staring at Finch with black buttons of eyes. Finch stopped talking to him, looked up and nodded as Kane entered. Finch said: "While you're steamin' around in circles, look what I got."

Kane looked and said: "Oh-oh. Zybrlowsky, the Pole with the unpronounceable name. When did they let you out?"

"He's out a week," Finch snarled. "And he damn near ruined two of my best men with a chair when they went after him in a North End tenement. I knew this guy was around, and I don't forget it was Hoban put him in stir. Five years in Charlestown is a long time to be thinking about sweet revenge."

"That's a fact. Where's Moroni?"

"Gone up to see that Lang woman."

"What a sap she'll make of him," Kane sighed.

"Meaning she made one of you?"

"Plenty."

Finch grinned, reached for the phone as it rang beside his elbow. He grunted into the tube, listened, jerked his head up. "There's a guy out front wants to see the detective who called on Miss Barbara Lang this morning." He frowned. "Listen. For God's sake don't actually tell anybody you're helpin' me out on this mess. If it got around—"

Kane walked out front, nodded to the desk man, peered at a well dressed young man sitting stiffly upright on a bench. He knew without asking that the young man was Barbara Lang's brother; he had the same tight features, slim build. The desk man said: "O.K., buddy, here's your man," and Lang stood up, came stiffly forward.

"I—my name is Roger Lang." He put out a hand, let it drop as soon as Kane had touched it. "May I talk with you alone?"

Kane walked into a side room, pushed the door shut.

"I'm here on my sister's account," Lang said. "It—well, frankly Mr. Kane, it's about those letters."

"I thought it would be."

"They're very personal. Having read them, you must know what I mean. My sister is about to be married. If those letters were to be made public, if they appeared in the newspapers, Mr. Kane—"

"Beacon Hill'd be shocked, eh?"

"Yes. I've come to you to—to do what I can, for Barbara's sake. You have the letters yourself?"

"I have the letters myself," Kane nodded.

Lang stared at him, seemed to grow older, more mature after ten seconds of silent contemplation. The boy stood straighter, stopped fumbling with his hands and assumed an attitude of sudden desperate quietness.

"I won't try to bribe you, Mr. Kane. I came here with that intention, but I don't think it would work. May I have the letters, and destroy them in front of you?"

"Sorry." Kane pursed his lips, rocked his head sideways. "Not a chance."

"May I ask—why—not?"

"Moe Finch'd lose his job; it'd put both of you in a spot; and the letters won't be in the papers anyhow." Kane held the door open, put a hand on the boy's arm and steered him over the sill. "Better go home and keep out of this. Bad enough for one of the family to be roped in."

Roger Lang walked out very slowly, stiffly, paced past the desk man and closed the outer door after him. Kane said to the desk man: "Listen. If anyone else wants me, I'm over to Limpy's. This is beginning to get my nerves somethin' awful. You'd think I even worked here."

CHAPTER THREE
CALLERS FOR KANE

KANE HEADED for a cab stand on the corner of LaRonge Street, changed his mind and walked briskly uptown. He felt rotten with a hangover, and the best cure for a hangover was one of Limpy's long cold drinks with ice and absinthe. Afterward the absinthe would do things to you, but for a while at least it took some of the blur out of your eyes and deflated an oversized windpipe.

He walked all the way to Limpy's, stayed there an hour and walked back again. He was very drunk and he did a military right-face on the sidewalk in front of headquarters, climbed the steps and paraded into Moe Finch's office with a broad grin on his face. He knew he was drunk and it made him feel good to be drunk, because Moroni would gripe about it and Finch would whine complaints about the negative value of plastered pals.

Moroni and Finch were both present, and Barbara Lang was sitting very white and still in the chair recently occupied by Zybrlowsky. Moroni was saying: "Sister, bein' in the Blue Book won't get you out of this. You were in Smiley's apartment that night, and sure as hell you'll admit it!"

"How you do find out things," Kane drawled.

Moroni swung to face him, glared. "Yeah. And the next time you bribe a dame not to give me information, I'll push your funny face in, mister. I don't forget you're nothin' but a cheap private shamus. One of these days you'll muscle in just one time too often."

Finch played a piano on the desk, sighed heavily. Moroni swung back to the girl. "Now listen, sister. You were in Smiley's place that night. The janitor's wife saw you go in. She was drunk when she admitted it, but she wasn't drunk when she saw you, and she'll spill the whole thing to a jury if necessary."

"You just came from there?" Kane demanded. "And the lady was drunk?"

"She was paralyzed."

"My, my. She must've killed that pint just like that."

"What?"

"Oh, don't mind me. Carry on."

"Listen," Moroni said to the girl. "I'm not asking you, I'm telling you. You went to Smiley's joint that night to get those letters. You blew Smiley's brains out. Then you heard someone comin', and you got scared and scrammed before gettin' your hands on the letters after all. The guy you heard comin' was DiVina, and DiVina was wise enough to know what you were after, so he grabbed those letters and put 'em in his pocket, figurin' to use 'em later to good advantage. Then some of Smiley's pals rubbed out DiVina, thinkin' he done the job you did."

Moroni swung on Finch. "Understand, I ain't interested in who rubbed out DiVina. Not just yet, anyway. But I'm sure as hell gonna prove this dame killed Smiley. I never did like society dames for nuts."

"How you go on," Kane murmured.

The girl said: "It's not true. I didn't go there that night. I haven't seen Smiley in two years." She was breathing hard and fast. She was scared, Kane thought, but she had not yet lost that certain high-hat disdain. She had guts under the fancy veneer. She was young and dumb, but the cream-puff was solid inside.

"All this leaves me flat," Finch croaked. "I ask you two birds to find out who killed Hoban, so you go chasing after a dame, just to be smart."

Kane said softly. "You're not talking to me."

"Hell no! Far as I can find out, all you been chasing is another drink! What a swell pal you turned out to be!"

"Drink," Kane murmured, "has slain more people than all the women in this forlorn world. Whatever became of Zybrlowsky, the Pole?"

"He took a fit."

"I beg pardon."

"He took a fit, I said. He's about ready for the hearse. He's in the back room, sleeping, and Doc says leave him there. His lungs are gone; he's been hittin' the pipe and drinkin' too much rotgut. That's what'll happen to you if you don't lay off."

Kane scratched the side of his mouth with a blunt fingernail, grinned widely and walked to the door. "I guess I better go."

"Where to now?"

"Places, then home to bed." He peered casually at Moroni. "With Mr. Moroni on the job, we can all take a vacation. But listen, marvelous. Before you wrestle with society any more, do a little memory work. Seems to me when they found Smiley he had a gun in his fist with one slug fired out of it, and there wasn't a sign of that slug anywhere in the apartment—which proves Smiley hit what he aimed at. And I don't notice any bullet holes in this gal's chassis."

He closed the door behind him, aimed his feet at the street end of the corridor, and paraded leisurely out.

ON THE way uptown to Limpy's, he thought of the slug which had been fired out of Smiley Smythe's gun and which had not been found in Smiley's apartment. He drew a mental picture of Smiley pacing leisurely into the kitchenette to mix drinks—of the party of the second part telling Smiley to turn around and take it standing up—of Smiley whirling, dragging out a gun, stumbling against the gas stove and jerking the trigger before getting a death-bullet in the brain.

It was something to think about.

Kane changed his mind about going to Limpy's, and took a cab to Smiley's apartment house. A big-boned, ruddy-faced Swede was polishing mail boxes in the front entry. Kane said: "You Groler, the janitor?"

The Swede stopped polishing, straightened slowly. "I'm Groler. Yuh."

Kane showed his borrowed badge. "I could use another look at Mr. Smythe's apartment."

"Well, I got work to do. I'm sick and tired of havin' to show you policemen—"

"Save it. I won't keep you long."

Groler lumbered up the steps, opened the buzz-door, made grumbling noises all along the corridor to the elevator. He had a can of polish in one hand; he shoved the can into a hip pocket, jarred open the door of Smiley's apartment, stood staring sullenly in the doorway as Kane paraded in and looked around.

Kane walked into the kitchenette, peered at dried blobs of blood on the gas stove. He made a thorough investigation, began to frown, said suddenly: "Give me a hand here."

"I was told not to touch nothin'."

"Forget it. Help me get this out."

The Swede slouched forward, put both hands under one end of the stove, hauled the thing out from the corner without waiting for Kane to help. He let go with one hand, made a face. Kane peered behind the stove, scowled and said slowly: "H'm. Guess I had the wrong idea. I thought—"

With one hand, Groler pushed the stove back again, straightened, leaned against the wall. He stared, said nothing as Kane looked around some more.

After ten minutes Kane made a growling sound, said curtly: "Well, thanks anyway."

"You all through in here?"

"All through. Go back and play with the mailboxes."

AT TEN P.M. Kane left Limpy's and walked home. He was slightly drunker than usual, and spent three minutes looking for the keyhole before letting himself into his apartment and leaning against the door to shut it. Without haste he tramped into the living room, turned on the lights and radio and sat on the studio couch. The radio came in too loud, so he got up and turned the volume down. He took off his coat, hat, tossed them on a chair, lit a cigarette and read the paper. The apartment was warm; after a while he got up and opened a window.

He wondered, then, how Moroni had made out with the girl, and he remembered dimly that Moroni had wandered into Limpy's place about an hour ago with the information that the girl had been released. Moroni himself had let her go and put a dick named Donovan to keep check on her. Considering Moroni's mental deficiencies, that wasn't a bad idea. Moroni, being usually very dumb….

Kane dozed.

There was an alarm clock on the desk in the other room, and the run-down alarm had been set for eleven that morning. When eleven P.M. came, the alarm made a weak jangling sound and jogged Kane out of his doze. He bent over and pulled his shoes off, took a half-full pint bottle from his coat on the chair, went into the kitchenette for a glass.

The kitchenette was warm because the door had been closed and the pilot on the gas stove was burning. Kane opened the window and leaned out over the fire escape, breathed deep and dragged cold air into his lungs. After pouring and downing a drink, he put the empty glass in the sink and the bottle on the fire escape. The window he left open, and returned to the living room.

The letters written by Barbara Lang to Smiley Smythe were in the pocket of his coat on the chair. He took them out and went through them, scowled over them. After a while he shoved them back, hung the coat on the back of the chair, got up and turned the lights and radio off, went into the bedroom and sprawled on the bed.

He was drunk and he went to sleep thinking about Moroni. When he awoke, the window of the kitchenette was creaking, and something thumped on the floor in there. Then the kitchenette door creaked and rubber-soled shoes made a sucking sound across the hardwood floor.

Kane lay very still with his eyes open, breathed through his mouth and listened intently. The footsteps stopped when the shoes making them reached the living-room carpet; then Kane inched himself off the bed, stood erect in stockinged feet, moved slowly to the door.

He was drunk, but not drunk enough to be clumsy. He went down the hall on the balls of his feet, saw the gleam of a flashlight streaking the living-room threshold. When he reached the threshold the glare swept up into his face.

In the middle of the room Roger Lang was standing on rigid, wide-spread legs beside the chair which supported Kane's discarded coat. The boy had the flashlight in one hand and a small black gun in the other. He said harshly: "Get back or—I'll shoot!"

Kane stood still, stared; his eyebrows came together and formed bat-wings above unblinking eyes. He saw a pack of letters on the chair and said softly: "Boy, you sure have a yen for those things."

"I mean to have them. I told you this afternoon."

"You'll do time for armed robbery."

Lang put the flashlight on the chair, scooped up the letters. He glared triumphantly. "I don't care a damn what you do to me after these letters have been destroyed. But by God, you leave my sister alone or—"

The drone of a bell in the next room silenced him. He stiffened, turned an impulsive half-circle, stuffing the letters in his pocket. When he realized his mistake and turned back again, Kane had already taken two steps and Kane's fist was finishing a vicious upswing. The fist made loud, crunching contact with Lang's jaw, rammed him back into the wall. The gun exploded in his hand, belched thunder with its muzzle pointing floorward. The boy made a hoarse sobbing sound in his throat, flattened himself against the wall and stared with bulging eyes as Kane lunged at him. Then his face changed expression, became hard, snarling with youthful rage; he dropped the gun and hurled himself headlong into Kane's bulk.

Sober, Kane could have put two hands on the kid, bent him into a knot and flung him aside without indulging in over-exercise. Drunk, he went back off balance when Lang made contact; the kid's flailing fists worked like pistons, stung his face, chest, scorched an eye. Together, he and the kid staggered in circles, tipped over an end-table and sent a lamp crashing, rammed the studio couch away from the wall on protesting castors, reeled drunkenly into a corner and ruptured the fancy fabric front of the radio. In the other room the doorbell still droned.

THE KID tripped, sat down backward and dragged Kane with him. He was crying, sobbing hysterically, snarling at the same time. He had strong hands but his blows failed to keep Kane back, and he was like a small boy hammering futilely, in childish rage, at an assailant too big for him.

Kane said, "Well, you asked for it!" and drove a knotted fist twice into the boy's face. Then he groped to his knees, swayed there, got to his feet and stared down at Lang's body. The kid was out cold, face smeared with tears, mouth drooling blood at one corner.

Kane laid him on the studio couch and bent over him, ran exploring hands over the kid's clothes. He pulled the pack of letters from Lang's pocket, saw another letter hanging half out of an inside pocket and pulled that out too. He looked at it; his eyes tightened. The envelope was pale blue, addressed with a typewriter. In the upper left corner was the typewritten name J. DiVina and a post-office box number. The letter was addressed to Miss Barbara Lang.

Kane opened it, read the typed contents.

> Dear Miss Lang—
>
> The night your friend Smiley Smythe was rubbed out, it was my good fortune to be coming up the stairs of his apartment house at the same time you were coming out of his apartment. Most likely the police would be able to make something of that fact if I was to inform them. I think maybe you had better come to see me and we will talk this thing over before I make up my mind what is the proper thing to do.
>
> > Yours truly,
> > Joe DiVina.

Kane looked at the kid and the kid was conscious again, staring at him. Kane said: "This kinda makes the wheels go round. Where'd you get it?"

"That's my business."

"Listen, son. Being tough won't get you to first base even." Kane clamped a hand on the kid's shoulder. "As I already told your sister, I'm not a regular dick and I don't tell all I know, many a time. DiVina sent this letter to your sister and you got it before she did, eh?"

"Yes."

"I guess you had a pretty fair idea of what it meant, huh?"

"I'm not dumb."

"No. You're not dumb." Someone was hammering insistently on the hall door, and Kane shoved the letter back in its envelope, jammed the envelope in the kid's pocket. "Kid, you've got guts, even if you are kind of wacky like most of the rest of these college boys. I bet it was the first time you ever used a machine gun, too. I bet it was."

He walked down the hall and opened the door. Moroni came in with Donovan. He was sore; Donovan, sloppily dressed and sucking a cigarette, seemed indifferent. Moroni growled sullenly: "What the hell is this? Are you so drunk you don't even hear doorbells?"

Kane said, "My, my, you're always mad with me," and walked back to the living room. Moroni, trailing him, took a long look at Roger Lang, at the ruptured radio, the upturned end-table.

"You breakin' up house-keepin'?"

"I been taking lessons in these new Bode gymnastics," Kane grinned.

"You look it." Moroni ploughed to the couch and curled a fat hand around Lang's arm. "I'm movin' this mugg to headquarters."

The kid stared, sat very still. Kane flopped into a chair, gazed darkly at Moroni, said with apparent indifference: "What'd he do?"

"You'd be surprised."

"I would be."

"Well, get a load of this!" Moroni turned a triumphant face, hooked his mouth into a sneer. "Donovan, here, tailed the girl home and then hung around to watch the place. See? She didn't come out again, but this mug did. Donovan tailed him here, saw him come up the fire escape, then gave me a ring and waited for me downstairs, like I told him to. The kid was after those letters you're luggin' around."

"Really?"

"And that ain't all. While Donovan is watchin' the girl's house, I'm workin' on a new angle, and what do I find? I get hold of the cop who was on the spot when DiVina and Hoban got rubbed out, and from him I get the name of a dame who seen the actual rub-out. She tells me she got a good look at the guy behind the gun, and he was a young guy, kind of good-lookin', with curly hair. So now—" Moroni glared venomously at Roger Lang— "I got a damn good idea who wiped out DiVina and Hoban!"

Kane was silent for twenty seconds. He looked at Lang and Lang's face was chalk-colored, cheeks sucked in around bulging muscles. He looked at Moroni and Moroni was swaggering on widespread legs, chest bloated, mouth curled in monstrous satisfaction.

Kane said softly: "It's amazing how you guys find out things."

"Yeah, it is. And this kid goes to headquarters with me, and then we get the girl down there, and then," Moroni declared, "we settle this whole business in one big smash. What you do, I don't care a damn. Go ahead and finish your Rover gymnastics."

"Bode, Moroni. Bode."

"Bode hell and boil," Moroni growled.

CHAPTER FOUR

COCKROACHES IN MORONI'S COFFEE

HALF AN hour later Kane got out of a cab, climbed the stone steps of Smiley Smythe's apartment house, opened the outer door and pushed a hard thumb against the janitor's bell. The door release buzzed and he went in, went downstairs. Groler, the Swede, was standing in the door of the janitor's suite, scowling. He had on corduroy trousers, worn-out leather slippers, no shirt. He had a razor gripped awkwardly in one hand and shaving soap on one side of his big face. He said: "Well, what you want this time?"

"I'm in a spot," Kane said, "and I need a guy with your intellect to help me out."

"What you mean?"

"Want you to come down to headquarters with me."

"Listen. I can't go nowheres this time of night. I got to stay here. I can't go to no headquarters."

"Oh yes you can."

"I tell you no! I—" The Swede stopped raving, made eyes at the revolver in Kane's fist. He stood stiff, stared for ten seconds, raised his head and peered into Kane's face.

"Go put a shift on," Kane said.

Groler put a shirt on and wiped shaving soap off his face with a dirty towel while Kane leaned in the doorway and watched him. The Swede walked very slowly through the cellar, went upstairs and out of the building with Kane close behind him, and got into the waiting cab without saying a word. He sat stiff and awkward while the cab rolled downtown through late traffic, and when the cab stopped he got out, walked up the steps into headquarters and stood like a big-boled tree in front of the desk.

Kane said to the desk man: "Where's Zybrlowsky, the Pole?"

"He's out back yet. The doc says—"

"I know. The doc says he's dying. I'll go talk with him. Keep an eye on this guy until I get back."

The desk man leaned on bent elbows and peered at Groler. He began humming a song, tapping an accompaniment on the desk with the end of a pen holder.

Groler said: "I—I ain't under arrest, am I?"

"What do you think?"

"Well, I ain't done nothing! That guy, he said he needed me to help him out. I don't know what I'm here for, even."

"I dunno either, mister. If you were drunk, I'd say Kane brought you along to keep him company. Stick around and maybe we'll both get wise."

Groler licked his lips and remained standing. The desk man hummed the song through, began over again. After ten minutes Kane walked into the room.

"Finch out back?" Kane demanded.

"Him and Moroni both, with the Lang girl and her brother. Nobody sleeps around here."

"Swell," Kane said. He put a hand on the Swede's arm. "O.K., mister. You wouldn't want to miss this."

He paced down the corridor, pushed open the door of Finch's office and motioned Groler inside. Moe Finch was sitting sideways at the desk, long legs stuck out in front of him, hands folded majestically over a protruding stomach. He looked contented. He glanced at Kane, rolled his gaze to the Swede and said indifferently: "Who's your pal?"

"He's interested in Moroni," Kane smiled. "He came all the way from Stockholm just to listen to Moroni."

Barbara Lang and her brother were sitting in chairs ten feet apart against the wall, and Moroni was wearing out the floor between them, parading back and forth with relentless strides. Moroni was raving in a harsh, booming voice, punctuating his words by slapping a hard right fist into a cupped left hand.

His ugly face was scarlet, his mouth drooling brown juice from a chewed cigar; his hair was in his eyes and he kept tossing it clear with savage snaps of his outthrust head. "My, my," Kane murmured. Finch said, without shifting his fat-man-for-emperor pose: "The party's just getting warmed up. Sit down; make yourself to home. Moroni's in rare form."

MORONI PAID no attention. He was saying to the girl: "All right, get a load of this. The night Smiley Smythe was killed, you visited him. DiVina saw you come out of the apartment after you did the job on your boy-friend. I had that all figured out long ago, and now this letter proves it." He waved an envelope. It was the envelope Kane had taken from Roger Lang's pocket; the one addressed to the girl, from DiVina.

"Well," Moroni bellowed, "am I right or am I right?"

The girl said stiffly: "You are altogether wrong. I did go there that night, but I didn't kill him. Perhaps DiVina thought I did, because DiVina did see me come out of Mr. Smythe's apartment; but I didn't kill him. He was dead when I went in. I had my own key and I let myself in, and he was lying there on the kitchen floor, dead."

"Yeah."

"Yes. Mr. Smythe forced me to visit him often. He had some letters that I wrote to him when I was very young and foolish, and he threatened to show the letters to the man I am going to marry, unless I—I did as he wished."

"Well, you'll need more than that, sister. Before you get out of here, you'll change even that! It was you killed Smiley Smythe, and it was this baby-faced brother of yours that rubbed out DiVina and Hoban. Why? Because he knew DiVina was all set to rap you off for a pile of dough and maybe other things more personal. If he'd known what you were to Smiley, he wouldn't've worried so much about that c'm-up-sometime letter DiVina wrote you. But he figured you were a nice innocent little girl in the clutches of a big bad wolf, so he rubbed out the wolf. Hoban wasn't supposed to be in on it; he just happened along accidental and took the works. Deny that one." He swung on the girl's brother. "Or maybe you'll deny it, push-face!"

Roger Lang was sitting stiff as wood, feet rooted in the floor, hands curled on his knees. His face was carmine, his eyes wide and smouldering.

"Well," Moroni growled, "are you gonna talk?"

"He doesn't need to," Kane said gently. "You do very well without help."

Moroni rocked around, glared. "Listen. When I want any wise-cracks from an agency mug like you—"

"I know a million. I know something else, too, that you forgot all about."

"Yeah? What?"

"When Smiley croaked, he had a gun in his fist and there was a shot fired out of it. And he hit what he aimed at."

"Meaning?"

"I don't see any slug-holes in either this kid or his sister."

"And I suppose that proves something," Moroni scowled.

"Sure it does. This is indeed going to be a pleasure. It so happens, Mr. Moroni, that Smiley had other female friends, and one of them, being quite close at hand, did a whole lot of playing in his apartment. Matter of fact, she's quite the little playgirl. Even tried it on me."

"She must be hard up," Moe Finch droned.

"Check. Anyway, she did a lot of playing with Smiley, and her old man didn't like it a little bit. So he went up there one night and let Smiley have it. And Smiley, being very fast with a gun, found time to return the compliment.

So this guy is now suffering from a winged shoulder, and that is a pity."

Moroni said sullenly: "What the hell you handin' us?"

Kane was standing near the door. Moe Finch took a cigar out of the desk, lit it, blew smoke through frowning lips. Roger Lang and his sister were staring, and the girl was leaning far forward in her chair, breathing rapidly, deeply, with her mouth open. Groler, the Swede, had not moved his feet on the floor since entering the room; he stood rigid, fists clenched against thick thighs. He, too, was breathing hard.

Kane glanced at him, said softly: "Show the people where Smiley plugged you."

THE SWEDE took a step sideways, glared at the door and hurled himself toward it with a sudden lunge. He tripped over Kane's outthrust foot, crashed headlong against the door jamb, rocked erect and swayed his face straight into Kane's arcing fist. The fist made a loud crunching sound against flesh and teeth, carried through and sent the Swede over backward in a sprawled heap. When the Swede groaned up on hands and knees, Kane's gun was out, covering him.

Kane said softly: "Thanks. That kind of dynamite is better than a written confession and doesn't take half so long." He looked over the Swede's head into Moroni's gaping face. "When you get around to it, sweetheart, have the doc look at this guy's shoulder. Chances are, Smiley's bullet is still in there. The guy's arm is plenty sore, anyway. I found that out when I chiseled him into moving a heavy gas stove this afternoon."

Moroni made a rumbling sound, wiped wet lips with the back of his hand. Moe Finch had an idiotic expression on his face, as if he had just watched rabbits walk out of a magician's hat. Barbara Lang was sobbing, and her brother had an arm around her, a trembling hand cupped under her chin.

Moroni said: "So you're a wise guy. You wouldn't spill this before; you had to make a sap out of me." He strode forward, jammed a hand against the desk and swayed there on wide-spread legs. "Well, you're not so wise after all, wise guy. Maybe the Swede did rub out Smiley Smythe; maybe the girl didn't have a thing to do with it. But that don't clear the girl's brother. The Swede didn't turn that machine gun on DiVina. Lang did—and I got a witness to prove it!"

"A female witness, sweetheart. And when a middle-aged female gets excited that way—phooey!"

"What?"

Kane pulled a folded square of paper from a coat pocket, flipped it to the desk. "Worry through that. Zybrlowsky, the Pole, gave it to me fifteen minutes ago."

Moroni unfolded the paper, studied it. He dropped it on the desk, scratched feebly at disheveled hair. He said thickly: "Well, I'm damned. I'm damned."

"The Pole," Kane said, "didn't have a thing against DiVina; he was out to get Hoban. Hoban put him in stir, and the yen for revenge was deep and dirty. But the Pole is all washed up, ready for the hearse. I had a talk with him. As a result, he handed me the whole works, put his name to the paper here, and said he'll take pleasure in keeping the fires stoked up till the rest of us drop in on him."

Kane strolled to the door, grinned broadly, realized that the girl and her brother were staring at him with deep, silent gratitude. He glanced at the Swede, said indifferently: "Watch out he don't do a Tarzan. He's tough and nasty. Me, I'm so dry it's painful, and I got a date with Limpy."

AT ELEVEN A.M. Kane let himself into his apartment, took two pint bottles from his coat and ceremoniously placed them in the middle of the living-room floor. He sat on the studio couch and stared at them. His eyes were bloodshot.

At eleven-thirty the doorbell rang; he got up, pushed the release, walked a snake-track down the hall and gaped at Roger Lang as Lang came up the stairs.

"C'm right in," Kane said cheerfully. "I b'n expectin' you."

Lang sat in a chair, stared. He had aged ten years in the past few days. His face was dirty gray from lack of sleep.

"Don't mind me, I'm just drunk," Kane said. "Matter of fact, I'm most always drunk. I like to be drunk."

"Mr. Kane," the boy said slowly, "I—"

"Yeah, I know. I know all about it. I made pretty damn sure I knew all about it, because Hoban was a pal o' mine, see? I had to make sure as hell I wasn't lettin' a pal o' mine down."

"I was half insane," Lang said. "If I hadn't been, I would have seen Hoban. But I didn't. I was blind to everything but DiVina."

"Who was drivin' the car?"

"A friend of mine. I showed him the letter DiVina wrote to my sister, and he felt the same way I did. We room together at the University and—"

"Just a couple of college boys with big ideas," Kane sighed. "Ain't it funny? I used to think that way about women, myself."

"Mr. Kane." Lang leaned forward, put out a groping hand. "Mr. Kane, my sister and I owe you more than—"

"You owe me five grand, sonny. Five thousand dollars. Me, I'm broke as always, but I promised Zybrlowsky. He's gonna die, see? He'll be dead before they even get a chance to work on him. But he's got a girl in boarding school, about thirteen years old, and he's nuts about her. A lot of these tough guys have soft spots. This girl, she don't even know she has a father, but she's his and she means a lot. So I promised Zybrlowsky I'd put up a five-grand trust fund for the girl, in return for the favor he did me. So—you owe me five grand."

Roger Lang said: "God, you're white!"

"Don't be a sap," Kane growled. He gathered one of the two bottles off the floor, unscrewed the cap and leaned back on the couch with the bottle upended in his mouth. He gagged, glared resentfully at the bottle. "Day by day Limpy's stock gets lousier. Listen, don't be a sap. I'm just a dumb agency dick without a conscience. All I live for is to do favors for Moe Finch and put cockroaches in Moroni's coffee."

HELL ON HUME STREET

THERE WERE ONLY THREE THINGS THAT MATTERED TO KANE— DOING FAVORS FOR HIS PAL, FINCH; PUTTING COCKROACHES IN DETECTIVE MORONI'S COFFEE— AND, MOST IMPORTANT OF ALL, DRINKING QUANTITIES OF LIQUOR. HE'D BE DAMNED IF HE'D INTERRUPT THAT LAST JUST FOR A LITTLE THING LIKE MURDER. AND ANY-WAY IT WAS EASY ENOUGH TO HELP FINCH, HAND MORONI A RAZZBERRY AND STILL KEEP PLASTERED, ALL AT THE SAME TIME.

HUME STREET runs from Baker to Harriman, through a tenement-house district where cops walk in pairs and street lights are rare as fresh air. At night, Hume Street is a dark graveyard, full of prowling ghost-shapes, black spectres, low-voiced mutterings and odors of unwashed human flesh. The good Lord didn't design Hume Street. It was transplanted out of hell and left to rot.

In front of Zanelli's Delicatessen stands a grimy-faced sidewalk clock. The clock told Kitty Dolan that midnight was ten minutes gone, so she pulled her pretty head and bare shoulders back over the windowsill of her third-floor tenement down the street and finished dressing in a hurry. Zanelli's clock was usually accurate, and the old guy up the street was supposed to have his medicine at midnight or else—

Dressed, Kitty walked to the door. She was a good-looking girl, as girls who worked uptown in Horgan's mammoth department store had to be. She was small and trim and Irish and had a face that smiled without provocation. Tonight, as she inched open the door leading to the landing, she didn't smile.

She narrowed her eyes, scowled, peered both ways along the landing and exhaled a murmur of relief as she closed the door behind her. For once, that Heinfein was off the job. For once that glue-faced woman-chaser who lived behind the ogre-door at the head of the staircase wasn't standing there in his doorway in pants and undershirt, black eyes open and unblinking and waiting to stare holes in Kitty's soul.

Funny, what Heinfein's eyes could do to you. Kitty shuddered.

ON TIPTOE she went past Heinfein's door and descended the stairs. Before closing the street door behind her and going down the filthy steps to the sidewalk, she looked up and down Hume Street, just to be sure. Then, quickly, she ran down the steps, turned left and walked toward the clock in front of Zanelli's Delicatessen.

Above her—three stories above, on the roof of the tenement house from which she had just come—something moved. Something shadowy, human in form, leaned over the roof-edge and peered down. An arm snaked out and hung poised above the sidewalk. Gnarled fingers at the end of the arm were closed around something that gleamed dully. The fingers opened when Kitty passed beneath them. The gleaming thing, released, fell of its own weight, fell swiftly in a plumb-line. It was made of steel and it was long, like a pencil; but it was fatter and heavier than a pencil and the end that fell first was a whole lot sharper than a pencil point.

Kitty Dolan, with even stride, walked straight into the thing's line of descent. The thing had dropped three stories and it was heavy. It made dull, crunching contact with Kitty's bare head and buried itself, point first, in her brain.

She did not scream. She stood stock still, opened her eyes wide in sudden unbearable agony and lifted one hand toward her face. Her slender body trembled, then crumpled and lay very still in a small limp heap on the dirty concrete.

Two minutes later by Zanelli's clock, the door of the tenement house jarred open and a long-legged, gangling, half-dressed human form catapulted over the threshold, leaped down the steps and lunged along the sidewalk to stand gasping above Kitty's dead body.

The man was Heinfein—Antole Heinfein. And the eyes that Kitty Dolan had lately learned to dread gaped down at her wide open with horror.

Heinfein rocked backward, turned a convulsed face toward the tenement doorway, and screamed. He made mumbling sounds in his throat, stooped to gather Kitty Dolan's dead body in his long arms, then shuddered away from it and stared in new horror at the steel shaft protruding from Kitty's blood-drenched hair. He was

He pawed empty air like a fanatic in a heathen temple.

still staring when Mrs. Mame Lorier, Kitty's landlady, came wallowing down the steps and sailed toward him like a blimp staggering through a storm.

"What is it?" Mame gasped. "What happened?"

"It's her—Kitty," Heinfein mumbled.

Other persons came. Kitty Dolan's father, drunk and in pajamas, came stumbling out of a tenement two doors down across the street, and lurched from curb to curb. He elbowed his way explosively through a gathering crowd and stood swaying, staring through bloodshot eyes. Maybe he recognized the dead girl; maybe he didn't. He said nothing. He was an ex-pug and a chronic drunk. No love was lost between father and daughter. They didn't even live together. More than once, Porky Dolan's fists had hammered the limp body and convulsed face that lay there now in death.

Old Fanner came, too, from the same tenement across the street. Old Martin Fanner, in a frayed khaki shirt and faded overseas cap, who had to push himself along on his bands, because his legless body squatted like a praying Buddha on a kiddie-car contraption that bumped and whispered along on rubber-tired wheels. But Fanner had seen death before— He gaped and said: *"Ah-h-h-h-h!* This time it is Kitty—dead like the—other—one!" Tears rolled down his twisted face.

Hume Street's denizens stood around and stared and talked in low voices. Only a week ago they had done the same thing in almost the same place; and the dead girl then had been Anna Procaccini, Kitty Dolan's girl-friend.

Now Kitty Dolan was dead, too. Murdered the same way.

Who would be next? They asked one another that, and were terrified. Then the cops came.

LIMPY'S PLACE, uptown on Stuart Street, had one customer the morning after Kitty Dolan's death. The customer sat not at the bar but in one of Limpy's back-room booths, his long legs jammed under the low table, his elbows denting the cloth, his unshaven chin cupped in his hands.

Peter Kane, number-one man on the Beacon Agency gumshoe list, was drunk. Kane had been drunk more or less, mostly more, for a period running now into its third liquid week. He knew he was drunk and he liked to be drunk. Right now, as Limpy pushed open the back-room door and came toward him, he was staring soberly at a small black object that moved jerkily across the white cloth, and when the thing stopped jumping he picked it up, rewound it, and made it jump some more.

Limpy said: "There's a lady out front wants to talk to you, Kane."

"Meet Moroni," Kane said.

Limpy stared. "Huh? What the hell—"

"Someone must've left it here." Kane grinned. "I found it on the floor a couple of hours ago. Look. It jumps just like a real one."

Limpy stared again. The black thing leaped toward him across the cloth, scaring him back. It was a mechanical bug. It looked like a cockroach.

"I got it all named," Kane said. "Meet Moroni. Moroni—jump for the gentleman!"

Limpy sighed. "Aw, nuts. There's a lady outside, I'm telling you, wants to talk—"

"Send her in." Kane shrugged.

Limpy went, shaking his head dolefully. A moment later when Kane ceased playing with "Moroni" and again looked up at sounds of intrusion, a youngish good-looking woman was advancing toward the booth, advancing slowly as if she wanted to be somewhere else.

Kane put both hands on the table and pushed himself up, stood staring. He wished suddenly that he were not so drunk, at least not so drunk that it showed in his face, in his actions. He said thickly: "Alma. Say—" Then he wanted to be very drunk, because there was something in the woman's dark eyes, something accusing and—and pitying—that made him feel rotten down inside.

She put a hand on his shoulder and pushed him down again, then sat facing him and looked at him soberly. Those dark eyes missed nothing. They had known Peter Kane a long time, and knew him better than he knew himself.

"Very drunk, Peter?" Alma Finch asked quietly.

He shook his head negatively, palmed the mechanical cockroach into his pocket and tried to sit straight.

"I had to come," the woman said. "Moe needs you. He wouldn't come himself. Said you've done favors enough for him already." Again those dark eyes searched Kane's lean face. "Moe's in a spot, Peter. You've seen the papers?"

"Not for three weeks," Kane sighed.

"You mean—you've been drunk for three weeks?"

"Three weeks tomorrow."

"Eight days ago," Alma Finch said slowly, "a girl named Anna Procaccini was murdered down on Hume Street. For eight days the papers have been riding Moe's heart out and blaming the department for not finding the killer. Now—it's worse. Last night a second girl was murdered, the same way, in the same place. Moe is desperate. He needs help. We need help, Peter, because if Moe loses his job—"

Kane nodded. He was drunk, but not too drunk to read what lay in the anxious face of this woman who sat staring at him. She loved Moe Finch, loved her big, good-natured, small-boy mug of a husband who sat down there in head-quarters behind a butt-scarred desk. Once, a long while ago, she had loved Peter Kane and he her. But he had celebrated that love by getting soused about it—too often. And he had killed it.

No, not killed it. Changed it. Changed it to a different kind of love. Alma Finch still loved him, still came to him when in trouble. But good girls don't marry drunks. Good girls may stay in love with drunks after marrying elsewhere; but the "marry a drunk" business is out, if a girl has sense. Alma had sense.

Moroni had had a hand in it, too. Big, know-it-all Moroni of the city payroll. Moroni had soured because Peter Kane, drunk, had caught results. Moroni, with a drag on the higher-ups, had seen Peter Kane heaved off the department. And, to a sensible girl, a drunk without a job is an even poorer bet than a drunk with a job. So Alma had married Moe Finch.

Kane stared at the girl and thought about it. He liked her. Maybe it was more than just that. He liked Moe Finch, too. And despised Moroni, for good reason. He said suddenly, leaning forward with one hand outpushed to grip the girl's arm: "Listen. Is Moroni on this job?"

"Yes," Alma Finch said. "Yes, of course."

Kane said, with a drunken snarl: "O.K., pal. Count me in."

THE SIDEWALK clock in front of Zanelli's Delicatessen said eleven five when Kane, still drunk, hiked down Hume Street toward Mame Lorier's tenement house. Half-naked urchins were playing noisily in unclean gutters; a pushcart man was shrieking his wares at frowsy women

who leaned out of upper windows. Across the street, two
doors up from Mame Lorier's, old Fanner, the legless one,
trundled himself down a short flight of wooden steps and,
using his bare hands on the dirty pavement, rolled himself
on his rubber-tired truck along the sidewalk. He was on
his way uptown to where he would spend the day selling
pencils and catnip in front of Horgan's Department Store.

Kane did a military left-face on the curb, climbed the
steps of Mame Lorier's, and hiked inside. He heard voices,
stopped in the hallway and listened, scowling. The voices
came from a half-open doorway at the end of the hall.
Kane strode forward, stood in the doorway and stared.

The room was small, filled to capacity with chunks of
cheap mahogany furniture, and all the remaining space
was taken up by Moroni, the Wise One, who stood wide-
legged, talking in a loud rasp to a big-breasted, big-hipped
woman who overflowed around the arms of a wooden
rocking-chair. The woman stared at Kane. Moroni turned,
stiffened, and scowled blackly.

"Oh, it's you," Moroni growled. "I figured you'd be around
after a while."

Kane murmured: "Don't mind me. I'm only sight-seeing."

"I guess Moe Finch told you we couldn't handle this
case without your valued help, huh?"

"If I'm intruding," Kane sighed, "I'm so sorry."

"And drunk, as usual."

"Inevitably, Moroni. Inevitably."

The woman put her fat hands on the chair-arms and
said: "If you two men want to talk alone—"

"Sit down, Mrs. Lorier," Moroni told her. "It won't take
me long to straighten this mug out." He glared at Kane.
"Listen. I'm a good guy. I'll save you a lot of time and

trouble. The job's all done and I'm here just to clean up some loose ends."

"Really!" Kane murmured.

"Yeah, really! We got a carload of dicks out walkin' the streets, lookin' for the two major suspects, and it won't take us long to tag both guys and drag 'em to headquarters. They cleared out and did a vanishing act right after Kitty Dolan was murdered. Maybe you know 'em. One's Heinfein; he's an oversexed, hungry-eyed furniture store guy who made so many plays for the Dolan girl that she was scared stiff. Her soul wasn't her own. He dogged every step she took, and she had to sneak in and out of the house to avoid him."

Moroni made a face, jammed a cigarette butt viciously into an overfilled ash tray. "The other mug is Kitty Dolan's own father. Fifty-five years old and a perpetual drunk of the mean variety. And an ex-pug to boot. Porky Dolan's his name, and I'm ready to prove right now, with Mrs. Lorier's help, that he's the guy who done both jobs!"

Kane leaned against a sideboard and said softly: "The speed with which you work amazes me, Moroni. Positively it does."

"So you think I'm nuts, huh?"

"A veritable Hawkshaw, Moroni."

"Well, I ain't drunk like you, that's certain! And get this: Porky Dolan had a damn good reason for bumping off both girls. Why? Because he was playin' the first girl for a long time, see? Him and Anna Procaccini were just like this." Moroni stuck out two fingers and crossed them. "If you want my opinion, he got the girl in wrong and had to rub her out before she raised a squawk. Then he found out his own daughter was wise to him—which was natural, because Kitty and the Procaccini girl were pals—so he put

Kitty out of the picture, too. Put that between your toes and use Absorbine, Junior on it!"

Kane sighed. The room was hot and stuffy, and instead of one big-bosomed woman sitting gaping at him there were two big-bosomed women. And instead of one bare-headed, sweat-faced Moroni raving in a loud voice, there were two Moronis. With a shrug, Kane swayed away from the sideboard and paraded unsteadily to the door.

"You wouldn't mind if I looked around, would you?" he said. "Me, I love souvenirs, and maybe I can find me a lock of the girl's hair—"

He went out, leaving Moroni alone with the woman. In the hallway he turned right and ascended a flight of uncarpeted stairs that led to the third floor. Alma Finch had told him the layout, back there in Limpy's, and he knew that Kitty Dolan's rooms were third-floor-front, overlooking the street.

THE DOOR was open and, judging from appearances, Moroni and the rest of Moe Finch's gumshoes had been through the place with a fine-tooth comb. Kane went in, eyed the bed yearningly. A little unsteady on his feet, he wandered from room to room, looked at Kitty Dolan's belongings. Going from the living room back to the bedroom, he tripped on a raised threshold and sat down with a thud that jarred his teeth.

He said aloud: "My God, you're plastered!" Reaching into a hip pocket he brought out a pint bottle half full that was miraculously unbroken. He emptied it, gagged, and reverently placed the bottle upright on the floor, then grabbed a corner of Kitty Dolan's dressing table and pulled himself erect.

The effort rocked the dressing table away from the wall. Behind it, something made a skidding sound and thumped to the floor. Kane leaned forward, looked down, and made a face. When he straightened again he had a rubber-banded package of letters in one hand and he was scowling.

"Moe Finch's dick's must've got their training out of correspondence schools," he growled.

The letters were addressed to Miss Katherine Dolan and bore no return address. The handwriting on the en-velopes, and on the pages of cheap paper inside, was crude, scrawly. It was a man's handwriting, and the same man had written all the letters. He signed his name Sammy.

Kane read every word of every letter and when he was finished, twenty minutes later, his eyes were tight and his mouth hooked in a thin hard line. He said aloud: "Boy, does this Sammy guy know his love-words! Does he and how!" Then he looked again at some of the crude handwrit-ing and pondered over words that made the love-lines seem sinister.

> ... Like I've told you before, Kitty, I know how much this Antole Heinfein wants you for his own. And I'm telling you, if you ever go out with that man even once I'll kill both of you, even though I love you more than anything on the whole earth, Kitty....

Kane shoved the letters into his pocket, looked around some more and walked out on the landing. Both Kitty Dolan and Anna Procaccini had been murdered by darts dropped from the roof of this same building. There ought to be a stairway leading up there.

There was, at the end of the hall. Kane climbed it, pushed open a heavy bulkhead and clambered out on the graveled roof. The roof was broad and flat, with clothes-yards and sky-lights bulging up to make a skyline. A foot-high ledge of painted tin ran around the rim. The sun was a bowl of bloody gilt up above, and the tin was hot against Kane's legs as he leaned over to peer down at the sidewalk three stories below.

Any man who could lean over here and drop a steel dart on the head of a moving pedestrian that far below, would need to be a good shot. That was something worth re-membering.

Kane walked to the rear of the roof and looked down on an alley littered with garbage cans and refuse. The height made him dizzy. He swayed around in a half-circle and paraded back to the bulkhead. When he got downstairs after pawing the rickety bannister to avoid taking a nose dive, Moroni was still chiseling information out of Mame Lorier.

Kane dug the pack of letters out of his pocket, pushed them against Moroni's elbow and said: "I found these up in Kitty's room. Read 'em and get a free lesson on how to make love."

Moroni stared, took the letters and pawed them. When he started reading them, he kept going until he had waded through them all. Then he frowned, said sullenly: "Sammy, huh? Sammy who?"

He swung on Mame Lorier. "You know any guy by that name? You know any of Kitty Dolan's friends named Sammy?"

"I know Sammy Ketz," the woman said.

"Yeah? Who's he?"

"I don't know who he is. I know his name is Sammy Ketz and he comes in there once in a while, not very often. He goes upstairs to the third floor, but I wouldn't know whether Kitty knows him or not. Heinfein lives on the third floor, too."

"That's the only Sammy you know, is it?"

"I can't remember no other," Mame said thoughtfully.

"Well, this stuff is hot, see?" Moroni gripped the letters in hard fingers. "Hot as hell. It puts a new angle on things." He glared at Kane. "Thanks, mug. Thanks a lot. For once you done me a favor."

"The only favor I could do you," Kane murmured softly, on his way to the door, "would be to drop arsenic in your coffee—or maybe a cockroach." He put a hand in his pocket and brought out the mechanical cockroach he had been playing with in Limpy's. "Moroni," he said, addressing the bug. "My pal, Moroni." Without haste, he closed the front door of Mame Lorier's tenement house behind him, teetered down the steps, and walked a straight course up Hume Street by watching the center crack in the sidewalk.

MOE FINCH was in the back room at headquarters on LaRonge Street when Kane opened the door and paced with drunken dignity over the threshold. Finch's square face was criss-crossed with worry-lines; his dark eyes looked darker than usual because they were sunk deep in hard rings caused by lack of sleep, and because he needed a shave.

He straightened his hunched shoulders, stared steadily at Kane and said, after an unnatural silence: "I been hoping you'd show up, Kane. So help me, I'm frantic. Alma was telling me you promised to get in on this Dolan business, and then you didn't come around—"

"I been down there," Kane grinned.

"What?"

"Maybe you'll do me a favor, if you can stop worrying long enough. I want a look at the things that killed Kitty and her girl-friend."

Finch exuded relief. "You been down there? You're a pal, Kane; so help me you are. I figured you'd be too wall-eyed drunk." He slid open a drawer of the desk, took two gleaming objects out of it and laid them on the desk-top.

Kane leaned forward, picked one of the things up and studied it, then studied the other. They were both alike, both needle-sharp, both heavy. After a five-minute inspection during which Finch's anxious eyes watched every changing expression of his face, Kane leaned back, pushed the steel darts away from him.

"You ever see murder-tools like those before?" he demanded.

"I never did, and I hope to God I never see another!"

Kane said: "No, you never did. You didn't go through what I did. You had flat feet or something." He made a sucking sound with his lips, and there was a hard glint in his eyes that had not been in them before. "It's a good thing I was curious enough to look at these things, Finch. A damn good thing. Now we got something to worry about."

He stood up and walked around the desk, pulled open a lower drawer that was jammed full of papers and junk. Fumbling under the junk, Kane hauled out a pint bottle, then fumbled again and produced a waxed-paper cup. Laboriously he poured a stiff drink, stared at the amber liquid before downing it. He snorted, crumpled the cup in curled fingers. "Lousy, Finch. Lousy. Sell it to Moroni and buy some stuff worth imbibing."

"Where you going?" Finch wailed.

"Hume Street."

"Again?"

"Again. Maybe I even have a date with the guy who dropped those steel toys."

"You mean—"Moe Finch jerked forward, sucking breath. "You mean you got a line on where Heinfein and Porky Dolan are hiding out?"

"Maybe I even mean that." Kane rounded the desk and paced to the door. "While I'm at it, your friend Moroni is out looking for free lessons in the art of making love. He's got a crush on the large lady that runs the tenement. When he comes in, give him my best wishes. And by the way"— Kane walked crookedly back to the desk and pocketed the pint bottle—"this stuff isn't so lousy after all. Maybe I'll need it where I'm going."

Finch gaped. This time, Kane navigated the threshold, marched out of headquarters and descended the steps to LaRonge Street. He walked half a block, thumbed a prowling cab and got into it. To the driver he said thickly: "Hume Street, buddy."

Uptown, a clock was striking two.

AFTERNOON SUN had baked Hume Street into a canyon of evil odors. The odors invaded Kane's sensitive nostrils and caused him to make a wry face as he prowled along the filthy sidewalk toward Mame Lorier's house. But Mame's place was not, this time, his destination. He crossed the street and climbed the steps of a building two doors up from the death house.

Porky Dolan had lived here before doing a fadeaway. Other people lived here, too, and Kane studied the row of battered mail boxes before thumbing the bell. A bald-pated Italian without any shirt answered the bell, gaped at the police badge that Kane palmed toward him, and backed away, staring. Kane walked in, walked upstairs.

He stopped on the second floor, looked at door numbers and brought hard knuckles into play on a paintless portal that bore a brass numeral—7. After awhile he rapped again and then, scowling, tried the knob. The door was locked. Kane shrugged, bunched his shoulder to break the barrier down, and then thought better. Turning, he went slowly down the stairs, strode past the gaping Italian in the lower hall, and paraded out of the building.

At the end of Hume Street he caught another cab and said: "Limpy's. Stuart Street."

On the way uptown he killed Moe Finch's pint and gazed longingly at the dead bottle.

Half a dozen men were stooled at Limpy's bar and Kane joined them, pushed a half-dollar through a pool of beer suds and said to Limpy: "Scotch, *padre.*" He was drunk and he knew it, and he had a desire now, for no particular reason to get very much drunker. Later, he had an unpleasant job to take care of—perhaps a dangerous job. Meanwhile, Limpy had good Scotch, and Scotch was excellent medicine for clearing mud out of a man's brain. Certainly it was.

He downed three of them, climbed off his stool and walked to the other end of the bar. Three men at that end were harmonizing painfully on a song that needed some *boom-boom-booms* to give it depth. Kane supplied the *boom-boom-booms.* After a while he said, "Meet Moroni," and placed his mechanical cockroach on the bar. The men stared at him. One of them laughed and another said gently: "How long you been on this bender, Kane?"

Limpy, behind the bar, answered a phone and said: "For you, Kane. Important the guy says." Limpy passed the phone over the bar and Kane took it, mumbled into it.

A crisp, jerky voice said: "Listen, Kane. You know where Moroni is?"

"He is making love," Kane grinned, "to a large lady named Mame. Mame Lorier. You should go find Mame, and there also you will find Mr. Moroni."

"Listen," the voice jerked, "this is Kennedy talkin', and I'm down at the Lorier place now, and Moroni ain't here. Break away from Limpy and get down here quick as hell!"

"Certainly," Kane said. He passed the phone back to Limpy. *"Tsk, tsk.* Always when I'm enjoying myself. May I be excused, please?"

Limpy nodded knowingly: "You're plastered."

"But never too inebriated to be of service, my friend." Kane scooped up his mechanical cockroach, shook beer suds off it and dropped it into his pocket. Elaborately he walked to the door. "I shall be back, Limpy. Never let it be said that I run from my liquor."

Outside, he caught a cab. When the cab squealed to a stop twenty minutes later in front of Mame Lorier's tenement on Hume Street, Kane stepped gingerly out, teetered while paying the driver, and zig-zagged slowly up the steps.

KENNEDY WAS in the small, stuffy room where Moroni had talked with Mame. She was there with him, and so was a thin, mouse-faced youth who sat stiffly erect in a straight-backed chair. The youth gazed at Kane with pop eyes as Kane leaned against the door-frame, steadying himself. Kennedy, a red-haired, wide-shouldered-head-quarters dick, turned on large feet and said jerkily: "It didn't take you too long, mister. Look what I got here."

Kane pushed thick fingers through his hair and blinked his eyes. After he had succeeded in condensing the six people he saw first down to three, he peered steadily at the youth and realized things.

The kid was young, not more than eighteen or nineteen. Judging from the sheen of his eyes, he was coked; and judging from his match-stick thinness, his muddy complexion, his uncontrolled nervousness, this load of coke was not his first. Right now he was scared stiff.

"This," Kennedy declared triumphantly, "is the Sammy Ketz that wrote those letters."

The kid made convulsive movements. "I didn't write no letters, I'm tellin' you! So help me God, I never wrote no letters to the girl! I didn't even have a speakin' acquaintance with her!"

"And so help me God," Mame Lorier snarled, "I seen you come in and out of this house at least a dozen times, and I seen you go upstairs to the third floor!"

"I—I went up there to see Heinfein. I done odd jobs for Heinfein."

"And you never even knew Kitty Dolan," Kennedy sneered.

"That's the God's honest truth and strike me dead if I'm lyin'!"

Kennedy turned, glared at Kane. "You see what I got on my hands? A dirty, doped-up liar. Even when I grabbed him, he was on his way into this house."

"I come to see Heinfein, I told you!"

"And you wouldn't know, of course, that Heinfein don't live here any more?"

"I don't know nothin', except what you been tellin' me," Sammy Ketz wailed.

Kennedy shrugged, gazed again at Kane. "The reason I sent for you—someone's gotta stay here while I take this mug to headquarters. I been expectin' Moroni, but somethin' must be keepin' him. You ain't too drunk to hang around?"

Kane sighed, took four uncertain steps and lowered himself into a chair. "There's nothing I'd enjoy more than hanging around, sweetheart. Nothing on earth. Especially"— he raised his eyebrows at Mame Lorier—"with Moroni's loved one."

Kennedy said, "O.K.," and put a hard hand on Sammy Ketz's arm, hauled the boy erect. "Let's go, mug." Stolidly he herded Ketz to the door, marched him down the hall.

Kane swayed erect again and lurched after them, grinning. To no one in particular—certainly not to Mame Lorier—he murmured aloud: "Always do I have a yen to watch a first-class detective earn his living. Always do I have it." In the street doorway he pawed Kennedy's arm. "You wouldn't have a little liquid lubrication on you? Such a lovely time I was having at Limpy's when you dragged me away—"

Kennedy snorted, pushed Sammy Ketz down the steps and along the sidewalk. Sighing, Kane leaned in the doorway, watching them. On the roof at the far end of the building, something moved. Kane saw, jerked to abrupt attention. For six seconds he stared, then bellowed a yell of warning.

The yell spewed from his lips after the shape on the room had leaned forward and leaned back again. Then it was too late. Sunlight made a gleaming arrow of the steel dart as it fell. A single line of bright silver, like water streaking thinly from a sharp-nosed faucet, extended from the roof to Sammy Ketz's bare head.

Ketz stopped in his tracks. He had a long thin neck, but the neck vanished as his head was driven down between his bunched shoulders. He jerked both hands up and clawed wildly at his hair as he went to his knees. For seconds there on his knees he was like a fanatic in some heathen temple, pawing empty air and shrieking in a voice so high and so shrill that it racked Kane's eardrums. Then the boy collapsed in a contorted heap, face down, and Kennedy stood gaping above him, gulping great breaths of air.

In the doorway of the tenement, Kane whirled, leaped like a mad bull along the hall. His outthrust left hand slapped the bannister and made a whining sound as he lurched up the stairs. He had been drunk down there in the doorway. By the time he reached the second-floor landing he was drenched with cold whiskey sweat and beginning to be sober.

Midway between the second and third landings he stumbled, swore bitterly as the uncarpeted stairs took skin from his face. Blindly he heaved himself up again, staggered down the top-floor hallway and made for the stairway leading up to the roof. Blood was dribbling onto his shirt from the torn flesh of his face before he succeeded in slamming the bulkhead open.

HE WAS too late, but almost not. At the rear end of the roof something moved, slithered over the edge. Kane lunged forward, felt the roof tremble under him as his big feet crunched down on loose gravel. He had to skid sideways to avoid ploughing through a low skylight, had to bend double at the hips, lowering his head and shoulders to avoid being hung in a maze of bare clotheslines. It took time.

Took too much time. Sucking breath, he sobbed to a stop at the roof-edge, jammed his hands against the tin ledge and looked over. A rope snaked over the ledge beside him, and the top end of the rope was bowlined around a foot-high iron pipe that elbowed above the roof.

The rope hung in a plumb line down the rear wall of the building. Its lower end dangled a foot above the filthy floor of the alleyway that separated Mame Lorier's tenement house from houses that fronted on the next street. Aside from garbage cans, ash barrels and piles of accumulated refuse, the alley was empty.

Kane stared for two minutes, waiting for signs of life that failed to materialize. Scowling, he backed away from the edge, turned on the balls of his feet and ran back to the bulkhead. Cold sober, he groped down to the third-floor landing and found the upper end of a rear stairway that led him to the alley. The stairway was dark, narrow, and looked as if it had been used not more than twice in the past twenty years. The door leading to the alley was open.

He prowled down the alley and peered with narrowed eyes into every possible hiding place. It took him ten minutes to go seventy yards. When he got to the alley mouth he relaxed, made a growling sound through tight lips. There were too many avenues of escape, too many blind doorways through which the killer could have fled. Besides, the murderer had planned his escape—or her escape—beforehand. Any fiend who could slaughter three victims—and get away with it—was not dumb.

Kane turned the corner into Hume Street and walked back to Mame Lorier's. The sidewalk where Sammy Ketz had died was empty. Kennedy, being wise, had carried the body inside before a crowd could smell blood.

Kane prowled into the house. Kennedy, leaning against the wall in the first-floor hallway, was staring mutely down at Sammy Ketz's sprawled body. Kane stared too, and looked away, feeling suddenly ill, after examining the steel dart that was imbedded inches deep in Sammy's skull. Blood was on the worn carpet, and blood was on Kennedy's clothes.

Kennedy said in a low voice. "I wonder if that thing was meant for me instead of him."

Mame Lorier was standing stiff as wood in the doorway of the small, stuffy room ten paces distant. She looked, Kane noted, as if she had walked backwards along the hall, and probably she had done that very thing, gaping at Kennedy as the headquarters dick had carried Sammy into the house. She looked scared. Her eyes were like flat glazed buttons in a fat face drained of all color. Her hands were clamped on the door frame.

Kane said: "I guess we better take Ketz to headquarters. I guess we better do that right away." He glanced at Mame. "You wouldn't mind if I used your phone to send for the wagon. And, if you got a drink in the house—even shellac— this is one time when I feel justified."

MORONI AND Moe Finch, both in the back room at headquarters, gaped in silent amazement at the killer's latest victim, and then, like mated love birds, turned their bewildered gazes on Kane and Kennedy as blue-uniformed policemen dumped Sammy Ketz's body onto a wooden bench and paraded from the room.

"Meet Sammy Ketz," Kane said.

Moroni stiff-armed himself out of a chair and strode forward, stared down into the dead youth's face. "You're telling me this here is Sammy Ketz?"

"In person."

Moroni's big face took on an expression of triumph. He made fists of his hands and jammed them against his hips, stood swaying on spread legs. "O.K., mister. Again you done us a favor, even if you didn't mean to. You tell me, 'meet Sammy Ketz.' So I'm telling you, meet the rat that rubbed out Anna Procaccini and Kitty Dolan!"

Moe Finch sucked on a fat cigar and said, beaming. "That's right, Kane. We got the whole works."

Kane was silent, scratching the side of his mouth with a blunt fingernail. He glanced at Kennedy, grinned, aimed his gaze laconically around the room and ambled to the door. "Fine! Now I can go back to Limpy's and—"

"So you're a wise guy," Moroni sneered. "You're so big-headed you don't even want to know how we figured this guy out. Just because you fell down on the job yourself, you ain't interested no more."

"I'm all ears."

"Yeah? Well, grab yourself an eyeful of these!" Moroni strode to the desk, scooped up a handful of letters and thrust them forward. "Me, I've been doing some quiet investigating on my own hook, while you been messing around. Where did I get these? I got 'em in the Procaccini girl's rooming house, where she was living at the time she was bumped off. And who wrote 'em? Sammy wrote 'em! This same Sammy Ketz guy that's lyin' here right now, dead as hell!"

Kane looked at the letters. They were love letters, ad-dressed to Miss Anna Procaccini and scrawled in the same crude handwriting as those that he himself had discovered behind Kitty Dolan's dressing table. Judging by the post-marks, the Procaccini girl had received at least one missive a day up to, and including, the day of her death.

Kane put the letters on Moe Finch's desk and paced slowly forward to peer down into Sammy Ketz's dead face. He stared a long while, scowling. Then he bent over, emptied Sammy's pockets and dumped a handful of junk on the bench, between the youth's stiff legs. The junk included keys, cigarettes, a cheap billfold, an aspirin box that contained cocaine, and, finally, two cards of matches.

Frowning, Kane pawed open the billfold and extracted papers that had handwriting on them. One paper read, *See Heinfein Tuesday 4 o'clock.* Another, *Brass Monkey in the sixth, R'ingham, Friday.* Another was apparently a list of phone numbers. Kane smiled softly, took the papers to Finch's desk and spread them out beside the stack of letters. His gaze met Moroni's.

"Just why," Kane demanded, "should Sammy Ketz want to murder two nice girls all of a sudden like?"

"I got that figured out," Moroni growled.

"You would have."

"You're damn right I would have! This Anna Procaccini was Sammy's girlfriend, see? I found that out. And I got a pretty safe idea he was playing around Kitty Dolan, too—or else why was he always hanging around the house she lived in? So what? So Anna found out he was two-timing her and maybe threatened to tip the Dolan girl off as to what kind of a guy he was. So Sammy rubbed her out, maybe in a fit of temper and maybe just in cold blood. Then he got rid of Kitty because Kitty smelled a rat. What's wrong with that?"

"Nothing," Kane murmured. "Nothing, really. And after he'd murdered both girls he felt bad about it, so he rubbed himself out just to make it all even, huh?"

A puzzled expression spread over Moroni's large face. He turned slowly to peer at Sammy Ketz.

"He's dead," Kane said. "Deader'n hell, honest. You never thought of that." He sighed, shook his head in mock pity. "And Sammy didn't write these letters. Didn't write these, or the ones that were stowed away behind Kitty Dolan's dresser. Sammy's handwriting"—he poked the papers that had come from Katz's billfold—"is nice and neat. These letters are a mess."

Moroni and Moe Finch compared handwritings. Kennedy stood looking on, sucking a cigarette he had forgotten to put a match to. When Moroni finally looked up, glaring, Kane said softly: "If you and Kennedy want to visit Hume Street again, maybe we can snag the eagle that dropped all three of those darts. Or if you don't feel that ambitious, I'll mosey along alone."

Moe Finch leaned over the desk, mouth agape. Moroni made mumbling sounds. Kennedy, lighting his cigarette, said indifferently: "O.K. Anything to oblige."

A SLOW drizzle was making LaRonge Street dark and gray when Moroni slid behind the wheel of a police car and waited for Kennedy to climb in beside him and slam the door. The drizzle was a pelting rain by the time Kane leaned forward from the rear seat, jarred Moroni's shoulder and said: "Never mind Mame's place. Pull up to the house across the street there."

It was the house formerly occupied by Porky Dolan. The house Kane had invaded, unsuccessfully, only a few hours ago. Moroni, scowling, growled out: "What the hell are you handin' us? Kitty Dolan's old man—"

"Sure," Kane said. "Sure. Kitty Dolan's old man used to live here. I know."

The car's right-front tire scraped the curb and Kane got out, dragged a deep breath while waiting for Moroni and Kennedy to untangle themselves. Quietly he led the way. While he was thumbing the bell, Moroni said irritably: "Listen. What is this? Are we after Porky Dolan?"

"We're after hell on earth," Kane said, and pushed past the bewildered Italian who opened the door.

He said no more then, until he had climbed the stairs to the second floor. Once before, he had climbed those stairs and thumped on the door marked 7. Now he banged it again and stood waiting, with Moroni and Kennedy standing impatiently behind him.

Kane knocked again, waited another two minutes and said softly: "O.K. We'll break in." The hallway was dark, because the rain outside had turned Hume Street into a canyon of gray gloom. Kane locked his arms, heaved his shoulder against the door and said, *"Ugh!"* Breath exploded from his lips. He tried again, and Kennedy stepped up beside him.

"Now!" Kane rasped. Both men heaved. The door groaned open and clattered back against the wall inside.

Moroni, staring into gloom across the threshold, said sullenly: "So this is Porky Dolan's hangout, huh?"

Kane could have answered but did not. He fumbled for a light switch, found one and looked around. There were two rooms, connected by a wide doorway. One room contained a cheap divan and two overstuffed chairs to match; the other held a bed, a wooden chair, a scarred bureau. Kane walked through the living room into the bedroom and dumped the contents of the bureau drawers, one after another, on the bedroom floor. He said: "Now don't be asking me what I expect to find, because—"

Breath whined between his teeth and he stabbed a hand downward, snatched a pack of letters. There was a glint in his eyes that meant something, and a trace of a smile on his mouth. He sat on the bed, unhanded the letters and pawed through them, slowly.

More than twenty letters were in the pack. About half of them were addressed in one feminine hand; the other half in another. All were for Sammy Stanton, Box 47, Back Bay Station. Kane opened the letters and saw that half of them had been written by Anna Procaccini, the other half by Kitty Dolan. He said: "Dear me!"

He handed the letters to Moroni and said: "I had an idea we'd find something queer like this. Read 'em." Moroni read them and began to scowl, and continued scowling as he waded through page after page of feminine script.

"Combining these here letters with the ones we found in the two girl's rooms," Moroni said, "it makes a funny set-up. Who is this Sammy Stanton guy, anyhow? He writes first to the Procaccini girl and tells her he seen her walking on the street and she's the angel of his dreams, and he just had to write to her because he loves her so much; and then he plays the same tune on Kitty Dolan. And both girls fall for it, separate. Sammy writes a pile of swell romantic letters and both girls are sap enough to answer 'em, even though they never seen this Sammy person and don't even know what he looks like. What kind of a romance is this?"

Kane said: "It's the sort of thing you'd expect from this Sammy Stanton."

"Yeah, but what the hell? What kind of a guy would swap love letters with a couple of broads and never actually meet the broads, and all the time keep each dame in the dark about the other one? What kind of a guy, I ask you?"

Kane was leaning forward, fumbling again with the mound of junk dumped from the bureau drawers. He had a cardboard shoe box in his hands, with the cover off, and was gaping wide-eyed at a pair of evil-looking steel darts and a large number of small tin-foiled packages side. "This kind of guy," Kane frowned. "There's enough coke here to—"

THE CLICK of a light switch cut his talk and he dropped the box and sat suddenly stiff as the room went black. For three seconds he didn't move. Moroni slapped a hand on the bedpost and growled out: "Say! What the hell—"Kennedy, more phlegmatic, flattened silently against the wall and hauled a .38 from his pocket, leveling the gun at the doorway between the two rooms.

A soft creaking sound began near the hall door and came slowly across the living room toward the connecting threshold. Kane stared and stood erect, stood wide-legged with his hands dangling and his head tilted a little to one side, the tip of his tongue caressing his half-parted lips. He had no gun, so he balled his hands into fists and set himself for a swift leap.

Kennedy against the wall was gazing sullenly at a spot in the doorway, where the head of the creeping intruder would first loom in the dark. He paid for his mistake. The intruder's head, when it came, was no more than four feet off the floor and the man's outstretched arm ended in a leveled gun.

Kennedy's .38 belched, sent a slug screaming through space a foot above the mark. The other gun roared in answer, then leaped in a half-circle and roared twice more, as Moroni lunged forward.

Kennedy said: *"Ar-r-r-gh!"* and thudded back against the wall, hung there like a spread-winged bat before crumpling to the floor and clutching his stomach. Moroni staggered sideways, fell against the edge of the bureau and sobbed to one knee, groaning. Before the killer's gun could make more thunder, Kane had stooped with uncanny quickness, stabbed both hands under the mound of junk on the floor and, with a swift scooping movement, raked the stuff into the man's face.

The man floundered in the doorway, clawed madly to free his arms, face and shoulders from a tangled mass of shirts, underclothes, bed sheets and bureau-drawer dumpings. Before he came out of it, Kane had a chair in both hands and was swinging the chair in a vicious circle.

The killer's gun roared, roared again as Kane leaped forward. Kane's left side went white hot but he did not stop. The gun belched again and the slug hit the chair in Kane's hands, sent an electric shock through his arms and shoulders. Then the gun whined through space, missed Kane's cheek by fractions of an inch and thudded against the wall behind him.

The killer clamped both hands, bare, against the floor and whirled forward. He didn't leap; he had no legs to leap with. His body in the dark was a monstrous black spider-shape crouching on a four-wheeled kiddie-car contraption. His big head was thrust forward. His curled lips frothed out snarling sounds that chilled Kane's blood.

Kane sobbed, brought the broken chair down with all his strength and knew that he had missed. The chair cracked up on the floor, but Martin Fanner was not under it. Fanner could move more swiftly on his rubber-tired truck than Kane could on two feet. The man's hands were iron, hardened by years of contact with the streets. He could make his kiddie-car do tricks, make it leap and lunge and dodge with amazing swiftness. How—in the name of God—could a man like that fight—a freak—

Agony blurred Kane's eyes. The gun-wound in his left side had stirred a three-weeks' supply of alcohol inside him, making him suddenly drunk, sick at his stomach. He staggered, hit the bed-end with the small of his back and jabbed both hands out, gripped the brass knobs of the bed posts. Both his feet lashed out and kicked savagely, blindly, at the spider-shape clawing toward him. Steel fingers gripped one of his ankles and twisted as if they were twisting limp rope.

Kane let go the brass knobs and spilled sideways, turned a half-circle. He had to or his leg would have snapped. Before his face and arms slapped the floor, Fanner was on top of him and Fanner's clubbed fists were falling like twin pile-drivers. Teeth went loose in Kane's mouth. He spat blood from a torn tongue. The blows that raked his chest and throat were strong enough to break bone. Fanner's face above him was a crooked gargoyle white with foam at the mouth, and the man's eyes were distended, red as gobs of congealed blood.

Kane rolled clear, rolled under the bed and lost face-flesh on the iron bed frame. He was sick, but scared stiff with an icy dread of annihilation, and when he slid free of the bed on the far side, desperation gave him sense enough to lurch erect. The spider-shape shot toward him and Kane leaped to the bed, swayed there like a drunk on a heaving ship. He saw himself in the mirror of the bureau, saw blood gushing from the gun-wound in his side, saw a pair of long arms stabbing toward him over the bed edge.

He leaped, made the bureau in two stumbling strides and gripped the side frames of the mirror to steady himself. Fanner came at him again, swift as a monstrous fiddler crab. The mirror broke out of its side arms and Kane gripped the jagged arms for handles.

You killed spiders with anything you could get hold of. They were vermin—

He lurched on spread legs, brought the heavy mirror down with a sweep that sent new agony through him. Fanner's snarling face went under glass, broke through and reappeared with one eye gouged, blood spurting from cheeks and mouth. Again and again Kane struck. More glass broke. Jagged edges raked Fanner's face and throat. Fanner's hands stopped clawing at Kane's legs. The hands trembled, curled up like the legs of a dying spider.

Kane's foot shot out, kicked against the man's bulging chest and sent him savagely across the room. The kiddie-car made thudding contact with a wall. Fanner swayed sideways and the kiddie-car tipped over, two wheels spinning slowly. Fanner did not move.

Sobbing, Kane wiped bloody hands on his shirt and walked drunkenly into the next room to click the light switch. He came back and stood over Kennedy, peered down and saw that Kennedy was dead. Moroni was moaning, twitching on the floor. Kane stretched Moroni on the bed, left him there and went downstairs to use a phone. He wanted a drink more than anything.

MORONI HAD bandages around his head and was staring at Kane through a horizontal gap in the white strips. Moroni sat on the bench in the back room at headquarters, and Kane leaned against Moe Finch's desk, and Moe Finch sat like a wooden Indian in the chair behind the desk, gazing at Fanner.

Fanner was not dead. His face was raw meat under layers of bandages and one of his arms hung limp because the muscles had been slashed by broken glass, but his eyes were still loaded with malice and he was able to utter sounds that were unpleasantly alive. Handcuffed, he squatted on his truck with his back against the wall. Dicks and uniformed policemen were in the room. The door was closed.

Moroni growled at Kane, through bandages that muddied his voice. "Listen, we admit Fanner's guilty; we know that. But what'd he kill the Procaccini girl and Kitty Dolan for, and how in hell did he get up on that roof to do it? And why'd he kill Sammy Ketz?"

"Answer 'em yourself," Kane shrugged pleasantly. "I'll have mine with Scotch."

"I'm askin' you for information, damn you!"

"O.K.," Kane said. "Fanner's queer. He's queer with gas and shell-shock and with another kind of queerness that comes to any guy with half his body cut off. As Sammy Stanton, he was living a life of swell romance—the kind Martin Fanner never could lead. Maybe he really loved the girls he wrote those goofy letters to. Maybe he wrote to a lot of girls. Anyway, he killed the Procaccini girl because she was playing with either Porky Dolan or Heinfein or both." Kane turned his head toward Fanner. "Which one was it?"

"Go to hell," Fanner growled.

"All right. Call it Porky Dolan. We know she played with him, and we're not sure about Heinfein, so call it Porky. What difference does it make?" Kane put a hand against his injured side and exhaled slowly. "Fanner killed Kitty Dolan because she got wise to him and learned about the first killing—or because he thought she did, even if she didn't." He turned again to Fanner. "Want to deny that?"

"Go to hell!" Fanner screeched.

"Sure, but you'll be there first." Kane forced a crooked smile and peered at Moroni, who was glaring. "About Sammy Ketz, the cokey, I'm not sure. My guess is that Sammy was buying coke from the kiddie-car Romeo here. Fanner got panicky when, from his window across the street, he saw Kennedy grab Sammy and drag Sammy into Mame Lorier's. He thought Sammy would blab the works, and for peddling coke a guy gets plenty time in the jail house. So he hustled around the block, went up on Mame's roof by the back stairs, as he always did, and gave Sammy the works while Kennedy was taking Sammy to headquarters. Then, using a rope—also as usual—he did a fade-out."

Moroni scowled. Moe Finch, leaning forward, said: "What I don't get, even yet, is how you sorted Fanner out of the crowd."

"I'm tired of talking," Kane sighed. "My throat is so dry—"

"You spill that, and you can go back to Limpy's for the rest of your life."

"O.K.," Kane murmured. "O.K. Those steel darts are *flechettes*, same as were used in the war. In the war they were dropped out of planes and did plenty damage. It takes a good man to use 'em right. Takes a man with training." He glanced at Fanner and nodded slowly, meaningly. "Plenty of training. So I looked around for a war vet and there was Fanner, living right across the street. Now, if you don't mind, I'm thirsty as all get-out, and—"

He straightened away from the desk and walked toward the door. No doctor had looked at him yet, and there were no bandages on his injured side. He took four steps, stopped, turned suddenly pale and began to sway. Moe Finch was out from behind the desk in a flash, reaching for him.

On the floor, Kane grinned up into Finch's face and said: "Ain't it sad? The older I get, the less I can take it." Finch had a pint bottle open and was baring the wound. He spilled whiskey into his cupped palm and slapped it against the gash that was spurting red blood.

Kane said: *"Ugh!"* and did a convulsion as the alcohol bit. His hand stabbed out, clamped around the neck of the bottle. "Honest, Finch, you can think of more ways to waste good whiskey—" The neck of the bottle went into his mouth. When he stopped drinking, the pint was three quarters empty and Moroni, across the room, was growling: "Listen, Finch. After what I been through, I could use some of that, too."

Kane gave the bottle to Finch and Finch put it on the desk. Moroni lumbered forward, took a lily cup from the desk drawer and poured the cup half full. He stared at Kane as Kane groped erect. Kane was grinning. Kane said drunkenly: "Wait a minute. I forgot something."

He swayed to the desk and leaned there, with one hand fumbling in his pocket. "This here is my party. I gotta mix the drinks myself." He put a finger in Moroni's lily cup and stirred elaborately before handing the cup to Moroni. Then he turned, grinning, and paraded drunkenly to the door, and this time he made it.

Moroni, glaring at him, took a mouthful of whiskey and suddenly choked, spat the mouthful over Moe Finch's desk. Moe Finch stared. So did the rest of the room's occupants.

A small black thing sat on the desk-top in a pool of whiskey. The thing had passed from Kane's pocket to the lily cup to Moroni's mouth and out again. It was a mechanical black bug that looked like a cockroach, and as Moroni stared the bug made a soft whirring sound, shook itself and leaped toward him.

Moroni cursed, went red in the face. On the threshold, Peter Kane grinned drunkenly and murmured: "A cockroach—in Mr. Moroni's coffee—*tsk, tsk.*"

BOTTLED IN BLONDE

IT WAS THE GREATEST
OPPORTUNITY OF KANE'S
DRUNKEN CAREER—KEYS TO A
LIQUOR STORE AND ALL NIGHT TO
SAMPLE WHAT LAY BEHIND THE
LOCKS THAT GUARDED IT. BUT
EVEN HE MIGHT HAVE HESITATED
TO BARGE IN ON THOSE SERRIED
ROWS OF CASE GOODS IF HE'D
KNOWN THE FIRST SWALLOW
WOULD MEAN MURDER—

CHAPTER ONE
MURDER PASS-OUT

R AIN CAME out of a 3 A.M. sky and drummed hollowly on the box-kite sign-above Kane's head. The sign's neon tubes were dead, but for the benefit of occasional disinterested passers-by the curled glass letters said: Bonney's Class A Liquors.

Kane moved a rum-heavy head sideways, made *tsking* sounds and said aloud, sadly: "Why a guy who owns a liquor store should close up shop at midnight and make a bee line for Limpy's to get himself drunk, I don't fathom. Nuts, just nuts."

Albert Bonney could be a good guy when drunk. He had been drunk fifteen minutes ago in Limpy's place on Stuart Street, had propped his pointed elbows in a suds pool on the bar and grinned at Kane. "Listen. If you actually wanta buy some package goods to go home and get plastered with, don't be a sap for Limpy's stuff. Me, I sell Limpy all his package goods so I know how lousy it is. Grab these keys and go help yourself to what I got in stock."

Two keys. One to fit the door, the other to be used in turning the electric alarm whose outside lock lurked behind an arm of the awning. "Help yourself to anything on the shelves and leave the dough on the counter on your way out," Bonney had mumbled. "And if you see DeSanto, the cop who is on the beat this time of night, tell him it is O.K. and I am not crazy but just feeling generous."

Kane made a face in the rain and looked both ways along South Center Street. Up the line half a block, an

There she lay, behind the counter.

owl restaurant threw yellow light across the gleaming sidewalk; the street itself was abandoned. Kane sighed, slouched forward. "Me," he murmured, "I intended to buy one pint of Limpy's lousy liquor and go home like a gentleman. Now I got a whole liquor store to sponge up. *Tsk.*"

He was drunk and his six-foot-two frame swayed from lean hips as he gripped the awning arm and aimed the smaller of Albert Bonney's two keys at the lock of the alarm. The key slipped sideways because another key was already in the slot. The lock was turned to Off.

A scowl corrugated Kane's brow. He said: "Huh?" He put a hand on the doorknob and the door opened when he leaned against it. He pushed his hat brim higher, rubbed his uncombed gray hair and peered into the store's dark interior.

"Something," he said, "is screwy."

He had a flashlight in his pocket and used it, swayed drunkenly over the sill, closed and locked the door behind him before scuffing forward. The flashlight's beam made gleaming doll-shapes of many bottles on shelves. It swept the floor, the counter, and the dark rectangle behind the counter. Albert Bonney's establishment was small and neat and the light had but a short distance to travel.

Kane went in behind the counter. The flashlight beam touched a cash register, roamed down and played over pasteboard boxes filled with bottle caps. It slid lower and jerked to a stop, went out when Kane's fingers tightened so convulsively that the contact was broken.

He shook the light, leaned forward when it blinked on again. The beam touched a slender silk-clad leg, moved sideways and encountered naked thigh-flesh and the torn fringe of a black rayon dress. Kane snuffed a deep breath.

The light beam came to rest on a pertly good-looking feminine face, on blond, wavy hair stiff with coagulated blood.

The girl was young, not more than twenty-five, and her tall slender body under the black dress was the kind of body men would turn to look at on the street. Kane said: "Fern Becker! What in—" His right knee slapped the floor and he bent forward, gaped into the girl's face. The face was a pale tableau of surprise and terror; the dark eyes were big in their sockets. A reek of strong Scotch whiskey clung to her glossy hair and to the floor around her head. Chunks of a broken quart bottle gleamed on the dark linoleum. Her head was bashed in.

Kane rocked around, felt sick instead of drunk. He knew Fern Becker. Had known her a long while, not intimately but well enough to like her. A good kid despite her chiseling, gold-digging habits. She had worked various sucker rackets to ensure her living.

HE CLICKED a light on and looked around, saw a blood line on the floor. The blood thinned, became a broken red trail leading crookedly into Bonney's back room, a small, grimy enclosure containing washstand, lavatory. Gobs of red stuff gleamed at a trap door that opened on Bonney's cellar.

Kane descended steep dark stairs and used his flash. The beam snaked over racks of beer, unopened cases of whiskey, high shelves stacked with cans of malt. The cellar was long, narrow, and the blood-trail ran through it. Kane followed, stopped beside an upturned box that supported a half-full gin bottle and a quart of lime-and-lithia.

He killed the gin, glared resentfully at the green lime bottle and stalked on again. The flash beam met a patent-leather-shoed foot that toed out of darkness. Kane hunched forward and the gin soured in his throat. He put the flash down on a box where its glow flooded the shape before him. Then he bunched his eyes and studied the sprawled body that lay between boxes and wall.

He knew this one, too. Louis Healey was the name, the age about thirty-two. Liquor fumes stabbed Kane's nostrils and the fumes came from Healey's cavernous mouth. Dirt and alcohol stains mingled with gouts of blood on Healey's tight-fitting tan suit, two-toned vest. The man's brilliantined hair was unruffled.

Louis Healey—suave, too-good-looking, pseudo-cultured thug, as cheap as the initialed necktie that bulged above his yellow shirt. A race-track lizard, Rockingham and Narragansett, but veneered with hair-slick, form-fitting toggery and the features of a tanned Apollo. And blood.

Kane sobered, made sounds like the grumblings of an aroused hound and bent closer to stick his chin out in a scowl. Louis Healey was not dead, not even hurt. Drunk, yes. Stupefied, paralyzed drunk and messy with blood. Blood on his clothes, his shoes. Blood on gray rubber gloves that masked his lean hands.

Rubber gloves? Kane's eyes were question marks, his forehead a maze of small creases. He reached down.

One of Healey's rubber gloves had a jagged rip in the palm—a rip that could have been caused by broken glass. The bottle that had slain Fern Becker upstairs....

Kane breathed slowly, removed the torn glove and peered at the uncovered hand. A flabby, long-fingered hand, smeared with blood but ungouged. He replaced the glove and stood up, turned on the balls of his feet and paraded slowly to the cellar stairs. Drunk, but no longer staggering.

It was Peter Kane, private shamus and number one man of the Beacon Agency, not Kane the souse, who stood over Fern Becker's bashed head, upstairs, and murmured through a thin-lipped scowl: "She comes in here with Healey and when he gets tough with her she tells him where to get off—so, smack! Nice people. But how'd she get in here?"

He knew how. Fern Becker was a friend of Bonney, who owned the joint. Too good a friend, according to some of those in the know who dubbed Bonney a fool for falling so hard, especially for a gold-digger like her. Keys? She had them, all right. Bonney would have seen to that.

Kane scooped the girl's handbag off the counter. From the looks of things she had come up from downstairs to grab a bottle from one of Bonney's shelves. The tout, sore about something, had trailed her up and swung on her before she could dodge his drunken attack. Then, plastered, he had gone down-cellar again, got drunker and passed out. But those gloves—

Kane dumped the handbag, pawed through powder, perfume, cigarettes—only a woman could carry that much junk. His lean fingers spider-legged around a pack of small white cards, calling cards, that were rubber-banded together.

Kane read names. Luther Gleason, contractor. J. Mark Allen, attorney. Dr. Paul Lafey. Bill Malkey, Station WLSO. Jacques Fournier, caterer. Others. She had been popular as a dance partner and this sucker list showed she'd made the most of her opportunities for profitable chiseling.

Kane pushed the cards into his pocket, stuffed the rest of the junk back into the bag and slouched to the door. Hand on the knob, he hesitated, scowling. If he were seen leaving—

He turned the knob slowly and thighed the door open. His big body tensed on the sill. Above him the electric alarm shrilled a jangling clamor loud enough to wake the dead!

THE ALL-NIGHT restaurant up the street ruined his chances. High buildings caught the alarm's cacophony, flung it in distorted echoes that reached the restaurant and sucked lurching figures onto the sidewalk. Kane stood wide-legged, heaved a step forward and jarred to a halt again when a hoarse voice blurted orders to stop.

He might have made it, but not with liquored legs. The restaurant vomited dark shapes that fumed along the wet sidewalk toward him. Kane's mouth formed a sickly grin. He thought of Moroni, the Wise One—Moroni, the headquarters dick who for months had vainly been trying to squelch Peter Kane. Moroni would like this, would revel in a chance to turn on the heat.

Fat fingers curled on Kane's arm and a uniformed hulk bellied against him. Bonney, the liquor-store owner, had said back in Limpy's: "If you see DeSanto, the cop who is on the beat this time of night, tell him it is O.K." That was a laugh. You couldn't tell DeSanto anything, now.

The cop was big, swarthy, with black bugs of eyes and white teeth gleaming through a snarl. He said nasally: "What is this, huh? What is it?"

A crowd filled sidewalk and gutter, made Kane the focal point of rubbernecked curiosity. Kane exhaled a sigh. "I'll save you trouble, DeSanto. In there you'll find two people; one's a stiff. I didn't do it; I don't know a thing about it. I didn't bust into the joint, either. I had Bonney's keys and walked in like a gentleman to acquire some booze. While I was in there, someone turned the alarm on me."

DeSanto said thickly: "What you talkin' about?"

"It's a mess," Kane sighed.

It would be. Moroni would see to that. A dirty, odious mess with Moroni doing the leering and Moe Finch, boss of headquarters, worrying himself sick but incapable of action.

DeSanto moved a big head up and down knowingly and clung to Kane's arm. "We'll go inside and see what you're talkin' about. You're lit." He shoved Kane through the crowd, stopped shoving and grunted with relief when a brother cop elbowed through to his side. "Breakin' and enterin'," DeSanto snarled, "and maybe more. Go look around, Joe."

Kane's gray gaze swept the mob of night owls hemming him in. Mugs, most of them. As unlovely as the average early-morning restaurant crowd. They choked the sidewalk and overflowed into the gutter. To the left, maybe twenty long strides beyond the end of Bonney's store window, a black alleyway snaked between high brick walls and a sign said: Look Out for Trucks.

Above Kane's head the electric alarm was still wailing a devil's bombilation.

Saber-toothed Moroni would make mountains of this. Would fasten his claws in it and gnaw it to shreds. Black a man's eyes for months on end and then give him a chance for a snarling comeback and—curtains. Moroni would ignore logic, override Moe Finch's protests, and rip out Peter Kane's heart—if he got the chance.

DeSanto's pal was inside, nosing around, and the buzzards on the sidewalk were gawking, muttering, some of them laughing. Kane peered drunkenly into DeSanto's leathery face and said plaintively: "Listen. I didn't do a thing. Honest to Gawd, I—"

He wrenched his left arm free and swung his right fist with pile-driver power. The fist made crunching contact, raked DeSanto's jaw and cheek and spilled the cop across Bonney's threshold. Kane leaped sideways and whirled on the wet walk.

His headlong charge broke the crowd apart and opened a lane, and before DeSanto was erect again and lunging forward the buzzards had milled together, formed a block-ade. Someone cheered. DeSanto's violent oath spewed through the cheer and a gun belched. The slug sobbed within inches of Kane's face.

His face was tense, lips agape and sucking rain. His arm hooked the brick wall; he spun on lunging legs, heaved his big body down the alley. Darkness shielded him. A police whistle whinnied behind him and the sound thrilled between high walls, accompanied by a rush of feet. Kane swung left again and wallowed through mud, came out on a board platform and raced along it.

For a big man he was fast, fast enough to be a zig-zagging shadow when DeSanto fired again from the alley mouth. The bullet splintered a wooden wall. Kane grunted, leaped into more mud and kept going. He turned two more corners and the tumult faded behind him.

He came out on a sidewalk four streets east of South Center and hiked across the street, kept going toward the corner. Two cabs were parked before an all-night drug store and Kane peered into the first, strode past it and shook the drowsing driver in the second. He said: "Come out of it, Nick."

The driver blinked at him and mumbled: "Uh? Oh, 'lo Kane. You soused?"

"Limpy's," Kane growled. "In a hurry."

CHAPTER TWO
THE GIRL-FRIEND

L IMPY'S BAR stools were empty of customers. Kane pushed forward, opened the door of the back room and said nasally: "Clean-up time, huh?"

Limpy folded small dark hands on a broom handle and wrinkled his thin face into a frown. "Listen, Kane. I'm closin' up, see? There ain't no business on a sloppy night like this. After I sweep up—"

"Sure," Kane said. "Sure." He slouched into a booth, put his back against the wall and his feet on the booth bench. "What time did Bonney desert you?"

"No sooner was you gone with his keys," Limpy scowled, "than he was on his way, too."

"Huh?"

"Maybe he wanted his keys back," Limpy grinned.

Kane eyed the toes of his drenched oxfords and thinned his lips. His brain worked slowly, took time to form ugly thoughts. He said aloud, almost inaudibly: "Sure. Bonney hands me the keys and says, 'Go help yourself.' I'm sap enough to go do it, and what do I find? While I'm in there, someone turns the key in the alarm so the cops will sit on me when I walk out. Sure." He jerked his head up. "Say— what time did Bonney breeze in here tonight?"

"You should ask me," Limpy shrugged.

"I was soused. What time did he arrive?"

"He come in," Limpy said over the broom handle, "about ten minutes after you did. You and him got sentimental over a pint of blue ruin, and then he give you the keys and you barged out. He wasn't here no more than two minutes longer."

Kane pulled a match from the upright box on an ashtray and dug holes in his outthrust chin. He took more matches, spread them on the table, grouped them and made mumbling sounds through pale lips.

"Sure. Here's Fern. She falls for the tout." He pushed two matches together. "She's Bonney's large moment and when he gets wind of this double-cross he hangs around and keeps tabs on her. He is nosing around with one eye cocked when she takes Healey into the liquor store tonight."

Kane pushed a single match near the first two and scowled at it. "Bonney sees them go in, bides his time and while they're downstairs he sneaks in and plants himself. The girl comes upstairs alone and Bonney brains her."

He broke one match and sighed. "Then what? Bonney prowls downstairs, finds Healey in a state of suspended animation, and plants the tout with blood-smears, rubber gloves and much murder evidence. And then—"

He flicked a solitary match across the table, plunked another one beside it and peered at Limpy. "This is most interesting, Limpy. Here's me; here's you. And here"—he paraded Bonney over the board—"comes friend Albert. He comes in here, hands me the keys and is very generous. 'Go help yourself,' he says, 'to the very good package-goods in my store.'

"Because why? Because someone has to bust into his place and yell murder before the tout comes to and does a sneak-away. Me, I'm ossified enough to think Mr. Bonney is a swell guy. I barge over there and he follows me. Because why again? Because he figures to turn the alarm on me while I'm in there, just to be sure I don't fade from the scene without first reporting to the cops."

Kane exhaled softly, moved his head up and down on a stiff neck. "My pal, Bonney. He loves me; he's in a jam;

he looks for a sap to get him out of it, and I'm the sap. My pal."

"What the hell are you ravin' about?" Limpy demanded.

"Listen," Kane growled. He leaned forward, swept the table clear of matches and scooped a rubber-banded pack of small white cards from his pocket. "Abandon the broom and gaze at these. You're in a lot of know around here. You ever hear of a girl named Fern Becker?"

Limpy sat down and draped his smallish body over the edge of the table, made squint eyes at the cards. "Yeah, I know her. She rooms over on Verndale Street with a girl name of Anna Sproul. Why?"

"Skip it," Kane growled. Methodically he fanned the cards over the board. "How many of these mugs was she strong with?"

Limpy looked, grinned. "A whole lot more than her boy-friend Bonney was wise to. She even played DeSanto, the cop on the beat, for a sucker. I'm tellin' you!" He sorted the cards, stacked them and thumbed two into Kane's palm. "She had them two guys eatin' out of her hand. Wouldn't it astound you, the kind of birds that get taken in by a chiseler like her? Man, if the payin' public only knew what its trusted servants did on the side! Shameful, I calls it!"

Kane eyed the two cards, scooped the others up indifferently. "You sure?"

"Positive."

"I could use a drink."

"Listen. I'm closin' up, I told you. I got to open up early in the mornin' and—"

"Scotch," Kane murmured. "Straight."

Limpy sighed, brought Scotch. The bite was still in Kane's throat and the pint bottle in his sodden coat pocket when he hiked across Randall Square and turned into Verndale Street, twenty minutes later.

THIRTY-NINE VERNDALE, Limpy had said. The house was a red-brick apartment building across the street from the broad green lawn of a private residence. A quiet sector, and high-brow. Evidently the income of the Becker girl had been in keeping with the type of men she was used to gold-digging.

Kane climbed wet white steps and let himself into a tiled vestibule. Brass mailboxes studded the wall, and a row of push-buttons with brass-rimmed name-plates. Kane saw the names through a blur that came in pint bottles. He shook his head, palmed the wall to steady himself. Aloud he said: "Always that guy Kane is nunkis bendums. Always. You'd think he'd lay off at least when the cops are on him for murder."

He pushed the bell under the name Becker-Sproul and unhooked the phone. Minutes passed and a girl's voice droned drowsily: "Hello?"

"Want to talk to Anna Sproul," Kane said.

"I'm Anna Sproul."

"Listen. Something's happened to your girl friend. I got to see you about it."

"The hell you have. Not at this time of night!"

"I'm a dick," Kane growled. "Beacon Agency. Maybe you'd rather talk to the cops."

The door buzzed in answer, and he got up the steps to it before the buzzing ceased. A night light glowed in the inside corridor, showed him the stairs. On the floor above, a door opened. Anna Sproul was standing on a threshold, staring, when Kane reached the stairhead.

The girl was small, blonde, too sleepy to be good-looking. She wore crumpled yellow-and-black silk pajamas, slippers with glass-eyed bunnies on them. She blocked the doorway and said in a throaty whisper: "What's wrong? What's happened to Fern? Spill it!"

"Not out here where the whole house can tune in," Kane shrugged. "Invite me in, sister. I don't bite."

She looked him over with cold blue eyes that seemed capable of reading men's motives. Jerkily she stepped back and let Kane sway past her. She closed the door quickly. Kane looked around a small, lamplit living room, gazed yearningly at a square gin bottle that squatted on a window sill between bright drapes, and lowered himself wetly onto a studio couch. The girl stood wide-legged, facing him with her hands hipped.

"This is the wrong time of night for funny business," she said acidly.

"It's not funny, sister." Kane took a cigarette from an end table beside him and lit it. "Your girl friend was rubbed out tonight in Bonney's liquor store."

"What?"

"A guy by the name of Louis Healey—maybe you know about him—was framed for the killing. Maybe he did it; maybe he didn't."

Anna Sproul opened her eyes to coat-button bigness, backed into a chair and sat down as if pushed in the face. Her hands clutched the chair arms. She leaned stiffly forward, looked at Kane as if he were unreal, and croaked: "Oh my God no!"

"Sorry," Kane said. "It's true."

"It isn't! You—you're—"

"I wish to God I were, sister. It so happens the cops are on the prowl for me right now because they think I swung the bottle that brained your girl friend." He sucked his cigarette and sprayed twin shafts of smoke at the girl's pajamaed legs. "That's why I'm here."

ANNA SPROUL closed her eyes, shuddered, and slowly opened them. Her small chest swelled with indrawn breath, sagged again when she exhaled a sniveling moan. She went limp, slumped in her chair and sat staring.

Kane said: "I don't think Healey did it, and I know damn well I didn't. I'm a dick and I can unravel the mess if I get a lead to work on. I'm asking for help. And"—he pushed his head forward, scowling—"even if you're cold to my end of it, you ought to be hot for getting the tramp who did kill your friend."

"You're drunk," the girl mumbled.

"I'm always drunk." Kane fished two white cards from his pocket and spilled them in the girl's lap. "Take a look at those."

She gaped at him, seemed drugged by the low drone of his voice. When she picked up the cards, the movement was mechanical; she had them in her hand ten seconds before lowering her gaze to stare at them.

"One of those men," Kane said, "maybe had good reason for bumping off Fern. Do some deep thinking."

Anna Sproul's eyes lost their scared bigness, narrowed slowly and spawned significant shadows. In an adjoining room a clock ticked hollowly while Kane scrutinized the girl's tensing face and checked each changing expression. He caught a slow breath, balled his hands into fists and waited impatiently, knowing he had fired a hidden fuse.

"You know something?" he demanded softly.

Anna Sproul yanked her head up and her eyes were smoldering. "You're damn right I know something!"

"Spill it, sister."

"To you? Don't make me laugh!"

"Listen," Kane snarled. "I'm on the level with you. I'm in a jam and what you know will get me out of it—and burn the rat that killed your girl friend."

"I'm not saying a word."

Kane got off the studio couch and swayed forward, glared down into the girl's defiant face. "Yes you are, sister."

"Make me! Just try it and see how far you get!"

Kane's left hand stabbed down, closed like a vise on the girl's bare arm. He flipped his last ace. "You talk, sister, or you go with me to the cops—right now."

"Any time you say, I'm ready."

"Get your clothes on!"

"Sure. Why not?" She wrenched her arm free and stood up, put a warped grin on her face. "Maybe you think I'm scared the cops will ask questions. Let 'em ask! To them, I'll talk and tell all I know. But I'm not sap enough to spill it to you, see? What are you? A tanked-up mug that chisels in here this time of night and gets nasty."

Like a tin soldier she marched into the bedroom, dressed with the door open and paraded out again. "O.K., shamus. Lead me to the bulls and see if I get cold feet!"

"You're on your way," Kane shrugged. "Only—" He stared at her, inhaled deeply. "Listen. I'm not the wise guy you think I am. If I walk you to the cops, I put my neck in a rope—unless you've got talk that's strong enough to drape that rope around someone else's neck. Are you on the level?"

She frowned at him. "I guess you're not so drunk after all."

"Cold sober, pal."

"O.K. I'm on the level."

Kane grinned sheepishly and slid a pint bottle from his pocket. "You almost scared me to death, sister. Have one."

She took one, downed it without catching a breath and had another for a chaser before handing the bottle back. Kane emptied it and said: "Whether you know it or not, Fern and I were pretty good friends. The name's Kane."

She stared with one hand on the knob. "Why the hell didn't you say so?" Snorting, she jarred the door open and stepped into the hall.

CHAPTER THREE

JUGGED

THE HALL was deserted, dark except for a dim night light burning near the stairhead. The girl's high heels clicked on hardwood to send rattling echoes through the building's dead silence. She was four strides from the threshold when Kane closed the door and turned to follow her.

Something moved in the deep end of the corridor and Kane jerked his head, glowered. The thing moved again. Kane went stiff, bellowed: "Look out! For God's sake—" But he bellowed it too late. A gun belched, belched again and made scarlet daggers in the darkness.

Anna Sproul turned a slow half circle on one foot and pitched floorward, one hand raking empty air, the other jammed against her face.

The girl moaned and Kane lurched toward her. Heavy feet pounded the corridor's deep end. Kane whirled in a crouch, glared for two seconds and hurtled forward.

His fists were clenched and he ploughed blindly between dark walls, but he was too slow. He was snarling when he passed the stairhead. A door clanged shut ahead of him. The door was big, heavy, faced with sheet-iron and marked with red letters, Fire Exit.

It was locked on the far side. Kane clawed the latch, banged it with clenched fists and cursed gutturally. His own voice was the only sound in a silence pregnant with black mockery. He ran back to Anna Sproul and when he bent above her, the girl lay sideways in a gathering red pool and her heart was thumping slowly, heavily, as if weary of the effort.

Behind Kane a door jarred open. He rocked around on one knee to see a cold-creamed face glaring above a night-gowned torso. The woman snorted explosively and said in a voice that rasped on Kane's wire-tight nerves: "You might have some consideration at least! Just because this is an apartment house, that don't mean it's a madhouse! Some decent people live here!"

"Sure," Kane growled. "Sure, sure. Where's the nearest doctor?"

"What?" The woman's head jerked out, turtle-fashion, and her eyes popped. "Mercy's sakes, the girl's hurt! She—"

"A doctor," Kane snapped. "Where is one?"

"There's a doctor across the street in that big white house. But what on earth happened? Is she drunk? Is she—"

Kane gathered Anna Sproul in his arms and stood swaying, cursed the liquor that made his legs wobbly. Other doors opened in the corridor as he lurched to the stairs, floundered to the floor below. The woman's shrill voice yawped after him: "It's the house right across the street—"

Kane stood on the sidewalk in drizzling rain and looked into the lolling face of the girl in his arms. One slug had viciously mangled her jaw; the other had smashed a shoulder. Blood was on Kane's clutching hands.

He hiked across the street, forced his rubber legs to follow a straight line up stone steps and along a red-brick walk. On the puddled lawn beside him a cast-iron sign said neatly: P.W. Lafey, M.D.

Kane climbed the wooden steps of the front porch and punished the bell. Waiting impatiently, he shifted the girl's dead weight and hooked a heel on the stoop. Minutes passed. He was ringing the bell a fourth time when a light gleamed behind the door window.

The door opened and Kane pushed unceremoniously past a plumpish, gray-haired man who stood gawking. He took two steps, rocked around and returned the man's sleepy stare. "This girl's hurt. Hurt bad. Where'll I put her?"

P.W. Lafey, M.D., blinked small blue eyes in a pasty face and worked salmon-hued lips to make words. He wore crumpled striped pajamas with short sleeves, and his pink feet toed outward in leather slippers. He closed the door nervously. His leather slippers slapped the carpet as he came closer to Kane's swaying bulk.

"What is the trouble?"

"She's been shot. Twice," Kane snapped.

The doctor gaped, then stiffened. "Come this way. My office—"

KANE TRAILED him, crossed a threshold and lowered the girl on a red-leather divan. He stood back, hipped his hands and stared narrowly while Lafey stooped above the girl and tore the blood-drenched dress from her shoulder. The doctor's head weaved back and forth; his hands were faster than Kane's eyes. He straightened, went quickly into an adjoining room and fingered a light switch. Returning with short, jerky steps he said curtly: "I'm afraid it's too late. Help me to carry her."

The girl sagged between them as they lugged her into the next room and stretched her small body on a white-topped table. Lafey brought tools, bent above her. Kane, breathing deeply, blinked at the floodlight above the table and would have sold his soul for a drink.

He watched Lafey, and Lafey was no longer half asleep but professionally deliberate. Hunched above the girl, Lafey swabbed her wounds, said gutturally: "The bullet is still in this shoulder. I'll remove it, but I'm afraid—"

"She's a good kid," Kane growled. "Keep her alive!"

Lafey probed with the gleaming point of a knife. He was nervous again. More than likely it was the sight of blood. In a hospital operating room, blood would probably have made no impression; but blood on a strange girl at this hour in the morning—

Lafey uttered a sharp "Oh!" and half straightened, made dabbing movements at the palm of his right hand. Kane bent closer, staring. The doctor exhaled impatiently and returned to work. Blood trickled from a gash in his palm.

Kane counted seconds into minutes and licked sour lips with a dry tongue while he waited. The doctor's silence got on his nerves. He shifted from one foot to the other, stared, tried to relax against the wall and knew the whiskey inside him would sour if he let go. In the end Lafey stepped back, turned slowly and shook his moon-face from side to side. Blood was on the man's hands, on the knife. "It is—too late."

Kane nodded, caught a grip on himself and aimed a cigarette at his mouth. His eyes ached from staring so long. He looked at Lafey's knife hand and said mirthlessly: "I guess doctors don't have any stronger nerves than the rest of us."

"It is nothing. Only a scratch." Lafey poked at the gash with a clean handkerchief. "I shall have to report to the police about this girl. If you will excuse me—

Kane looked into the face of Anna Sproul. The girl was dead. He said softly: "It's tough, kid; tough as hell." He turned, said to Lafey: "No need to phone the police. I'm a detective." Casually he flashed a police badge.

"A—detective?"

"M'm." Kane glanced at the girl again and knew what he was up against. She would have talked, cleared him. Now she couldn't. He was back where he had started from—a hunted man on the prowl, with the cops watching every street corner. By now the murder-yell would have passed through headquarters and been spilled out over short wave to every cruise-car in the city. And Anna Sproul's lips were forever sealed.

It would not do for Lafey to phone the police. After what had happened in Bonney's liquor store, such a call would bring results before Kane could get clear.

"Listen." He put a hand on the door and stared with forced indifference. "I'm on my way to headquarters. I'll make a report of this and save you trouble."

He walked out, closed the front door behind him and hiked down the veranda steps. In the pockets of his drenched coat, his hands were balled into fists.

IN RANDALL SQUARE, a news truck rumbled over broken macadam and a shirt-sleeved kid in the rear heaved bundles of papers into a drug-store doorway. Kane slouched across the street, flicked a paper loose, plunked two pennies on the pile and walked away.

Fifteen minutes later, after slopping through side streets and back alleys, he thumped on the rear door of Limpy's place. His shoes sucked water; his clothes were drenched; his face was a gray mask, empty of humor. The folded newspaper was jammed hard in his coat pocket.

Limpy opened the door and stared from the threshold. Limpy's eyes bulged, filled with consternation. His voice came in a croak. "Geez—it's you! I can't hide ya in here, Kane! It's the first place the cops'll look."

Kane pushed forward. "I need a place to dry out and think."

"But, Geez! You'll be gettin' me in hot water! They're on ya for murder, Kane!"

Kane closed the door after him and walked into the back room, sank sloppily into a corner booth. Scowling, he unfolded the morning paper and glared over the sodden top of it. "Can a man buy a drink in here?"

"But Geez, Kane—"

"I didn't lay a hand on the Becker girl," Kane said quietly. "Scotch, Limpy. In a bottle."

Limpy mumbled incoherently, wiggled his head from side to side and waddled away. Kane forced a thin smile, studied the paper. When Limpy plopped a bottle and glass on the table an instant later, Kane reached for the bottle without looking at it, stripped tinfoil from its neck and gurgled until the stuff kicked back in his throat. Through blurred eyes he scanned the paper's black banner and glared at smaller print beneath.

"So Moroni made a statement. He would. Big-mouth Moroni, the wise detective. Bah!"

Moroni had come out with a loudmouthed opinion and the news-hounds had gobbled it up. "The department's ace detective is positive," the paper said, "that his friend and former associate, Kane, is responsible for the atrocious slaying of the Becker girl, and promises that Kane will be apprehended within the next few hours."

"Sure," Kane nodded. "Sure." Moe Finch was different. He, too, had made a statement, apparently not too willingly. According to Finch, the evidence was as yet incomplete. Surface evidence, so far uncovered, pointed not to Kane but to Healey, who had been found intoxicated in the basement of the liquor establishment.

"One regular guy," Kane murmured, "in a bunch of lizards."

HE READ further, skipped the usual padding and found something more significant. His eye caught the name DeSanto, and he thought suddenly of what Limpy had said, not long ago, about DeSanto and Fern Becker.

The paper said: "Jerome DeSanto, in a statement made early this morning, cleared up the mystery of why Kane, in prowling from the scene of the crime, happened to make the blunder of sounding the electric alarm which led to his apprehension.

"In the course of duty," DeSanto stated, "I was walking up South Center Street and saw that the alarm was turned to 'Off.' I tried the door, found it properly locked, and did not suspect anything wrong. Albert Bonney had more than once locked up of a night and forgotten to set the alarm. I thought he had merely forgotten again to set it, so I turned the key and went about my duties. Less than five minutes later the alarm sounded."

Kane leered at the paper and said: "Sure. You were eagle-eyed enough to see the alarm was off, but you didn't see Fern go in the store with Healey, and you didn't see me go in either. Maybe!"

The "maybe" came thickly through sour lips. Kane shoved the paper aside and stuck the neck of the whiskey bottle in his throat, glared drunkenly at Limpy. He gagged, lowered the bottle and said sullenly: "Sure. It was an accident DeSanto turned the alarm on me. A pure accident. And it was mere coincidence he was waiting in the restaurant, only half a block away, when the alarm went off. Sure it was."

"Listen," Limpy whined. "Don't be a damn fool, Kane. You can't hang around here! Why, the cops are certain to come in here—"

"My pal, Moroni," Kane gurgled. "The chance of a lifetime."

"Listen, Kane. For God's sake—"

"I gotta get drunk. When I get drunk, I'll scram. Whose funeral is this? Don't look so sad!"

"I'm sad for you!" Limpy wailed, gesticulating with upturned palms. "They can't do nothin' to me—maybe." He turned nervously and blinked at the door. Out front, the street door had opened, thudded shut. Footsteps were audible. "I got a customer," Limpy mumbled. "Be a good guy and don't shoot your mouth off too loud. I don't want no trouble—"

He limped across the room and was scuffing over the threshold when a hand shoved him back. Past him, and looming big against him, came a uniformed figure that dripped water. Brass buttons gleamed dully and the cop's face was a wet scowl. Kane had the whiskey bottle upended in his mouth, lowered it slowly and stared through blurred eyes.

"Just like that they find me," Kane said sadly.

The cop strode forward, made movements with the barrel of a police .38 and rapped out: "You better come easy, Kane. I'm takin' no chances."

Limpy stared and the cop stepped back, waiting for Kane to slide from the booth. Kane pulled a deep breath that smoothed the wrinkles in his soaked vest. He shrugged, palmed the table with both hands and pushed himself up. "O.K., brother. Already I can see the smoke in Moroni's eyes."

He killed the pint, gazed at the empty bottle and sighed. The cop's free hand clamped on his arm. Kane blinked bloodshot eyes at the gun, swayed unsteadily on rubber legs and murmured: "Be a good guy and put that thing away. I know all about 'em."

CHAPTER FOUR
ACES FOR KANE

IN THE rear room at headquarters, Moroni, the Wise One, stood with feet apart and hands hipped and let his leering gaze travel over Kane from head to legs. His black hair was an oily mop and his face sallow with pock marks. He was bigger than Kane and when he thrust his large head forward to glare, his thick red neck swelled against the unclean collar of his striped shirt.

He said: "So the smart agency dick couldn't dodge even a flock of dumb flat-foots. Huh!"

Moe Finch looked small and worried behind the desk. An unlighted cigar rolled between his lips and his nicotined fingers were like the restless forelegs of a horse fidgety at the post. His face was stubbled and his sparse gray hair damp with sweat. His watery gaze traveled from Kane to Moroni to Albert Bonney. He worked his jaw muscles as if chewing a cud, but maintained silence.

Albert Bonney sat in a straight-backed chair and gaped.

"So you couldn't dodge the cops even for a few short hours," Moroni sneered. "You're a smart private dick and you catch crooks as easy as you guzzle bum liquor, but when we put the screws to you, you bogged down and squeaked for help."

"Go right ahead," Kane murmured. "I love it."

"Hell, I can't be bothered."

"I'm so sorry."

"Listen." Moroni lurched forward, stuck his face out and curled his lower lip belligerently. "I could put the tongs to you in a minute, see? I could even send you to the chair, maybe, with the evidence I got. Maybe I couldn't do all that, hut just by talking the D.A. into putting you on trial for murder I could pour so much mud on your cheap reputation that you'd be done for life. It's easy as that, wise guy! But why should I? What's it to me?"

He leaned back, spread his hands palms upward. "I'm a good guy, Kane. I'm doin' you a favor by lettin' you off. If I wanted to, I could put a foot on you and push your face in the mud, but I'm lettin' you go free. Because"—he rocked around, stabbed a thick forefinger at Bonney—"we got the guilty party right here and he knows it!"

Albert Bonney's eyes bulged in a pink face. His plump body jerked forward in the chair and his hands were pink crabs clawing space. "It's not true! I didn't do it!"

Moroni ignored him, continued to leer at Kane. "Fern Becker was Bonney's special girl friend, see? To him she was an angel, and I don't mean a street angel. Then he found out she was two-timing him and chasing around with Healey, so he kept his eyes open. He saw his chance, took it, and framed Healey for the killing. And to make sure the cops reached the scene before Healey came to and did a fadeout, Bonney made a sucker of you with the keys to the store. Get it?" Moroni's mouth fish-hooked into a leer. "Makin' a sucker of you was the easiest part of his whole scheme."

Kane was silent. Moe Finch, behind the desk, said feebly: "I guess you're lucky all right, Kane. You were in a tough spot, sure enough." Bonney, lurching erect, clawed Moroni's arm and spilled blubbering sounds that shrieked into words. "I didn't do it, I tell you! It's a frame-up! So help me God, I never even knew Fern and Healey were friends! I—I—"

Moroni shoved. On limp legs Bonney staggered back and flopped into the chair. Moroni glared at Kane and said curtly: "Scram, shamus. And next time keep out of trouble. Only for me and my brains you'd be in a hell of a mess."

"Wouldn't I though?" Quietly Kane slouched to the door, stopped again when Bonney's treble voice squalled after him. Bonney was erect again, wringing sweat-soaked hands.

"You gotta get me out of this, Kane! They're tryin' to frame me for somethin' I never done! Oh my God, if I ever needed a pal—"

"Skip it!" Moroni rasped.

Kane eased over the threshold and pushed the door shut behind him. Perspiration beaded his forehead and dampened the palms of his hands. Outside headquarters he stood on the wet curb, exhaled explosively in the rain and muttered aloud: "Ugh! That guy Moroni would give even a cockroach the creeps." He walked slowly because there was no cause for hurry. For a while, at least, Moroni's army would leave him alone. In time, P.W. Lafey, M.D. would smell a rodent and phone headquarters to report the killing of Anna Sproul. Bonney couldn't be guilty because Bonney had been in custody at the time. Moroni would go red in the face, issue new orders, and again the cops would look for Peter Kane.

He stopped walking, lit a cigarette and cursed the whiskey that muddled his brain. What Peter Kane did in the next hour or so would maybe count a great deal in deciding Peter Kane's future.

When he began walking again, he had a destination.

IT WAS raining hard, and when he turned at last from drooling concrete to the sodden grass of a lawn, his thin-soled shoes made sucking sounds to accompany his slow advance. A house loomed through the downpour. Kane reached it, prowled to the rear and was careful to make no betraying noise while turning the knob of the rear door.

The door was locked. He paced away from it and peered up at kitchen windows. He tried two windows and the second yielded, slid open with a soft squeak. Kane boosted himself, hung grotesquely on the sill and wriggled through onto a linoleum floor.

He was drenched and his mop of hair shed water in his eyes, blinding him. Water squished in his shoes when he toed forward. He stalked warily along a carpeted hall, turned left, passed through two small rooms and emerged in a short corridor. An alien sound jarred him to a halt.

The sound came from just ahead, and was made by water running from a tap. A closed door muffled it. Kane moved forward, stood near the door and listened. The muscles of his face tightened under pressure. His hand sought the knob.

He opened the door quietly, but not so quietly that the sound failed to reach the man who stood hunched over a wash bowl against the far wall. The man whirled, stood gaping, his eyes protruding like bright buttons. The wall at his back was of white tile and the room a bathroom. The man was Dr. Paul Lafey.

Lafey's body was bare from the waist up, clad from there down in pajama trousers and leather slippers. Half naked, he looked less womanish than before—looked plump, but powerful despite his obesity. Behind him, water ran into the bowl and turned milky white because the bowl contained disinfectant. The room reeked.

A small brown bottle was in Lafey's left hand; his right hand was turned palm up. The palm still had a gash in it. The gash was wet with disinfectant. Lafey stood rigid, kept his large eyes wide open and said shrilly: "What is the meaning of this? What are you doing here?"

"I guess broken glass makes a dangerous cut," Kane murmured.

"You guess—what?"

"Broken glass." Kane nodded. "You know—when you bash somebody over the head with a bottle and the bottle breaks."

Lafey stared at the wet palm of his hand. His bare chest swelled with indrawn breath; blood seeped from his face. He squared his fleshy shoulders, took a step backward and glared. His lips were tight-pressed and his cheeks hollow. He said slowly: "What do—you—mean?"

Kane stood wide-legged in the doorway. "Your big mistake, Lafey, was in putting the rubber gloves on Healey.

The right-hand glove was gouged and Healey's hand underneath didn't have a mark on it. You shouldn't have worn rubber gloves in the first place. They smell too much like the medical profession. And then"—he took a step forward and stared holes in Lafey's face—"that gag about cutting yourself with a knife while you were working on Anna Sproul, when you knew I was a dick and thought I had the eagle eye on you—"

Lafey was big, and his near-naked body ballooned across the narrow bathroom with weight and strength behind it. He lunged from the waist and heaved forward like a wrestler. His pudgy hands were outflung, his fingers working, his thin lips drawn over blunt white teeth.

He was big enough to have ploughed through Kane and smashed clear, but the wet floor spilled him. Kane's fist whined through four feet of space and sank into fat flesh, then stabbed up and rapped one-two, one-two against Lafey's face. Lafey croaked, "Aarrrgh!" and pawed the wall with limp fingers while he slid to the floor.

He rocked backward, cracked his head against the side of the tub and lay in a heap. His legs twitched a moment, then stiffened.

Kane looked downward and murmured: "It's a cinch you don't play much poker. Only a sap would show his cards in a hurry like that."

IN THE back room at headquarters, Kane leaned against Moe Finch's desk, gazed solemnly at Moroni's scowling face and said softly: "It's like this. Lafey is one of the best physicians in town and has a reputation to keep up. On the side he's human and kind of a sucker, and he plays Fern Becker, or rather, she plays him. Then, for some unknown reason he suddenly gets scared and decides he has to close Fern's mouth." He turned his head to peer at Lafey. "You mind telling us what that unknown reason was?"

Lafey had shoes on, and wore pajamas under an overcoat. His lips were puffed to twice their size where Kane's fists had ruptured flesh. There was a dead, glazed sheen in his eyes and he sat like a ventriloquist's dummy on the wooden bench against the wall. At Kane's question he raised his head, shuddered, and spoke dully.

"Fern and Healey had been blackmailing me for weeks. Every time I met their demands they promised to leave me alone. Their last demand was more than I—than I could pay."

"So," Kane shrugged, "the good doctor awaited his chance, got rid of the girl and framed Healey for the slaughter. But being an amateur at the murder business, he made mistakes. He wore rubber gloves, and when the bottle broke over Fern Becker's head the glass ripped one glove and gashed the good doctor's hand. He planted the gloves on Healey, downstairs, and spilled blood over Healey's clothes, but neglected to dig a chunk out of the tout's hand—and the whole set-up was thereby phony.

"Also, one of the good doctor's calling-cards reposed among others in Fern's handbag, and he forgot to remove it. That was a fatal oversight."

Words rolled easily from Kane's throat. The throat was lubricated, and the glow in his eyes was a whiskey glow. He leaned against Moe Finch's desk as if timid about trusting the rigidity of his legs.

"Later," he shrugged, "the good doctor spent sleepless hours of worry and kept a close check on Anna Sproul. He feared that the police, being clever, might question the Sproul girl because she was Fern's girl friend. And if the police did that, it might not be so good for the good doctor, because Anna Sproul knew all about his little difficulty with Fern.

"So, when he saw me—me, Peter Kane—go into Anna Sproul's apartment house, and recognized me as Kane, the private shamus, he got the horrors, sneaked into the house, and was hiding there when the girl and I walked out of her rooms. Maybe he overheard what we talked about; I wouldn't know that. Anyway, he successfully closed her mouth for all time. He didn't know then, you understand, that I—me—Peter Kane—was under suspicion for the killing of Fern Becker. He just knew I was a dick.

"And," Kane smiled, "when I lugged the Sproul girl into his office about two minutes after he'd shot her, he was scared stiff that I'd see how nervous he was. He was also scared that I'd notice how his right hand was banged up from broken glass, so he made a bluff at sticking a knife into it. And even a dumb dick like me knows that a good doctor doesn't go around sticking himself with a knife, even if he is supposed to be half asleep."

Kane sighed, transferred his soulful gaze from Moroni's mud-colored face to Moe Finch's amazed one. "Maybe I can go now, huh?"

"You're a good guy, Kane," Finch blurted. "So help me, you're aces. You want a drink?"

"I drink nothing but the best."

"Huh?"

"Nothing," Kane declared, "but the very best." He pulled a long-necked bottle from his pocket and caressed it fondly. "It was necessary that I revive the good doctor before escorting him here. As a consequence, I had to snoop around his office in search of arousing-fluid. Elegant taste the good doctor has. Nothing but the best!"

"I guess you're already soused," Finch nodded. "But just the same, Kane, you're aces. Only for you, Moroni would've sent an innocent man to the chair. For what you done, Bonney will be a friend of yours for life."

"I thought of that." Kane caught a deep breath and smiled. "And I don't forget, either, that Bonney runs a liquor store."

THE MAN WHO LOOKED SICK

KANE HAD WANDERED OUT TO
THE TRACK TO DO A LITTLE
DRINKING AND PUT A SMALL
SUM ON THE NOSE OF HIS
FAVORITE GEE-GEE, NOT GET
HIMSELF MIXED INTO A SERIES
OF COCK-EYED MURDERS. BUT
THE BEST LAID PLANS OF EVEN
THE SMARTEST DICK CAN GO
ASTRAY, AS HE SOON FOUND
WHEN SOULFUL SAMMY MARKED
HIS PROGRAM FOR A KILLING
THAT COULDN'T BE CASHED IN
ON AT ANY TOTE WINDOW IN THE
WORLD.

CHAPTER ONE
THE BODY AT THE TRACK

THE PONIES came down the stretch and thundered past the rail where Peter Kane stood glaring. Five of them were bunched, scrapping for the lead. The sixth splashed through mud on the outer rail after running wide on the turn.

Kane made a face as the trailer wallowed by. The mud-splattered Number 4 on the nag's broadside, under the cricket boy's flailing leg, matched the Number 4 on the tote ticket that Kane hauled from a vest pocket. From atop the judge's coop, a basso voice boomed through the address system: "The public is cautioned not to destroy any tote tickets. Remember, the result of the race is not yet official."

"Phooey!" Kane snorted. His lean fingers ripped the ticket twice, flicked the scraps over the rail. "Phooey!" Disgustedly he reached for the pint bottle in his inside coat pocket.

"Your luck ain't so good, mister, huh?" A wet gray figure sidled close to Kane's big bulk and turned a sallow face so Kane had to look at it. The face was sad and looked as though it had been that way since birth. It had large protruding ears and a pointed nose and puckered lips and dark soulful eyes that seemed on the verge of tears. It had lived maybe twenty-five years.

"Listen, mister," the face murmured. "Nobody ever beats the ponies by shootin' blind. My goodness no. *Tsk.* Now if I was to put you wise to some inside dope on the next race, would it be worth your time listenin', huh?"

"Scram!" Kane growled.

"Now listen, mister. Honest, I ain't foolin'. It don't cost you a dime. You shoot the works on this nag here see?" Sad-eyes thrust out his program and underscored, with the black crescent of a sharp fingernail, the name of a horse. "You go on Moralist, see? Go the limit. This here is a muddy track and on a muddy track Moralist could shed a foreleg and still gallop that bunch of goats into the ground. See? You do like I say, mister, and if you feel like passin' me a ten spot after you clean up, I'll be seein' you here after the race."

Kane glared, stuffed the pint bottle back in his pocket, choked, and hiked away. A sigh gurgled in his throat. "Maybe I change complexion when my nag chases them all home," he mumbled. "Something must be wrong with my looks when Soulful Sammy picks *me* for a sucker. My God!"

The "My God!" had nothing to do with Soulful Sammy's dumbness. It came convulsively, as Kane's legs stiffened under him and he stood stock-still, gaping. He forgot about Soulful Sammy. His eyes bulged and he took a hesitant step forward, caught a quick noisy breath that inflated his chest.

FACING HIM, a dejected figure sat propped against the red front of a refuse barrel. The man's head hung on his chest and the word *Waste* gleamed above his mop of hair, as if tagged to him.

"I yanked the dough and told him to figure it for hush money."

His eyes were wide and his rubber legs snaked out in front of him with the toes of his buckskin shoes pointing to ten past ten. He had a look of pain and amazement on a face strangely empty of color. Above the V of his vest his pink-striped madras shirt was clotted with sticky-looking red stuff that bubbled from within, and out of the red stuff protruded the bone handle of a knife whose blade was deep out of sight.

Kane said again: "My God!" And added almost inaudibly: "D'Amino. Louis D'Amino. Croaked!"

Louis D'Amino had a reputation around town for being a greasy-faced, self-satisfied racketeer, a pool-ticket dispenser, a dealer in spurious "import" whiskeys, and the unperturbed focal point of innumerable hates.

"Dead," Kane said. "Dead as hell."

He was drunk, and the sight of D'Amino's blood-soaked shirt made him feel vaguely ill below the belt. When he knuckled open the door of the track police office, moments later, he had to lean against the door jamb and take time out to steady himself before mouthing his report.

Then, while pop-eyed officials went out to collect D'Amino's body, Kane sat down and played an imaginary piano on the table top. With the body came Moroni.

"Always when I get a day off," Moroni snarled, "some punk gets rubbed out in front of my nose." He had been losing money and was sore. Sore, too, because a gawking crowd had accompanied the passage of D'Amino's corpse from the refuse can to the track police office, and Moroni, spotted by an alert track cop and drafted into service, had consequently been pushed, mauled, stepped on until wrath had exploded within him.

Kane smiled discreetly, said nothing. It was a pleasure to see Great Brain Moroni slaving while he, Peter Kane, private shamus and therefore ineligible, could sit and observe. A pleasure indeed.

Moroni labored. In half an hour Moroni had netted three very dissimilar individuals, had herded them into the office and, behind closed doors, had worked on them in typical Moroni fashion, linguistically, with gestures. Kane, nursing a quarter-full pint bottle, looked on with interest and maintained silence. Track officials regarded Moroni with awe and respect.

"Listen, you," Moroni growled. "What's your name?"

The lady's name was Mabel Jilson. She was a good-looking lady if one looked not too close. She was perhaps thirty-five years old and running to fat. She sat with one shapely leg crossed over the other, revealing the rolled top of one sheer stocking. She had been Louis D'Amino's broad until Louis had "gone nuts over a flat-chested, bedroom-eyed doll." The words were her own, muttered vindictively through very red lips that curled above an angular chin.

"What's more," she snapped out, "I used to be on the stage and I done a knife-throwing act. Make something of that, Glue-face!"

"I'll make plenty of it later," Moroni threw back. "And get this, sister. I knew who you were and what you were before you even opened your mouth. And you were seen talking to D'Amino less than half an hour before we discovered his corpse. That's why you're here." He swung on Number 2 of the round-up and spat cigar smoke in her face. "And you're D'Amino's new dame, huh? You're the broad with the bedroom eyes."

"I'll thank you," Miss Birdie Brooks said acidly, "to leave personalities out of this!" Certainly her eyes had no bedroom look in them now. They were smouldering coals in a face so devoid of color that the generous applications of rouge and lipstick stood out like splashing from a paint-pot. She was small and twitchy and as high-strung, though perhaps not as high-bred, as some of the nags in the paddock.

She had been with D'Amino all afternoon. Had left him, so she maintained, to go cash a tote ticket. On her return, she had failed to find him at the appointed meeting place, and spent the next ten minutes rubber-necking through the crowd in search of him.

She had not in the least wanted to come to the track police office. Would not have had to come, either, if Mabel Jilson had not pointed her out to Moroni and said viciously: "There she is. That's the little squirt Louis dropped me for. Ask *her* who knifed him!"

NOW THAT Birdie was in the office, she vehemently desired to get out of it. She said so, with an outburst of temper that sent the words shrilling between her very white teeth. Moroni said: "Sit still and shut up!" and turned to exhibit Number 3.

Number 3 was Soulful Sammy, the sad-eyed tout.

"Listen, mug," Moroni growled. "When I last talked to D'Amino he had an eye open for you. It's a good thing for you he's turned into a stiff, otherwise he might have caught up with you and squared things for the sucker tip you handed him. What I'm figuring is maybe you knew he was out to get you, so you fixed things first. That wouldn't've been too hard, even for a skinny rat like you. D'Amino was plenty drunk this afternoon." He narrowed his eyes, took a menacing forward step and applied the famous Moroni psychology. "What'd you kill him in a place like this for?"

Sammy's soulful orbs expanded to enormous bigness and took on white rims. "I didn't do it! So help me, mister, I never went near the guy after I sucked him in. Geez, I only took him for a fin. A guy with all his dough wouldn't be out to get me for a measly fin!"

Birdie Brooks uttered words that compelled attention. "Listen, dick. When I last saw Louis he had a roll. Abe Brolberg looked us up and handed Louis a roll, a bank package of ten new century notes. I knew because it was me that took the wrapper off and counted the notes, on account of Louis was too drunk." She peered past Moroni's looming bulk and focused her gaze at a pile of junk on the table. The junk had come from Louis D'Amino's pockets. "I don't see any hundred-dollar bills there," she said.

Soulful Sammy swallowed hard and made a stabbing movement toward a pocket of his wet gray trousers. He caught himself before the movement was completed, but Moroni saw, snarled, and jerked forward.

"Search this mug," Moroni said nasally to the track police.

Sammy cringed in his chair and his big eyes grew bigger. Terror thickened his tongue. He wailed despondently: "You don't need to search me. Geez, I admit it, I got the dough." His hand trembled violently but finally got in and out of his pocket and held a wad of bills toward Moroni's snarling face. "But I didn't knife the guy for it, so help me! I—I seen him get what was comin' to him, and I seen the killer frisk him, and then I mooched over and spoke my piece and got the dough for hush money. Honest to God, that's how it happened! I ain't lyin'!"

The bills fascinated Moroni. He gaped at them and unfolded the wad and bunched it together again. He glared into Sammy's terrified face and rasped: "Say that again, slow!"

"It was like this," Sammy moaned. "I was moochin' around out back of the grandstand and I seen this guy proppin' the body up against one of them big waste barrels. I figured the droopy one was drunk. Then I seen the blood all over the front of him, and a knife stickin' out, and I seen who he was. The killer guy didn't see me because he was too busy fishin' through D'Amino's pockets." Sweat gleamed on Sammy's pale forehead and he wiped it off with the tips of his fingers. "So then I moseyed over and grabbed this guy's arm, and while he was standin' there gawkin' at me, scared stiff, I yanked the dough out of his hand and told him he could figure it for hush money. Then I lammed."

"And maybe you know what this guy looked like?" Sarcasm dripped from Moroni's question.

"Well, I didn't get no close look on account of it was rainin' so hard. He was a thin, sallow-faced guy, kind of, and he looked sick. He had on one of them lap-around trench coats, and white shoes like what I got on, only cleaner." Sammy pushed thin fingers under the bead of his hat and swallowed again.

"Why didn't you call a cop?"

"Geez, why should I? The cops never done me no favors, did they?"

Moroni said acidly: "You can't even lie straight and make it sound convincing. If you want to tell fairy stories, tell 'em to Kane here. He's got imagination." He slapped the wad of bills on the table behind him. "Maybe you can tell us where your thin, sallow-faced guy went after he handed you the hush money."

"He beat it."

"Where to, sweetheart?"

Sammy was rattled. "I ain't sure. But he didn't lam out of the grounds, I know that! He made a bee-line for the clubhouse and I seen him hoofin' it up the stairs like bloodhounds was after him. Honest, I ain't kiddin'."

"Honest," Moroni sneered, "you ain't kiddin'." He waved one arm in a sweeping gesture that included Sammy, Mabel Tilson and Birdie Brooks. To the track cops he said indifferently: "Send for the wagon and give these mugs free transportation to headquarters. I'll be down later. This is my day off." Still sneering, he hiked to the door and barged out. Peter Kane stretched up from the table and strolled out after him.

KANE STEERED a crooked course for the clubhouse and the amplified voice of the public-address system growled around him: "The horses are approaching the barrier. You still have time to make your wagers." He made a face and snorted. An acquaintance pawed his arm.

"My Gawd, Kane, did you see who won that last race? Moralist by three lengths! Three hundred and eighty bucks for ten!"

Kane thought of Soulful Sammy's "hot tip" and felt the need of a drink. He had a long one that gagged him. When he got upstairs in the clubhouse he had four legs instead of two and prowled down the corridor like a seasick first-timer on the upper deck of a liner.

According to Soulful Sammy the sallow-faced guy who looked kind of sick had made a get-away in this direction. Maybe. Kane looked around and scowled. The crowd here was leaner than the crowd in the grandstand. Aloud Kane said: "Sure as hell the guy never chased up here to lose himself in the mob. Must be he had a destination."

He poked around and did a little bleary-eyed snooping. After a while he tried a door marked *Private*, and the door jarred open to his shove, let him into a small office. The office was empty but a washbasin in an alcove was wet and dirty and a damp towel hung from one of the faucets.

Kane looked around, slouched out, closed the door and caught a uniformed attendant. He said: "Listen, buddy. Whose hangout is that?"

It was the private office of Mr. Anson Lacey, who was fortunate enough to own a large slice of the track and conjunctive interests. "Mr. Lacey," said the attendant, "went south several days ago to look over a string of horses."

"That office supposed to be locked all the time?"

"Certainly. Mr. Lacey has the only key."

"That's what you think," Kane murmured. "Look again."

The attendant was astounded. Undoubtedly Mr. Lacey had gone away and left the door unlocked. Was there anything else the attendant could do?

"Sure," Kane mumbled. "You can find for me a thin, sallow-faced guy who looks sick and—" He sighed, shook his head sadly. "Never mind. Skip it. Remind me to fill a Christmas stocking for Moroni. He believes in Santa Claus."

CHAPTER TWO

THE BROLBERG ANGLE

IT WAS late when Kane got to the Beacon Agency offices on Washington Street. The office was empty; a stack of mail had been placed neatly on Kane's desk, had fallen and fanned out. He pawed through it, stuffed most of it into his pocket and went uptown to Limpy's Place. After three hookers of Scotch and a fistful of saltines he hiked downtown to police headquarters on LaRonge Street and found Moroni, Moe Finch and some men from the track gathered in the back room.

"We been wondering when you'd sober up and pay us a visit," Moroni said irritably. "Don't forget it was you that discovered D'Amino's body. You got a few questions to answer for the record book."

"You're always picking on me," Kane whined. "I won't stay another minute—"

"Cut the comedy."

Kane sighed and sat down, tipped his chair back against the wall and hooked his heels in one of its rungs, hunched himself comfortably. Apparently the racetrack men had been here a good while. Moe Finch, behind the desk, looked tired and exasperated and was biting little pieces out of a thumbnail and spitting them at the floor. Moroni had an air of largeness and importance. One of the race-track men said wearily: "We don't care what you do or how you do it, but this business has got to be kept out of the papers. It's the wrong kind of publicity."

Kane said quietly: "Whereabouts down south did Anson Lacey go to?"

"Who?"

"Lacey. You heard the first time."

One of the track men scowled. "Lacey's at Bowie, looking over some yearlings. He won't be back till the first of the week."

"Where's he live?"

"What the devil difference—"

"Where's his home address?" Kane insisted.

Anson Lacey's home address was in the 800s on Commonwealth Avenue. Kane puckered his lips and murmured, "Dough, eh?" The front legs of his chair bumped the floor and he stood up. "I got a date, Moe. Maybe later I'll be back."

He went out and took a cab. It was a long ride. Limpy's three hookers of bad Scotch began to take effect long before the meter had reached its total of five dollars and twenty cents. When the cab stopped and Kane got out, Lacey's home looked three times as big as it was and it was big enough in actuality to be an eyesore. Kane told the cab-driver to wait and walked crookedly up a flagstoned path that played tricks with his feet. A French-looking maid with much front opened the door to him. Kane said warily: "I've an appointment with Mr. Anson Lacey."

"Mr. Anson Lacey?" The girl wrinkled her face out of shape. "But he is not at home."

"It's important."

"But he is not here. Only Mr. Gerard Lacey is here."

"Anson's son?"

Gerard Lacey was Anson's son. "Tell him," Kane said, "I want to talk to him. Kane's the name. Peter Kane. From headquarters."

The girl's eyes opened wide and she retreated step by step down the corridor. Kane had a drink while he waited, was stuffing the bottle back in his coat pocket when the maid returned. The younger Lacey was standing wide-legged, midway down the hall, and stared holes in Kane as Kane advanced.

He said: "You're—an officer?"

"Detective."

"Well," Lacey frowned. "I—I guess it's all right." Apparently he was not sure. He walked slowly into a big living room, sat down and continued to stare. "May I ask," he said, "what is the trouble?"

HE HAD a face that Kane at once disliked. A thin face, habitually pale, with puffs under its eyes, pale wet lips, and a line of loose flesh under the chin. A dissipated face and a scared one. The hands that went with it were soft and flabby and moist. Something about the face was familiar, and Kane tried in vain to figure out what.

"We'll skip the preliminaries," Kane shrugged. "I guess you know what happened this afternoon at the track. I guess they told you."

"Yes, of course. But—"

"Spend a lot of time out there, do you?"

"No, I don't." Lacey's wet lips whitened in a sheepish grin. "As a matter of fact, I'm forbidden to set foot inside the gates."

"Huh?"

"I may as well be frank with you. My father is the old-fashioned type, Mr. Kane—stern and strict. He didn't like the way I went through college and, well, after college I got into one or two scrapes that annoyed him."

"What kind of scrapes?"

"Well, gambling if you want to call it that. Father is quite convinced that gambling is a grave weakness of mine. Therefore I'm forbidden to go wherever gaming instruments are found, and that includes the racetrack. It's a lot of silly nonsense, but father controls the exchequer and I do what I'm told."

"You've never been out to the track?"

"I won't say never, but never except in father's company."

Kane scowled, said curtly: "When do you expect father back?"

"Not until the first of the week at the earliest."

"H'm. O.K., son." Halfway out of his chair Kane stiffened, dropped back again. "Say. How long have you been out of college?"

"A year."

"Was it your picture they plastered all over the front pages for taking part in that college play that raised such a stink?"

Again that sheepish grin ran to the bulges under Gerard's eyes. "That was just another of the things that got father sore." Unaware of Kane's narrow-eyed scrutiny, he leaned forward to take a cigarette from the package Kane held out.

"Well"—this time Kane got fullway out of the chair and reached the door—"thanks anyhow." Scowling, he hiked down the hall, took an eyeful of the French maid and went out.

On the way back to town he sprawled in the cab, stared at the label on a pint bottle and said aloud: "Maybe the Brolberg angle goes deeper." He was thinking of what Birdie Brooks had said in the track police office, about ten one-hundred-dollar bills. Brolberg had looked up Louis D'Amino and delivered the dough. Brolberg had then faded.

Abe Brolberg, short, fat and of questionable nationality, ran a downtown dine-and-dance joint called The Palms. On the side he ran other things including a big lottery ring that rivaled the one controlled by Louis D'Amino, a gambling layout where everything was crooked except the wires of the police alarm, and a South End print shop which turned out, for fights, football, hockey games and similar sporting contests, the best no-good tickets a sucker ever paid top price for.

Abe Brolberg and Louis D'Amino, big shots in competitive, small-scale racketeering puddles, had seldom professed any great devotion for each other.

Kane went to The Palms.

IT WAS a frowsy joint on a one-way side street off Stuart, and he looked both ways along the street before entering. He was not known here; the doorman peered at him suspiciously because he was not wearing evening clothes. Funny, Kane thought—the dumpier a joint got, the more the suckers doll up to come to it.

He left his hat and coat with the check-girl, lit a cigarette and pushed forward through darkly draped swing doors that muffled a drone of dance music from the room beyond. The hour was about nine; the band was playing for the benefit of a few scattered couples, mostly half-scared kids who thought they were being hellions and went through dizzy contortions on the dance floor. Kane stood and looked around until a headwaiter came up to him and said: "Yes, sir. A booth?"

"I'm here to see Brolberg." Kane flicked ashes on the carpet and glared into the waiter's eyes. "Where'll I find him?"

"Is he expecting you?"

"Yeah."

The waiter seemed to doubt it, but turned and walked stiffly down an aisle between booths and tables. At the end of the aisle he held a door open for Kane, said, "This way, sir," and took the lead again. Out back he stopped with his back toward Kane and knocked on a small dark door.

After a while he knocked again, then tried the knob, found the door unlocked and opened it. He took one step over the sill and called out not too loudly: "Mr. Brolberg? Mr. Brolberg?" As if bewildered by Brolberg's apparent absence, he paced slowly forward. Kane reached the threshold in time to see him timidly push out an inner door that had tacked on its panels a magazine picture of a leggy girl with tights on.

The other room was dark and the waiter spoke Brolberg's name again before fumbling for a light switch. Kane had a feeling dynamite was about to explode.

It did when the light went on. The waiter stiffened, made saucer eyes at a thing that sat humped up on the floor with its back jammed against the front of a desk and its head lolling. He said hoarsely, "Brolberg!" and took a faltering step forward.

Kane beat him to it. On one knee, with one hand palmed against the floor to steady himself, Kane raised Brolberg's lolling head and peered into the man's face. It was a scared, contorted face. The mouth was agape and the tongue was jammed way back in. The eyes were wide-open, rimmed with white, and glassy as frosted marbles.

A bullet had drilled the starched front of Abe Brolberg's dress-shirt just above the second of three black studs. Blood had oozed from the hole and drooled in a thin stream to his trousers, puddled the floor between his splayed legs.

Kane said slowly with a knot in his voice: "That guy's— dead."

He felt funny inside and it was not Limpy's bad Scotch that made him feel that way. A minute went by before he could lean forward to move the body. He had an idea the bullet had gone clean through.

It had, but there was no mark on the desk. Kane stood up, walked around the desk and examined the wall. The wall was flecked with spatterings of blood, and the plaster was pulverized where a slug had smacked into it. Kane gazed at the waiter and said: "Whoever shot Brolberg took time out afterwards to prop the corpse on display, just like D'Amino's corpse was propped." The waiter stood pop- eyed, wringing an imaginary dishrag with his perspiring hands.

THE SLUG-HOLE in the wall was not deep; appar- ently the bullet itself had fallen to the floor. Kane stopped, stared, straightened and said grimly: "Whoever gave Brol- berg the works was careful not to leave any souvenirs. Listen, you!" He swung to the waiter's gaping face. "Who was in here this evening? Who had a date with Abe?"

The waiter had to swallow twice before his voice worked; then it was thin and whiney. "I—I won't do any talking. I should call the police."

"You're talking to the police!"

The man's mouth sagged and he caught a quick noisy breath. "You—you mean you—" Kane palmed a badge that Peter Kane, private shamus in the employ of the Beacon Agency, had no legal right to possess.

"Who was here to see Brolberg this evening?"

"I wouldn't know. I wouldn't know for sure." The badge had a numbing effect on the waiter's ability to concentrate. "I only been on since five o'clock."

"Brolberg's only been dead an hour or so, mug."

"Well—well then, it might have been a man who came in here about eight thirty." The waiter was again wringing dishrags. "The place was empty and he said he had a letter for the boss. He showed me the envelope and said he had to deliver it in person, and he knew where Mr. Brolberg's office was, so I let him go in—"

"What'd he look like?"

"I don't remember. I didn't pay much attention."

"Damn your soul, *think!*" Kane roared.

"Well, he—I think he had on a gray suit and a gray hat, and he was kind of thin and he looked sick, sort of. That is, he was pale and sallow in the face, as if he was sick most of the time, not sick with anything in particular. I mean—"

"I get what you mean," Kane said slowly. "I—get it."

"About half an hour before that," the waiter said, "a woman came in and went straight to Brolberg's office. She looked as if she knew what she was about, so I didn't pay any attention to her."

"Who was she?"

The man made a feeble gesture with his hands. "I wouldn't know."

"You work here, and you don't know the names of the dames who have free tickets to Brolberg's private office?"

"I've only been here two weeks," the waiter mumbled.

Kane glared at him and felt resentful. The man's hands were red and sticky and were still wringing dishrags. Kane slapped them apart, growled: "For God's sake, don't do that! You give me the creeps!" The waiter stared at him pop-eyed as he strode out.

He hiked with long lithe steps past the dance floor and into the lobby, jammed his big frame into a phone booth, thumbed a nickel into the slot and dialed headquarters. The desk man answered the call and Kane said tersely: "Gimme Moe Finch."

Then he said: "Listen, Moe. Get this down. Abe Brolberg was murdered tonight, shot, by either a dame or a thin, sallow-faced guy that looked sick. Yeah, the same guy that looked sick at the track. The job was pulled on the quiet and was a nice clean job without any labels. Me, I'm on my way out of here. Moroni can mop up what's left."

Moe Finch wailed: "Kane! Where you goin'?"

"I got a hunch this is a grudge killing. D'Amino, then Brolberg, see? Those two guys liked each other so much they wouldn't even spit on the same sidewalk. Brolberg's boys rub out D'Amino, so D'Amino's boys return the compliment." Kane's lips left a wet ring on the mouthpiece. "Get it? I'm gonna call around and see what I can catch."

He hung up. The pop-eyed waiter was standing in the middle of the lobby, nervously wringing his hands. Kane glared, said savagely: "Someone ought to put you in a strait-jacket." On his way out he slammed the door so hard that the glass shivered.

Hours later when he let himself into his own three-room apartment on Queensberry Street, he was bleary-eyed and top-heavy on his feet. Calling around at various joints frequented by the hirelings of D'Amino and Brolberg had involved the imbibing of some very bad liquor. The Kane constitution, though inured to such things, had taken a terrific tossing.

He threw hat and coat on the studio couch, kicked his shoes off, hiked into the bathroom and mixed a double bromo, gulped it and gagged. When he went to bed, the electric clock in the living room was chiming the half hour between three and four, and Kane's last thoughts were of hands, human hands—the restless, sweaty paws of the head waiter at The Palms and the thin, flabby hands of young Gerard Lacey.

CHAPTER THREE
THE CORPSE THAT LOOKED SICK

MOE FINCH took a sodden cigar butt out of his mouth at eleven o'clock the next morning, stared over the headquarters desk into Kane's hang-dog face and whined plaintively: "I thought you were gonna help me out and be a pal o' mine. Now look! Plastered to the gills!"

"Someday," Kane said, "you'll discover the difference between a skinful and a hangover. I got the hangover." He put his hands behind his back, teetered up and down on his toes and gazed with innocence at Moroni. "And what have you got that's eating you up, sweetness?"

Moroni had an important look on his face and for the past three minutes had been making strange, uncouth noises that went with the Moroni process of deep thinking. He came out of his trance, aimed a stiff forefinger at the top of Moe Finch's near-bald head and growled with much distortion of the lips—

"Listen. Last night's killing may be mob stuff like Kane thinks. Also it may be something else, see? Two times we been told about this thin, sallow-faced guy that looks sick. When a tip comes twice, from parties that don't even figure to know each other, it means something!" Moroni lowered his big body into a chair and hunched forward. "Listen now. That thin, sallow-faced stuff fits Soulful Sammy, don't it? Isn't he thin and sallow and sick-lookin'? And we gotta get this guy before he bumps someone else off, don't we? I say let Sammy loose, put a couple of men on his tail, and watch what he does!"

Kane murmured softly: "What a large brain you have, grandma!" But he didn't feel funny. His head had cobwebs in it and the bad liquor of last night had lined his mouth with flannel. He made for the door. "You guys can argue all you want. Thank God I'm just a private shamus and can ring out when I feel like it."

Moe Finch gripped the sides of the desk and wailed frantically: "Kane! Where you goin' now?"

"I gotta see Limpy about a pick-up," Kane said, and went out.

He went to Limpy's, prowled into Limpy's back room and sat in a booth. He had three of Limpy's unfailing revivers and decided, after the third, that he was sober enough to begin getting soused again. He was very soused when Limpy wallowed through a fog of cigarette smoke, thrust an anxious face forward and said: "Moe Finch is on the phone and near crazy from wantin' to talk to you."

Moe Finch said over the phone: "Listen, Kane. It must be I'm crazy or something. So help me, I let Moroni talk me into turnin' Soulful Sammy loose. Do somethin', will you? Kennedy and Mowens are tailing him and neither one of them could tail an elephant down Tremont Street!"

Kane grinned at the phone and gurgled: "For you, *padre*, I'd even do that." When he forked the phone and turned around, he was scowling. To Limpy he growled: "Moroni. Bah!" He was thinking not of Moe Finch but of Moe's wife, Alma. Before marrying Moe, Alma had tried hard to separate Peter Kane from liquor and make marriageable material of the Beacon Agency's ace dick. She had failed through no fault of her own, had finally, in despair, accepted Moe Finch as the next best alternative. But there was still a big something between her and Kane. There always would be.

He thought now that if Moe Finch went on the mat and lost his job, the chief sufferer would be Alma. He thought also that Soulful Sammy, on the loose again, would most likely have gravitated back to his habitual haunt, the race track.

Kane went to the race track.

THE CASH customers were hopefully wagering their savings on the second race when he got there. The ponies were on parade. Kane elbowed through the crowd drifting from paddock to track, hiked down the slope to the judge's stand and peered around. He was drunk, but it was a good clean drunk now and not a hangover. He spotted Kennedy and Mowens, the headquarters dicks, first, then saw Soulful Sammy and eased himself down to the rail where Sammy was operating.

He did so without attracting Sammy's attention, and for that matter it would have been difficult indeed to attract Sammy's attention at that moment. "Listen," Sammy was saying to a large-bosomed lady who listened closely. "Listen, lady. It ain't possible to beat the races by shooting blind. Now I been around the horses for many years, lady, in fact I was once one of them little cricket men that you see aboard the ponies this very moment, but I got overweight and had to become what is known as a trainer. It is not possible to beat the races unless you are in the know, lady, because the races are very crooked. Now I am in the know on this race and I say to you, bet every cent you own on this goat named Happy Lad. A goat is race-track language for horse, lady."

The lady was much impressed. She was facing Kane at a distance of about six paces but she either failed to see, or did not realize the significance of, the dry smile that played about Kane's face. She said to Soulful Sammy: "Are you *sure* Happy Lad will win?"

"Lady," said Soulful, "this race is what is known locally as in the bag. If you will look in the book you will see how in his last four starts Happy Lad has been a terrific last, which means, lady, that he was held back so the odds would be very much higher on this occasion today. I am not a tout, lady. I am giving you good information and if you are in the mood to hand me one or two fins—that is, five-dollar bills to you, lady—after you have cleaned up, I will be seeing you here after the race."

The lady made gurgling sounds and hurried away to bet much money. A grin wrinkled Soulful Sammy's thin face and with the black crescent of a tapered fingernail he underscored the name of Happy Lad on his program. All other horses in the same race had been underscored similarly, with penciled notations marked beside their names so that Soulful Sammy would not be confused when he sought out his winning client after the contest was over.

With a gentle sign indicative of work well done, Sammy relaxed against the rail and lit himself a cigarette.

Kane was staring at something else.

The object of Kane's stare was apparently trying to be as inconspicuous as possible. He wore a soft felt hat with the brim turned low to shadow his face, and looked about him with anxious eyes, furtively, as he maneuvered through the crowd near the rail. He stiffened with a convulsive jerk when he met Kane's level gaze, and he stood stock-still, gaping, as Kane bore down on him.

Kane said: "I thought father never let you hang around here."

Gerard Lacey essayed a weak-lipped smile and took a backward step as though fearful of being slapped. "Father doesn't know," he said. "He isn't back yet."

"Oh."

"I had a tip on a sure thing," Gerard faltered, "so I—well, I sneaked out here." He made movements with his hands to show Kane that he was wearing shabby clothes, apparently his own brilliant idea of a disguise. "Listen. You won't let on you saw me, will you? I mean, if father should be talking to you some time—"

Kane snorted, moved away and centered his attention again on Soulful Sammy. Sammy had moved, because the large-bosomed lady had made a reappearance and if a horse by the name of Happy Lad failed to win the coming race—as a horse by the name of Happy Lad figured to do—Sammy wished to be where the large-bosomed lady would fail to find him.

It was a mile event and the horses were lined at the barrier in front of the judges' stand. They were off as Kane aimed a cursory glance into the crowd. A wave of sound belched from the grandstand and Kane saw Moroni hoofing down the slope.

HE SIGHED, because he thought Moroni had money on the race. But he was wrong. Moroni was steering a frantic course for Kennedy and Mowens, the men assigned to tail Soulful Sammy. He saw Kane, changed his course, pawed Kane's arm and blurted: "I can use you, Kane. There's been a killing in the clubhouse."

Kane said sourly: "Save it. I'm not that drunk."

"I said I could use you!" Moroni bellowed. "Get Kennedy and Mowens and tell them to drag Soulful Sammy over to Anson Lacey's office. Be a help for once!"

Kane stared, saw the fever in Moroni's eyes and hunched his shoulders. "Anything," he said, "to oblige." He wondered vaguely who had been murdered, and how.

He found out five minutes later when he hiked down the second-floor corridor of the clubhouse and pushed open the door of Anson Lacey's office. The office was jammed to the walls with men in uniform and men not in uniform, track attendants and track police and chiselers who had managed to wriggle in for an eyeful of what lay on the table. There was much talk, and Moroni, in the hub of the mob, was yelling above the others to make himself heard.

The thing on the table was a thin, sallow-faced man of about Soulful Sammy's build and looks. His ankles over-hung the table-top, the Adam's apple in his neck bulged toward the ceiling, and a trickle of blood ran from under him into a crack in the table where it had formed a dark red pool.

Kane peered into the man's face and said: "His name is Coutu. Paul Coutu. He's a small-time thug and was up two months ago for peddling fake tickets on a sweepstakes. Who did it?"

Moroni said nasally: "How the hell do we know who did it?"

Coutu had been stabbed in the back. "We found him," a track attendant told Kane, "hanging over the verandah rail, like he was looking down at the people below. He didn't look dead; he looked sick. He might have been there like that for a long time."

Kennedy and Mowens came in with Soulful Sammy between them. Sammy looked scared, was trying to make words of protest come through pale lips that twitched convulsively. Moroni said grimly: "Listen, you guys. Did this mug get out of your sight even for a minute since we turned him loose?"

"Not even for a minute," Kennedy said.

"Was he up here in the clubhouse at any time?"

"He was not. He spent all his time fishing for suckers in the grandstand."

"Then he's out," Moroni growled. "And this here looks like another link in a series of gang killings. First D'Amino was rubbed out, then Abe Brolberg, and now Brolberg's boys have taken care of the mug that shot Abe. This here is the sallow-faced, sick-lookin' guy we've been trying to check on."

"And they all," Kane murmured, "lived happily ever after."

"Huh?"

"Hooey," Kane snorted. "Hooey and more hooey." Mumbling to himself, he elbowed his way out of the office. Deep down inside he felt ornery and disgusted, and the only cure for a feeling of that kind was a quantity of Limpy's very bad liquor.

AT NINE P.M. by Limpy's clock, Kane was sprawled in a booth at Limpy's, languidly studying the manner in which whiskey burned with a pale blue flame when spilled on the table and ignited with a match. At nine thirty the phone rang and Limpy came in back to say grumblingly: "It's for you, from Moe Finch, if you ain't too plastered to get up."

Moe Finch said: "If you hadn't been in such an unholy rush to get away this afternoon, mister, you'd've been in on something. First place, Moroni found the knife that killed Paul Coutu. Yeah. Found it jammed behind a pipe in the washroom in Lacey's office. Second place, Lacey himself was prowling around, trying to keep under cover."

"I had a talk with him," Kane said.

"Not with this Lacey you didn't. This was Anson Lacey in person, the old man himself. We tagged him for questioning but he swore up and down he don't know a thing about the murders. Says he got wind that his son was gambling again, so he sneaked up from the south to check up. Maybe so, maybe not. Anyhow, Moroni claims the whole thing is gang stuff."

"So what now?" Kane sighed.

"So we're keeping an eye on Brolberg's place and on the side we're tabbing the Laceys. Also Soulful Sammy."

"What," Kane demanded, "ever did become of Birdie Brooks and that Mabel Jilson dame?"

"They're around if we need 'em. What I'm telling you is to be careful, kind of. You been acting like you knew a lot. Maybe some of Brolberg's boys will be worried about guys that know a lot. I don't have time to attend any funerals."

"Thanks," Kane said. "I already thought of that angle."

He went back to the booth and Limpy said: "For God's sake, Kane, do you *got* to burn my tables? Ain't it enough you come in here to get plastered, without—" With gestures, Kane got into his overcoat and jammed his hat on his head. He felt good, but he felt sleepy. He put both hands on Limpy's shoulders, murmured gently: "My pal. You'd come to my funeral, wouldn't you?" Unsteady on his feet, he prowled out the back way and walked home.

Twice, on the way home, he lingered in dark doorways and tried to get a good look at the man who was deliberately following him. But the man had very good eyesight and was clever enough to keep just far enough behind to be only a shadow.

"Moe Finch," Kane muttered, "had the right idea." He was thinking of the funeral.

When he let himself into his apartment, he was careful to close the door until the lock very definitely clicked; then he paraded into the living room, turned on a couple of lights and the radio, and poured a drink.

He didn't need the drink now, but reflected grimly that he might need it, and more like it, before the night was over. When Brolberg's boys figured you knew too much, you sometimes abruptly ceased knowing anything at all.

THE RADIO played dance music and Kane sat on the studio couch, made a church-and-steeple with his hands while the Kane brain worked overtime. In the end he hiked into the bedroom and dragged back the sheets of the bed, pulled a mound of blankets from a bureau drawer and went to work with the blankets, a length of rope and a wad of towels. It took him fifteen minutes to arrange the resulting contrivance on the bed, pull the covers over it and add the finishing touches by poking and patting wherever necessary.

"So help me," he said proudly, "it even looks like me."

He tossed a coat and a pair of pants on a chair near the bed and threw a soiled shirt, two socks, undershirt and shorts on top of them. Then he kicked two shoes across the floor and the whole thing looked very much as if Peter Kane, drunk, had sloppily discarded his wearing apparel, sprawled into bed and was now dead to the world, slumbering blissfully beneath a warming tangle of covers.

Kane put out the light, went back to the living room and turned off lights and radio. Then he pulled a chair into deeper darkness away from the window and sat there nursing a pint.

Half an hour later a window creaked in the kitchenette and Kane opened his eyes very slowly, turned his head toward the hall doorway—and stared.

The window stopped creaking. Something heavy thudded to the floor. In a moment the something heavy moved again, tiptoed warily along the hall and steered a course for the bedroom, moving with such sluggishness that Kane had both shoes off and was on his feet before the bedroom door creaked open.

Sitting still so long had made Kane drunk. Prowling into the hall, he came within an inch of colliding with the door frame, had to stand there holding his breath and shaking his head to get his bearings.

The hall was empty. In the bedroom a loose floorboard creaked as the intruder tiptoed toward the bed. Kane heard a dull thud, a sudden squeak of the bed-springs and a guttural exhalation of breath. Next instant a dark shape streaked over the bedroom threshold and lurched down the hall toward him.

Kane heaved out from the wall and swung a knotted fist at the man's head.

He missed because he was too plastered to see straight, and because the killer, after plunging a knife into the dummy on the bed, had gone panicky and acted with unforeseen speed. Ordinarily such a killer would have stabbed three or four times with the knife, then realized that something was not according to Hoyle, and been easy prey for the surprise attack Kane had figured on. This one had messed things up.

Kane's fist made crunching contact with a wiry shoulder and the killer staggered in midnight, let out a hoarse grunt and careened against the wall. In the dark of the hallway Kane's eyes focused too slowly to be of any help. He swung again wildly, missed, went off balance. The killer made whimpering terror-sounds and streaked past him, made a bee-line for the kitchenette. The window groaned and the fire-escape rattled to an impact of pounding leather heels.

With a scowl on his face that would have soured milk, Kane pushed himself up, hipped his hands and stood swaying. He was drunk and sore with himself for getting drunk. He said aloud: "You dizzy damn dope, maybe some day you'll learn." Muttering maledictions, he clicked on a light switch and limped into the kitchen.

CHAPTER FOUR

THE GROOVED KNIFE

THE WINDOW was wide open and from the alleyway three stories below, under the fire-escape, came a noise of fast-moving feet thumping over concrete. Kane closed the window and hiked dolefully into the bedroom, thumbed another light switch. Gaping at the bed, he made a wry face and his stomach did a turnover.

The killer had evidently known the lay-out of the apartment, the exact location of the bed and the probable position of any prospective victim who might be slumbering therein. The hilt of a long, wicked-looking knife protruded unpleasantly from that portion of Kane's dummy which in Kane himself would have been the heart. With a shudder, Kane drew the knife out and made eyes at it.

It was a very ordinary cheap knife with a soft, wood handle. The handle bore a number of thin grooves. Kane narrowed his eyes at the grooves, scowled, and thought they were interesting.

He carried the knife into the living room, parked himself in a chair and had a long, stiff drink to clear the fog out of his brain. During the next half hour he had many more drinks and centered his attention on the knife and the grooves. Especially the grooves.

"I guess the guy was nervous," Kane said. "I guess, on his way here, he had the jitters."

He wondered if the killer actually thought that Peter Kane, the Beacon Agency's gumshoe, was dead. There was one good way of finding out. Go ask him.

He wrapped the knife in a sheet of newspaper and stuffed it into his pocket. While he was lacing his shoes the phone rang. He scowled, got up and answered it, and Moe Finch said: "Kane? That you, Kane? *You?* My God, I thought you were done for! Listen, never mind asking me questions, but get down here to headquarters in a hurry!"

Kane went to headquarters.

When he walked in, a sleepy-eyed desk man blinked at him without emotion and said: "They're waitin' for you in

the back room." In the back room Moe Finch was fidget-
ing at his desk, Moroni was chewing savagely on a thick
cigar, and Mabel Jilson, the ex-girlfriend of Louis D'Amino,
was saying things in a shrill, excited voice.

Kane looked around, sat down and said curiously: "Well?"

Moe Finch looked at Mabel Jilson and said: "Tell him,
Mabel."

"It's like this." Mabel caught a deep breath and leaned
forward. "I was on my way to your place to have a confidential talk with you. Never mind what I wanted to talk
about; it don't matter now. The point is, just when I got
there I saw this guy sneaking out of your place through a
window. I backed up and kept my eyes peeled, and the guy
came streaking down the fire-escape and faded around
the corner.

"Well, I followed the guy, see? I didn't get a good look
at him, but I know this. He went straight to Birdie Brooks'
apartment house on Camp Street!"

"And that," Moroni put in, "is where you and me are
goin' right now, Kane. Drunk as you are."

Kane opened his mouth to speak, changed his mind
and transferred his gaze from Mabel Jilson to Moe Finch.
He aimed a cigarette at his mouth, stood up and said
without blinking his eyes: "O.K., Moroni. Let's go."

Scowling, he followed Moroni outside and got into a
police coupé that stood at the curb. Moroni drove. After
a while Moroni said gutturally: "This sort of clears things
up, don't it? Either that or the Jilson dame is screwy."

"Either that," Kane said, "or we are."

A CLOCK, uptown, bonged the half hour between two
and three as Moroni braked the car on Camp Street. Kane
slid from the seat and stared at the apartment house where

Birdie Brooks had three rooms. It was a big house with dirty white pillars out front and an amber light glowing above the doorway. Kane hiked up the steps, entered the vestibule and ran a finger down the row of names.

He put a finger on the button beside the name Brooks and pushed hard. Moroni said nasally: "You got a gun, Kane?" Kane shook his head. Through the tube a woman's voice droned in weary sing-song: "Hello? Who is it?"

Moroni told her. Moroni also did the talking when he and Kane got to the door of Birdie's apartment. Birdie listened, standing with both hands jammed on the door-frame and her small, wiry body filling the entrance. She had pajamas on—pale blue ones, wrinkled from being slept in. Her eyes were circled and her mouth looked as if it had a bad taste. She said irritably: "Listen. I'm not even interested. I was in bed."

"One side, sister," Moroni growled. "We're lookin' around."

A scared look came into Birdie's haggard face and she stepped back, stood flat against the wall as Moroni and Kane walked past her into the apartment. Lights were on in the hall, the bedroom, the living room. Moroni put his head in the bedroom, peered at a crumpled bed and a chair full of feminine garments and growled: "I guess you were in bed, all right."

He put a hand on the girl's arm and said: "In here, sister, where we can keep an eye on you." She flung his hand off, walked stiffly into the living room and plunked herself down in a chair. She was sore. She said savagely: "Will you tell me what the hell this is all about?"

Moroni was already snooping. Kane stood in one place, stared around, picked out a chair and sat down. The apartment was hot and the heat did things to the whiskey in his stomach. He stuck his feet out and made himself comfortable.

"Listen." Birdie's voice had a wail in it. "For the love of God, what is this? Loosen up, will you, before I go nuts completely?"

"Ask Moroni," Kane said. "He thought it up."

"Thought what up?"

"Darned if I know."

The girl subsided with a noisy explosion of breath and an air of long suffering. After a while she turned the radio on. A dance band played two hot numbers and was beginning a third when Moroni appeared in the doorway.

Moroni's lips were curled, a cigarette drooping between them. His arms were full of junk. He dumped the junk on a chair, glared at Birdie and growled thickly: "So you can't figure out why we're here, huh?"

The stuff on the chair was mostly clothing. The main items were a man's gray suit and a pair of soiled white shoes. From a pocket of the coat Moroni pulled a .38 caliber automatic, a handful of loose shells and a bone-handled knife. "I found this mess," he said grimly, "under a pile of junk in one of the bedroom cupboards. That's all I want to know, sweetheart. Just as soon as we get you to headquarters, *you* can do the talking."

Birdie Brooks opened her eyes very wide and helped herself to a long, shuddering stare. Violently she lurched erect. Hysterically she wailed: "No. No! It's a frame!"

SHE SAID more than that at headquarters. Sitting in a straight-backed chair behind closed doors in Moe Finch's back room, with Moroni standing wide-legged before her, she hung onto her knees and stared mechanically at the bottom button on Moroni's vest and moaned: "I didn't do it. Honest to God, I didn't. It's a dirty plant."

Moroni was working up to a display of the famous Moroni psychology. Eyes narrowed, mouth rolling around a sodden cigar, he hooked his thumbs in his belt, pushed his shoulders up around his ears and glared holes in the girl's colorless face. "I'm warning you, sister, you'll save yourself a lot of grief by coming clean before we crack down on you. You killed D'Amino and Brolberg and Paul Coutu, or if you didn't do the jobs with your own lily-white hands you were working with the thugs that did. Spill it!"

Across the room Mabel Jilson was doing things to her scarlet fingernails, and seemed indifferent. Moe Finch had both elbows on his desk and his knuckles jammed against his jaw. He had a wife at home and a soft streak under his leathery skin. Apparently he was not enjoying Moroni's methods. Neither was Peter Kane.

Kane said: "If it's all the same to you, I'll get my entertainment elsewhere." He opened the door, took a last look around and went out. Moroni took off coat and vest, tossed them on the desk and went to work in earnest.

"Maybe," Moroni said to Birdie Brooks, "you can explain away the stuff we found in your apartment. Go to work on that."

"I told you it's a frame!"

"And you don't know how they got there even? Try again, sister. Maybe you think this is a kindergarten. Maybe you think I'm Kane."

Moe Finch said: "Listen, Moroni. Let me talk to her. Maybe she'll come clean with me."

He was wrong. She wouldn't. For half an hour she sat stiff and straight, stared with wide wet eyes and moaned the same answer to every question. "I don't know, I told you. The whole thing is a frame-up, so help me God!"

Moe Finch gave up in despair, went back to his desk and mopped perspiration from his face. Mabel Jilson gazed indifferently at Birdie and murmured: "Well, anyhow, the girl's got guts." Moroni got sore, let his voice rise to a hoarse bellow and worked himself into the usual Moroni lather.

"Sister, all I'm warning you is, don't get me mad! Don't make me lose my temper! If that happens—"

The door opened and Moroni jerked around, stood glaring. Over the threshold came Peter Kane, and Kane had one hand on the trembling left arm of Soulful Sammy. Moroni took a long look at the red welt on Sammy's jaw, at the crumpled condition of the greenish-gray suit he was wearing, at the frantic, scared expression on his face— and blurted out: "What the hell is *this?*"

"When I walked in on him, in the tenement where he lives," Kane murmured, "he wouldn't come quietly like I told him to. So I had to do a job on him."

Moroni wrinkled his face and gaped. Moe Finch stared. Mabel Jilson stiffened in her chair, stopped cleaning her fingernails, and focused a narrow-eyed, unblinking gaze on Soulful Sammy's battered face.

Kane said quietly to Soulful Sammy: "Have a seat, little one, and tell the people all about it." He shoved Sammy forward. Trembling legs let Sammy down into a chair beside the desk and he shot a startled glance around him, saw Mabel Jilson for the first time and shuddered violently. Evidently he and Kane had already had a long talk. Almost inaudibly he whined: "I—I gotta get a lawyer. Ain't I entitled to a lawyer?"

"Tell Moroni," Kane snapped, "how you knifed D'Amino at the track the afternoon D'Amino was plastered."

The answer came from Mabel Jilson. She was out of her chair, snarling as she heaved herself forward. "You can't believe a word that rat says! He's a dirty, damn liar!"

"Tell 'em," Kane insisted, "how you got five hundred dollars for putting a knife in D'Amino."

SAMMY MADE sobbing sounds in his throat and stared wide-eyed at Mabel Jilson. He didn't answer Kane. He jerked backward in his chair and shrieked: "Don't let her get at me! Keep her away from me, for God's sake! She'll kill me!"

She would have, if Moroni had not grabbed her and wrestled her into a chair. Kane was unscrewing the cap from a pint bottle. He took a long drink, leaned against the desk and wiped his mouth with the back of a blood-smeared hand. The hand was bloody from contact with Soulful Sammy's jaw.

"It's like this," Kane said. "D'Amino tossed Mabel over for Birdie Brooks, after he'd played around with Mabel for years and she helped make him a big shot. Tossing over a girl like Mabel is risky business. She got sore and paid Soulful Sammy five hundred bucks to square things for her. In order to keep Sammy out of trouble, she coached him on that hooey about a sallow-faced, sick-lookin' guy, so he'd have a talking point if the cops happened to tag him.

"The trouble was, Sammy yielded to temptation, mixed pocket-picking with murder, and made a mess of the whole business. And that was too bad."

Kane sighed, had another drink and successfully navigated the distance to the nearest chair. He was drunk and he was enjoying himself. "Well," he said, "it looked like Sammy might get out of it even at that, but someone else nosed into the affair. Abe Brolberg knew all about Mabel and D'Amino, figured things out for himself and called Mabel up to congratulate her—or something like that. Anyway, she had to get rid of him, so she went to his place and shot him, just like that.

"And, having killed him, she figured to build up this hocus-pocus about the thin, sallow-faced guy that looked sick, so she hired a guy who was sallow-faced and thin and sick-looking and paid him a few dimes to go to Brolberg's office and deliver a note or something. Just so the cops would find out that this very sinister sallow-faced guy, whom they had already heard a great deal about, was in Brolberg's office just about the time of the shooting. Damn clever, these Jilsons!"

"It's a dirty lie!" Mabel Jilson bellowed. "It's a rotten dirty lie!" She was not looking at Kane. Her eyes were smouldering coals in a face utterly drained of color, and if Moroni's paws had not been curled around her arms, holding her down in her chair, she would have been at Soulful Sammy's throat.

Moroni stared daggers at Kane and seemed very annoyed at the grin on Kane's face. Moe Finch and Birdie Brooks merely sat. Soulful Sammy huddled low in his chair and made whimpering sounds, stared at Mabel Jilson as if terrified that she would yet find some way of destroying him.

"That Coutu business," Kane sighed, "was exceeding clever, so help me. Just what Mabel told Mr. Coutu, I wouldn't know for sure, but the guess is that she instructed him as follows: 'Mr. Coutu, you go into Brolberg's outer office with this letter, and if Brolberg is not there you wait a few moments and walk out again.' In that way she made very sure that Mr. Coutu would not discover Abe's body and report to the cops about it, because Abe's body was in the inner office behind a closed door.

"Or on the other hand, maybe Mr. Coutu knew all about everything. Anyway, it was very good pinochle to get Mr. Coutu out of the way so the cops could not tag him and make him talk too much, so Mabel trailed Mr. Coutu to the racetrack and bumped him off. She used Anson Lacey's office to clean up in afterwards. I imagine Soulful Sammy, being that sort of person, had a number of keys to various private places about the track. I found some of them in his room. Also I imagine Mabel has been involved in many gang killings in the past, and the art of murder is nothing new to her. Furthermore she was once very clever in a knife act in vaudeville.

"And finally," Kane murmured, "Mabel decided to get rid of me because I was supposed to know many things which I did not know." He had another drink to drown the frog in his throat. "She dispatched Soulful Sammy to my place, to destroy me, and at the same time she arranged an elaborate frame on Birdie Brooks, because Birdie is the gal who stole Louis D'Amino away from her in the first place. It is very sad business, being in love."

HE EMPTIED the bottle, put it on the floor beside him and relaxed with a sigh of contentment. "And that," he said, "is that. Am I not very good, even if I did have to throttle Soulful Sammy to get the most of it out of him?"

Moroni, red in the face, made sputtering noises. Moe Finch said feebly: "What are you, one of these guys that play with crystal balls and tea leaves?"

Kane said elaborately: "I never use tea leaves because I never drink tea. It was like this. Soulful came to my apartment and murdered me and left a knife sticking right in my tummy. Or maybe it was my heart. Anyway, here is the knife." With exasperating lack of haste he fished the weapon out of his pocket, unwrapped it and held it in the palm of his hand.

"It is a very cheap knife for such a noble task, but look. It has many little grooves on the handle and the grooves were made with a sharp fingernail. Now many times at the track I have seen Soulful Sammy use a fingernail to underscore the name of a horse on his program. In fact he did it to me, myself, when he advised me one time to play Moralist, which I will always regret not doing.

"Anyhow, I looked at this knife with which Sammy murdered me and I said to myself, 'Mr. Kane, undoubtedly the owner of this knife is Soulful Sammy. Because why? Because these are fingernail marks. Undoubtedly,' I said to myself, 'Soulful Sammy was very nervous when he came here to commit murder. He had this knife in his pocket and he kept digging at it with his fingernails because he had a case of the jitters.'

"So then I thought: 'if Soulful Sammy is the man who murdered me, perhaps he is also the man who murdered D'Amino and Brolberg and Paul Coutu. I will have a talk with him about those things, and I will ask him about these fingernail marks. They are very little things, to be sure, but little things are sometimes very important.' So I had a talk with Soulful Sammy and—"

"And now," Moroni snarled, "you're soused to the gills. Bah!"

Moe Finch said softly: "What I think is, we should get some of Kane's liquor and feed it to some of the big-mouthed dicks in this department. Maybe it would save us a lot of running around."

Kane opened his eyes wide and gazed lovingly at Moroni. "It is very good liquor," he said. "It is much too good for Mr. Moroni."

With a sigh of contentment, he passed out.

THE SCREAMING PHANTOM

KANE WAS A VERY DRUNK
DETECTIVE WHEN HE GOT TO
OPAL LAKE PARK—SO DRUNK
IN FACT THAT HE COULDN'T
BE SURE WHETHER THE
SCREAMING PHANTOM OF THE
ROLLER COASTER WAS REAL OR
SOMETHING OUT OF HIS OWN
ALCOHOLIC IMAGINATION. BUT
IT DIDN'T TAKE HIM LONG TO
FIND OUT THE ANSWER. D.T.
CREATURES DON'T LEAVE MURDER
IN THEIR WAKE—AND MURDER
WAS WHAT HE FOUND WHEN HE
STAGGERED INTO THAT HOUSE OF
HORROR.

CHAPTER ONE
THE COASTER-CAR
PHANTOM

THE SIGN was a modernistic creation dangling on cables above the state highway. Neon letters, colorless now and topped with nightcaps of snow, marched along the shaft of a neon arrow. The letters read, OPAL LAKE PARK, and the arrow pointed off to Peter Kane's right.

"Well, for goo'nesh sake," Kane said without enthusiasm.

The name, Opal Lake Park, was vaguely familiar, even though this was a strange road in a strange part of the state. The name, Opal Lake Park, had something to do with a Mr. Daniel Kingsley, who lived in a town called Northvale or Westvale or something, which was up this way somewhere.

Mr. Daniel Kingsley was the gentleman who had written a nice letter to the Beacon Agency, enclosing a generous check and suggesting that one of the Beacon Agency's competent detectives hasten at once to Northvale or whatever it was, to look into something.

The letter had mentioned things about Opal Lake Park. Certainly it had. And this modernistic sign hanging above the snow-covered highway, here in this remote part of nowhere at one half hour after midnight, said OPAL LAKE PARK.

"Well, for goo'nesh sake," Kane said.

He was very drunk and he wondered what Mr. Daniel Kingsley would say when a very drunk private shamus arrived at the Kingsley home about one or two o'clock in the morning, many hours overdue. Probably Mr. Kingsley would be angry. Mr. Kingsley was principal of a high school or something.

Kane took a long look at the sign and helped himself to a drink from the pint bottle that lay on the seat beside him. Turning his head, he peered in the direction of the arrow. The side road into which the arrow pointed was a lane of white, sloping gently downward into the park itself.

The fantastic array of buildings and amusement devices lay about one hundred yards distant from Kane's idling sedan, along the shore of a frozen, snow-covered lake that leveled away like a smooth white sheet in the moonlight.

Mr. Daniel Kingsley's letter had mentioned a roller coaster. The coaster itself loomed like a Rube Goldberg distortion in black and white above the structures beneath it. Kane stared and shuddered. The thought of being subjected to the stomach-turning thrill of that ninety-foot drop did things to the whiskey in his inwards.

"I better get goin'," he said. "That Kingsley guy will throw a fit."

He put a hand on the gear-lever, took the hand off, turned, and peered again at the distant roller coaster. Above the purr of the car's idling engine had come a chug-chugging sound that was strangely out of place in so much snowbound desolation.

The sound was fantastic because it was undeniably the kind of noise made by the heavy car of a roller coaster beginning the long, sluggish climb in preparation for a death-defying descent. Kane blinked both eyes and groped

The gargoyle face turned to peer at the girl.

for the whiskey bottle. Then, thrusting his head forward, he gaped.

"Well, for goo'nesh sake!" he said for the third time.

The front car window was dirty and he rolled it down, but even then he could not see clearly. The coaster was a long way off and the moonlight gleaming on its snow-crusted superstructure was not too brilliant.

But, unmistakably, a car was climbing the long, gradual ascent to the structure's peak, and unmistakably the car contained a lone rider. And, now, the rider was uttering loud screams of terror!

Kane's eyes went big in his head and he pushed himself onto the running board, stood like a man swaying at the edge of an excavation, gazing in utter fascination at the unbelievable dexterity of a mammoth steam shovel. Only this wasn't a steam shovel. It was a streamlined roller-coaster car traveling over icy rails in the I dead of night, in an amusement park which by all things logical should be abandoned for the winter.

And, judging by the unending scream of soul-searing terror that came wailing across that same snow-covered desolation, the car's lone passenger was not enjoying her midnight excursion!

The car had reached the top of its climb. Horrified, Kane watched it level off and go creeping around the wide curve. It was like a small red bug creeping against the emptiness of the sky. Slowly it gained momentum. The girl's lurid voice rose to an ear-splitting note of horror.

"Good God!" Kane whispered.

Those rails would be covered with ice. The car was rolling toward the brink of a dizzy ninety-foot plunge, which, even under normal conditions, must be dangerous. In another moment—

The red bug dipped, hurtled downward. Kane closed his eyes and opened them again. Like a living thing gone mad, the car rocketed straight down, swaying on icy ribbons of steel. With a thunderous roar it shot up again, hurtled to the peak of the slope on the far side. The girl's arms— naked arms, they seemed to be—fought the gale of wind that rushed against her.

Kane stood stiff with horror. The red bug had to lurch at frightful speed around a turn before making its next plunge. If it left the rails at that speed, at that height....

It didn't. The roar of its mad progress came like a rumble of distant thunder to Kane's ears. Madly it swerved around the bend, straightened, shot again into the depths. When it reappeared, it was racing along a lower level at slackened speed. The peril was over.

KANE LURCHED forward, gasping breath. Ploughing through ankle-deep snow, he ran jerkily along the park's private road. The thunder of the coaster car was in his brain, spurring him on. It was still throbbing in his head when he staggered drunkenly past a leering row of snow-capped park buildings, minutes later, and reached the entrance to the coaster.

A ticket booth loomed there beside a turnstile that led to a wooden ramp. The ramp angled up to a platform where passengers were supposed to embark. Above the stand a sign shrieked out blatantly— THE SERPENT! MILE-A-MINUTE RIDE OF DEATH-DEFYING THRILLS!

Kane pushed against the turnstile and went up the ramp with his eyes wide and his hands balled into fists. A crimson, streamlined bullet car stood on the rails and he hiked toward it, stood on the edge of the platform and gaped down at it. It looked like the same car that had almost carried a shrieking girl to eternity.

The platform was empty. There was no longer a sound of rumbling mechanism. The entire layout was as silent, as dead, as it should be at this time of night in the middle of winter.

Kane blinked his eyes and looked around him, paced the length of the platform and back. The place gave him the creeps. Hiking back down the ramp, he went through the turnstile, paced out into the open, stood in the midst of a snowbound desolation and gazed up at the coaster's frowning superstructure.

"What the hell is this?" he snarled.

He knew what it was, and knew what he had seen. Less than five minutes ago, that coaster had been active. Now it looked as though it had lain dormant for months. Across the way, a big, dome-roofed building loomed in moonlight, and huge letters above its doorway said, THE HOUSE OF FUN. Beyond stood a circular structure, boarded up and abandoned, which was probably a merry-go-round. Farther down the midway bulked a massive frame building with a wooden cut-out sign depicting a man and a maid engaged in the business of dancing.

It seemed inconceivable, now, that anything had really come to life in this graveyard of abandoned buildings. Utterly inconceivable. "Maybe," Kane mumbled, shaking his head in bewilderment, "I was seeing things."

That was possible, too. Since early afternoon he had been guzzling enormous quantities of mongrel liquors. Maybe he had been seeing things. Maybe that improbable vision of a streamlined car hurtling over icy rails, with a screaming girl for its lone passenger, had germinated in his befogged brain because of certain bewildering comments in the letter which Mr. Daniel Kingsley had written to the Beacon Agency.

Anyhow, Peter Kane was a very plastered shamus. "Yeah," he said aloud. "I'm drunk as a goat."

Still shaking his head, he began the long trek back to his parked car.

IT WAS two A.M. when Kane arrived in Northvale. At two A.M. the town was as dead as a cemetery. Kane stopped his car in the main street and debated the wisdom of seeking the home of Mr. Daniel Kingsley at such an hour.

"Well," he shrugged, "the guy sent for me. Is it my fault if I got plastered and spent half a day getting here?"

He looked at the letter in his pocket and asked a sleepy-eyed cop where Elmgrove Street was. At ten minutes past two he braked the sedan in front of a large private residence on Elmgrove Street, got out and steered himself up a concrete walk between knee-high hedges. Grimly he poked a finger at the doorbell.

The door was opened by a smallish woman whose graying hair came about level with the bulge of Kane's necktie. Before taking even a second look at him the woman said irritably: "Well, it's certainly about time! You nearly frightened the wits out of—"Then she peered into Kane's face, gasped, and stepped abruptly backward.

"Who are you?" she faltered. "What do you want?"

Behind Kane the concrete walk echoed to a *clump, clump,* of unhurried footsteps, and the sound was so out of place in the hitherto deserted street that Kane swung about scowling. The gray-haired little woman peered past him. Up the walk came a man of Kane's own height, a thin, long-legged man, bare-headed, his hands jammed into his pants' pockets, his lean body devoid of an overcoat despite the early morning chill that made Kane shiver.

The woman said sharply: "So you've finally decided to come home, Daniel Kingsley! Well, I must say you choose queer hours for your idiotic walks!" Again she peered suspiciously at Kane. "And who might you be?"

"The name is Kane," Kane said softly. "From the Beacon Agency."

"What?"

He didn't have to explain. Daniel Kingsley, ascending the steps, gaped at him and said abruptly in a booming voice that came from his shoes: "Eh? What's that? You're from the Beacon Agency?"

"Yeah."

Kingsley was both impressed and displeased. He said something about his opinion of people who failed to keep their appointments on time. In the same breath he told the gray-haired woman that everything was all right, quite all right, he'd only been out for some air, and she shouldn't let herself get so upset over nothing. Then he took Kane's arm, ushered Kane into the house, led him into a roomy parlor, asked him his name and introduced him to a gentleman who was camped there.

"Doctor Clement Upham—Mr. Kane, from the Beacon Agency, come here to look into this ghost business at Opal Lake. What the devil are you doing here, Upham?"

Dr. Clement Upham had the facial expression of a professional man who had been aroused from bed in the middle of the night by a fussy female with indigestion. He was a middling-large man with wrinkles of red flesh under sunken, piercing eyes, and he had a forehead so high and broad that his head resembled an ostrich egg with appliquéd human features.

"Your wife," he said tersely, "became worried when you walked out without a word of where you were going. You don't seem to realize, Kingsley, that you're not a well man!"

"Nonsense! I'm well enough." Screwing his lean face out of shape, Kingsley jerked to Kane. "Sit down, sir. Let me tell you why I sent for you."

KANE SAT down. Dr. Clement Upham snorted, gathered up hat and coat and paraded to the door, banged it violently after him.

"It's like this," Kingsley said, plodding about the room. "Between Northvale and Maybridge there's a place called Opal Lake Park. I have no desire to repeat this, sir, so get it the first time. Opal Lake Park was owned by a Mr. Paul Upham, a brother of the man who just walked out of here—if you can conceive of a despicable blackguard being the brother of a reputable physician."

Kane listened, gathered facts. "Paul Upham was a scoundrel," Kingsley declared vehemently. "He made money by putting on obscene performances at the park. When his actions became intolerable, a group of Northvale citizens put the law on him.

"The place needed a thorough overhauling anyway. Last summer a girl was killed when one of the coaster cars jumped the track. That fact was brought up in court and aided the reformists in their campaign to have Paul Upham ousted. The park was closed. It has been closed ever since."

Kingsley stood wide-legged and glared into Kane's face. "Paul Upham," he declared, "drank himself to death, squandered his money and left Opal Lake Park to his brother— the man I just introduced you to. Clement Upham wanted no part of the property, so he sold it. And now there are wild reports circulating around town that the place is haunted. Haunted! No less than a dozen persons have reported seeing the coaster in action, seeing a lone car speeding around the rails with a screaming, terrified girl for its solitary passenger. In the dead of winter, mind you, and at night!

"Well, sir"—Kingsley aimed a bony forefinger at Kane's frowning countenance—"I have my own ideas about that. It so happens, sir, that a young woman who teaches at my high school has been mysteriously missing for more than ten days. She is one of the four reformists who succeeded in inducing the police to close Opal Lake Park. And I believe that the 'ghost girl' is none other than my missing school teacher!"

"What's wrong with the local police department?" Kane murmured.

"The local police, sir, are grossly incompetent. I've told them so."

"*Mmm.* They'll appreciate your dragging a private shamus into the mess. All right, Kingsley, I'll take the job. I—" Kane stopped talking. A door had opened out in the hall, and feminine laughter trilled pleasantly into the parlor. The parlor door opened. Kane jerked to his feet, stared.

CHAPTER TWO
DEATH'S-HEAD

THE GIRL on the threshold was worth staring at. She was young, not more than twenty, and she had a buoyant, carefree face above a perfect body. The body was garbed in a fetching rig of gray and blue, low at the throat, tight at the hips. The girl's coat was thrown back. She ignored Kane, grinned at Kingsley and said: "For goodness sake, daddy, don't you ever go to bed?"

A man trailed her into the room, and Kane's admiration took a nosedive. It was always the way, he reflected glumly. A good-looking girl usually had something utterly hopeless in tow. This chap looked like something that had been dunked in oily water, hauled out and propped up to dry.

"Leroy picked me up at the bridge party, daddy," the girl said, "and brought me home."

Daddy was not enthusiastic. He mumbled something to the gentleman named Leroy and introduced Kane to both the intruders. The girl was his daughter, Anita. He called her Nita. Mr. Leroy Bird, her escort, meticulously called her Anita, employing every syllable and rendering the first "A" as though it were intended to be a sigh of rapture.

Mr. Leroy Bird was handsome in an ascetic, languorous manner. He was tall and slender and had womanish hands that continually messed with each other. He was, explained Kingsley when Bird and Anita had gone out of the room, a Northvale artist and exceedingly clever.

Kane thought he was a disgrace to the male of the species.

"Getting back to the park," Kane said, "who owns the place now that your doctor friend has sold it?"

"A man who also owns concessions at various New England resorts. Tierney is his name. As yet he hasn't shown himself in Northvale."

Kane nodded slowly. "I suppose there's a hotel in town?"

There was. Kingsley tendered detailed instructions for finding it. Kane said, "I'll be around tomorrow," and slouched to the door.

He felt more like sleeping in a gutter than seeking quarters in a hotel. The warmth of the parlor had aroused all the lethargic potency of the liquor he had consumed during the past many hours, and the doorway swam before him as he went toward it. And suddenly he stopped, aware that the hall was full of a loud buzzing noise.

It was the doorbell. Kingsley said, "Excuse me, please," and opened the door. Kane gaped at uniforms and steadied himself against the wall. Over the threshold came a pair of hard-faced scowling gentlemen who were evidently emissaries of the local police, and an expensively dressed, dark-eyed youth who said cockily, "Evening Mr.

Kingsley," and bobbed a smile up and down on his upper lip while he said it.

Kane's path to the door was blocked. He sighed, made *tsking* sounds and relaxed against the wall. One of the uniformed policemen demanded gruffly: "Whose car is that parked out front?"

"Mine," Kane murmured.

"Yours, is it? I guess we want to talk to you. What's your name?"

The Kane disposition was not too good. It resented being yapped at. "What's it to you?" Kane growled.

That was a mistake. You don't, without perilous results, ask a hick cop what's it to him when you're a stranger in town, and plastered, and your car may have been seen leaving the scene of strange happenings. Especially you don't say such things to a lieutenant, because a lieutenant is important.

The lieutenant, whose name was Cleves, stiff-armed Kane into the parlor, pushed him into a chair and made a speech. He called upon the expensively dressed young man to corroborate his statements.

Tonight, near midnight, the ghost girl of Opal Lake Park had again ridden one of the streamlined, bullet cars of the Serpent. The expensively dressed young man, whose name was Rupert Varley, had seen the girl with his own eyes while driving home from a date in the next town. Also he had seen a lanky, loose-limbed, apparently plastered individual messing around the park grounds, and had seen that gentleman drive away in a sedan.

Rupert Varley had trailed the sedan here to the home of Daniel Kingsley, had carefully noted its number, and had, forthwith, hastened to the police.

"And this," Lieutenant Cleves demanded, jabbing a stiff forefinger at Kane, "is the man you saw prowling around the park?"

"He's the man," Varley nodded.

KANE SCOWLED, appreciated the delicacy of his position. Already he had aroused the good lieutenant's ire by displaying a drunken lack of respect. Moreover, the police of Northvale were in a spot. They had been called incompetent. They were ready to crack down at the first opportunity.

The set-up was perfect. Here was a stranger, caught on the scene of trouble, acting suspiciously. Here was a chance to slap a man in jail without arousing the wrath of anyone except the man himself.

Kane sighed, gazed solemnly into the scowling face of Lieutenant Cleves. "Listen. I'm a private dick, Beacon Agency, Boston. Kingsley sent for me. I stopped in at the park just to have a look at the place."

"You're a—what?"

"A dick. A private shamus. A detective. The Beacon Agency."

The lieutenant was impressed. He stared, frowning. "The Beacon Agency? Well, then, answer me this. Did you see that coaster car go around tonight?"

"No."

"You sure?"

Kane peered at the expensively dressed young man whose name was Rupert Varley. The young man had an air of self-importance and a look-me-over-I'm-good at-titude that aroused Kane's abrupt dislike. "Positive," Kane growled. "And if it's all the same by you, I was on my way out of here when you barged in. My local address in case you want me is—" He swung to Kingsley. "What's the name of that hotel again?"

"The Granville House," Kingsley supplied.

"The Granville House," Kane murmured. "What more could a distinguished guest of Northvale demand? Provided," he added, "they have anything to drink in this lousy town."

Scowling, he paraded down the hall and closed the front door after him. The run-in with Northvale's police department had sobered him; he felt rotten. Climbing into his car he adjusted his long legs under the wheel, killed what was left in the pint bottle and sucked on an unlighted cigarette.

It had all the earmarks of a dirty business with Peter Kane nominated for chief sucker. A dangerous job, running counter to the police department of a small town where strangers were bound to be scrutinized with suspicion.

"Most likely," Kane sighed, "they'll gather me up drunk some morning and plunk me in the can for vagrancy. *Tsk.* My God," Kane sighed, "what an outfit!" But the unlikable young man, Rupert Varley, had said something back there that was of importance. Varley had sworn to seeing a shrieking girl riding the coaster at Opal Lake.

"So I wasn't drunk," Kane nodded. "I *did* see it."

He put the car in motion and sent it growling away from the curb, but his destination was not the downtown section of Northvale where, according to Kingsley, the Granville House lay in wait for unsuspecting guests.

The Kane brain, aided by what had come out of the empty bottle which now lay on the seat, had spawned a hunch. Opal Lake Park was the car's destination.

THE PARK was as forlornly abandoned at three A.M. as it had been at midnight. Kane turned the car's lights out, braked the machine at the end of the private road, and got out.

The park's grotesque buildings loomed black and silent on both sides of him as he paced forward. Crusty snow crunched under his weight. He went slowly past a row of booths boarded up now for the winter, went past a nightmarish structure whose front was shaped like the face of a grinning gargoyle. The House of Fun stuck its domed roof into chill darkness on the left of the midway.

Suddenly Kane stopped.

The thing that stopped him was a thin wail that came from the depths of the Fun House. The sound was not much, but in the nerve-racking silence of a deserted amusement park, it resounded. It came again, even less distinct than before, while he stood rigid with his head jerked toward the building's angular doorway.

It sounded like a scream.

Kane screwed his mouth out of shape and strode forward. With his gaze glued on the doorway, he went past a ticket booth, ascended a slippery runway and put both hands on an iron bar that angled across a pair of sliding doors. The bar refused to budge. The platform was dirty white with hard snow that bore no marks of footprints.

Kane jerked away, slid down the ramp and prowled to the rear of the building. He found wooden steps, climbed them, and used his shoulder against a narrow door that went down under his assault. The echoes of the crash chattered back to him from the building's depths.

He had a feeling that Peter Kane was being a damned fool. A freak building like this would be full of traps and pitfalls. Any intruder who went prowling into those pitfalls without a light and without knowing a little something of the layout, was inviting disaster. But a girl had screamed for help....

Scowling, he pushed forward, was lost in gloom before he had gone a dozen steps. For a long straight drink of whiskey at that moment, he would have swapped a month's pay. Instead he stood suddenly motionless, listening to a low moaning sound that came from far ahead in darkness. An unpleasant sound, as of someone feebly attempting to cry out through a throat racked with torment. A woman all right!

Kane lurched forward, blundered into a railed enclosure where the floor dipped grotesquely. A curse ripped from his lips when he sprawled headlong. But that was only the beginning.

It was a house of fun. Kane had fun. The darkness flung mirrored walls at him, sucked him into a labyrinth of glass panels that toyed with his blundering body. The darkness concealed a thousand and one trick gadgets—wooden floor-discs that revolved when he stepped on them, balanced stairways that bucked under the weight of his lurching body, floor-waves of sheet metal that humped and sank with a noise like thunder when he ventured onto them.

Sweat ran in rivers from Kane's forehead. He stopped at last and stared around him, with no idea of what lay ahead or behind; no idea where the door was.

He stood where he was and clung to a polished metal bar that extended from floor to ceiling. Then he heard something behind him.

It was a low, whispering chuckle and sucked Kane around on stiff legs. The eyes in his head widened to enormous bigness; breath stuck in his throat and gagged him. The thing that swayed slowly toward him, through evil darkness, was a face. Not a human face, but a face.

It was a mask. It had to be a mask. Kane clung to the thought and kept his sanity because of it. If that thing were alive—if it should prove to be something more than a covering for a normal face beneath it—he had no hope.

It was green and horrible. Like a floating death's-head it stole forward, hanging suspended in darkness. The eyes in it were sunken, glittering holes of green; the nostrils were open cups of bone without flesh; the mouth was a vile gash, grinning hideously.

And Kane was not drunk. He was sober and knew it. His eyes were not playing tricks.

HE FOUGHT free of the numbing sensation that had crawled through him. Pawing his thighs he took two steps backward, but the thing followed him and the floating face did not stop grinning. The grin was a threat. The face was sure of itself, knew what it could do, knew what it *would* do!

Somewhere, in this vast hell of crazy darkness, was a girl who had already discovered what that face could do. Kane knew it.

His stumbling feet encountered a bulging section of floor and he leaped sideways, feared to retreat farther, feared even to move. If he blundered into some treacherous pit now, it would be the end. Standing where he was, he gathered his lean frame together, tensed himself for a forward lunge.

That face was a death's-head but something behind it was human. It could be battered back. It had to be!

The thing came on, and with it came a sound of bare feet whispering over the floor beneath it. Kane drew both arms back, sucked his stomach in tight. His own feet scuffed the boards, bracing themselves. He muttered aloud: "All right, damn you, come on! Keep coming! By God—" Then he hurtled forward.

He lashed out with a flailing fist first and then struck with the whole weight of his lunging body. The face and the shape beneath it had no time to get out of his way. The face stopped grinning; the green gash of mouth spat breath explosively. Kane threw fists into a contorted body that was human.

The body went back on stiff legs but came lurching erect again, like a weighted salt-cellar that can't tip over. The death's-head blurred against Kane's own, belching snarling sounds that curdled his blood. Savage arms whipped around him; a foot shot between his knees. Kane went down, dragging the thing with him.

Even then, even while rolling in vicious combat over the floor, he saw only the face. The rest of the thing he fought was garbed in jet black; it had to be, to be invisible in darkness. The face was a mask. His clawing fingers raked it, encountered hard stuff that was not flesh. A mask, masterfully created with luminous green paint and stuff that flaked off like soot. The thing behind it, the thing under it and around, was human.

Human or not, the fiend possessed abnormal strength. Hooked fingers sought Kane's throat, tore at his Adam's apple. Naked feet lashed at his groin and came within inches of disemboweling him.

But the thing was human. That was enough! Peter Kane, ace-shamus of the Beacon Agency, chronic drunk, two-fisted, hard-headed private dick with nothing to live for except the next drink, had encountered tough guys before.

This was just another tough guy, with a ghoulish mask that was supposed to terrify all other tough guys.

That was a laugh!

Kane slammed both fists with sledgehammer strength, kicked himself clear of the serpentine arms that sought to encircle him. The Kane method of dealing with potential death was not gentle. Lurching erect he swung one foot in a vicious arc, went off balance when the foot buried itself in soft flesh and brought a gurgling gasp of agony from livid lips. Like a cat, the keeper of the Fun House fumed erect and sprawled on top of him.

After that he was not sure what happened. A knotted hand, invisible in the dark because it was encased in a black glove, kept hammering at his face. The hand held a blunt, black instrument of torture. Sobbing, Kane got to his feet, staggered back, slammed a clenched fist into the midst of the face that growled toward him. The face spun sideways.

Kane blundered clear, reeled drunkenly through darkness. But he was not drunk. His brain was laden with torment and his face was wet, sticky with blood. When he rocked around, looked back, the death's-head was swaying grotesquely about two feet above where the floor should be. Apparently the keeper of the house was on hands and knees, groggy from the last frantic blow of Kane's fist.

But Kane was all done. Oblivion clawed at him; agony drove him forward. He had no thought for the girl whose cries of anguish had lured him into the building. He wanted air.

CHAPTER THREE
IT'S MURDER!

IT TOOK him a long time to find the door.

He was drunker then, from the pain that racked him, than he had ever been from whiskey. Staggering blindly, he navigated the impossible miles of cockeyed darkness to the exit. Cold air slapped him when he lurched over the threshold and stumbled down the steps.

"My God," he moaned, "I'm plastered." But he wasn't. He was out on his feet.

He went away from the House of Fun in a staggering contortion, his knees buckling beneath him. How he got through the maze of park buildings, and finally reached the car, he was never sure. He did reach the car, and managed somehow to get the door open. His outstretched hand clawed the wheel and let go again.

Lurching around, he stood staring.

The park was no longer a place of silence. With uncanny abruptness, an alien sound—a sound horribly familiar—had come into being and was jarring its way through the agony-haze that enveloped Kane's warped brain.

The roller coaster! Once more the sleeping mechanism of that huge thrill-device had awakened and was sending forth a guttural growling noise that presaged horror!

Kane's outstretched hand was white and hard on the car door, holding him erect. In his present battered condition he could no more hope to lurch down the snow-covered midway to the roller coaster than he could hope to be of any use if he got there.

And on the coaster platform, something was moving. Something dark, visible only because it was moving. Kane's eyes bulged, watched the shape step back, watched one of the streamlined bullet cars begin its journey of terror.

A girl's screams shrilled across the park.

The car groaned forward, dipped out of sight, reappeared again on the long upgrade. Sucking breath, Kane pushed himself clear and stumbled forward.

He did not get far. Agony went with him for a dozen lurching steps and then dragged him to a halt, sent him groaning to the ground. On hands and knees he swayed drunkenly, gazed with bloodshot eyes at what was happening.

The car had reached the top, was silhouetted against the lesser darkness of an empty sky. Its lone passenger, a girl, was screaming in the front seat.

Slowly the car gained momentum, roared with a crescendo thunder down the ninety-foot drop. Whirling wheels shrieked on the ice-coated rails as the car scooped at the bottom and streaked up again. Like a mad, living thing, lurching and swaying with the force of its unchecked momentum, it soared to the top of the second rise and swept around the turn.

Once before, Kane had watched the same car, or one of its mates, scream around that perilous curve, while the Kane intestines had clogged with horror and the car's imprisoned occupant had flung out shriek after shriek of fear. This time the horror was real.

Like a monstrous red bullet the streamlined car shot clear of the rails, hurtled into space. Kane, lurching erect with an effort more than human, stumbled blindly forward, bellowing idiotic words of warning.

The car shot out and down, turning grotesquely in mid-air. With fantastic abruptness, the whine of steel wheels

on icy rails had ceased; the girl's cries of terror knifed clear
and shrill now above Kane's booming voice.

Heaving and twisting like a thing in torment, the car
crashed through the structure's interlaced timbers, smash-
ing and grinding its way earthward. Weight and momentum carried it through, gave it the power to destroy everything in the path of its headlong plunge.

Peter Kane took half a dozen staggering strides and
stopped, stood retching. The world around him was a world
of screaming madness, of horror come to life in a prolonged,
grinding roar of annihilation. But Kane could do nothing
about it.

Blood bubbled from his gaping mouth as he rocked
grotesquely on spread legs. A groan welled up from his
throat. Headlong he pitched forward, sprawled face down
in the midway, his feet beating a feeble tattoo and his
bloody lips crimsoning the snow.

REGAINING CONSCIOUSNESS, hours later,
was like crawling out of a thick dark fog that had eaten
its way into brain and body. He stared around him, realized
dully that he lay on a couch in a room that had four walls,
rain-wet windows, a carpeted floor. Above him hovered a
face that was vaguely familiar, a face he had seen before
in the home of Daniel Kingsley. It belonged to Upham—
Dr. Clement Upham. And this room was apparently a
doctor's office—

"The police brought you," Upham declared quietly. "They
followed you from Kingsley's home last night, lost you,
and then discovered you lying half dead in the midway at
Opal Lake Park. What happened to you, man?"

Kane stared at the drooling windows, at a clock that
said ten thirty. Ten thirty A.M.

"Something else," Upham muttered, "happened at the park last night A girl was murdered."

"I know. I—saw it."

"Murdered." Upham's face was abnormally pale, had deep circles under both eyes. "Horribly murdered. As yet the police haven't been able to identify her. The body was found in the wreckage of a coaster car, so horribly mangled and torn that identification may not be possible. The police want to talk to you, Kane. You are to remain here until they come."

"Yeah?" Kane pushed himself up and leaned against the wall, pawing his bandaged head. His head felt enormous and his aching body was loaded with sickness, but he could still think.

He thought of Lieutenant Cleves of the local police department. Thought of a girl's torn and mangled body which had been found in the battered wreckage of a roller-coaster car. It was murder now. Before, it had been merely an annoying business of a "ghost girl" riding a roller coaster in the dead of night in a deserted amusement park. Now it was murder.

Now, more than ever, the police of Northvale would be desperately anxious to clamp their claws on someone.

"Where's my car?" Kane demanded.

"Your car? Outside. But I warn you, sir, I can't permit you to leave here."

"Listen." Kane pushed himself clear of the wall and stood with his head shoved forward belligerently. He felt sick, but the Kane constitution had long ago learned how to fight its way out of hangovers. "Listen, I was brought into this goofy business by Daniel Kingsley. If your cock-eyed local cops want me, they'll find me at Kingsley's house."

Dr. Clement Upham reached nervously toward a spindle-legged table that stood against the wall. Upon it lay a police revolver which the police had evidently left with him, just in case.

The good doctor's intent was obvious.

Kane's foot slid between Upham's knees. Kane's left hand, open, made sudden, hard contact with the good doctor's face. Upham executed a clumsy half-turn, rocked off balance and crashed into the wall. Kane strode out of the office.

On the way out he collided with Mr. Leroy Bird, the artist, who was about to enter. Mr. Bird looked ill and vaguely worried. He registered astonishment when Kane barged past him without so much as a word of greeting.

Kane went down two flights of stairs, hiked out of the building and found himself on Northvale's main stem in the heart of the downtown section. Rain was drizzling from a dreary sky; the sidewalk was dirty and wet. Across the street loomed an ungainly pile with a drooling sign that read, GRANVILLE HOUSE.

"The joint I was supposed to dwell in," Kane observed. "Well, well."

His own car was parked at the curb. He climbed into it, voiced a grunt of satisfaction that the Northvale police department had been dumb enough to leave the ignition key in the lock. Brooding over the events of the last night, he debated the wisdom of chucking the whole dirty mess and returning to the Beacon Agency.

That would be an easy way out. It might also be an unpleasant way of being dragged back in again. The Northvale cops would attach grave significance to a walkout at this stage of the game.

Grimly, Kane drove to the home of Daniel Kingsley.

KINGSLEY HIMSELF opened the door.

"Kane!" he gasped. "Then you're not under arrest! The police haven't—"

"Listen," Kane said. "There are two things I want, and the Northvale cop department isn't one of them. Give me the lowdown on what happened last night at the park, and—" He studied Kingsley soberly, shook his head. "Skip the other. I doubt if you ever tasted the kind of stuff I crave, anyhow."

Kingsley's good-looking daughter stood staring in the hall as Kane and the high-school principal went into the parlor. Kingsley closed the door, began talking even before Kane had found a chair. Evidently the man wanted to talk.

"The police, Kane, have not been able to identify the girl who was murdered last night. But I have!"

"But you have?" Kane scowled.

"Yes. My suspicions were correct. The murdered girl is the young woman who taught at the high school. She was naked, mind you, when they found her, and because of the frightful mangling of her body, identification was impossible. But I have been to the office of the medical examiner and viewed the corpse.

"There is an odd-shaped ring on the girl's hand, a ring which the murderer was perhaps unable to remove. I have seen that same ring every day for months, on the hand of Miss Dawes, the teacher I refer to!"

Kane hunched forward. "This Miss Dawes was one of the reformists who caused the cops to crack down on Opal Lake Park?"

"Yes."

"Who are the others?"

Kingsley chewed his lower lip and looked worried. "Well, it was really Miss Dawes and another young woman, Miss Eleanor Covell, who did the bulk of the investigating. There were others, of course. Mr. Bird, the artist, whom you met here last night, is one of the group. So is Mr. Bernard Varley, one of our wealthier townspeople. It was his son, Rupert, who brought the police here last night. Varley himself has no love for Opal Lake Park. He happens to own a rival park out Harrisville way."

Kane stood up. "Why the hell didn't you say that before? Listen. Write out those names and put some addresses with them. If your screwy police department doesn't tag me too soon, I'll maybe find out things."

He did. It was eleven A.M. when he hiked out of Kingsley's house and piled into his car. It was four P.M., in the expensive home of Mr. Bernard Varley, far out in the residential section of town, when the police caught up with him. And then, strangely enough, they were not looking for Peter Kane.

They were seeking Bernard Varley himself, and with them came the good Dr. Upham whom Kane had unceremoniously pushed in the face hours ago. They were much surprised to find Kane sitting in the spacious, elaborately furnished parlor of the Varley home.

They wanted to ask Mr. Varley a few personal questions. Would Mr. Varley condescend to answer those questions without making a fuss?

MR. VARLEY would, but was obviously annoyed at the intrusion of such plebeian persons as Lieutenant Cleves, Dr. Upham, and the rest. Mr. Varley himself was a bristling, bearded gentleman, Napoleonic in spirit and size.

"I was just telling Mr. Varley," Kane murmured pleasantly, "that he's in grave danger. Because of this affair at the park, you know. Or do you know? Maybe you haven't identified the body yet."

"We have," Lieutenant Cleves growled.

"Really? My! The police are efficient. Maybe you also know that another of the reformists, Miss Eleanor Covell by name, is also missing." Kane was enjoying himself. The pallor had long ago gone out of his bandaged face and the face was aglow now with a ruddiness produced by alcoholic stimulation. Northvale was not a bad town at all after you learned the location of its liquor marts.

"Miss Covell," Kane said, "supposedly left town over a week ago, to visit friends in Albany. Or maybe it was Pittsburgh. Anyhow, she left town. I spent a lot of time talking to her folks this afternoon. I also spent some time talking to Leroy Bird, the fellow who looks like Garbo and paints pictures and things. He's scared stiff. He was on this reformist committee, too."

"And so you came here to warn Varley that he, too, is in danger, did you?"

"That's part of why I'm here," Kane admitted.

Lieutenant Cleves hunched forward and planted himself before the chair that supported Varley's Napoleonic body. "You needn't have bothered," Cleves snarled. "I don't think Varley's in any danger of being murdered. Not when he, himself, is the man who owns Opal Lake Park!"

The expression that crossed Varley's face was a queer one. His eyes widened and he looked bewildered. "What?" he said.

"You heard what I said, Varley."

"Are you insane? Who told you that I'm the owner?"

"The man who sold the park to you. Upham!"

Upham stepped forward, nodding. "I'm sorry, Varley," he mumbled. "I know I promised to keep the sale a secret. But, Lord, man, a murder's been committed."

Varley got out of his chair and stood wide-legged. "You're a confounded liar, Upham. I've never had any dealings with you, and you know it!"

"That isn't so. You've got the papers that will prove it." Upham turned feebly to Lieutenant Cleves and his eyes blinked rapidly in their wrinkles of loose flesh as he ran a trembling hand over his smooth, pinkish billiard-ball of a head. "It's he who's doing the lying, Cleves. I swear it. There are papers—"

Cleves had his own blunt, blundering methods of proving things. He jerked around, barked orders to the men behind him. "Search the place!" he growled.

The policemen searched. Bernard Varley reseated himself and sat like a smoldering volcano. Dr. Upham stood off at a safe distance and mopped a perspiring forehead. Kane looked on.

Kane was thinking that the party was incomplete. Young Mr. Rupert Varley, the playboy son of the enraged Napoleon whose home was now being ransacked, was not present and should be. Perhaps the youth had a reason for remaining away.

Meanwhile, if Upham had sold the park to Mr. Bernard Varley, Bernard would have a great many questions to answer.

Kane patiently awaited development.

They were not long in coming. One of the uniformed policemen returned presently from a foray in Mr. Varley's library and thrust a wad of papers into the hand of Lieutenant Cleves. "I guess these are them," the policeman said. "It says Opal Lake Park on them, and it says the park is hereby sold to Mr. Bernard Varley."

Varley rocketed from his chair. "Let me see those!"

Lieutenant Cleves said: "You'll see them at headquarters. You're going there right now."

Kane said, pushing himself lazily erect: "If all you nice gentlemen will excuse me, I tank I go home."

HE WENT downtown to the Granville House. Obtaining a room on the second floor, he dumped the contents of a battered suitcase onto the bed, poured water into a bowl, washed up and changed to clean clothes.

"About the best thing a guy can do in this goofy town," he observed, "is get drunk."

He had obtained a pint bottle hours ago in a Northvale liquor establishment. He guzzled half of its amber contents, left the bottle on the bureau and went out to a barroom. When he returned to the hotel at eight P.M. he was inebriated. "You should be ashamed of yourself, Mr. Kane," he *tsked*.

Yes, he was plastered, but the Kane brain had functioned in full force during the past two hours. From the suitcase on the bed he took a neat, palm-fitting S.&W. automatic, and from the bureau he took the half-full pint bottle. The phone rang while he was stuffing the bottle into a coat pocket.

"Mr. Kane," the desk clerk said, "a young lady has tried several times to get in touch with you while you've been out. Miss Kingsley, she said her name was."

Downstairs in the lobby Kane looked up the number in a book and called it. Anita Kingsley answered.

"Mr. Kane!" she sobbed. "Oh, I've tried so hard to get in touch with you!"

"For what?"

"It's my father, Mr. Kane. He's in one of his strange moods again. An hour ago he got up from the supper table and said he was going to Opal Lake. And he's gone!"

"I'll look into it," Kane said.

FROM THE looks of the layout when he braked the Kane chariot at the end of the park's private road, half an hour later, the girl's suspicions anent her father were founded on nothing much. The midway looked as deserted as ever. There were no lights. There was no sign of any prowling intruder who might be Daniel Kingsley.

Mechanically Kane pulled the pint bottle from his pocket, uncorked it and helped himself to a sizable amount of its contents. Then he got out of the car and hiked forward.

He was in no hurry. His plan of action called for a complete, comprehensive search of the park's buildings. It would take time and he would be a very drunk shamus before he got through, especially if the job got on his nerves.

If it got on his nerves? It was already doing that. Something was happening to his insides, to his eyes, to the aching, pulsing thing which a few moments ago had been his head.

That old sickness, coming back....

Kane stood still, put a faltering hand to his eyes. The darkness around him had begun to heave and roll alarmingly. Black hulks of buildings blurred into fantastic shapes and merged into undulating gloom. Every separate thing was in motion.

The snow-crusted macadam underfoot rose and fell as if tossed by a subterranean tidal wave. Wide-legged, Kane stood like a seasick inebriate on the deck of a wallowing ship.

Savagely he jerked from his pocket the whiskey bottle that had lain unguarded on the bureau of his room in the Granville House. It took him a full minute to get the cork loose. A long, deep suck of breath carried the odor of the bottle's contents to his internals.

A whiskey odor, yes, but blended with something else, something vaguely pungent and bitter.

"Doped," Kane mumbled. "Doped—and me so soused I never noticed." Again he sniffed at the bottle, screwed his face into a scowl of self-denunciation. "Chloral hydrate." The words drooled in a sick, drunken gurgle. "And morphine. Imagine me drinking that stuff—"

He stood retching, then, and staring into the weird world around him. Presently his attention centered on a distorted, two-legged shape that seemed to be advancing toward him—a menacing, mask-faced form in a shadow-world that was too fantastic to be real.

Kane stiffened, sucked breath to his laboring lungs and cursed the drugs that had made a half-blind scarecrow of him. The whiskey bottle still lay in his hand and he raised it, flung it feebly at the center of that leering mask. The bottle missed its mark.

Kane's right hand groped for the gun in his pocket, but the hand was no part of him; was, instead, a nerveless appendage that refused to do what he willed. Retching, he lurched forward, heaved himself blindly at the shadowed shape before him.

A clenched fist leaped from the midst of the shape and crashed with sledgehammer force into the pit of his stomach. Breath whined from Kane's drooling mouth. He was unconscious before his contorted frame hit the snow.

CHAPTER FOUR
HOUSE OF HORRORS

SOMEWHERE IN a world of crawling, undulating gloom a yellow light was struggling for existence. It lived, died, lived again in fitful spurts. Finally it took form and became constant. Kane stared at it, held his eyes half open with a superhuman effort and forced his drugged brain to concentrate on that one vague blur.

The awakening from mental oblivion had been an aimless, agonized groping through abysmal blackness. Now, after an eternity, that yellow light was something to cling to.

It became, after his blood-rimmed eyes had stared long enough, a pot-bellied lantern that leered out at him. It stood on an upturned box, and the box stood on a dirty stone floor that sloped away into crowding walls of darkness.

Kane peered around him. From the looks of things he had been dragged into some remote part of the House of Fun and left there. Perhaps the man behind the mask had believed Peter Kane to be permanently scratched from the list of contestants. The Kane torso lay in a twisted posture against the sloping side of what was apparently an enormous barrel—one of those huge revolving barrels which, when mounted endwise on rollers, provided amusement no end for kids who climbed into them and made them go round at terrific speed.

A low, moaning sound lured Kane's attention to the darkness beyond the potbellied lantern. He stared, bewildered. At first he did not see the thing that loomed there, did not separate that significant shape from the gloom around it. A thick, circular pillar rose from floor to ceiling.

At its base bulked a weird, shadowy mass of silent machinery.

Yes, this was the cellar of the Fun House. This was the mechanical heart from which all those screwy devices in the building above obtained life. But the place was dead now. Dead and deserted.

No, not deserted. Again that half-audible moaning sound sobbed through gloom and worked on Kane's brain. Again he stared. Then he saw, and stiffened.

Part of that looming pile was human. Part of it was an ill-defined shape which could move, which *was* moving in a futile attempt to free itself from encircling ropes that bound it. A girl, roped there against an iron shaft! A girl, moaning incoherently, sobbing her heart out, staring at Kane!

Kane dragged his legs under him and made an effort to get to his knees. The effort sent a wave of sickness undulating through his big body and he slumped back again, his shoulders jammed against the curved side of the big barrel. Then he heard footsteps.

His eyes remained wide, staring into gloom beyond the mound of dead machinery. Then the thing took form. A face—*the* face—materialized in darkness. A leering green gash of mouth became hideously visible; green-rimmed eyes glared as they advanced.

This was no House of Fun. It was a House of Hell. And this gargoyle-faced horror was its master!

Kane watched, wide-eyed, as the robed figure paced into the ochre glow of the lantern. There the creature stopped, turned to peer at the girl, turned again to gaze at Kane's sprawled body. The leer of those uncouth lips became more menacing.

But Kane's spasm of horror had passed. The muscles of his lean frame tightened. He licked his lips, slowly inflated his chest with indrawn breath. And then abruptly he realized that he would have to fight not one killer but two!

THE SECOND robed shape had come silently out of darkness behind the first. This one wore no fantastic mask of horror. A black cowl concealed the man's features, merged darkly into the robe that enveloped his bulging torso. Glittering eyes studied Kane through slits in the cowl. A mocking voice issued from hidden lips.

"So the great Peter Kane has discovered our meeting place."

The man's voice was low, deliberate. "Undoubtedly, Kane, you *think* you know my identity. One thing you *will* know, soon, is that I have every reason in the world for despising the meddling busy-bodies who saddled this place with a bad reputation. I want revenge for that, and I'm having it."

The glittering eyes studied Kane's twitching face. "Already, Kane, Opal Lake Park has received wide publicity through the antics of its ghost girl of the roller coaster. This other female, Eleanor Covell"—a black-clad arm stabbed out, pointing—"is another of the meddlers who sought to ruin me. Tonight, she dies, too."

A snarl leaped to Kane's lips and expired there. He knew vaguely that silence was his best weapon. This man wanted to talk, to gloat.

"A few weeks from now," the hidden lips said softly, "when the police are frantically looking for you and Miss Covell, and your names are blurbed over the front pages of every newspaper in the east, the police will receive a mysterious tip to come here to Opal Lake Park and investigate the House of Horrors—the wax museum.

"They will discover that two of the painted wax figures strangely resemble you and Miss Covell. When they look closer they will learn the secret of your strange disappearance. And that discovery, Kane, will make a sizable fortune for me when the park is reopened this summer. People will come from far and wide to visit the place where such sensational things happened. Do you see?"

Kane saw, shuddered. Mutely he gazed past the cowled shape and stared into the fantastic, cleverly painted death's-head mask beyond it. The man in the mask was slowly advancing upon the girl who was to accompany Peter Kane to hell.

But the man did not get that far. A wave of revulsion seemed to jar him. He turned, shuddering, and pawed the arm of his companion. "I—I can't do it!" he wailed. "I can't!"

The other's reply was amazingly soft, soothing. "You're ill? Is that it?"

"Yes. I—I need—"

"I know what you need." One lean hand slid into a pocket of the black robe, reappeared holding a smallish tube of crystalline stuff that gleamed white in the lantern-light. With unholy eagerness the whimpering killer snatched it.

"You won't need the medicine much longer," the other declared softly. "Not much longer. Soon you will be cured. Now, are you ready?"

The change that came over the man in the mask curdled Kane's blood, even though Kane had seen dope addicts before. Eagerly the gargoyle-faced one swung toward the girl.

KANE, ON the floor, inched the far-flung parts of his sprawled body together and tensed himself. The Kane brain, laboring, had borne fruit. Within it, a fantastic scheme of action was festering.

He addressed himself to the man in the cowl. "Listen," he said glumly. "You've got no reason for hating me. If I've got to go through hell, how about giving me some of the stuff you just gave Bird?"

The effect of his words was fantastic. The man whirled, glared at him through the slits of his hood. The man in the mask stopped as if impaled. He, too, turned and gaped.

Kane essayed a sheepish grin. "Sure," he mumbled. "Am I any worse than Bird here? You got him all doped up with coke. Maybe he thinks it's medicine, but I guess he'll find out the truth some day."

The man in the painted mask took a jerky step forward, not toward Kane but toward his cowled companion. For silent seconds he stood rigid. Then his hands clawed up, raked the gargoyle head-covering loose and flung it aside. The face beneath the mask was a thin, sallow face with drug-dilated eyes. The face of Leroy Bird, the artist. And it was convulsed with dope-augmented rage.

"Is he right?" Bird snarled. "Is it dope you've been giving me? Is it a drug you've been feeding me all these weeks when you swore you were curing me? Is it?"

"From the looks of things," Kane drawled, "you've been eating dope, mister, for breakfast, dinner, and supper."

That was enough. Bird's face turned scarlet, his swollen eyes filled with a hate so intense that the other lurched backward in gurgling terror.

Kane said dryly: "You asked for it, *Upham*."

The man in the cowl would have had no chance if Leroy Bird had chosen to use his gun as a firearm. Instead, Bird snarled forward, swung the weapon as a bludgeon. A clenched fist caught him with pile-driver force in the precise center of his drooling mouth. He reeled sideways, gasping. The gun spilled from his paralyzed fingers.

Peter Kane went for the gun in a frenzied, headlong leap.

He got it, raked it into his fist. At the same instant, the cowled master of the death house crashed down on him.

The weight of that big body slammed the breath out of Kane's lungs. It all but broke the bones of his chest. But he had been storing up strength for more than half an hour now, in preparation for one desperate stab at freedom. Breath sobbed to his lungs and he heaved himself clear, lashed out with both feet and sent the cowled shape away from him, sent it crashing against the sloping side of the big barrel.

One clawing hand pawed at a pocket in the black robe. The hand came clear again, jerked up a gun—the same gun that had lain on the spindle-legged table in Dr. Clement Upham's office.

Kane's automatic and the police revolver belched in unison. Upham, on braced legs, fired from a standing position with his gun hand outthrust. Kane was on the floor, his weapon wedged under the hook of one arm.

Liquid fire streaked through Kane's thigh and the impact of the bullet twisted him. Clement Upham went back with a grinding thud against the barrel, blood bubbling from the bulge of his stomach, his arms outflung, his mouth full of a gasping, choking cry of agony.

He dropped his gun, took two stumbling steps and spiraled to the floor. Kane, on hands and knees, crawled crookedly toward him and snarled down at him. Then Kane turned, stared at the slumped body of Leroy Bird.

Bird was out, unconscious. Upham's fist and the skull-cracking impact of the stone floor had put him to sleep.

Kane swayed erect, groped past the sputtering lantern and released the girl who had been slated to go to hell with him. He had to keep shaking his head violently to retain consciousness. Feebly he pawed the girl's arm, mumbled words into her colorless face.

"Listen," he told her, "listen. Get out of here and get to a phone and call the cops. Tell 'em to make it—snappy—and—"

He swayed backward, propped himself against a pile of dead machinery and stood like a dynamited tower ready to crash. "And tell 'em," he croaked, "to bring some fire-water. A lot of it. A whole lot—for—Peter Kane."

KANE SAID, days later, to the competent blonde in the front office of the Beacon Agency: "It was this way. A guy by the name of Clement Upham had a standing grudge against a small flock of Northvale reformists because they put the skids to his lousy brother and indirectly sent the brother to an alcoholic grave.

"Me, I can't see what's so terrible about an alcoholic grave, but this Upham guy figured to get revenge. He figured to murder some of the reformists and hook the blame on another one, a swell guy named Varley, through a planted bill of sale which would make Varley look crooked. Underneath all this, he planned to combine his revenge with a whole lot of swell publicity for his amusement park."

Kane raised a pint bottle from the desk and gurgled contentedly. "The queer part of it was, this Upham didn't have to do the dirty work himself. Not at all. He had a patient by the name of Leroy Bird, an artist who had been going to Upham for a long, long time, getting himself treated for what he thought was a serious disease. And Upham hooked him for a sucker.

"Bird was scared stiff and easy meat for Upham's schemes. Upham fed him dope, made a slave of him, and Bird had to obey orders or else go crazy from wanting his 'medicine.' As a matter of fact, the disease he was supposed to be suffering from was so serious that they could have put him away for it—so he would have done what the doctor ordered anyhow, to keep Upham's mouth shut.

"Anyhow," Kane sighed, "the guy was doped to the gills and did what he was told. And now he'll burn."

The competent blonde studied Kane pensively. "And the great Peter Kane saw through all this?"

"The great Peter Kane," Kane gurgled, "had several run-ins with this Leroy Bird guy while Bird was wearing a death's-head mask. Also the great Kane was sap enough to guzzle some whiskey that'd been spiked with opium and chloral hydrate during his absence from a hotel room.

"After a long while, sweetness, Kane figured out that only a very clever artist guy could create a mask like that, and only a doctor in good standing would have access to opium and so forth in a hick joint like Northvale. The hell of it was, by the time Kane got around to figuring those things out, he was in a position where figuring wouldn't do him no good. And the Beacon Agency almost lost its best dick."

"What you mean," the blonde said, gently removing the pint bottle from Kane's semi-paralyzed fingers, "is that Limpy, the local liquor dispenser, almost lost his best customer."

THE BRAND OF KANE

THE *CONCORD* BECAME A HORROR SHIP THAT NIGHT IT RAN AGROUND—FOR SCORES DIED IN THE CRASH OR WERE DROWNED AFTERWARDS. BUT IT WAS MURDER THAT BROUGHT PETER KANE TO THE BATTERED HULK. SOME CRAZY KILLER HAD PICKED IT AS A CONVENIENT DUMPING SPOT FOR HIS VICTIMS AND, MUCH AS HE HATED MIXING SEA-WATER WITH HIS SCOTCH, IT WAS UP TO KANE TO STOP THE CORPSE PARADE.

CHAPTER ONE
WATER-LOGGED CORPSE

MR. MICHAEL ALOYSIOUS KELLY, night watchman on board the steamship *Concord*, took a corncob pipe out of his face and stretched himself. Being alone on board the half-submerged hulk of a wrecked steamship did not annoy him so much as did the endless yammering of rain around and about him. Rain-mutter had been disturbing the Kelly eardrums for hours.

He peered around the ship's dining room, spat smoke from his wrinkled lips and slouched erect. It was not easy to walk without staggering. For one thing, though the *Concord* had been aground since yesterday noon, the distance between ship and shore was alarmingly great, and the moiled waters in which the *Concord* now rolled were apparently suffering a severe hangover from the storm which had aroused them.

The *Concord*, after crashing head-on into the side of a Tampico-bound freighter, had shivered herself loose, wallowed helplessly through more than a mile of mountainous seas, and finally bogged down in shallow water offshore. And though the ship still lay in a reasonably upright position, the carpet beneath Mr. Kelly's feet was damp, and the floor pitched and swayed disturbingly as he made his way into the ship's salon. From adjoining staterooms came sounds of sea-water sloshing sluggishly against walls and bunks.

Mr. Kelly swayed to a slow stop, stood listening, and puffed his red face into a scowl. He was hearing things. The sound that disturbed him was a dull thumping noise that accompanied the gurgling of sea-water in a nearby stateroom.

He opened the stateroom door and thumbed a light-switch. When the switch failed to function, he unhooked an enormous searchlight from his belt and used that. The glare of the searchlight showed him an inundated oblong of floor, a stool, a washbasin, and a double bunk.

Mr. Kelly stared at the floor. He took a step backward and opened his eyes to white-rimmed bigness. Breath rattled in his throat. The hand that gripped the flashlight began to tremble.

The thing on the floor was not pretty to look at. Its feet were somehow wedged

Kane pawed empty air and let out a yell.

beneath the bunk, and from the looks of things the rest of it had been wedged there also, until dislodged by the ship's continued lurching.

It had been dead a long while. Its face was white and bloated, its mouth hung open, and its wide eyes peered glassily into Mr. Kelly's own. With every sluggish roll of the ship, the body lurched as though alive, its pajama-clad torso wallowing in dirty water, its head thumping the base of the washstand in rhythm.

Mr. Kelly backed away from it and quickly pushed the door shut. His heart was pounding furiously. His legs were limp with terror as he hastened back to the dining room.

On a sideboard in the dining room, the police had installed a telephone. Michael Aloysious Kelly seized the instrument in trembling fingers and called police headquarters.

PETER KANE, ace shamus of the Beacon Agency, sat in a backroom booth at Limpy's on Stuart Street and stared moodily at a dark, square bottle of Scotch on the table before him. The bottle was half empty. An hour ago it had been full.

Life, Kane reflected, was very good. With a bottle of Scotch on hand and nothing to disturb a man's drinking time, life could be very pleasant indeed.

Limpy, proprietor of the establishment, waddled into the back room and tapped Kane's shoulder. "Listen, Kane," Limpy said, "Joe Henderson is out front lookin' for you. Will I tell him where you are?"

Joe Henderson was a fellow slave on the Beacon payroll. His presence was ominous. Kane sighed, tamped out a half-smoked cigarette, and realized that life was no longer pleasant.

Henderson peered searchingly into the Kane countenance. He sat down, pushed the square bottle out of the way. "You're assigned to the *Concord* job, Kane," he grinned.

"The police," Kane said, "are already—"

"This is private. The steamship company just called up the office and hired Peter Kane. It seems a dead guy was found on board the wreck last night, after they thought all the bodies had been removed. It also seems the dead guy is a company official. So you're hired to look into things. It must be they think you're good."

Henderson helped himself to a drink. "Me, personally, I think you're a hollow-legged souse, with a taste for a lousy brand of likker," he grinned. "Have a good time, pal. They tell me Moroni is doing the snooping for the police. I feel for you, Kane, I feel for you!"

Life, for Kane, had suddenly become very lousy. He groaned. It was not enough that the peaceful routine of his drunken existence was about to be disturbed. On top of that, the job was one that would necessitate close contact with a lot of bilious-looking green ocean.

"Sure as hell," Kane mumbled, "I'll get seasick. I feel sick already."

He was more than sick when he climbed out of his own coupé a couple of hours later and hiked across a broken-down wharf that fronted on a bulging, heaving expanse of that same despised ocean. The *Concord* had gone aground off Sanders Cove, and Sanders Cove had apparently been used from time immemorial as a dumping ground for clam shells, deceased fish, and sea-spawned refuse that stunk to high heaven.

The odors assailed Kane's innards as he paraded forward. His face had taken on a hue that matched the pale, muddy green of his battered hat. The mingled stenches of things dead and decaying did not harmonize with the quantities of liquor already reposing in the Kane stomach.

"I'm gonna hate this job," Kane groaned.

He went toward an end of the wharf where a large individual in hip boots and dirty clothes was messing about on board a fishing boat. The fellow looked up and blinked watery eyes.

"Take you out around the wreck for a dollar, mister," the fellow said.

Kane stepped aboard. "Take me to it, not around it," Kane groaned. "And for God's sake avoid the bumps. Water—especially a whole lot of it like this—always does things to me."

He had a ghastly upside-down feeling in the pit of his stomach when the fishing boat finally chugged alongside the *Concord*.

Resolutely he climbed the ladder that hung over the steamer's side. The broad grin on the fisherman's leathery face did not bother him. He was beyond being bothered by trivialities.

Kane said, "Stick around, guy," and steered a crooked course along the *Concord's* deck. Opening a door, he marched through a narrow passageway and went down a flight of stairs into the salon.

MORONI AND another dick from headquarters were talking near the newsstand and turned to eye Kane as he approached. A scowl hooked Moroni's large face and the scowl became a broad grin. "Well, look what's here," he beamed. "The great Peter Kane himself, in person. You don't look so good this morning, Kane. You sick?"

Kane stared at the bulge of Moroni's big stomach. He thought dully that if Mr. Moroni's large belly were as full of sickness as Peter Kane's little one was, Mr. Moroni would be a very sick man indeed—and that would be swell.

Lowering himself onto a divan, he pulled a pint bottle of whiskey from his pocket and had a long drink. On a job like this, with Large Mouth Moroni and a lot of heaving green ocean all over the place, the only thing to do was get thoroughly plastered and remain that way.

Moroni said: "Sorry, Kane, but you got to clear out. We're under orders from the steamship company to bar anyone who don't have official business or a permit."

"The trouble is," Kane groaned, "the steamship company hired me, so I got to stay." Wearily he helped himself to a long look around the salon.

The place had several occupants. On the other side of the room sat a dumpy, red-faced man who had a corncob pipe stuck in his face and was slouched down in a big leather chair, intently watching everyone else, but saying nothing.

Most likely the fellow was Mr. Michael Aloysious Kelly, who according to the papers, had discovered the body last night.

Mr. Kelly seemed particularly interested in a woman who, at the moment of Kane's arrival, had been opening and closing stateroom doors but who was now standing very still and straight at the foot of the staircase. She was a small woman with dirty-gray hair and a woodenish body that had no curves. Her face was gray and one side of it kept twitching. She had small dark eyes that drilled holes in Kane's soul and made him feel itchy all over.

From the looks of things the woman was either going to throw a fit or fall into a nervous collapse.

Upstairs a couple of men who looked like insurance dicks were nosing around and yelling back and forth to each other.

"Whereabouts," Kane demanded, "is the body?"

The body was on a bunk in the stateroom where Michael Kelly had reputedly discovered it. Kane prowled forward, pushed open the stateroom door. With Moroni trailing him, he entered and took a long look around, bent over the body and stared down into a white, unlovely face that was very dead.

"The dame out there," Moroni said, "is this guy's wife. Says she's positive he was a passenger on the boat and was traveling under an assumed name because he had some other dame in tow. The way she prowls around here, snooping into this and that, would give anybody the living creeps."

Kane said: "Who is this guy?"

"The name is Mr. Clarence Waite—with an 'e'. He's a big shot with the steamship company."

KANE BRACED himself against the hulk and made a careful inspection, had to forcibly hold down the contents of the Kane stomach while he turned the body over and examined it. It was bad enough to be drunk and seasick both, without having to mess around with a pajama-clad body which was bloated with sea-water and had already begun to decompose.

"You won't find anything," Moroni shrugged. "The guy was drowned. Chances are he tried to get out of bed when the crash came and got himself jammed under the bunk. That's why the body wasn't discovered until later when the roll of the ship dislodged it."

Kane felt the need of another long drink from the bottle in his pocket. He had one. "This guy's name on the passenger list?" he demanded.

"I guess you don't read the papers," Moroni said. "They didn't have no passenger list. The purser's office downstairs was wiped out in the crash, and, thanks to a lot of official dumbness, there wasn't a duplicate list on shore."

Kane made a rumbling noise in his throat. On his way out of the stateroom he again peered at the woman who stood near the staircase. If she was the wife of Mr. Clarence Waite, she probably knew things that might be of importance.

He started toward her, changed his mind and stopped. Someone else, coming down the stairs, was apparently bent on engaging the woman in conversation.

Kane put a cigarette in his mouth, walked unobtrusively to a divan and sat down. A scowl twisted the corner of his mouth that was not filled with cigarette. He wondered what Dr. Nicolas Ackerman was doing on board the *Concord*. Ackerman, tagged with a shady reputation which extended far back into the past, was supposedly the head of a private hospital in Plymouth. The man towered above Mrs. Clarence Waite, had a hand on the woman's elbow as he talked to her in low tones that failed to reach Kane's ears.

He had a string-bean body and stooped shoulders, an angular dark-skinned face that would have harmonized nicely—and probably did—with operating rooms and the midnight moans of patients. When he was through talking he gently patted the woman's arm, shook his head to toss a mop of black hair away from his high forehead, and walked away. Kane watched him.

The man nodded to Moroni, peered darkly in Kane's direction and strode along the passageway that led to the dining room.

Kane stood up, blew cigarette smoke through quivering nostrils. He had met Dr. Nicolas Ackerman before; had, in fact, been assigned to investigate certain shady dealings in which Ackerman had been involved. The presence of Ackerman aboard the *Concord* was something to think about.

Moroni had evidently thought about it. "That guy," Moroni said, "gives me the creeps, Kane. How he got a permit to snoop around here, I wouldn't know. He says one of the crash victims was a staff member at his hospital, but if that's any excuse for him to go prowling around like a walking corpse—"

Kane had the neck of a pint bottle in his throat and was gurgling noisily. He gagged, spat a spray of whiskey at the floor, muttered darkly: "With guys like him hanging around, and a water-logged corpse to mess over, and a floor that won't keep still under a man's feet, this is one lousy job."

He paced forward, pawed the wall in an effort to keep the Kane torso on an even keel. Then, because someone called him by name, he dragged his unsteady feet to a stop and turned.

THE YOUNG man who came toward him had, for the past half hour, been sitting at the desk in the salon, methodically filling pages of paper with what was probably an official report. He was slender, good-looking, and had a lick of black hair curling gracefully over one temple.

He said: "You're Detective Kane, aren't you?"

"I was," Kane growled, "before I came aboard this damn barge."

The young man did not smile. His gray eyes scrutinized Kane from head to foot. "I'm Frank Deasy," he said. "The company sent me down to make an estimate of the financial loss. If there's anything I can do—"

"You work for Coastal Steamship?"

The young man nodded. "Mr. Waite," he said, with a movement of his head toward the door of the stateroom where Clarence Waite lay sprawled on the death-bunk, "was my superior."

Kane exhaled slowly, put a hand on the young man's arm and steered him to a divan. If the corpse cargo of this wrecked barge had formerly been Mr. Deasy's superior, it was just probable that Mr. Deasy might be able to furnish pertinent information.

Mr. Deasy could and did. "It's probably true," he said, sitting with his knees apart and his gaze focused on the floor, "that Mr. Waite was on the passenger list under an assumed name." He glanced at Kane quickly and put a hand out to touch Kane's arm. "Understand, I have no proof. I only know that Waite took frequent trips to New York whenever home conditions got too stiff for him. Usually he took along a companion."

Kane nodded, glanced across the room to where Clarence Waite's wife had been standing at the foot of the staircase. The woman was no longer there. Evidently she had quietly gone upstairs.

"So you think Waite was a passenger?" Kane murmured.

"Yes, I do." Frank Deasy blew ashes from the glowing tip of a cigarette and screwed his good-looking face into a scowl. "In the first place, he'd been working hard at the office, preparing the semiannual financial report for the auditors. It was at times like that that he usually helped himself to impromptu vacations and slipped away without saying a word to any of us." Deasy stood up. "If I can help you in any way, let me know. Right now I've got to get back to the office."

KANE SAT for ten minutes with his legs stuck out in front of him and his gaze focused on his shoes. The Kane brain was at last beginning to function, probably because of the increased amount of liquor in the Kane stomach.

In the beginning, this thing had looked like a case for an undertaker, not for a private shamus who disliked messing about in surroundings where people got seasick. Yet the Coastal Steamship Company had hired Peter Kane to investigate the discovery of Clarence Waite's body.

That meant that the officials of Coastal Steamship were inclined to disagree with the theory that Clarence Waite had been a passenger.

Perhaps, after all, Mr. Clarence Waite had not been a passenger.

Kane pushed himself erect and found Moroni. He said: "Has the medical examiner seen Waite yet?"

The Moroni countenance wig-wagged sideways. "Not yet. We're taking the remains with us when we get through here."

In the chair beside Moroni sat the chalk-faced form of Mr. Michael Aloysious Kelly. Mr. Kelly was obviously frightened. From the looks of things, Moroni had been doing a great deal of involved thinking and had arrived at the conclusion that Mr. Kelly would bear questioning. Having decided upon that, Moroni had apparently, in the usual Moroni manner, taken Michael Aloysious Kelly apart to see what made him tick. Mr. Kelly looked very ill.

Kane glanced into Kelly's gray face, sighed, and took himself away from there. The pint bottle in his pocket was empty, and the sickness in his own stomach was insidiously creeping higher.

He took himself out on deck. A grunt of relief gurgled in his throat when he saw the guardian of the fishing boat had obeyed orders and hung around.

CHAPTER TWO

A SHADOWY ASSASSIN

IT WAS two P.M. when the Kane chariot groaned to a stop on Atlantic Avenue in Boston, in front of the building occupied by Coastal Steamship Lines, Inc. Kane had used up the best part of two hours in driving back from Sanders Cove; had stopped twice en route, parked himself in drinking establishments, and consumed large quantities of liquor in a vain attempt to rid his mind of the ghastly, unshakable vision of green ocean that clung there.

Nothing but a prolonged diet of good Scotch whiskey would ever budge that ghastly vision and return the Kane innards to normal.

He got out of the car and steered a crooked course up the steps of the building before him. Instinct warned him to avoid such stomach-lifting vehicles as elevators, so he used the stairs.

For half an hour he sat in conference with the officials of Coastal Steamship and acquired information concerning the past history and habits of Mr. Clarence Waite.

The information checked quite nicely with that which had already been volunteered by Mr. Waite's underling, the athletic young man whose name was Frank Deasy.

Waite had made frequent trips to New York on the quiet. Undoubtedly his very angry and very nagging wife had known a great deal about it.

And it was unfortunate that Waite had seen fit to return from his last New York visit as an incognito passenger on board the ill-fated *Concord*. Most unfortunate. It meant that the company's financial report would now be unavoidably held up, and would have to be completed by Waite's understudy.

"How come you're so positive," Kane demanded, "that Waite traveled under an assumed name? I thought the passenger list was lost."

"Yes, yes, the passenger list had been lost. But the purser, whose duty it was to see that all passengers were duly listed, was a man who had a good memory. He was positive that no such name as Clarence Waite had appeared on the list.

"So you see, Mr. Kane," murmured one smirking gentleman who apparently did the most of Coastal's hiring and firing, "we were really on the wrong track when we requested your services. There is nothing now to investigate. We really won't need you after all. I'm sorry."

A sigh of relief whispered on Kane's whiskey-sweet breath. "That," he murmured, "is a break. You don't have any idea."

He felt so good that he took the elevator on the way down. That was a mistake. The sudden drop of the elevator car pushed the contents of the Kane stomach into the Kane throat and brought a weird whiteness to his face.

When he got into his car he sat very still for ten long minutes, while the heaving sensation in his mid-section subsided to normal. Then he drove to Limpy's on Stuart Street.

IT WAS six P.M. when Joe Henderson, fellow slave on the Beacon Agency payroll, again found him in Limpy's back room. The quart bottle on Kane's table was two-thirds empty. Kane was plastered.

A grin was on Henderson's large face. He sat down, murmured gently: "I hear you got relieved of that steam-ship job. That made you mad, huh?"

Kane had a silver cigarette case in one hand and a pony of Scotch in the other.

"About fifteen minutes ago," Henderson went on, "the Coastal Steamship outfit called the office and re-engaged the services of a guy by the name of Peter Kane. It seems the medical examiner found some interesting stuff in the stomach of Mr. Clarence Waite. Poison, in fact. And so the whole thing looks very dark and dirty all of a sudden, and your vacation is over."

Kane stared, made rumbling noises in his throat. A look of pain came into his countenance. "I'sh a cruel world," he said solemnly.

"The boss," said Henderson, "told me to tell you to hie yourself down there to the wreck and get on the job before you get plastered or something. He figures you'll stay sober down there."

DARKNESS HAD blurred the greenish-gray hue of the Atlantic when Kane got out of his car in Sanders Cove and paced sluggishly across the wharf. A light glowed in the window of the wharf shanty. At Kane's drunken "hallo," the guardian of the fishing boat emerged from the shack's doorway.

"There ain't a livin' soul on board except Kelly, the watchman," the fellow informed Kane while guiding his chug-chug boat through restless waters that disturbed the Kane intestines. "Mr. Moroni, he told me not to take no one out there tonight unless they got a written permit, but I guess you're all right, seein' as how you're a detective."

Kane was silent. His mouth was clamped shut and he kept it that way for reasons best known to Peter Kane. When he had climbed the ladder and gained the *Concord's* deck, he closed his eyes and hung onto the rail.

The chug-chug man called up to him: "You want me to wait?"

Kane shook his head, opened his mouth, said, "Come back in a couple of hours," very quickly, and closed his mouth again. Then he pawed his way along the deck and descended into the steamer's bowels.

A ship's lantern was burning in the salon, and Kelly, the night watchman, came scuffing from the dining room, staring with big eyes and gripping an enormous searchlight in one outthrust fist.

"Oh, it's you," Kelly mumbled. "I was wonderin' who in the name of Gawd at this time of night—" He shuddered, peered fearfully around. "This job is enough to give a man the holy shakes, Mr. Kane."

Kane said: "You all alone?"

"I—I think so. But sometimes I ain't so sure. I'll be sittin' here, readin' out of a magazine or somethin', and I'll hear the strangest noises."

Kane walked crookedly to a chair and sat down. He had come here to do things, to look around and make his own kind of investigation without the interference of Moroni and others who might veto the Kane method of research.

The lantern swung slowly back and forth. Malshaped shadows, created by its yellow glare, did the same thing. Kane's innards followed suit.

A groan of misery spilled from Kane's lips. Then, very suddenly, he stared straight ahead.

His hands tightened on the arms of the chair he was sitting in and his big body stiffened. His eyes widened, refused to blink.

At the head of the stairs, some twenty paces distant, stood a dark, ill-defined shape that did not belong there.

THE SHAPE was grotesquely tall in actuality and looked gigantic because of the shadows that enveloped it. It had two glowing eyes that returned Kane's stare. For twenty seconds Kane's blood ran cold with creeping dread of things sinister and supernatural. Then the menacing monster moved.

It descended the stairs slowly and paced forward into the glow of the lantern. Kane relaxed, dragged breath into his numbed lungs and pushed himself erect, scowling. His left hand slid into a pocket of his coat.

"Good evening, Mr. Kane," the shape said.

Kane growled, "Is it?" and stood wide-legged, glaring. If the presence of Dr. Nicolas Ackerman on board the *Concord* had been ominous before, during daylight hours, it was doubly so now. The man's thin-lipped smile was ominous, too, and in the ochre glow of the lantern his shadowed face possessed a corpse pallor.

The man had stopped within five feet of Kane and was standing motionless, smiling as though fully aware of

Kane's uneasiness. He stiffened slightly as Kane jerked toward him.

Kane said grimly: "All right, Ackerman. What's the big idea?"

The man's eyebrows and shoulders went up in unison. "I do not understand what you mean."

"You're here, aren't you? What for?"

"I have a permit—"

"Your permit's no good at night and you know it! How'd you get aboard?"

Again that ominous half-smile curled Ackerman's mouth. "It is really quite simple, Mr. Kane. I hired a man to bring me here in a rowboat."

"Where is he now?"

Ackerman calmly raised one arm and peered at his strapwatch. "By now he should have returned. I told him to come back in an hour. Really, Mr. Kane, my motive for coming here tonight was quite reasonable. I'm neither a vampire, as you seem to think, nor a thief in the dark. I came here to take pictures."

"To what?"

"To take pictures." Quietly, Ackerman displayed a small but expensive camera, foils of films, flash-sheet equipment. 'This morning, while I was here to check in the unfortunate death of one of my assistants who was a passenger, I was deeply impressed by the macabre atmosphere of the ship. Photography is my hobby, Mr. Kane—especially the photographing of things weird and unusual. So I took the liberty of returning here to-night—"

Kane's eyes narrowed, clouded with suspicion, but the vague smile did not fade from Ackerman's thin lips. With a shrug the doctor stepped backward. "Now, if you are quite reassured, Mr. Kane, I had perhaps better be leaving."

Kane watched him go, felt damp and clammy all over. He returned slowly to his chair and helped himself to a long stiff drink from the quart container he had brought with him. He needed it. The evil stare of Ackerman's eyes had eaten right through to the Kane arteries and soured the blood that coursed there.

His gaze focused again on the ship's lantern. The lantern was still swaying horribly to and fro, and the floor of the salon was doing the same thing. Kane groaned, closed his eyes and gulped hard. But closing his eyes did not help.

Peter Kane, ace dick of the Beacon Agency, was a sick shamus. Nothing less than a team of mules could have dragged him out of the chair he was sitting in. He wanted very much to die and get it over with.

Instead, he spent the next half hour guzzling from the quart bottle. And for the first time in his eventful life he passed out before the supply of liquor was finished.

THE STRAPWATCH on his wrist said four twenty A.M. when he came to, but he did not know it. His gluey eyes jerked open, focused groggily on the swaying lantern. His mouth was full of a whiskey-thick tongue and his big body was piled like a deflated blimp in the chair.

He groaned, hauled himself to a more upright position. And the sound which had aroused him from his drunken stupor came again, whispering its way into his consciousness.

He hunched forward, stared. From a passageway upstairs, in gloom beyond the head of the staircase, came a sound of slow footsteps.

Frowning, Kane pushed himself to his feet and swayed forward.

He was seasick and suffering from a monstrous hangover but he managed somehow to keep on an even keel as he swayed across the salon floor. Sometimes, despite its usual load of Limpy's bad liquor—or perhaps because of that—the Kane brain functioned clearly when other brains might be expected to wallow in darkness. Right now the Kane brain was full of a disturbing intuition that something was very wrong.

The gloom around him was alive with strange noises that might be considered normal on board a wrecked hulk which lay at the mercy of heaving seas. But that other sound—that sluggish whisper of footsteps in the passage above—was somehow ominous.

Kane pawed the bannister, ascended slowly. Hangover-hammers pounded a dull dirge inside his skull and his throat was gummy with the fusel oil in Limpy's liquor. When he reached the head of the stairs he stopped, dragged breath into his lungs and gathered himself together.

The sound of footsteps had ceased.

Kane moved slowly into gloom, tip-toed along a corridor where stateroom doors frowned darkly on both sides. Ahead of him a sliver of light crept from beneath a closed portal and yellowed the floor.

In a dozen slow strides Kane reached the door, thrust a hand toward the knob. From inside came sounds of a bunk creaking. The light was suddenly extinguished.

The stateroom door swung open in Peter Kane's face.

The liquor in Kane's big body went to his legs as he lunged sideways to avoid the pile-driver fist that lashed out at him. His shoulder crashed the side of the doorframe;

the impact spun him off balance, left him wide open. The fist raked one side of his face.

It was a hard fist full of knuckles. The blow jarred Kane's head on his shoulders and drew blood. It would have knocked a sober man out. Instead of doing that to Kane, it shook some of the whiskey-mist from his eyes and brought a savage snarl from his bleeding lips.

He staggered forward, cursed the darkness that blinded him to the flailing arms that sought to drive him back. One thing he was sure of—he was fighting a man who knew how to fight. An upthrust knee ground into the pit of his stomach. When he stumbled back, gasping, his assailant rushed him with lowered head, both fists working like pistons.

One of those fists held something big, solid—probably the searchlight whose glow had lured Kane along the corridor. The weapon crashed down on Kane's head, crashed again and again as he got his arms around the killer's body and tried to drag the man down.

It found a vital spot. Blood trickled from Kane's gasping mouth. He stumbled, clawed the wall as he collapsed.

The killer lurched away from him, turned, wrenched open a shuttered window that gave access to the cat-walk outside. For an instant Kane's eyes, blurred by hot blood, focused on a contorted shadow-shape that clambered through the aperture.

The shape thudded loudly on the deck outside, made more noise as it clambered onto the ship's rail. Through the shattered window Kane caught a dim vision of something big and dark leaping out into space. A muffled splash echoed up from the sea below.

Kane didn't hear the splash. It was smothered by the groans that issued from his own battered mouth as he crawled on hands and knees into the corridor.

He clung hard to consciousness, refused to pass out. At the end of the passage he clutched the bannister at the stairhead and hauled himself erect.

"Kelly," he croaked hoarsely. "Kelly!"

Then he collapsed in a gurgling contortion and slid grotesquely down the carpeted stairs, to land in a sprawled heap on the floor below.

CHAPTER THREE
CALL FOR KANE

A SIDEWALK clock on Huntington Avenue said four thirty P.M. when Kane hiked out of the Peter Bent Brigham and thumbed a passing cab. Getting out of the hospital had not been as easy as getting into it. He had known nothing whatever about getting in. Michael Aloysious Kelly and a Sanders Cove doctor had driven him to the city in his own car, after Kelly and the pilot of the fishing boat had lugged him ashore. When consciousness had finally filtered through the blood-mist in Kane's brain, his blurred gaze had focused in bewilderment on the hovering face of a hospital doctor and the white walls of an accident ward.

Getting out of the place had necessitated a lot of loud talk, threats, and the signing of certain papers which relieved the hospital of all responsibility for what might happen after the exodus.

Kane said grimly to the cab driver: "I got a car parked in the Huntington Garage, or so they tell me. Drive over there."

It was after six when he reached Sanders Cove. The ocean was a monstrous caterpillar that crawled away into gathering gloom. The owner of the fishing boat, lured from his wharf shanty by the sounds of the car's approach, stopped abruptly in the lighted doorway and gaped as if seeing a ghost.

Kane said huskily: "I hope to God you got a drink around somewhere. I need one. My brand is Scotch, but anything you got will do."

When he climbed the *Concord's* ladder and descended into the ship's salon some ten minutes later, he felt better. The owner of the boat had possessed a pint of amber-hued liquid that smelled like the concentrated juice of crushed bedbugs and tasted worse than it smelled. Even that, however, felt better than the ether fumes which had worried the Kane stomach for the past many hours.

He walked crookedly across the salon and was oblivious to the amazed stares of Moroni, of Mr. Michael Aloysious Kelly, and of others who were assembled there. He looked worse than he felt. One side of his face was swathed in bandages and his greenish hat was cocked at a grotesque angle because of the strips of adhesive that humped his forehead.

Moroni, recovering from the shock, gasped out: "Where the hell did you come from?"

Kane made a face and sat down. "I guess you heard what happened."

"Yeah, sure. Some guy beat you up with a flashlight. We got the light right here. Found it in the stateroom. But how—"

Kane stood up stiffly and walked to the news counter, peered down at the searchlight. "Any fingerprints on this?" he demanded.

"The guy must've worn gloves," Moroni said.

KANE STARED around him, encountered the gaping stare of Kelly's big eyes and saw a thin, hawk-faced woman talking to one of Moroni's men on the other side of the room. The woman was Mrs. Clarence Waite. Kane hooked his mouth into a puzzled frown and took a long look before turning his attention elsewhere.

He wondered how it was that some women, after nagging their husbands all through life, suddenly took a large interest in them after death.

He poked a cigarette into his mouth and sat down. To Moroni he said, suddenly: "Has Ackerman been around?"

"Thank God, no. He gave me enough creeps yesterday." The Moroni jaw-muscles tightened ominously. "Whatever Ackerman does from now on, I'll know about it. I put a man to keep tabs on him."

"When?"

"Last night."

"Last night," Kane said, "the good Doctor Ackerman was—" He stopped talking, peered across the room at the approaching figure of Frank Deasy. Deasy had come from the dining room, was staring at Kane in open-mouthed astonishment as he paced forward.

"Last night Ackerman was what?" Moroni demanded.

"Skip it," Kane said. "I want a look at that stateroom upstairs." He put his feet under him, stood up.

Frank Deasy, gaping at him, exclaimed loudly: "Good Lord, Mr. Kane, what are you doing here? Kelly told me you were at the Peter Bent Brigham!"

"They serve lousy liquor in hospitals," Kane said, "and they're stingy as hell with it. I didn't like the joint."

He strode across the salon and went upstairs, felt wobbly in his legs as he prowled along the upstairs passageway and pushed open the same door that had opened in his face the night before.

Before entering the stateroom he shot a quick glance both ways along the corridor. Inside, he closed the door behind him, pulled a flashlight from his pocket and looked around.

The room contained nothing worth looking at.

He strode to the shuttered window and peered out. A moment later he was on the cat-walk outside, leaning over the ship's rail. The sea was an undulating carpet far below. The light in the wharf shanty, on shore, was a long way off.

Scowling, Kane went back downstairs, knew before he reached the foot of the big staircase that something had happened during his absence. Moroni was hiking the floor, chewing savagely on a sodden stump of black cigar.

He looked up and glared as Kane approached. "I just had a phone call," he said thickly, "from Moe Finch at headquarters. It seems Finch had a hurry call from some girl who works for Coastal Steamship. The girl was one of Clarence Waite's secretaries."

"This has possibilities," Kane murmured.

Moroni evidently thought so. "This girl's been out of town on vacation, see? Just this afternoon she got back to the city and heard about Waite's death. So she calls up police headquarters and says she knows where there's some very important information to be had."

Moroni spat cigar smoke out of a twisted mouth. "So Moe Finch, being too busy betting on the ponies or something, tells her to come down and tell me all about it. Then he calls me up and tells me to hang around till she gets here."

Obviously Moroni did not relish the idea of hanging around. Neither did Peter Kane. Kane murmured softly: "So she works in Waite's office and she knows something, does she?" Rocking around, he hiked toward the stairs.

Moroni said: "Hey, what's the idea? Where you goin'?"

"Only a dumb dick like you," Kane grunted, "would even think of hanging around after getting a phone call like that."

IT WAS after eight o'clock when he got to Boston and later than that when he parked his car on Atlantic Avenue in front of the Coastal Steamship Building. He used up half an hour in rounding up a sleepy-eyed night janitor and convincing the man that Peter Kane, being currently in the employ of Coastal, had a right to be let into the Coastal offices.

The janitor, after much deliberation, turned on some lights, reluctantly manned an elevator, and ushered Kane into the very dark and very gloomy rooms on the building's fourth floor.

Kane went straight to the private office of Mr. Clarence Waite but he had a feeling he would be too late getting there.

He was.

With a hand on the light switch inside the door, he gaped at the scene of upheaval before him. The carpeted floor was strewn with papers; the contents of desk drawers and filing cabinets had been dumped out, pawed through and flung aside. Wax records of a dictating machine had been spilled from their containers and smashed into chunks of black, gleaming stuff that crunched under Kane's feet as he advanced.

He turned a slow circle, stared around him. Half an hour later, when he paced wearily out of the office, the hangdog look on his face would have soured milk. He had listlessly waded through all the stuff that the intruder before him had condescended to leave behind. He had methodically explored Clarence Waite's domain from end to end.

The sullen curve of his mouth was proof enough that he had wasted half an hour of good drinking time.

When he left the building he drove uptown to Limpy's and from there drove to the Back Bay apartment house where Peter Kane's name adorned a brass mailbox. The ache in his battered head had grown to alarming proportions. Letting himself into his three-room apartment on the third floor, he savagely kicked the door shut and paraded into the living room.

AT FOUR THIRTY A.M. the next morning, when the phone rang, Peter Kane was sitting deep in a big easy chair with his stockinged feet propped on an end-table and a large bottle of Limpy's very bad Scotch squatting on the floor beside him.

The voice on the phone was vaguely familiar.

"Mr. Kane!" the voice wailed. "This is Frank Deasy. You've got to come down here!"

"Down where?" Kane mumbled.

"Here—to the *Concord!* Something frightful has happened! You've got to come, Mr. Kane. Our company hired you—"

Kane made loud grumbling noises and asked questions, hung up when he realized that Frank Deasy was too excited to supply coherent answers. Something undoubtedly had happened. It was essential that Mr. Kane rush at once to the scene of the happening.

"If ever there's a lousy job around," Kane groaned, "I'm elected."

It occurred to him later, as he sat behind the wheel of the car, that after all he might as well be glad of a chance to get the job over with. During the past few hours the Kane thinking apparatus had spawned several loose ends of ideas that were beginning to blend together.

He had to get the owner of the fishing boat out of bed, had to bang on the shanty door and bellow loudly before a light went on in the shack and the fellow appeared. Out on the steamer's hulk other lights were visible, and between steamer and wharf lay an expanse of bulging ocean that looked dark and mean.

"You wouldn't have any more of that brimstone-branded brew of yours around, would you?" Kane said. "Sure as hell I'll be sick as a goat without some little thing to bolster me up."

The fellow had some. But despite the liquor's potency, it was sea-sickness, not the pale contents of the bottle, that caused Kane to stagger drunkenly when he entered the ship's salon some ten minutes later.

The salon was empty.

From the direction of the dining room came a murmur of voices that dragged Kane to a halt, made him stop and peer around. He went slowly past the foot of the staircase, paced along the passageway. The voices emanated from a stateroom set back in a small side-passage off the end of the dining hall.

Moroni was doing most of the talking.

Kane pushed over the threshold, stood staring. It was a big stateroom and had a pair of iron beds instead of a bunk. Moroni, in the middle of the floor between the beds, had his hands hipped and his legs spread wide and was glaring into the dark, unlovely face of Dr. Nicolas Ackerman.

Michael Aloysious Kelly stood with his back against a wall, his big eyes bulging, his face, for once, empty of the corncob pipe.

Frank Deasy was methodically rummaging through a small overnight case that lay opened on a chair.

"Well, for goo'nesh sakes," Kane croaked.

The occupants of the room turned toward him, and Moroni grunted disdainfully: "Oh, it's you." Frank Deasy had a sheepish look on his face as he straightened above the overnight case and came forward.

"I guess I should have waited a while before I called you, Mr. Kane," he said. "There really was no need for you to come down here."

"Thanks," Kane said. Slowly he paced toward the cot on the far side of the room, stood there and peered down.

CHAPTER FOUR

DEATH IN A DUMB-WAITER

THE GIRL who lay there had a crumpled blue dress on, and the dress was soiled and wet looking. The girl was young. She lay with one leg bent at the knee and the fingers of one hand pressed rigidly into her stomach. Her face was gray and dirty and her hair was a stringy mop that bulged out over the pillow.

From the looks of things, she had been dead some time.

"Where," Kane demanded in a low voice, "did *this* come from?"

No one was in a hurry to answer him. Michael Kelly was gawking. Moroni had jerked his large head in Kane's direction but was still standing over the stiff, chalk-faced form of Nicolas Ackerman, who sat like a propped-up wax figure on the other cot.

Frank Deasy said, slowly: "Kelly was the one who found her. He was making his rounds, and when he entered this room he heard a kind of creaking noise that seemed to come from over there." He aimed an unsteady hand at the corner of the room, where a door hung open. "The noise came from behind that door, but he couldn't get the door open, so he went and got help."

Kane said softly: "The door was locked?"

"No, it wasn't. It was stuck. Mr. Moroni and I got it open and found—her."

Kane strode forward and would have hiked over the threshold. He stopped just in time, used a searchlight from his pocket and screwed his face into a puzzled frown. It was a queer layout. The enclosure beyond the threshold was a small-sized closet of some kind, but the closet had no floor.

"When the company bought this ship," Deasy said, "the dining hall was half again as big as it is now, and these staterooms didn't exist. Apparently this was a dumb-waiter leading down to the kitchen. When the staterooms were built, the dumb-waiter was blocked up with a false door."

Kane leaned forward, peered down into the depths and heard a gurgle of water down below. "You found the girl in here?"

"Yes. She was wedged in the shaft. The creaking noise Kelly heard was caused by the pressure of her body against the walls, every time the ship rolled."

Moroni said grimly, from the other side of the room: "The idea is, the girl was a passenger on the night of the crash. She got panicky and made a dive for the door. The door was supposed to be locked but it wasn't—or else the lock was so damn ancient that she had strength enough to get it open. She thought she was getting out into a corridor or something, and instead of that she took a nose-dive down the dumb-waiter and got jammed tight. And she's been there ever since. That," said Moroni, "is what Deasy thinks, anyway."

Kane peered at the overnight bag. "Where did that come from?"

"We found that down in the shaft with her," Moroni shrugged. "Deasy thinks she snatched it up when she made the break. Maybe Deasy is right about the whole business. Me, I think different."

"And just why do you think different?"

Moroni scowled, jerked his head toward the girl's body. "It so happens, Kane, that this girl's name is Helen Tilson. It also happens that she's the dame who was supposed to come to me a long time ago with some important information. About two minutes after you barged out of here, the gal called up and said she'd be late. Said she was going to the steamship office first, to get the papers that contained that important information. Well—here she is."

Moroni had his theories but was not sure of them. He went into doubtful detail. "Maybe," he said, "the phone calls to Moe Finch and me were just gags. Maybe the gal who did the phoning had a good reason for using this gal's name. It's possible, all right, that this dame was a passenger the night of the crash. Sure as hell, this corpse could have been jammed down that dumb-waiter for a couple of centuries without ever being discovered except by accident."

Moroni screwed his face around to glare into the gray features of Dr. Nicolas Ackerman, "But it also happens that I found *this* mug snoopin' around here about an hour ago, and so help me, he says he was takin' pictures!"

Moroni had evidently worked long and hard on the good doctor. Ackerman showed pathetic signs of having been subjected to the usual Moroni method of third-degree. "I—I *was* taking pictures," he insisted.

Kane took a long drink from the pint bottle of vile-smelling liquor he had acquired from the owner of the fishing boat. He felt wobbly from being so long in a stuffy stateroom. "If it's all the same to you people," he mumbled, "I'll go take a walk."

He closed the stateroom door behind him and was scowling as he paraded across the dining hall and went out on deck. The Kane brain had begun to do a great amount of deep thinking.

HALF AN hour or so later, when Moroni and the others appeared, Peter Kane was apparently plastered and his eyes had taken on a sickly green hue from peering so long at so much ocean. Moroni had a look of triumph on his face and a firm grip on the arm of Dr. Nicolas Ackerman.

The expression on the face of Mr. Michael Kelly, who shuffled along in the rear of the procession, was strangely enigmatic. The Kelly mouth seemed to bear a slight suggestion of triumph, too.

Moroni said: "That's where you're goin', Ackerman. Right straight to headquarters until you come clean. I got this thing all figured out, and it ain't often I figure things out wrong." He shoved Ackerman to the rail and yelled down to the admiral of the fishing boat. To Kane he said: "Hang onto this mug a minute."

"Poshitively," Kane gurgled.

Kane was plastered, and when he released his grip on the rail and turned around, his feet crossed and he went off balance. The deck was slippery with spray. Less than three paces distant, the railing had a break in it where the ladder hung over the ship's side.

Kane pawed empty air and let out a yell. His big body teetered, went out on one foot and hung over vacant space. Moroni stabbed a hand at Kane's legs, missed. Frank Deasy yelled incoherent words. Kane went overboard.

He struck with a huge splash, went down a long way into undulating wet darkness and made blubbering sounds when he broke surface. A searchlight gleamed yellow on deck and the beam picked him out, clung to him as he dog-paddled wildly in a frantic effort to stay afloat.

From the looks of things he either couldn't swim or was too drunk to remember how. He was blubbering under a second time when a hurtling shape shot head foremost from the steamer's deck and sliced the water beside him.

The hurtling shape was Frank Deasy.

Deasy could swim. With a minimum of effort he dragged Kane up from under, lugged him to the ladder. Moroni and Michael Kelly hauled Kane to the deck. Moroni growled: "Well, of all the drunken souse-brained idiots, you're it."

Frank Deasy came up the ladder hand over hand and spat out a mouthful of sea-water.

Kane stood up. "Thanks, Deasy," he said. Oddly enough he did not look half as plastered as before. His eyes were narrowed and there was nothing fuzzy about the metallic rasp of his voice. "Thanks, Deasy. That's all I needed to know."

Moroni gaped at him. Deasy took a step backward, staring, and said: "What?"

"It was either you or Ackerman," Kane murmured. He took a police thirty-eight from a pocket of his drenched coat and toyed with it. The gun dripped water, but the chances were ten to one it would work if called upon. Deasy made large eyes at it and stood stiff as wood.

"At first," Kane said, "I figured it was Ackerman. I figured he and Mrs. Clarence Waite were in cahoots and engineered Waite's murder between them. That was before the girl called Moe Finch and said she worked for Waite and knew where to put her hands on some important information."

KANE WAS drunk enough to be enjoying himself. The scared look on Deasy's face amused him, brought a twisted grin to his lips. "I guess you got into a jam with the finances or something, huh?" he gurgled. "Why not come clean?"

Moroni said, frowning: "For God's sake, Kane, what's eating you? Do you go nuts like this all the time?"

"This mug murdered Waite because Waite knew things," Kane shrugged. "He'll tell us all about it in a minute. Just stick around. He murdered Waite, and figured to do it in a way that would leave him a loophole in case things got hot. You can't burn a man for murder unless you first prove the victim was murdered. The poison in Waite's stomach didn't mean a thing. The guy might've been drinking poisoned liquor the night this barge cracked up.

"The fireworks began when this Helen Tilson girl, or whatever her name is, came back to town and called Moe

Finch. Maybe you don't remember it, but Deasy here was in the salon when you were blabbing to me about getting the call from Moe—and you weren't talking in a whisper. I guess Deasy was still there when the girl called you and said she was going to the steamship office. The chances are, you even told him all about it."

"Sure I did," Moroni growled. "Why wouldn't I?"

"Sure you did. So Deasy faded out of here and got to the steamship office ahead of me, and got his paws on the girl, and went through the joint with a cootie comb. I bet you never even knew he left the ship."

Moroni put thick fingers into his hair and scratched. He seemed to be remembering things that heretofore had seemed unimportant.

Kane said: "Until I took a look around Waite's private office, I was on the wrong track. I figured on Ackerman and Waite's wife being in on some dirty scheme that spelled murder. But there were some funny things done in that office. For one thing, a whole bunch of dictating-machine records were smashed."

The Kane orbs drilled holes in Deasy's white face. "Only a guy who worked pretty close to Waite," he said, "would even figure to suspect that Waite might have put that important information on the dictating machine. I guess you better come clean."

Frank Deasy's nerves were in good shape. Despite the lack of blood in his stiff face, he forced a sickly grin to his mouth. "You're altogether wrong, Mr. Kane," he said. "I assure you—"

"There was another thing had to be figured out," Kane mused. "The mug who murdered Waite and Miss Tilson had to be a good swimmer. He couldn't have lugged those bodies aboard by boat, because the risk was too big. So he had to be a guy with enough swimming ability to tote them through the water. I figured on finding out if you could swim well enough to tote a dead man through the ocean, Deasy."

Moroni jerked a step forward, stood glaring. He was no longer interested in Dr. Nicolas Ackerman. "So you weren't plastered when you went overboard? You can swim?"

"I can—" Kane caught his answer, changed it quickly. "I can swim like a hunk of lead pipe, mister. It was a chance I had to take." The gun in his fist drooped a little as he swung again on Deasy. "How about coming clean, mug?"

DEASY WENT limp, had a look of resignation in his face. He had an eye on the opening in the rail where the ship's ladder hung over the side. He shrugged his shoulders.

"Did you get the important information or is it still in the steamship offices somewhere?" Kane demanded.

"It—it's still there," Deasy mumbled. A glint of black hate gleamed in his eyes. "I couldn't find it. Only for that, I'd have a chance to get out of this, damn you!"

"Tell us about it."

"You know about it already." Deasy's voice dropped low, became a mumble. "I was in deep. I—well, I'd stolen enough to send me to prison for—a long time. I'd been playing the horses." He put a trembling hand to his face and wiped away beads of perspiration. "Waite was preparing a report for the auditors," he groaned, "and he found out what I'd done. I—well, I had to shut him up. I despised him anyway."

"And being a bright young man," Kane grunted, "you figured to plant the body on board ship where it would look like Waite had been a passenger the night of the crash. What's the rest of it?"

"You know the rest," Deasy mumbled. "When Helen Tilson called up, I realized that Waite must have made out some kind of a report before I killed him. I had to get to the office before she did. I—I guess I should have hidden there and waited for her to find the papers, but I was nervous. When she showed up, I—"

He shuddered, stared helplessly at Kane. "Then I got her into my car and drove down here and dumped the body into the dumb-waiter shaft. The overnight case didn't belong to Helen. It was something I found in one of the other staterooms the day after the crash."

"You're not so dumb," Kane muttered.

"I didn't think the body would be discovered so soon," Deasy moaned. "When Kelly stumbled on it, I had to think fast. That's why I called you. I—well, I thought it would clear me of suspicion, and you'd be so drunk you wouldn't guess the truth anyway, and—"

Deasy's voice ended in a sucking intake of breath as he lunged forward. The distance to the rail was about eight feet. He took it in a headlong rush, cleared the opening with inches to spare and streaked down into darkness. The guttural drone of his voice was still alive on deck when the heaving black waters of the Atlantic sucked him under.

Moroni and Ackerman and Michael Kelly stood gaping. Peter Kane ploughed forward, stood in the open space above the ship's ladder and peered down at the widening rings of black water below.

The sight of so much water brought a pained look to Kane's face. He pulled a pint bottle from his pocket, dropped it and growled to Moroni: "Take care of that. I'll need it!" His big body shot out and down, sliced the water and reappeared almost instantly. A stream of gurgling white foam trailed out behind him as he surged away from the ship.

Moroni, gasping, said in a hoarse voice: "For God's sake!"

FRANK DEASY could swim, but the torpedo-like shape behind him caught up with him. Deasy twisted around, put both hands out of the water and raked savagely at Kane's face, battered wildly as Kane closed in. Terror made a contorted mask of his face and sucked a lurid shriek from his lips.

Kane growled, savagely, "I owe you this one, mug!" and drove a sledge-hammer fist into the killer's screaming mouth.

The fist crunched home, brought a sobbing sound from Deasy's throat. Thrashing wildly, he flung himself back, spun in the water and again headed for the distant light in the wharf shanty on shore.

He turned when Kane's big body again bore down on him. The surface in front of Kane was suddenly a boiling upheaval. Deasy shot down, vanished. Savage hands clawed at Kane's legs, dragged him under. Water rushed into Kane's breath-sucking mouth.

Twisting at the hips, Kane hooked himself double and got both hands on the shape beneath him. He was sore, and the sea-water in the pit of his stomach was making him sick. The fingers of his left hand tore into a mass of wet hair. His right hand, balled into a fist, struck three times with trip-hammer precision under water. Bubbles of blood gurgled to the surface.

After that, Peter Kane hooked one arm in a stranglehold around the limp neck of his assailant and swam wearily back to the steamer. Moroni and Michael Kelly helped him haul Deasy's unconscious form up the ladder.

"He figured," Kane mumbled, "I couldn't swim. *Tsk.* I was a Boy Scout once."

Moroni and Michael Kelly gaped at him. Walking crookedly around Deasy's crumpled body, Kane gathered up the pint bottle and stood swaying. His face in the broad beam of Moroni's searchlight was the color of seaweed.

"About one half the Atlantic Ocean," he groaned, "is inside my stomach. In a couple of minutes I'm gonna be sick. Awful sick."

He glared at Moroni, pulled the cork from the bottle and gurgled until the container was empty.

"When I come to," he said thickly, "the first guy that hands me a drink of water—any kind of water—will get—" His legs buckled under him, let him down. A groan of torment mumbled up with the heaving contents of Kane's stomach. "Will get—hell," Kane finished. "It ain't my brand."

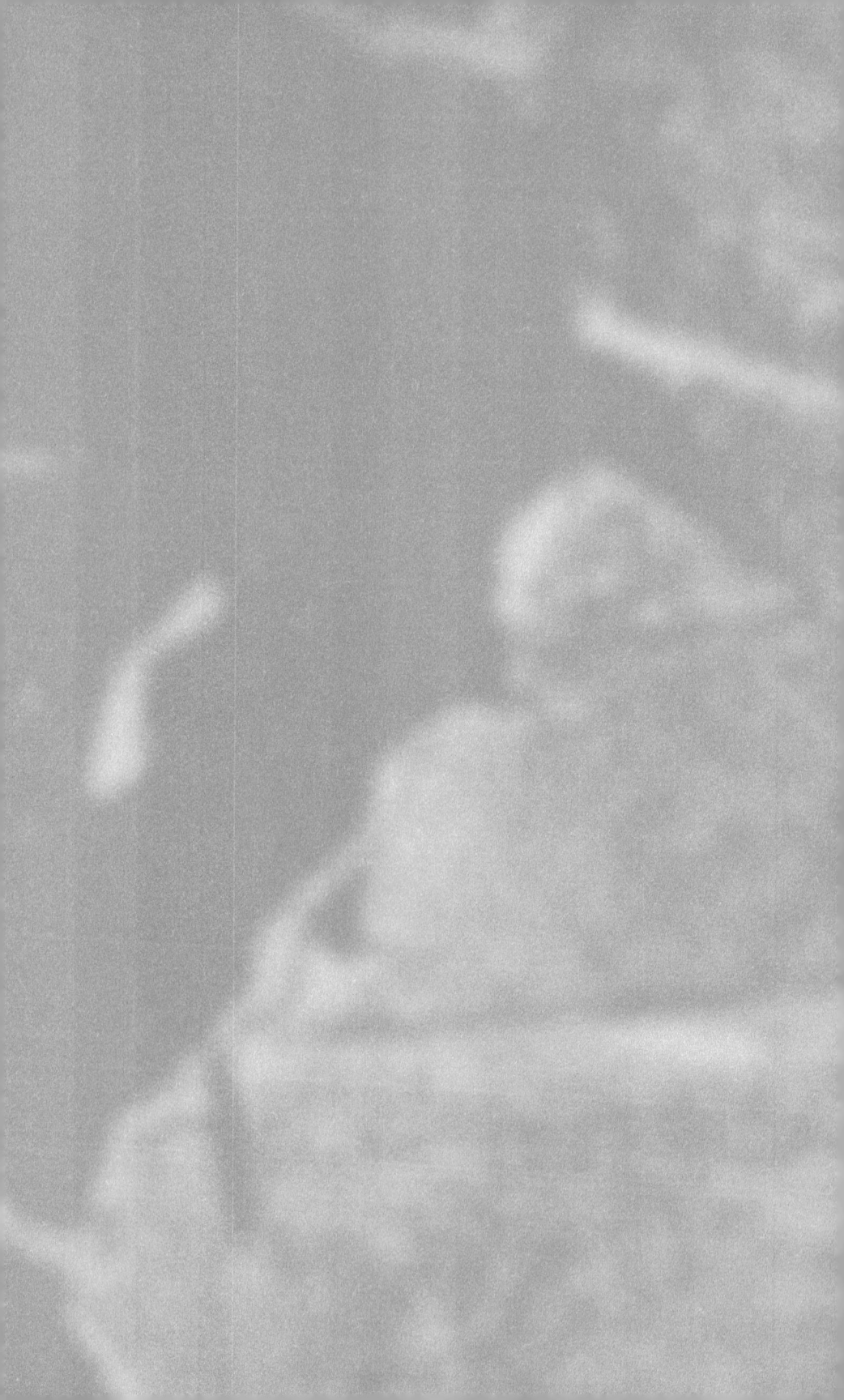

DING DONG BELLE

A GORGEOUS MODEL, CLAD ONLY IN A BATHING SUIT, FOUND SLAIN IN A PING-PONG PARLOR ON A WINTRY NIGHT. THAT WAS A PUZZLE TO DETECTIVE MOE FINCH. BUT TO HIS THIRSTY FRIEND, PETER KANE, IT WAS A CHALLENGE—AND WELL-WORTH A BEATING—TO PUNCTURE THAT WINDBAG OF THE FORCE, THE "GREAT" MORONI.

DETECTIVE LIEUTENANT MORONI was in a mood. "And you, Kane, you keep your nose out of this!" he snarled. His fat neck was red against the collar of his pink-and-white striped shirt, and his big face was puffed. "You hear?"

Kane grinned drunkenly through the amber sheen of his beer glass. "What intrigues me," he murmured, rolling his eyes at the buxom beauty in oils above Limpy's bar, "is that the gal was un-draped at the time—or anyway, in a bathing suit. A bathing suit in the middle of winter, friend—"

"You keep out of this, Kane!"

"And playing ping-pong, of all things! Ping-pong in a white bathing suit at midnight, in the middle of winter. Why that's—"

"It ain't ping-pong any more," Limpy declared gravely. He was a little man who seldom smiled. He'd been pickpocket, cop, night-club owner, had lost half a knee in the war, and this quiet, high-class liquor trough on Stuart Street was Kane's favorite hangout. "They call it table tennis now," he declared. He poured Scotch and placed it beside Kane's beer. The beer was a chaser.

"And I'm warning you, keep out of this!" Moroni snarled again. "I had my fill of you when Moe Finch was in his prime, Kane. I got more to say now, and I'm tough!" He slapped his glass savagely on the bar and turned away.

"Dear, dear," Kane murmured. The phone was ringing and Limpy hobbled along back of the bar to answer it.

It was a queer case when you thought about it. Kane thought about it. The girl's name had been Dolores Trent before she married the Anderton bankroll, and as Dolores Trent she'd been on the covers of a lot of magazines. A lot of people had paid out nickels, dimes and quarters just to take her home with them. She'd been framed and placed on mahogany bureaus. She'd been thumb-tacked to fraternity-house walls. She'd made old men young and young men reckless.

Day before yesterday at three o'clock in the morning, a newspaper photog named Hulett had found this gal's husband dead on the stairs in the Goodwin Building. He'd followed the dead man's blood up the stairs to the table tennis parlors on the floor above, and found Dolores Trent Anderton dead under one of the dark green tables—in a ravishing white bathing suit.

Kane wished he were back on the cops. This kind of case stirred the bloodhound in him. He gulped his Scotch and swayed a little and realized he was drunk. That was all right, too. As an agency dick he was seldom sober. He disliked being sober.

Limpy said: "For you, Kane."

It was a girl's voice and it called him Peter. The voice jarred him. He lowered his gaze quickly from the oil painting above the bar, because the painting was lewd and that sort of art was way out of line when you talked to a girl like Anne Finch. He'd been in love with Anne before she acquired the Finch. He'd been on the cops then, with a glorious future. The liquor had licked him with both the future and the girl.

He listened and said, scowling: "Moroni was just here. He must have figured you'd call me. He warned me to keep out of this."

The girl said: "Then I won't need to beg very hard, will I?" Her voice was low and cultured, as always. It was as soft and clean as Anne herself, but Kane caught the tremor in it. He guessed she was pale and desperate.

"Meaning?" he countered, not knowing what else to say.

"You've never turned down a Moroni challenge yet, Peter!"

"This is different," Kane muttered. "He's a lieutenant now."

"Then—you're afraid of him?"

That did it. Kane's mouth twitched and a dull red crept up his jaws. He was

Dolores Trent was found dead under one of the dark green tables.

drunk—he'd been drunk for days—but there was a part of him the liquor never touched, and the girl had reached that part with a thrust that cut deep.

"Afraid of Moroni?" Kane snarled. "The hell I am! Where are you?"

She told him where she was.

"Wait there," he snapped.

Limpy said with a sigh: "Now look, Kane. Look what you done to my phone! Now how will I explain that to the telephone people?"

Kane poured a drink and downed it. It gagged him and he made a face. He slapped his last dollar bill on the bar to pay for it. "Tell 'em Superman was in," he leered, and went out.

SHE LOOKED just the same. He hadn't seen her in six months, but she was the same girl with the same warm brown eyes and sensitive mouth and straight, slim body. The sight of her did things to him. He never could look at her without remembering the night three years ago she had told him she loved him, and always would love him, and never could marry him. Life with a perpetual souse, she had told him, was not her idea of security.

He'd been drunk that night. He'd spent the next two weeks in an alcoholic fog, and groped out of the fog at last to find her married to Captain of Detectives Moe Finch, his boss and best friend. Soon after that he'd quit the cops to go to the Beacon Agency as a private shamus. He and Finch were still friends, but there was a difference. Kane didn't try to define the difference—he just knew it existed.

She put her hands on his arms now and said, "You're drunk, Peter," and Kane said defensively, "I like to be drunk." They never talked of that other thing.

She drew him into the apartment and shut the door, steered him to a chair in the living-room. She was worried. Her eyes had a hunted, desperate look and her hands shook as she reached for a cigarette. Kane lit it for her, stared at her and waited.

"It won't be the first time you've helped Moe out of a spot, Peter."

There was no answer to that. He just shrugged.

"This time," she said, "it means his career. Moroni's been waiting for a big, sensational job like this. You know."

Kane knew. He knew that the man she was married to was just a big, sober, hard-working cop with no flair for showmanship. When Moe Finch muffed a job, the papers tore him apart. When he cleaned up a city sin-spot or sent a killer to jail, the newspapers' silence was ear-splitting. Moe Finch had never learned to yell from the house-tops. He was good but not brilliant.

The newspapers were promoting Moroni for Moe Finch's job. Moroni the Mouth, the Great I Am. Moroni the swaggerer.

If Moroni solved the mystery of the girl in the bathing suit, he was in.

"Did Moe ask you to call me?" Kane demanded.

"No, Peter. He asked me not to." She took the cigarette from her lips and looked away from him, the lips trembling. "Moe says he's determined to sink or swim on his own, this time. You've held him together for three years. You've kept him up there. It can't go on, he says."

"He's a sap."

"Then you—you—"

"He's the biggest damn fool in the world," Kane growled, "with the biggest heart and the biggest conscience." He reached for a newspaper on the divan, and scanned the headlines. "What do you know about this case?"

"The girl, Dolores Anderton, used to be a model."

"I know that."

"Wednesday evening, she and her husband went slumming with another couple. That isn't in the papers because the other two, the William Singsens, were influential enough to hush it. The Singsens took Dolores and her husband home at one A.M., then went home themselves. That's all they know. At three, this newspaperman found the Andertons in the Goodwin Building, dead."

"How'd he happen to be in the building at that hour?"

"He has a studio there."

Kane studied his fingernails and wished he had a drink. His brain worked better when lubricated. The trouble was, he had to lubricate it often, because his system was pickled and the effect of each new drink quickly wore off. He was so sober now that it hurt.

He said: "These Singsens—who are they, pal?"

"William Singsen is one of the vice-presidents of Anderton's machine-tool company. With Anderton dead, he'll move up."

"Anderton boozed a lot, didn't he?"

"Moe says he did."

Kane stood up. He had an idea this job was going to unravel him. It was a boat race. Moroni had the official oars and a long head-start, and Moroni, though still blessed with more bluster than brains, had learned a lot about rowing since the old days. It was going to be a hell of a hard job to scuttle Moroni's boat this time.

"I'll give it my old-time best, pal," Kane said. He reached for her hand and held it a moment, then looked into her eyes, pulled a deep breath into his chest and abruptly turned away. His best, he promised himself would be good.

WILLIAM SINGSEN'S private secretary was a pert little chick with Jean Harlow hair and a way of using her eyes and voice that shrank a man down to size. Kane wished he had his old police badge to impress her with. Lacking it, he sat and munched his tongue while she phoned his name in to her employer.

He waited. The surroundings were magnificently modern and he was their only occupant. He stood up, said. "May I?" and snaked a newspaper off the girl's desk. It was full of pictures.

That was the hell of this mess, the pictures. A newspaper photog had discovered the bodies and taken enough pictures of them to make him happy for life. They were good, too. They were sensational. They made this the biggest murder case in a decade.

He discovered something in the paper that Anne Finch had not told him. Both the girl and her wealthy husband had been shot with a thirty-eight. The same thirty-eight. The gun was missing.

Moroni had passed that out to the newsboys. "Detective Joseph Moroni, ace sleuth of the city's police department, revealed this morning…."

Kane threw the paper aside with a snort. He smoked a cigarette, squashed it. His mouth was dry and he needed a drink. The liquor that was already in him was beginning to sour, and he had a headache. He looked at the clock and scowled at the pert little chick behind the desk. She ignored him.

Twenty minutes he'd waited. He was stewing. Then the inner sanctum door opened and he stood up, strode forward.

He stopped. He was face to face with the man who'd come out of there, and the man was Moroni. Moroni's face was a thundercloud.

They were Dempsey and Firpo, confronting each other. Moroni filled his barrel chest with air and let it out in a swift, noisy stream, jabbing a fat forefinger at Kane's face. "I told you to keep your nose out of this, Kane! By God, if you pull any tricks on me this time—"

Kane took out a handkerchief and elaborately wiped his face. "You spit too much." He tossed the handkerchief into a wastebasket beside the desk. Moroni lurched about and strode back into the sanctum, slamming the door.

What was said in there, Kane couldn't know. The phone rang on the waiting-room desk and the blonde answered it. She said, "Yes, Mr. Singsen," and hung up. She looked at Kane, her dark red lips faintly scornful.

"Mr. Singsen will be in conference the rest of the day," she said.

Kane glared at the sanctum door and slowly unclenched his fists. His knuckles were white. "Round one," he muttered.

Round one had gone to Moroni.

HE WONDERED if Moroni had phoned Mrs. Singsen at her Chestnut Hill home and told her to throw him out, too. It was a pretentious place with an acre of winter-dead lawn and a driveway that curved between lanes of soldier-straight poplars. He punished the bell. A maid with a blank face and a large blank bosom opened the door and blinked at him.

Kane said unctuously: "I am Mr. Hadley. Mr. Singsen sent me with a message for Mrs. Singsen."

The maid thought it over. She let him in. She changed her mind about halting him in the hall and let him into the living-room, which was almost too large for an Elks' convention. "Wait here, please," she said.

Kane prowled. He stopped beside a table on which lay a pair of gloves. They were a man's evening gloves and lay on a bright red rectangle of cardboard that bore the words, *Wop Willy Offers.*

He reached for the red cardboard and changed his mind when a door opened across the room. He turned. "Ah," he said. "Mrs. Singsen!"

She was no chicken, this Mrs. Singsen. She had several auxiliary chins and she wore a nondetachable life-preserver of blubber around her middle. The motif was nautical: embroidered anchors on a navy blue dress that hugged the hull-like armor-plate. She was designed to plow through heavy seas, this lady.

She frowned at him, fluttering her eyelids, and Kane said: "I'm investigating the Anderton affair, Mrs. Singsen. Your husband suggested that I come here and talk to you."

"Indeed!"

"He tells me that you two were out with the Andertons Wednesday evening, and—"

"One moment, Mr. Hadley," she said. Kane scowled at the broad of her back as she headed majestically for the hall.

He heard the dial-clicks of a telephone and guessed what she was doing. She'd been tipped off, then, that Peter Kane might come calling. Kane rolled the name Moroni under his tongue and in less refined surroundings would have expelled it vehemently. He stepped back to the table and snatched up the bright red oblong of cardboard. It was in his pocket when the woman cruised in from the hall.

She dropped anchor a few feet from the door, hipped her hands and delivered a broadside. "I have just spoken to my husband," she snapped. "*You* are without doubt the private detective we were warned about! You are Peter Kane!"

Kane sighed. With some ceremony he put his hat back on his head and headed for the door.

"And don't dare show your face here again!" the woman lashed. "Of all the underhanded, sneaky tricks—why, in all my life I—"

"Lady, lady," Kane growled, "you're not slumming now." With what dignity he could muster, he went past her and out.

THE BRIGHT red folder was a menu, and was something special. The menu you usually got in Wop Willy's was a greasy typewritten sheet covered with fly-tracks as big as moose-prints. This was different.

Kane held it against the wheel of his car and studied it. It was Wednesday's menu. Wednesday had been Wop Willy's eleventh anniversary. Wop Willy's was a dump on a North End side street.

Kane slipped a pint bottle of rye from the glove-compartment and shut his eyes while the whiskey gurgled down his throat. He looked at the last inch in the bottle and decided to save it, decided not to and killed it. He felt better. He thought of Mrs. Singsen and laughed, and that was a step in the right direction.

He drove downtown to the North End, parked his car and went into Wop Willy's where among other things you could buy the best spaghetti and meatballs in town.

A waiter smiled and said, "This way, Mr. Kane," and the checkroom girl smiled, too. Kane shook his head and said, "Willy." He went upstairs. He went along a hall up there, past the men's room to a door marked private, and knocked. A pleasant, cultured voice told him to come in.

Willy Sakarian was not a wop, he was a Greek with his B.A. from Harvard, but this was a wop district and Willy knew his business. He was small and swarthy, with beautiful teeth and beautiful blue eyes. He had the build of a sixteen-year-old girl, a handclasp gentle and soothing.

Willy had a gold mine here. He served cheap, noisy entertainment and the city's finest food. He lured the wealth that went slumming. He was grateful to Kane for a lot of ideas that had panned out and made him more money.

"You been reading the papers, Willy?" Kane asked him.

Willy nodded. As though by magic, a fifth of Scotch, a syphon of soda and two gleaming glasses appeared on his desk. He said while pouring: "The Andertons were here Wednesday night, Kane, with another couple. They came about eleven, left at one. Anderton himself was ugly drunk." He pushed a drink toward Kane's hand. "But if you hope I can tell you why they wound up the way they did, with that girl playing table tennis in a bathing suit—I can't."

"I was hoping you could."

"One thing did happen. Dolores Anderton had a drink with one of the boys in my band. I didn't like it, but it was her idea and what could I do? Her husband didn't like it, either. He never took his eyes off them. When she went back to her own table, he wouldn't speak to her. I was watching, I saw it. Soon after that, they left."

Kane rolled the Scotch under his tongue. His headache was gone and he was thinking better. "You speak to the boy in your band afterward?"

Willy shrugged. "Why should I?"

"Is he here now?"

Willy shook his head.

"Well," Kane said, "it may be nothing, but I got to start somewhere, and fast! Who is he?"

"Fred Patten. Nice kid, about twenty-five. He was down on his luck and asked for a job, three-four months ago. Said he could sing. I let him sing and never even heard him, he was so eloquent on the piano. He lives—" Willy pulled out a desk drawer and dipped into a neat row of file-cards—"at eighty Morris Street. No phone. Used to be a struggling artist. But wait a minute, Kane." Willy put down his drink, scowling. "Something else happened."

"Ah!"

"The Anderton woman used to be a model. You knew that, of course."

"I knew."

"Well, Carl Dolce was here Wednesday night, too. Carl Dolce, the photographer. She talked to him, and Anderton didn't like *that*."

"Hmm," Kane said. He stood up. "I'll look into that, Willy. Has Moroni been around here?"

"Not yet."

"You encourage me," Kane muttered. He had another drink, a quick one, standing, and put a hand on Willy's shoulder. "Thanks, pal. The more I know you, the better I hate Yale." He thought that was a dumb crack, but Willy found it funny and was still grinning when Kane closed the door.

CARL DOLCE did covers for the magazines. Photographs of beautiful girls skiing, beautiful girls eating grapefruit, beautiful girls looking beautiful. He was a furtive, pop-eyed little man of unguessable age, with a prodigious reputation. His studio was the last word.

Kane hiked into the chrome and plastic reception-room and leaned on the desk. He said to the pale young man there: "Like to see Mr. Dolce. Police business." That was cutting the corners pretty close, but Carl Dolce was known to be a difficult man to get close to, and time was precious.

The pale young man shook his head. He said Mr. Dolce was not in. He said he didn't know when Mr. Dolce would be in. He talked with a slight lisp and was very arty.

"Tell you what I want, then," Kane scowled. "Some of those pictures Dolce took of Dolores Trent before she was married."

The young man was perturbed. "I'm sorry, sir, but Mr. Dolce took all those pictures out of the files yesterday afternoon and—" He pulled up short. His face crimsoned and he seemed angry with himself. "You'll have to see Mr. Dolce," he said curtly, dropping the arty accents.

Kane said, "Sure." His eyes had a glitter in them and he wore a wolfish smile. "Just where does Dolce live?"

The young man glared, eloquently silent.

"O.K.," Kane said. He leaned across the desk and slid a phone book toward him, opened it and found the name without any trouble. "Carl Dolce," he read aloud, "three-four-one Riverway.... Thanks, pal."

He didn't ask the pale young man if Moroni had been around. He was reasonably sure that Moroni hadn't, and felt for the first time that he might have at least a Chinaman's chance of crossing the finish line first.

"We're in the stretch, fella," he told himself. "It's time to go all out!"

He drove hard out to Riverway. Three-four-one was a horseshoe-shaped apartment house of red brick and ivy, old and ornate. The apartment number was thirty-one, which meant third floor front. There was no response to Kane's steady pressure on the bell.

He tried the foyer door and it was unlocked, and his leather heels beat a tattoo on the tile floor to the elevator. So Carl Dolce had cleaned Dolores out of the files, had he? This was a lead. It was so hot it smoked.

But the door of Dolce's apartment was locked, and persistent knocking brought no answer. Kane curled his lips around an oath. He folded his fist around the knob and shook it savagely, swore again and went down the stairs. "If I were Moroni," he muttered, "the guy would be sitting on the steps waiting for me."

He kicked a long-handled broom leaning against the wall, and it fell with a clatter, and a voice in the hall said petulantly, "Hey!"

"Ah," Kane said, braking himself. "The janitor!"

The fellow was big enough to be two janitors, and had a face as empty of guile as a goldfish bowl. Kane picked up the broom and carefully replaced it. "You're just the man can help me," Kane declared.

"Huh?"

"I'm looking for Carl Dolce. It's important."

"Him," the janitor said. He rolled his eyes and gazed at the ceiling. "Him! You think I know where he is?"

"Well, you work here."

"Listen," the janitor said. He came closer and lowered his voice to a chummy halftone. "When I try to find him, he is never here. Yesterday I go up to his apartment no less than twenty times, to give a registered letter I sign for. I could leave it in his mailbox, sure, but he is funny, sometimes he does not look in his mailbox for days at a time. So all right. I go up there twenty times. I don't catch him. So then, at half past two o'clock this morning, when I am fast asleep, he knocks at my door downstairs to ask me will I burn some rubbish for him in the incinerator!"

Kane let his breath out slowly. "A very queer duck," he agreed, "And did you burn the rubbish?"

"The rubbish he gives me at half past two o'clock in the morning? No, not yet."

"Ah," Kane said. His hand slipped into his pocket, hungrily, and then he remembered, with a pang, that he had spent his last dollar in Limpy's. Liquor, he decided ruefully, would be the ruin of him yet. "Friend," he said, his own voice confidential and cozy, "do you know why Mr. Carl Dolce sneaked down to your door at that unearthly hour?"

"Huh?"

"Yuh didn't peek at that rubbish, hey?"

"It was tied up," the janitor scowled.

"So! It was tied up. And you didn't untie it! Look, friend." Kane leaned closer, hypnotically staring. "You and I, we'll have a peek at that package, right now!" His leer spoke volumes. "Mr. Dolce is a photographer, friend, and photographers take some very interesting pictures!"

The janitor opened his eyes very wide. Kane had a mental picture of him peering furtively into a penny-arcade peep box, turning the crank very slowly to make his nickel last longer. They went downstairs. The big fellow plucked a package from the incinerator and stared at it.

"You have to open it," Kane reminded him.

"Y-you open it!"

"Sure," Kane grinned. He snapped the string and peeled off layers of newspaper. A very careless fellow, Mr. Carl Dolce. The pictures were intact, not even ripped through once.

There were at least two dozen of them and they were warm. Kane pawed through them, one by one—photographs of Dolores Trent in abbreviated bathing suits, of Dolores Trent in sport clothes and evening gowns. Of Dolores Trent in nothing. Very alluring, very seductive, with the stamp of art upon them. Especially upon those of Dolores Trent in nothing.

Kane shoved the pictures into his pocket and warped a scowl across his face. A very severe scowl. He glared at the janitor, who looked back at him puzzled and uneasy.

"These," declared Kane severely, "are not for the public eye. I'll take them with me. Official business," he added, clearing his throat. "The word, friend, is mum."

He went upstairs and out, the janitor too awed to stop him. He wondered how to go about getting hold of Carl Dolce, and decided to return to the apartment every hour until his efforts produced results. This was one lead Moroni was not likely to stumble upon. Therefore he had nothing to fear on that score.

Meanwhile, a few words with that piano-player might be of value.

MORRIS STREET is an odd little thoroughfare in the heart of the old business district. It is a dead-end lane of tenements. It is a dislocated wing of the red-light sector, surrounded by aged, dignified, once pretentious office buildings. Number eighty was a three-decker tenement.

There was a barroom next door.

Kane counted the loose change in his pocket and found he had eighteen cents. He hiked into the barroom and drank three nickel beers, placed the remaining three pennies in a pile on the bar and haughtily walked out, leaving them there. He climbed the aged steps of number eighty.

The tenants' names were penciled under the bells beside the door, and the name of the man he sought was under the topmost bell. Kane climbed to the third floor and was thirsty again. He knocked. The impact of his fist swung the door open.

He leaned over the sill and knocked again, on the open door, and got no answer. He shrugged and walked in.

No one challenged him.

There were three rooms and they were in keeping with the house itself, gloomy and gray. Yet they had a certain personality. This was supplied, Kane realized, by the pictures on the walls, by a colorful hand-painted spread that was thrown over the studio couch. He was puzzled.

He remembered Wop Willy's words to the effect that Fred Patten was a struggling artist, and that explained it. The atmosphere was vaguely arty. But Fred Patten was not here.

The place smelled of cigar-smoke that had a familiar, choking reek. A sodden cigar-end lay on the edge of a table. Kane went back to the door and peered at the lock and realized why the door had opened when he knocked. The lock was broken.

"Moroni's been here," Kane decided. It was only a guess, but the cigar smell was strong, and Moroni was famous for his grisly taste in tobacco.

He looked around. On the table lay a Southern Air Lines folder designed to lure winter-weary northerners to the paradise isles of the West Indies. A sunburned female rode a surfboard on its cover. Inside, on the margin, someone had done some figuring with a pencil.

It seemed unimportant. Everything else in the place seemed unimportant. Kane tired of the arty atmosphere and went out. He was so thirsty that his throat made small whistling sounds when he breathed, but his pockets were empty and his credit in this part of town was not tall enough to reach the suds on a glass of beer, even.

He walked around the corner into Nason Street and hiked across to the Goodwin Building.

It had been quite a structure in its day. Now it was occupied by a couple of sign painters, a rubber stamp manufacturer, a rug repair plant and Jerry Verall's Table Tennis Parlors. The signs outside told him this. Another sign said, Studio *space for rent.* Kane climbed the broad wooden stairs on which the body of Anderton had been discovered. Chalk-marks made by the cops were still in evidence. He tried the door of the table tennis parlors and found it locked.

He was disappointed. The idea of a gorgeous girl in a white bathing suit playing ping-pong at midnight in the middle of winter still intrigued him. The cops, he thought glumly, were always keeping him out of places he wanted to go. He scowled at the lettering on the door.

It read: *City Table Tennis Center. Jerry Verall, Prop. Registered T.T.A.*

"Hey!" Kane said softly, "Hey!"

HE LEFT the building and hiked down the street to a drug store, thumbed through a telephone book and found the name and home phone number of Jerry Verall. The name itself had a familiar ring. He supposed he'd seen it on the sports pages, because table tennis was an up-and-coming pastime, getting a lot of publicity. He stepped into the booth and remembered again, ruefully, that he was broke.

"Brother," Kane said soberly to the clerk, "I find it necessary to make a few phone calls. I have no nickels. I have nothing to change into nickels. But I have a watch, a very fine watch. You take the watch. You lend me three or four nickels with which to make phone calls. Can do?"

The clerk peered at the watch. He turned it over and read the engraving on the white gold case. "To Lieutenant Detective Peter Kane, for outstanding service. B.P.D."

"Gee!" the clerk said.

Kane made his phone calls. Three of them—the last to Willy Sakarian. He grinned at the clerk and walked out, as contented as though he had just wrapped himself around a fifth of the finest Scotch. He walked back to his car and drove to Wop Willy's, in the North End. It was now half past eight, and dark.

Kane went into Wop Willy's by way of the rear door, which was open. The door was open because Willy Sakarian had promised to open it. Kane climbed the stairs, went along past the men's room and entered Willy's office.

The slender Greek stared at him without smiling and said, shaking his head: "I'm sorry, fella. Moroni's here."

Those three nickel beers turned over in Kane's stomach. No other part of him moved except his fists. They curled into hard, white lumps.

"Five minutes after you phoned, Kane, the big slug walked in. He's downstairs with a couple of his men."

"Waiting?" Kane muttered.

"Waiting."

Kane walked the floor of Willy's office. He was sore now. He was sore with himself for having muffed the golden opportunity, sore with the croupier of his luck for having led him to believe he was winning. Losing was tough. Losing on the last throw of the dice was tougher. Losing when the future of an honest, sober, trusting pal like Moe Finch depended on you—when the swellest girl in the world had honored you with her faith—losing then was a numbing shock that twisted something deep inside you.

Kane felt the barb in that sensitive part of him that was never touched by the quantities of liquor he consumed. His lean face lost color and his eyes glittered. "Listen, Willy," he said. "You're doing me a favor!"

Willy listened. He didn't like it, and shook his head, scowling. He said: "Moroni will eat you up, Kane."

"You do what I say!"

"You want me to? You're sure of it?"

Kane pushed him toward the door.

Willy Sakarian went out, shaking his head. The door closed behind him and Kane went to work, hauling out the drawers of the desk, tossing papers around. In three minutes Kane had made a lot of progress. The office was a shambles, and he was snorting through the mess like a bull in a crystal-shop.

A snarling, guttural voice bellowed from the doorway, "All right, you! Hold it!" and Kane turned to see Moroni holding a gun on him.

Willy Sakarian was there at Moroni's elbow, and Willy was wringing his hands hysterically. "You see?" he wailed. "You see what he's done? He charged in on me and ordered me around! He said he was the police!"

"So you're the police now, Kane," Moroni snarled. He paced into the room, his big face oozing a leer of triumph. "This time, smart guy, you've gone too far!"

KANE STOOD stiff, defiantly glaring. He hoped the act was good because it was his last throw of the dice, his last chance. He didn't have to fake the trembling of his hands—that was genuine. Other things were genuine too. His disdain for the big dick who ploughed toward him. His determination to take a poke at that leering face, no matter what it cost.

He swung, and Moroni looked surprised. You had to belt that monkey-map more than once to change its shape. It was tough as granite. Kane swung again, awkwardly, and was knocked sprawling by an elbow to the side of his head.

He picked himself up, shook his head. His eyes were wild and he looked drunk, but at this stage of the proceedings he was more sober than he had been in weeks. He breathed hard and noisily, his hair hung in his eyes, but he was sober.

He said savagely: "You can afford to be tough, Moroni. You and your bodyguard!"

"Sure," Moroni sneered. He swung a fist and Kane drunkenly swayed away from it, in slow motion. Kane fell over a wastebasket and landed in a heap against the legs of the desk. Papers spilled out of his coat pocket.

Not papers. Photographs.

Moroni's eyes bugged. He pounced with surprising agility for one so big. He scooped up the pictures and pawed through them, the two cops crowding closer to peer over his shoulders. Willy Sakarian stood in the doorway, quiet now, sadly gazing at Kane.

Moroni stared at the undraped Dolores Trent and greed-ily sucked his lips. He said: "Well, well, Kane. You've been holding out on me!"

"You go to hell!" Kane snarled.

"Such language, Kane. Where did these come from?"

"Try and find out!"

Moroni pocketed the pictures and favored Kane with a thoughtful stare. "You shouldn't fight cops, Kane. People who fight cops get beat up all to hell. Legally, too." He grinned at his two henchmen. "You guys saw Kane slug me, didn't you?"

They nodded. Kane got to his feet and backed against the wall, breathing hard.

The two cops moved in on him with nightsticks, and Moroni said ominously: "I have seen guys go to the hos-pital for getting rough with the cops, Kane. They suffer from the damndest things, too—fractured skulls, busted ribs, kidney trouble—it's awful. But those pictures are hot. Where'd you get 'em?"

"You go to hell!"

The cops went to work on him, and there was very little Kane could do about it. He couldn't slug back, that would have left his head wide open to the rain of nightsticks. Kane crouched with his head under his arms, braced himself.

In the doorway, Willy Sakarian covered his beautiful blue eyes with his hands and uttered little moaning sounds.

Kane went to his knees, cursing. He called Moroni every name on the roster. He invented new names and snarled those. His arms felt like telephone poles, and he spat blood.

"The pictures, Kane," Moroni said patiently. "I want to know where they came from."

Kane rolled to the floor and glared up at him. He'd had enough. He'd put up a show, made it look good—more would be too much. "Carl Dolce took them," he groaned. "She used to work for him."

"That's better!"

"He was trying to destroy them. I got them away from him."

Moroni's leer was wolfish. He sucked air through his teeth, looked down at Kane and rubbed his big hands. "So why did you come barging in here to tear Willy's office apart?" he demanded.

"I had to know how hard-pressed Dolce was for dough. He owns a slice of this place. His papers are here."

Moroni's scowl was enormous. "Carl Dolce owns a piece of this dump? That's news to me, Kane!"

"A lot of things are news to you," Kane muttered, shielding his face.

Moroni could afford to take that lightly, and did. He grinned. "Go right ahead and snoop, Kane," he said. "Me, I'm a cop. I'll get my information from Dolce himself—the easy way." He patted the pocket that held the photographs. "Be good, Kane. I could be tough with you for all this, but I never kick a man that's down. Seldom, anyway." He put his heel against the end of Kane's tail, and shoved. "So long, sucker!"

Kane slowly stood up. He was a mess. His arms ached like ulcerated teeth and his head throbbed. He swayed to the desk and leaned there, and stared at Willy.

"You better go downstairs, Willy, and keep an eye open," he said.

Willy nodded. He went out.

Kane said softly, under his breath, "So long, Moroni!" and reached for the telephone.

IT WAS a tense little gathering. Kelley of the *Post* was there, languidly filing his fingernails. Murchison of the *Telegram* perched on a corner of Moe Finch's desk and asked innumerable questions to which no one else paid any attention. Sisson and McArdle, veteran news-hounds from the city's other two papers, leaned forward on their chairs and tossed pennies against the wall.

Moe Finch kept his mouth shut and tried to look wise, which was not easy because Moe Finch had a face as wide-open and guileless as his heart.

The door opened and Kane walked in.

Kane was not alone. With him was a dark-haired, good-looking young man who was so scared it was pathetic. Kane had a hand on the young man's elbow, and after marching him across the threshold and pushing the door shut, Kane gave the young man a shove, toward Moe Finch's desk.

"You were right, Captain," Kane said. "Here he is."

Moe Finch looked at the young man. He looked at Kane. Not knowing what else to say, he said, "Ah!"

"Shall I tell the boys about it, Captain?" Kane murmured.

"Do," said Moe Finch.

Kane leaned against the desk. "Well, gentlemen." He paused to push his fingers through his hair. "Would one of you guys have a drink on you?"

One of them had, and Kane put a large dent in the contents of a pint of bottle. It was newspaperman's rye. It hit his stomach and exploded, and he clung to the desk for support. But when the first cruel dizziness had passed, he felt tons better.

He began over again. "Gentlemen, there were certain aspects to this case that led Moe—that led Captain Finch to some definite conclusions. First, Dolores Trent was wearing a bathing suit and was slain in a table tennis parlor at midnight. You boys made a lot of that, because it was unusual, it bordered on the fantastic. There could be only one explanation for it."

The newsmen held their collective breaths.

"Captain Finch figured out the reason for it," Kane said, leering. "But that wasn't enough. It didn't tell him who was responsible for the girl's presence in the table tennis parlors at that hour. So...." He rubbed his tongue with the back of his hand and gazed soulfully at the man with the pint. The pint was produced again, and Kane put a second large dent in it. "Bad cold," he said. After corking the bottle he placed it on the desk.

"So at Captain's Finch's suggestion I found out from one Jerry Verall, head of the local T.T.A., the names of all those who have keys to the table tennis place. Sure enough, one of them—this lad here, Fred Patten—was an artist."

The newsmen stared at Fred Patten. The young man shuddered, clung to the desk with both hands.

"Investigation revealed," Kane continued, well-oiled now and thoroughly enjoying himself, "that Dolores Trent used to be very fond of this boy here. Last Wednesday night, while slumming with her husband and another couple, she had a chat with him at Wop Willy's. Investigation also revealed, gentlemen, a Southern Air Lines brochure in Mr. Patten's lodgings. The missing link!"

It made sense to no one but Kane. Even the eyes of Moe Finch were filled with question-marks. But the newsmen were too intent upon Kane to be watching Moe Finch.

"At Captain Finch's direction," Kane declared, "I telephoned Southern Air Lines and talked to their advertising department. Sure enough, they had commissioned our struggling young artist, Mr. Patten, to paint a picture for them. What kind of picture, gentlemen? Why, one with glamor! One with romance! What else but a picture of a lovely young woman in a very yummy bathing suit, playing table tennis against a background of southern sun and palm trees!"

The gentlemen of the press needed no more. As one, they took in air. As one, they wolfed at Fred Patten, backed him into a corner. Kane elbowed them aside and held up a hand.

"I can tell it much more simply than he can, gentlemen. Much more briefly. Mr. Patten was given the assignment to paint the picture we've been talking about. Wednesday night, when Dolores Trent slummed at Wop Willy's, he told her about it. They'd been fond of each other, those two. Miss Trent knew all about Patten's ambitions to be an artist. She offered to pose for his picture—to meet him later, if she could dodge her drunken husband.

"She did meet him. But her husband was not as dumb as she thought. He was wise. He followed her. And now, Patten, if you'd tell the boys what happened...."

THE YOUNG man raised a sweat-drenched face and tried to look at the half-circle of wolves that hemmed him in. He was a very sick young man, numb with terror. But there was something clean and decent and desperate about him that softened the newsmen's faces even as they crowded him.

"She—she was wearing the bathing suit under her dress," he said. "We went over to Jerry Verall's place and she started to undress. There was nothing wrong about it. Some artists can fake a picture but I can't. I have to have a model. But he—her husband—rushed in while she was undressing. He was drunk and he had a gun."

Patten looked at his feet and swallowed a sob that was not for the benefit of the newsmen. "He called her a—he called her names, and shot her. I went crazy then. I grabbed him and we wrestled all over the place, and the gun went off and he fell. He wasn't dead. I suppose he was fatally wounded, but I didn't know. I just knew *she* was dead, and I was scared. I took the gun and ran. After I left, he must have crawled out and fallen down the stairs."

"And the gun?" said Kelley of the *Post*. "Where's that?"

"I threw it in the river."

The newsmen took notes furiously. Their pencils raced, and made a noise like hens scratching in a barnyard. Peter Kane plucked the almost empty pint off the desk, gazed owlishly at Moe Finch, and killed it.

Murchison, of the *Telegram*, said: "I don't get your angle in this, Kane. You're not a cop any more. How come?"

"Captain Finch," Kane said solemnly, "is handicapped around here. He has to contend with the bullheaded blunderings of Moroni, and gets damned little cooperation. He asked me, as a favor, to do the roadwork for him. I'm unimportant. You can leave my name out of it."

"That right, Captain?"

"Why—ah—suit yourself," Moe Finch said.

"What do you think this kid will get, Captain?"

Kane answered that. He stepped up to Fred Patten and put a fatherly hand on the young man's arm. "I think he'll get a damned good lawyer," Kane said, "and if you boys are halfway human, you can win him the public's sympathy. He's a good kid and—"

There was a commotion in the hall. The door clattered open and into that room full of well-fed newspapermen surged Moroni. Moroni, the I Am.

The newsmen blocked Moroni's view of Kane, of Fred Patten. The Brain saw only Moe Finch and the press. He dragged a small, wasplike man into the room with him, flung the man forward. He and the man were handcuffed together.

"Boys," he said, flushed with pride, "take a good look at this guy! His name is Carl Dolce. You're looking at the man who murdered Dolores Trent!"

The silence was ear-splitting, but Moroni paid no attention. "Stick around, boys," he said, "and watch me slap a confession out of this guy!"

Carl Dolce was terrified. He squirmed against the desk and looked beseechingly at Moe Finch, rolled his large round eyes at the newsmen. "It isn't true!" he wailed. "Just because I got rid of some pictures that were in my files—I tell you it isn't true! I didn't have a thing to do with it! I just didn't want to have those pictures around if anyone questioned me, after what happened. Oh my God, I—"

"Shut up!" Moroni snarled. "I'll do the talking!"

Kelley of the *Post* snickered. Moroni gaped at him. The *Telegram's* Mr. Murchison said, "Dear, dear, such a commotion!" in a voice as mocking as an echo. Moroni widened his eyes and looked confused.

With Kelley in the lead, the press filed past Moroni to the door. He yelled at them and they paid no attention. He turned red, waved his arm. The press walked out.

On the verge of apoplexy, Moroni swung on Moe Finch for an explanation, and saw Kane. He stopped short. Understanding rushed into his eyes, and up his fat neck rolled a wave of crimson.

"You!" Moroni choked.

"Me," Kane leered. "And this, Moroni, is Fred Patten. Fred's already confessed. And I wouldn't get rough with Fred if I were you, Moroni. The newspaper lads definitely won't like it." He plucked the empty pint off Moe Finch's desk, drained the last amber drop of its contents onto his tongue.

Moroni, red to the roots of his hair, unlocked the manacle that linked him to Carl Dolce. He clenched his fists and blocked Kane's path to the door.

"You think so?" Kane said gently. "It won't be as easy as last time, fella. I only take a beating like that when there's a need for it."

Moroni faltered. Kane leered at him, plucked the empty bottle off the desk and tenderly placed it in Moroni's hand. "You look," Kane said, "as if you need a drink. Have one, pal, on me."

THE DEAD DON'T SWIM

SHAMUS PETER KANE IS ONLY
SLIGHTLY SQUIFFED AS HE SAILS
INTO THE CASE OF THE MISSING
RADIO OPERATOR WHO WENT FOR
A SWIM—BUT HE'S THREE SHEETS
IN THE WIND BY THE TIME HE
FISHES HIM OUT—TO THE GLORY
OF THE FBI AND THE CHAGRIN OF
LIEUT. MORONI THE MAGNIFICENT.

THE SIGN read *POSITIVELY NO ADMIT-TANCE!* and that was a laugh, because anyone with tenacity enough to find this place would never be scared into retreat by a placard. Kane read the sign from his car, got out and went up to the building.

The place had been hacked out of the woods, and a road gouged into it. It consisted of one flatroofed building and two tall radio towers that poked their points to heaven. It had been built here, Kane supposed, because land was cheap. Or for complicated reasons having to do with atmospheric conditions. Or something.

He knocked, and got no answer. He turned the knob and walked in.

Nine tenths of the building was taken up by hulks of machinery set on a concrete floor. The other tenth was a glassed-in office where a man wearing earphones sat at a desk. The man had a round, pink face that looked freshly scrubbed. He looked up. He was bald. Dits and dahs crackled through the phones, and with his gaze on Kane he swerved around to the typewriter beside his chair, rolled in an oblong of yellow paper and began tapping the keys. Every few seconds he leaned across the desk to make a few dots and dashes of his own. It was quite a game, Kane decided, watching from the office doorway.

This ended, and the fellow pushed the phones back on his gleaming head. His widened eyes said: "What is it?" His scowl said: "It better be good, with you barging in here like this!" His lips said nothing at all. They were pretty pink lips that belonged on a girl.

"You're George Bricklin," Kane said. "I'm Kane, private investigator, working on the Maitland affair."

"Investigator? You mean private detective?"

"That's right."

"Stand away from the door," he
said and blasted the lock.

Bricklin lit a cigarette. "Well?" he said. Visitors, Kane gathered, really weren't welcome.

"Do you always talk with those things glued to your head?" Kane asked pleasantly. "Or could you remove them for a while?"

"I wear them. It happens to be my job."

"Oh," Kane said. "I understand. Messages from ships at sea and all that." He sat down. A teletype machine crowded him on one side, a bulletin board covered with charts and maps on the other. "Well, my job is to find Paul Maitland. You being his boss I hoped you might be of some help."

Bricklin hooked his heels on a rung of his chair. He really was a little guy, five feet short. He had a scowl, though, that belonged on a six-footer with sinus trouble. "I'm fed up with this Maitland business!" he growled.

"So?"

"First the police, then the insurance people, now you! What the hell am I running here—a radio marine station or an autopsy?"

Nasty, Kane decided. Very nasty. "All I want, friend, is a word or two. It seems Maitland was working on some sort of gadget—"

"I don't know what he was doing, and I don't care!"

"It also seems he was having wife trouble," Kane went on, ignoring the outburst. "According to the papers, you said he'd been morose and moody for some time, that he hardly spoke to you when you showed up to relieve him that night. Trouble is, most of that stuff in the papers was supplied by Mr. Moroni, the city's ace sleuth, and Mr. Moroni is apt to be a little loose-lipped at times, for the sake of publicity."

"The papers," Bricklin declared tersely, "had it right."

"M'm. I'm surprised. Did you know Maitland was going for a ride that night?"

"No."

"He just went, hey? You three fellows live in a farmhouse up the road, don't you?"

"Yes."

"I suppose it gets kinds of boring at times."

"Maitland," said the little bald man, "was bored all the time. That was none of my business. My job is to see that schedules are kept and the work done. If a man wants to go riding at midnight, that's his own affair." His phones crackled. He slewed about in his chair to work the bug. Kane debated the wisdom of further probing.

THIS PARTICULAR ship, if ship it was, had a lot of traffic. After ten minutes of watching Bricklin's amazingly agile movements and listening to the static-blurred rattle of code, Kane sighed and reached for the pint in his pocket. He took a generous bite out of it and felt better. He decided suddenly that, what the hell, Bricklin was too cagy to let slip any information anyway. He stood up.

A car stopped outside and Kane heard its door slam. He stood still. He took one look at the big man who strode into the station—one long, unhappy look at the red neck bulging above the pink-and-white striped shirt, at the bulldog features and hostile mouth. "Oh-oh," Kane said softly, and sat down again.

Moroni loomed over him. Moroni the Magnificent. Moroni the Great Brain, the publicity hound, the poison in Kane's ivy.

"So, Kane! I rush out here to warn Bricklin about you, and you're here already!"

Kane stared at the red face and voiced a sigh. "Jed Clay's been talking to you, I see." That, Kane realized, was understandable and cast no reflections on Jed Clay, city editor of the *Post*, who was a smart man looking after his own interests.

With Moe Finch on the way out and Moroni on the way up, it was to Clay's advantage to play both ends against the middle.

But Moroni was genuinely sore this time. No horsing. The big dick's eyes held a dangerous glitter as he swung on Bricklin. "Has Kane been annoying you?" he snapped.

"Everybody annoys me," Bricklin grumbled.

"He tell you he was the police, or anything like that?"

"No, he didn't say that."

"I'm surprised," Moroni snarled. "And disappointed." He glared at Kane again. "You make one little slip this time, Kane, and all the Moe Finches in the world won't grease you out of it! You hear?"

"My ears are ringing."

"I'll wring your neck!"

"But, my dear man," Kane murmured, "I'm only doing my duty as a citizen. You yourself planted the seeds of thought in my troubled mind. Didn't you tell the papers this was an espionage case?"

"I'm telling you to keep out of it!"

"Surely my memory is not at fault, Mr. Moroni," Kane said. "Didn't you tell the papers that the men out here— Payne and Maitland and Bricklin—were natural prey for foreign agents, with their intimate knowledge of the position of ships at sea," and all that? It seems to me I read—"

"I refuted all that, Kane, and you damn well know it! This case is closed!"

"But poor Mr. Maitland is still missing," Kane murmured. He stood up. "Ah, well, Mr. Moroni, perhaps I'm wrong. Time alone will tell." His smile was annoyingly unctuous. "Farewell, gentlemen." He walked out to his car and got in, and with a languid wave of his hand, drove away. As usual, Peter Kane was not quite sober.

He drove along the rutted road a quarter mile and stopped at the farmhouse in which Bricklin and the other radio men maintained quarters. The radio station was something new; accommodations for the men were still primitive. Kane hauled a newspaper clipping out and studied a diagram of it—a diagram of Paul Maitland's last ride. He drove half a mile more, turned left at an intersection.

This road snaked through the woods and emerged suddenly in a waste of sand dunes. The waters of the Atlantic rolled sullenly against a mile-long strip of empty beach, under a leaden sky.

It was here, according to the papers, that Paul Maitland's car had been found, with an unopened bottle of hydrate of chloral crystals in the glove compartment. The glove compartment was locked, the key in Maitland's clothes. Therefore he must have put the poison there himself.

His clothes had been found down there in the dunes. According to the eminent Mr. Moroni, only one conclusion was tenable: Paul Maitland had removed his clothes and deliberately swum out to his death. The presence of the poison in the glove compartment indicated a contemplation of suicide by other means, then a sudden decision to simplify the method. The motive, Moroni said, was marital trouble.

To be sure, the Great Brain had first talked of foreign agents, kidnaping, espionage and so forth, but after thus building up copy for the papers, he had backtracked gracefully to the more simple solution.

Kane gazed at all that ocean and shuddered. He disliked water. He felt the need of a drink and had one, but it helped matters only slightly. This, he decided ruefully, was a sad and screwy case.

IN THE first place, it was Moroni's case from start to finish. Moroni had built it up out of nothing. In the words of Moe Finch's lovely and worried wife, Anne, it was just another Moroni attempt to publicize himself into Moe's job.

Kane had been over that angle with her. After reading the headlines until they sickened him, he called at the Finch apartment and demanded belligerently to know why he hadn't been sent for. "Damn it, pal! You know what's happening! Why wasn't I asked to stop it?"

Lovely in a red satin housecoat, Anne bit her lip. "I wanted to, Peter, but Moe—well, you know how he feels." For no good reason, the wall above the radio became a loadstone for her gaze. "You've helped him out so often. It can't go on, he says."

"Why doesn't Moe take some first-grade lessons in showmanship, and play Moroni's own game?"

"You know Moe."

Kane knew Moe. In the world of Moe Finch, just two things existed: his wife and his job. He had no time to buy drinks for the newsboys.

"Besides," Anne said wearily, "there's nothing *to* this case, Peter. Nothing you could do, even if Moe would have it."

"The guy is still missing."

"If that means anything."

"It could," Kane had insisted, helping himself to a drink from Moe Finch's little bar. "It could, couldn't it?" He had loved this girl once. He supposed he still did. Liquor and his hell-with-it outlook had licked him, and she had married big-hearted, dependable Moe Finch on the rebound. Kane couldn't see Moe Finch ruined without at least trying to stop it.

And then, of course, there was the Alma Payne angle. With Moroni riding his hand-made headlines, Alma Payne had paid Kane a visit in his Beacon Agency office. She was a nice girl. She was the wife of Dave Payne, an operator at the station. She didn't believe Paul Maitland had committed suicide.

"The papers, the police, and especially that man Moroni are all wrong!" she'd insisted.

She showed Kane a letter. It was typed on cheap yellow paper and read: "DEAR ALMA: I'M TOLD MY BETTER HALF IS PLAYING AROUND AGAIN— THIS TIME WITH SOME FELLOW IN THE APARTMENT UNDER YOU. WILL YOU LET ME KNOW THE SORDID DETAILS? THEY MAY COME IN HANDY WHEN I DECIDE, AS EVEN- TUALLY I MUST, THAT ENUF'S ENUF. REGARDS, PAUL."

He'd written it while on watch at the radio marine station, where the machines had only capital letters. And on the back of it were pencil scratches that looked to Kane like the doodlings of an inebriate. And a notation: "A.R. Co. 222 E. Layland." Kane had not as yet looked into this.

"He was probably working on some new invention," Alma Payne declared, "and just happened to write me on a piece of scratch paper. Paul is forever inventing something.

He's smart. Both Bricklin and my husband, Dave, are secretly jealous of his ability."

"And this wife of his who plays around—you and she share an apartment in town here, because there are no accommodations out there for women?"

"That's right. Yes."

"Does she play around?"

"Yes, she does."

"Who with?"

"Well, her latest is a man named Lett. Leo Lett."

That was what did it. The name Leo Lett. After shutting the door on her, Kane had lifted a fifth of Scotch out of his desk drawer, got middling drunk and thought about it. And decided, with typical Kane hot-headedness, to go all out, go overboard.

HE SWAYED over the telephone and dialed the number one used when desirous of speaking personally, and privately, with the grizzled city editor of the *Post,* Jed Clay.

"My friend," said Kane, swaying, "this is Peter the Kane, of the Beacon. I have news." He paused, listened to the reply, and murmured, "Dear, dear!" Then he plunged.

"About the Maitland case, friend," Kane said, "and the blatant publicity being dished out in behalf of the magnificent Mr. Moroni. Pull in your horns. The case is far from solved, friend, and Mr. Moroni far from knowing the all of what happened. The headlines will come later."

Jed Clay said suspiciously: "What the hell are you up to, Kane? You feuding with Moroni again?"

"I just want you to be geared," Kane said solemnly, "for the explosion. There *will* be an explosion. Take my word for it. Mr. Moroni may be blown up in it."

He hung up in the midst of Jed Clay's reply. He stared at the phone and was suddenly sober. He took a quick drink and wiped sweat from his face. "God help the Beacon Agency," Kane muttered, "if this is a dud!"

Now he stared at all that ocean, that mean, gray, ominous ocean into which Paul Maitland was supposed to have swum to a watery grave. And presently Kane became aware of a lank shape walking slowly along the beach.

About the same time, the lank shape became aware of Kane.

The fellow halted, peered at Kane's car. He came on again. He trudged through the sand and put a hand on the car door. "Nasty way to commit suicide, wasn't it?" he observed pleasantly. "You've read the papers, I suppose."

"Of course," Kane said. He wondered if the lank one was as guileless as his smile, and didn't think so. The gray eyes in that thin face were shrewd. The nonchalant attitude was a mite too obvious.

"Know this fellow Maitland, did you?" the man asked.

"He was a good friend of mine," Kane said. You opened the window and in flew info. Perhaps. It was worth a try.

"Well, say! That is something! Do you honestly believe he committed suicide, as the papers maintain?"

"Do you?" Kane asked.

"Why, I don't know. I suppose the police wouldn't make such a statement unless… but *you* should have an opinion on the matter, if you knew him well."

"I'll tell you," Kane said. "I think there's something screwy about this whole business. I'd look into it, too, if it weren't that I'd surely be questioned by the police and put to a lot of inconvenience. In my opinion, friend, Paul Maitland is no more dead than you are. No, sir. I think—"

He pulled up short and stared at the top of the man's head.

"There I go, shooting my mouth off again. Never know when to keep it buttoned."

The thin man underwent a slow but definite metamorphosis, shedding his nonchalance. He frowned. "My name's Bradley," he declared. "I'm an investigator for the company in which Maitland was insured. If you really know anything about this affair—"

Kane beat a hasty retreat, adopting a scared look that would have passed a screen test. "Me? Know anything? Oh, no!"

"My company is prepared to pay well for any information, Mr.—er—"

"Not me," Kane said. "Oh, no, not me! I'm not poking my nose into this mess, friend." He jabbed a foot at the starter.

Mr. Bradley, the insurance man, let go the door with great reluctance and was nearly bowled over. The car slewed through soft sand in reverse. Kane turned it, glanced into the mirror as he drove away. Mr. Bradley was angrily staring after him, and suddenly got out pencil and notebook and began writing.

THE TELEPHONE book listed an Arless Radio Company at 222 East Layland. Kane slapped the book shut with a grunt of satisfaction. He was in a bar two blocks from Layland, and the barkeep, calling him by name, had placed Scotch and tap-water on the mahogany without waiting for an order.

Kane poured a double dose from the bottle and downed it. He had done a lot of running around and was dry. He supposed it would help if he had a bite to eat, but food invariably lost its appeal when the bloodhound in him was running rampant.

He had another, a quick one, drank the tap-water to settle it and went over to Layland Street. The Arless Radio Company was a manufacturing plant in a block-long building. Kane climbed sooty stairs to a sooty office.

A plump gray man peered through spectacles at the hen-tracks on that yellow sheet of paper. He said finally: "It appears to be some sort of frequency monitor, Mr. Kane, but obviously this is no more than a preliminary sketch. If you could show me a more finished diagram—"

Kane said: "There may be something more in your files, under the name of Paul Maitland. It's possible he wrote to you."

Paul Maitland had written. Clipped to the letter were detailed drawings and diagrams. The letter wondered if the Arless Company could make up this piece of equipment from the drawings.

The Arless man consulted an appended carbon copy of the firm's reply. "We—ah—offered to do the job for fifty-five dollars," he declared, "but I don't see anything further here from Mr. Maitland. Wait, and I'll check."

He checked. In ten minutes he was back shaking his head. "No. That's the last we heard of it. Perhaps our price was too steep for him. I'm sorry, Mr. Kane."

Kane was sorry, too. "What other manufacturers could make up this gadget? Close to home, I mean."

"Well, now, there's the Driscoll Company on Atwells Avenue, the Trenchard-Biddle Company…." The gray man named two others.

Kane begged a loan of the drawings and made the rounds. It was slow work. It was throat-parching. Fortunately the manufacturing district was generously sprinkled with oases. Kane was very drunk when at last he got results.

Eben Snead & Company was the place. Eben Snead himself recognized the frequency monitor. "M'm," he said. He was a large, slow-moving man with a nose like a kingfisher's beak. "M'm, yes. We've made this monitor within the past two weeks, on special order, sir. Indeed we have. But not for a Mr. Maitland, I'm sure. I'll check."

He checked. "Made it for a man named Philip Smith," he reported after research. "Sorry I can't give you his address, but he called for the work personally. We have had another order from him since. Have some drawings and specifications of his in the files."

"You mean he's coming back?"

"Friday," Mr. Snead said.

"What does this man Smith look like?"

Mr. Snead was sorry, but he didn't remember. Perhaps someone else would know. He checked. He returned to Kane, shaking his head. No one, it seemed, had paid any particular attention to Mr. Smith's physical appearance.

"Did he know radio?"

"Why—ah—yes, he seemed to. On the other hand, I do recall that he seemed unwilling to go into any deep discussion of the article he wished us to make."

"Suppose we look at his drawings," Kane suggested, "and compare them with these." He tapped a restless forefinger on the papers mailed to the Arless Company by Paul Maitland. "You're an old hand at this game, no doubt. If the two sets of drawings were prepared by the same man, you'd be able to tell, wouldn't you?"

"Possibly," said Mr. Snead. He placed the two sets side by side and studied them. "Odd," he murmured.

"What's odd?"

"On the surface these were not prepared by the same man. Yet there are certain similarities that puzzle me."

"That's all I want to know," Kane said. "What time Friday is Smith expected?"

"We promised the work for two o'clock."

"I'll be here. I'll be seeing you,"

"Will you?" said a voice at Kane's elbow. "Now isn't that nice!"

Kane turned. He blinked into the beaming face of Moroni, who had oozed quietly through the doorway to take up a position behind him. Moroni was aglow with triumph.

"You've been a big help, Kane," Moroni gloated. "A great big help. Very nice of you, Stupid, I'm sure."

KANE WAS in an ugly mood as he drove across town to the apartment address given him by Alma Payne. It was a middle class neighborhood, the house too big to have any personality. Apartment thirty-four, Alma had said. Kane peered at the names besides the bell-buttons.

Thirty-four was right, and the card bore both their names: Alma Payne and Mildred Maitland. It was Mildred Maitland that Kane wanted. He rang the bell.

She wasn't much to look at. Too small and skinny for Kane's liking, she had mouse-colored hair and a small, discontented mouth. Her nose was a button, her cheekbones high, her neck so thin that her collarbone stood out like ropes.

She looked at Peter Kane with a good deal of interest, her frank scrutiny reminding him that he was supposed to be a handsome guy with a build the ladies liked. She said: "About Paul? Of course I don't mind! Come right in."

Kane parked on a studio coach that served as a divan. He accepted a cigarette. He bet himself a dollar she would offer him a drink, and won the bet handily. It was cheap rye. The bottle in his pocket contained better stuff, but he left it there.

In answer to his question, Mildred Maitland said with a shrug of her too-thin shoulders: "Frankly, yes. I do think he committed suicide."

"Why?" Kane asked.

"Well, Paul was a very moody man. Oh, very moody! And at times he was almost impossible to get along with. We quarreled a lot, and I simply had to seek the companionship of other men occasionally, in order not to go mad. He didn't like that. He threatened many a time to do something drastic."

"Meaning suicide?"

"Yes. Suicide. And then he was always working on some crazy invention, and never had any time for me."

"Do you know what he was working on at the time he disappeared?"

"Heavens, no, Mr. Kane! I never meddled in Paul's affairs!"

Kane wondered. "Did you know he'd bought those poison pills?"

"Did I know? Of course not!" She threw her hands about in dramatic helplessness. "If I'd known, I would have done something about it before it was too late!"

Kane wondered if she would have. A gal in love with her husband might have, but the way this scrawny wench was rolling her eyes and her voice at Peter Kane, it was obvious she could love no one but herself. It was also apparent that she considered herself utterly devastating to anything that wore pants.

Kane asked an important question. "Why do you suppose Paul suddenly decided to drown himself, Mrs. Maitland, after he'd gone to all the trouble of obtaining poison?"

She hesitated. She looked bewildered for a moment, then shrugged her shoulders, sighed, and somehow was all at once sitting beside Kane on the couch, with bottle and glass in her hand. "Dear me," she said, "I don't pretend to know all the answers. Here. Have another drink."

Kane had another drink. If she hadn't been drinking, too, he would have suspected her of trying to poison him, the stuff was that awful. It filled his stomach with smoke. "Pal," he thought, "get out of this dump!" Scowling, he said aloud: "Is Mrs. Payne around?"

The scrawny one's eyes flashed. "Mrs. Payne does not live here!" she snapped.

"No? She told me—"

"She moved," said Mrs. Maitland.

"Oh," Kane said. He thought he understood. He didn't think it was worth talking about. Rising, he placed his empty glass on a table. "Well, Mrs. Maitland, thanks. I'll run."

Her mouth fell open, petulantly. "You aren't leaving?"

Kane left.

HE DIDN'T go far. He didn't get out of the building. In the downstairs hall two men were waiting when he stepped from the elevator. Since Kane had never seen them before, he paid no attention. They took care of that. They moved in, one on each side of him. The one on his left, the young one, said gently: "Take it easy, pal, and nobody will get bruised." His fingers slithered over Kane's pockets.

Kane stopped. When he did this, a gun in the pocket of the other man quickly nudged his ribs, and he guessed it was wiser to keep moving. They marched him out of the building, across the sidewalk to a car that was parked behind his own.

Kane thought of the foreign agent angle expounded by Moroni, and strove for a look at his captors. They didn't fit his notion of what foreign agents ought to look like. They were very ordinary. They wore ordinary clothes. They were sure of themselves, and their nonchalance gave Kane the creeps.

The older one drove. The younger one sat beside Kane on the sedan's rear seat, with a gun against Kane's body. Experimentally Kane said: "This bewilders me no end."

The answer was to the point. "Go right on being bewildered, pal, in a nice quiet way."

The car zigzagged across town, avoiding most of the crowded arteries. There were times when Kane might have yelled for assistance, but he thought it might be too costly. The city slipped behind, and the man at the wheel stepped up the pace to a smooth forty.

Kane stared out the window and watched daylight turn to darkness. He hadn't realized it was that late. He wondered, metaphorically, how late it really was for Peter the Kane. The woods and fields became a shroud. Far out of town the car turned into a rutted road, bumped through blackened wilderness and stopped.

The place was a farmhouse of doubtful ancestry, and the man who opened the front door and came out on the porch was almost as scrawny as Mrs. Mildred Maitland. Face to face with him, Kane towered over him and stared, and said gently, with understanding: "Oh-oh. You."

The fellow smiled. He put out a hand. "How are you, Kane?" His name was Leo Lett. He had used a lot of other names while shifting from racket to racket, but Leo Lett, Kane knew, was the one on his birth certificate.

He didn't look born—he looked carved out of a briar root. The face of Leo Lett was knotty and dark, and huckleberry eyes and bat-wing ears, and the face sat upon a short, tough torso.

"Come in, Kane," Leo invited. "Where did the boys pick you up?"

"He was in and out of so many damn barrooms, we almost lost him," grumbled the man on Kane's left. "We finally caught up with him in Mildred Maitland's apartment house."

"You see, Kane? You get around too much. Where angels fear to tread, Peter Kane is the bull in the china shop." Leo's laugh was throaty. "I get those damned proverbs all mixed up, don't I, pal?"

"Don't you," Kane said.

In the old-fashioned parlor, Leo deftly ran his hands over Kane's clothing. "The boys take your gun, Kane?"

"I didn't have one, Leo."

"No? You getting careless?"

Kane sat down. "How was I to know this was a job for artillery?"

"That's right. How would you?" Leo gazed owlishly at his two lieutenants. "Leave us alone, boys. Mr. Kane and I wish to talk." He leaned forward as the door closed. "I got to apologize, chum, for the way you were brought here. It was unavoidable. No hard feelings, hey?"

KANE ALMOST laughed.

"What," Leo asked, "is this job getting you, pal, besides a crack at that dumb dick, Moroni? Is there any dough in it for you?"

"Not a sou."

"And what are you out to prove, pal?"

"It's like this," Kane said. His gaze wandered around the room and he wondered if he'd be leaving it. He thought probably he would, after a fashion. Leo Lett was not at the moment in bad with the cops. Therefore Leo would probably draw the line just short of murder, unless persuasion failed to get him results. "It's like this: A gal who knows Paul Maitland came to my place and said she didn't think he was dead, and asked me to find him. There's no dough in it, but if the gal's right and he is alive, and I do find him, the publicity will be terrific."

"Look, Kane. Paul Maitland committed suicide."

"So?"

"No matter what anyone told you, he's dead. He had a swell wife, see? But he commenced to play around. His wife found out and threatened to leave him, and he did the Dutch." Leo leaned forward, put a hand out and tapped Kane's knee. "There's nothing to this case, pal."

"You should know," Kane said, "with an apartment right under Mildred Maitland."

Leo Lett blinked one eye.

"So why was I brought here, Leo?"

"I think you should lay off," Leo said. "Hell, Kane, you're in business for dough, and there's no dough in this. All you're doing is causing a nice girl to lose sleep. You're a good guy, Kane. I never hope to meet one better. Suppose I buy you off this case, for say five hundred fish?"

The five hundred was in Leo's hand. Kane looked at it.

"The boys will ride you back to town," Leo said, "and everything will be hunky-dory, pal. All you do to earn the five hundred is forget the whole business. I got a soft spot for Milly Maitland, see? I want this mess to die down without no more headlines."

"Well, hell," Kane said, "if it means that much to you—"

Leo Lett hunched forward and tucked the five hundred into Kane's pocket, and stood up. His grin was as craggy as his face. "I thought you'd see it my way, pal," he said. "Hey, Clinker!"

The door opened.

"Give Mr. Kane a ride back to town," Leo ordered. "Take him wherever he wishes to go." He put a hand out and Kane took it. "Thanks, pal. If you're ever in a mess, look me up."

"Will I take Joe?" Clinker asked.

"Hell, no. Mr. Kane is a friend of mine."

"O.K.," Clinker said. "Let's go, mister."

Kane followed him outside, to the car. It was dark. It was so dark that Kane held a hand up in front of him for a bumper. It occurred to him that he never in a thousand years would be able to find this place again, unless, like the kid in the fairy tale, he tied a string to it and unravelled the string as Clinker drove him to the city.

With that in mind, Kane settled himself beside the driver as the car growled down the road. He looked perfectly relaxed. Half a mile rumbled under the wheels. Suddenly Kane sat up. "Hey! I forgot something!"

Clinker applied the brakes. Disgusted, he growled: "You forgot what?"

"My wallet. I left it back there on Leo's table."

The car stopped. "Hell of a note," Kane said. "I'm sorry." He really was, too. Clinker was a little guy, and the explosion of Kane's fist under his jaw was needlessly brutal. You couldn't help feeling for a man whose teeth had suddenly bitten off one-third of his tongue.

Kane eased him out of the car and laid him tenderly in a patch of poison ivy. It would be quite a while, he thought, before Clinker felt the itch. He appropriated a gun from Clinker's pocket. Behind the wheel, he moved the car off the road.

Alert for trouble, he walked the half mile back to the farmhouse.

WHERE THE fellow came from Kane never did know, but suddenly he was there at Kane's elbow, and Kane jumped as though touched by the clammy hand of a corpse.

There was nothing hostile about the lad. His hands hung at his sides, empty. He said, "Wait a minute, Kane," and his voice was low, persuasive, but not threatening.

Kane said: "Bradley, hey? The insurance man."

"Not Bradley, Kane. And I'm not an insurance man."

"I didn't think you were."

"Name's Kershaw, and I work for a friend of yours." A small gold badge glinted in the lank man's outthrust hand. "Your Uncle Samuel."

Kane looked him up and down and was not greatly flabbergasted. He peered ahead, through darkness, to the house. "You interested in Leo Lett, too?" he murmured.

"Should I be, Kane?"

"I don't know. I thought the espionage angle in this was just a Moroni pipe-dream."

Kershaw looked at the house, too. It was about a hundred yards away, a blur in the night. He said: "I was told to look into this business. First, I shadowed Moroni, who thinks I'm an insurance man. That got me nowhere. Then you seemed to be up to something, so I shifted the tail to you. How come you were driven out here?"

Kane told him. Told him, too, about Clinker and the patch of poison ivy. "So now I'm about to call on Leo again," Kane said.

"You think he knows the truth of what happened to Maitland?"

"I think he knows where Maitland is hiding out. I wouldn't be surprised if Maitland is in that farmhouse," Kane declared.

"I'll tag along."

Kane welcomed the company. You could depend on these federal boys, he mused. They were level-headed and competent. H'd been a bit leery about barging in alone on Leo Lett and the man named Joe, but with Kershaw along he felt better. They moved toward the house warily. "Cover the door, "Kane said.

Kershaw knelt beside the veranda railing, his gun out and ready. Kane climbed the steps and knocked. Standing at ease, his empty hands dangling, he heard furtive footsteps and called out: "Open up, Leo. It's me, Kane. We had an accident."

The door opened and it was Joe. Joe was bigger than Clinker. His bulk filled the doorway and he stared at Kane suspiciously. Kane said: "It happened down the road a way. The crazy fool was driving too fast, and—"

His left hand clawed at Joe's shirt and yanked. The yank was prodigious. It whipped the big guy clear of the doorway and sent him sprawling the length of the veranda, where Kershaw, the federal man, was waiting. Big Joe lurched to his knees, yowling. He pawed for his gun. The gun he got was Kershaw's, briskly across the back of his head.

With that settled, Kane slammed over the threshold in a power drive, head down and legs churning. He thought that would make him a difficult target for Leo Lett, inside, and he was right. Leo was a bug-eyed gnome at the far end of the room, frantically throwing lead at the empty doorway.

Kane lurched into a divan and dropped. He thought Leo's gun was about empty. The room was noisy as a bowling alley, though, and in all that din you couldn't count shot. Taking no chances, Kane sighted beneath the divan, along the floor, and located Leo's legs. He couldn't miss. He squeezed the trigger four times.

Leo sat down, knifing the gunshot echoes with a banshee howl that shook the windows. He grabbed at his legs with both hands and rocked back and forth on his rump, screaming curses. He was a tough little guy, as Kane had known. He spat like a cornered cat as Kane strode toward him.

Kershaw came in. Someone in another room was pounding frantically on a door, yelling for help.

Kane found the door at the end of the hall, and it was locked. A voice yelled through it: "Let me out! If you're the police, let me out! They've got me locked in here!"

Kane frowned. This didn't fit with certain theories he was stuck with. He said darkly, "Stand away from the door," and blasted the lock with a bullet. He had his fist cocked and his gun ready when the door clattered open and Paul Maitland, easily identified by his pictures in the papers, stumbled out at him.

"So you were locked in," Kane said. His scowl was terrific. He put a hand on the man's arm and led him into the parlor, where Kershaw and Leo Lett stared in taut silence.

"This man kidnaped me!" Maitland said hoarsely, stabbing an accusing finger at Leo Lett. "He and his friends have held me here all this time, a prisoner!"

THE CRAGGY face of Leo Lett underwent changes. His mouth dropped open, his eyes bulged, glittering. His face had been white with pain; now it turned beet-red with rage.

"You double-crossing louse!" Leo screamed. "Don't believe him, Kane! If he was locked in there, he locked himself in!"

"I don't believe him," Kane said.

"He's in this of his own accord! Now he's trying to slide out of it and slap a kidnap charge on me!"

"Tell us about it, Leo," Kane said.

Leo Lett bared his teeth. "You go to hell!"

"You tell us, Maitland."

Maitland backed up, trembling. He was not much to look at. He had a slack, unshaven face and his eyes were swollen with fear. "My word's as good as his," he mumbled defiantly. "I tell you I was kidnaped!"

"Well, Leo?"

"Listen," Leo Lett said. "I met this tramp through his wife, and he told me about a new two-way radio he was working on. I figured I could use that radio in my bookie business, for a sneak-proof tieup with the horse tracks. O.K. I made him a proposition and he went for it, on condition we help him engineer a clean break from his no-good wife and all his old ties.

"The suicide angle was his own idea, see? He bought the poison from a Mickey Finn dealer in town. He wrote letters to Alma Payne, to establish a motive. He staged the drowning gag. Then he moved in here with us and went to work on his radio."

"I never did think that drowning was on the level," Kane declared.

Kershaw said: "Why?"

"A bunch of reasons. First, the letter to Alma Payne. If he could find time to write to Alma, why didn't he write his two-timing wife and blame her for what he was about to do? Most men would. That's the one satisfaction a suicide gets—telling the world his grievances."

"That's theory," Kershaw said. "Not fact."

"Sure. Then he was supposed to have taken off his clothes and swum out into the Atlantic. But if the guy never intended to come back, why did he shed his clothes? I know damn well *I* wouldn't—unless I wanted someone to find them."

"Still theory, Kane."

"The poison business was phoney. Why didn't he use the poison? Or anyhow, why didn't he take some before his midnight swim, to ease the way out? I'll tell you why. The poison was a plant, to fortify the suicide angle."

The federal man shook his head. "You still haven't—"

"Hell!" Kane snorted. "You Hoover guys. Did Columbus know he'd find America?" He grinned at Leo Lett. "Who copied Maitland's drawings and took them to the radio company?"

"Joe."

"Smart of you not to use Maitland's originals."

"Oh, sure," Leo growled. "I'm smart." He held onto his legs and made a face with his eyes shut. "Look at me."

"You look at him, Kane," Kershaw said, "while I check the stuff Maitland's been working on."

It was valuable stuff. The government would want it, Kershaw declared. The government would also want to talk to Leo Lett and his buddies, and to Paul Maitland. "Can you keep quiet about this for a while, Kane? Publicity right now might hurt."

"Why not?" Kane said. He studied his fingernails innocently. "If this radio stuff is really important, there's some more of it you ought to pick up, friend."

"Is there? Where?"

"At the Eben Snead Company. They told me it would be ready Friday at two o'clock."

"Friday," Kershaw said, "at two. I'll be there."

HE WAS, and it was beautiful. It was gorgeous. At 2:07 by Kane's watch, Kershaw walked into the place and went up to the desk. "You made some equipment for Mr. Philip Smith," he declared. "I have the receipt here for the deposit. If I may have the equipment...."

For over an hour, Kane had been perched on a stool behind a row of filing cabinets, quietly sipping at a pint of bonded rye—ultra special stuff, as befitted the occasion. The rest of the boys were strategically hidden in other parts of the spacious office.

Moroni had come in half an hour ago, talked to Mr. Snead, and seated himself at a desk, where he was trying to act like a stenographer.

Moroni rose, now, in all his glory. His jaw was out, his eyes a-glitter, his big face bristling with triumph. He had a horse-pistol in his fist as he loomed at the counter.

"You're under arrest!" Moroni bellowed.

Flash-bulbs exploded. Murchison, of the *Telegram*, got a beautiful picture of Moroni's bellow, with emphasis on tonsils and epiglottis. Kelley, of the *Post*, caught the Moroni profile in all its splendor, with the amazed countenance of Kershaw in the background. Sisson and McArdle, veteran newshounds, were there to put it in words. Fat, juicy words.

Kane got off his stool. With flash-bulbs still exploding, and the Magnificent Moroni frozen in frantic amazement, Kane walked unsteadily to the counter and grinned at Kershaw.

"We're holding a little party here, Mr. Kershaw," he murmured, "for the press. This—ah—is Mr. Moroni, whom no doubt you've seen around. Mr. Moroni, meet Mr. Kershaw, of the F.B.I."

Out of there, then, weaved Peter Kane with his pint. The pint was about gone. He thought that was a shame. There was a definite need, he felt, for celebration at this time.

Then he remembered he had five hundred dollars of Leo Lett's ill-gotten money. That would buy him a lot of happy hangovers.

First, though, he had a call to make. Anne and Moe Finch would want to know the news.

NO PLACE TO HIDE

DOC ENDERSON'S BONE-DRY
LOONY BIN WAS NO PLACE FOR
A DRINKING MAN, AS TOSSPOT
KANE SOON LEARNED WHEN
HE WENT THERE TO PLAY
NURSEMAID TO C. PHILIP CULLY.
IF IT HADN'T BEEN FOR DRUITT,
THE FRIENDLY KLEPTOMANIAC,
THAT GREAT BIG MAN FROM THE
SOUSE WOULD HAVE SUCCUMBED
IN THAT PADDED-CELL SAHARA
IN ONE SHORT NIGHT. WHEN
DRUITT TURNED UP DEAD, THE
VERY LEAST KANE COULD DO WAS
CORRAL HIS KILLER—THE FIEND
WHO'D NIPPED HIS THIRST-AID
CLASSES IN THE BUD.

MR. CULLY patted his pink brow with a moist handkerchief. "Sh-shut the door, please, Kane," he said. "And lock it."

Kane turned the key and sat down. The rain, he observed, had doubled C. Philip Cully's terror, which had been pitifully enormous in the first place. Hopefully Kane gazed at his employer. "You going to bed?"

"To bed, yes. I think so. I think I should. My nerves...." Cully peered around him, shivering—a small, darting wasp of a man with more nerves than muscles. "This awful suspense, Kane! It's driving me mad!"

"Relax," Kane said.

"Relax! My God! You sit there and tell me to relax, when I must be on guard every instant!"

Kane sighed. For three days he had listened to the same frenzied stuttering. For three days he had followed C. Philip Cully about like a Great Dane guarding a chimpanzee. Endless strolls in the garden. Endless sessions of sitting on the long gray veranda. Dreaded mealtimes when Mrs. Featherby, the butterfly collector, chattered interminably about bugs, and Mr. Druitt glowered fiercely under his long white lashes, and the Pulkey sisters fought like cats over the salt.

Kane was fed up. The job was killing him.

"Look, Cully. I'll lock the windows, leave the light on and lock the door after me. You'll break an arm, shivering like that. You climb into bed."

Kane crashed through the juniper just
as Moroni's trigger finger tightened.

C. Philip Cully removed his sneakers, his pale blue shirt, his gray flannel trousers. He sat on the edge of the bed in his striped silk underwear, his mouth twitching, his watery blue eyes too big for his face. "M-my green pajamas, Kane," he begged. It was a sob. "In the b-bottom drawer."

Kane yanked open the bottom drawer. It was a mess. Expensive underwear, shirts, pajamas all tossed in a heap. He yawed through the heap and shook his head. "No green pajamas here, friend."

"Perhaps in the n-next drawer," Cully suggested, his teeth chattering.

Kane looked. "No green pajamas."

Cully got off the bed, scowling. He, too, pawed through his possessions. His blue eyes blazed and he balled his bony hands into fists. "I tell you, Kane, someone is stealing my things! This proves it!"

"I wouldn't put it past the wacky residents of this place to steal the corns off your feet," Kane growled.

"They're gone! My pajamas!" For a man whose advice on financial matters was sought by some of the biggest businessmen in the country, C. Philip Cully could certainly fly off the handle in most amazing fashion. "First my flamingo necktie!" he shrilled, throwing his arms about angrily. "Then my copy of *How to Win Friends and Influence People!* Then my gold pen-knife! Now my pajamas!"

He lunged at the door. "By heaven, Kane, I mean to find out who is stealing my things! I won't put up with it a moment longer!"

"Look," Kane said, easing him back to the bed. "It's close to midnight, Mr. Cully. We played Chinese checkers three hours, and it's way too late to go barging around this pecan palace. You can wear blue pajamas or pink ones. Be a good guy and go to bed."

Mr. Cully subsided reluctantly, but continued muttering through thin wet lips. He got into bed and petulantly kicked the blankets out of tuck. Kane retucked them with admirable self-control. Then Kane checked the two windows to be sure they were locked, turned to the door and said gently: "Pleasant dreams, Mr. Cully."

Cully didn't answer. Kane shut the door and went down the hall, spitting silent sounds of rage into the gloom. His own room was just down the corridor.

OWLISHLY HE surveyed his haggard countenance in the mirror above his bureau and wondered if it were possible for a man to get so wild, so uncivilized looking, in three days. In Dr. Enderson's rest home it probably was. The mirror was not kidding him.

Dr. Enderson's retreat was the last word in rest homes for fastidious patients. You had to present a check in three figures to get in. Once in, you had to use crowbar, hacksaw and gobs of ingenuity to get out. It was supposed to be tonic for the nerves.

But if, like Peter Kane of the Beacon Agency, you possessed arid nerves that required frequent and thorough lubrication, this place was a torture camp. Dr. Enderson was death on lubrication.

Kane swore fluidly and steadily for three minutes. He walked the floor, a thunderhead about to explode into bristling bursts of lightning. He was thirsty.

For three days he'd been thirsty. There were knobs on his tongue. And since he was here not as a patient but as C. Philip Cully's private bodyguard, there was no sane reason why he should be thirsty—except that Dr. Enderson refused point-blank, with glittering eyes and Olympian snorts of wrath, to permit anything stronger than root beer on the premises.

In this lovely little Connecticut retreat, the symptoms of thirst were met with proffered glasses of water, milk, buttermilk and pineapple juice. No trace, no smell, no slightest hint of alcohol.

Kane was burned up.

He sat down. He wondered darkly how Detective Lieutenant Moroni was doing, back in town. Moroni was on the case because C. Philip Cully was name for the headlines. Wherever there was a possibility of publicity, Great Brain Moroni worked overtime.

Moroni was endeavoring to track down two violent, typewritten letters dispatched to Cully by way of the U.S. mail. Kane remembered the letters very well indeed. In the first, the writer had promised to see that Cully paid for his crimes by the first of November. In missive number two, the writer had advised Cully to settle his affairs with God in short order, because the first of November was only just around the corner.

Cully had taken the letters to the police and sneered the whole thing off. But a day or two later, the financier had heard a clock ticking in the bedroom of his city apartment, where there were no clocks to tick, and—

Kane jerked his head up and peered at the door. He arched himself like a cat and was out of his chair, crouching at the portal, before it was time to draw another breath. In the hall outside—the dark, dreary, central hall of Dr. Enderson's dreary rest home—something was a-prowl.

Stealthy footfalls whispered past, and Kane inched his door open. He saw a gliding shape vanish around the bend of the corridor. Stooping, he swiftly shed his shoes and set out in pursuit.

This was the second time Mr. Druitt of the long white lashes had gone prowling past Kane's door in the middle of the night on some mysterious mission. Druitt might bear watching.

The house slept. Rain drummed its shut windows and the walls damply whispered their secrets. Kane followed the pale glow of a midget flashlight in Druitt's hand as the little man veered into the parlor.

The parlor was huge. Its furniture leaned darkly in the backwash of light. Druitt was an animated doll pedaling through the shadows, a Lilliputian overshadowed by yellowed hulks of piano and highboy. A grandfather clock bonged hollowly, once, and Druitt jumped as though a jet of live steam had been turned on under him. It was half past twelve.

Druitt pushed up a window and crawled through onto the veranda. He turned to close the window, and Kane waited. The little man vanished. Kane opened the window and went after him.

THERE WAS a wind that soughed mournfully around the many ells and dormers of the house. The night was black as a Dante dream, and the rain came gustily out of the blackness to chill Kane's bones. Far away now, Druitt's light winked among the trees near the high steel fence that enclosed the property.

Kane went across the sodden lawn in pursuit and saw, suddenly, the dark shape of a car parked on the dirt road outside the fence. The road that snaked through the mountains to the village. The serpentine ribbon of mud and skunk-smells that linked Dr. Enderson's nerve-nest with the sanities of civilization.

Mr. Druitt was flat against the fence, conversing with a dark shape that appeared to be human. Kane paused beside a big maple tree to watch.

Something shaped like a shoebox was pushed through the fence into Druitt's grasping hands. The little man turned. So did the one outside the fence. The latter hurried to the car, got in, and drove away, closing the door quietly and using no headlights.

Druitt blinked his puny flashlight once or twice to get his bearings, and with the package tucked under his arm hurried back toward the house.

Peter Kane stepped from behind the tree and said severely: "A-ha! Caught you!"

It was pathetic. Mr. Druitt was about the size of C. Philip Cully and was almost turned inside out, like a gale-blown umbrella, by the force of Kane's blast. He dropped his flashlight and came within an inch of dropping the package, too, but caught the latter with a frantic last-second clutch just before it reached the lawn. Then he stood quaking.

"Oh!" he gasped finally. "It's y-you, Mr. Kane. I—I thought it was Doctor Enderson. Oh, oh, oh!"

"What's in that package?" Kane demanded.

"I—I—it's nothing. Really, it's nothing!"

Kane was cold and wet and getting wetter. He thrust a rigid forefinger under the little man's nose. "Druitt, you're lying! Open it!"

"P-please, Mr. Kane. Not here!"

"Why not here!"

"I tell you it's nothing. Nothing of any—any importance to anyone but myself. Please!" The little man hugged his package protectively. "If you—if you will come to my room,

I'll show you. We can't stay here, Mr. Kane. If Doctor Enderson should discover us...." He shuddered.

The prospect of being caught by Dr. Enderson evidently terrified him more than Kane did.

"We'll go to your room," Kane said. "Lead on."

It was probably nothing, he decided glumly. The good Dr. Enderson had forbidden Druitt to eat bon-bons or pickled onions, maybe, and this was a smuggled box of the little man's favorite delicacy. Something like that. At any rate, the package didn't tick like the one C. Philip Cully had discovered under the bed in his town apartment. It probably wasn't a bomb.

Still... someone *had* planted a bomb in Cully's bedroom, and only by the grace of God had the financier discovered it before being blown to bits. The writer of those threatening letters undoubtedly meant business, whoever he was.

Kane wondered who he was. Chances were, he was some client of Cully's who had followed the man's advice at a bad time and lost his shirt in the market. Cully's advice wasn't always good, of course. It was good sufficiently often for him to charge all outdoors for it, but occasionally it did backfire and a few customers got burned.

The sender of those letters could be one of Cully's victims, convinced that the financier had deliberately tricked him.

It was not going to be easy to track the man down. Meanwhile, he just might make another bomb.

Kane trailed the diminutive Druitt back to the latter's room and with the door shut stood with his hands hipped, waiting. The little man blinked at him. About Druitt there was something pathetic. The wide brown eyes were soft as a seal's, begging to be understood. They could glare and glower, those eyes, and when they did so the white lashes lent them an unearthly glitter, but right now they were the orbs of a frightened child.

"You—you see," Druitt said, "I can't have what I want in this awful place, Mr. Kane. I'm a prisoner here. My wife"—he shuddered—"my wife made all the arrangements, and Doctor Enderson won't listen to me at all. So I've been smuggling things in."

He unwrapped the box and out of it lifted two cylindrical shapes wrapped in newspaper. "I hope," Druitt whispered, "oh, I do hope you won't report me to Doctor Enderson! Even if you personally don't approve, I hope you'll try to be understanding and—and sympathetic."

He unwrapped the cylinders. Kane looked at them. Kane's eyes bugged. His jaw dropped. Breath whistled between his teeth and flattened his tongue.

"Rum!" he blurted.

"You see," said Druitt hastily, "my wife doesn't think I should drink. She—she sent me here to be cured of the craving, Mr. Kane, though heaven knows I never drank very *much!* And I simply can't endure this place without something to—to soothe the nerves—and—" Pleadingly he gripped Kane's big arms. "You won't report me? Please!"

Kane scooped up one of the bottles and read the label, read every word of it. "*Good* rum," he whispered. A dreamy look crossed his face. "Druitt, this is Mecca. This is Nirvana. You're a friend for life. Break out a corkscrew and two glasses!"

After that, Kane did not remember too much of what happened. It was potent rum, and little Mr. Druitt poured generously. "There's plenty more," Druitt chuckled, "where this came from, friend. Tonight we celebrate. I thought everyone in this zombie den was against me!"

Mr. Druitt, it seemed, was a banker. Not a very big banker, but an honest, ambitious man whose great misfortune was to be married to a beautiful and domineering creature of society. Kane was not much interested. Kane sprawled in his chair and enjoyed the tingling sensation in the tips of his fingers. He liked the way the ceiling simulated a lazy, rolling ocean. He thought the little red and blue lights in the room's smoky atmosphere were as pretty as ornaments on a Christmas tree.

The rum was heavenly.

KANE TOOK a hangover to breakfast and found the antics of the filberts highly unamusing. So, apparently, did C. Philip Cully, who ate with his gaze glued to his plate.

The younger Pulkey sister, Sophia, was chided for being hoggish with the hot-cakes and thereupon sulked, refusing to eat. Her sister sang Wagner with a mouth full of syrup. Mrs. Featherby, the horse-faced butterfly addict, rapturously displayed—in a small mayonnaise jar which she placed beside the scrambled eggs—a large, hairy, red and yellow spider she had captured. Druitt was conspicuous by his absence. Too much rum, Kane decided.

Over all this presided with gaunt and watchful dignity the proprietor of the hostel, Dr. Edmund Enderson, who had little to say and said most of that with his eyes. They were the coldest eyes south of Davis Sound.

The non-eating Pulkey sister got up and sulked out of the room. No one missed her. No one seemed aware that she had gone until suddenly, about five minutes later, she raced up the veranda steps outside and burst back into the room, yelling from the roots of her hair.

"He's dead!" she shrieked. "Oh, my goodness, he's dead, dead, *dead!*"

Kane shot to his feet. Ethelda Pulkey stopped singing Wagner. The red and yellow spider began to run like hell around the mayonnaise jar. Dr. Enderson's icy eyes stuck out like lemon lollypops.

"Who's dead?" Kane demanded.

"He is! Out there near the fence! Mr. Druitt!"

Kane knocked her sprawling on his way out the door. He had to, because the doorway was only so wide and she used up the largest part of it, waving her arms. He leaped the veranda rail and ran straight for the fence. He ran along the fence until he found Druitt.

It wasn't the rum. That much rum could conceivably kill a little guy like Druitt, but this had been done with a bullet. With one bullet, neatly placed in the back of the little man's head.

He lay on a patch of rain-soaked turf where the grass grew thin and his footsteps were plainly discernible in the mud. He lay on his face, with his outflung arms pointing toward the house. There was something about his clothes that struck Kane as odd—even with all that blood on them. They didn't fit. They were sloppy. Mr. Druitt had always been neat as a tailor's advertisement.

And there was a lump in Kane's esophagus as he gazed down upon the man. He'd grown to like this friendly little fellow. He'd come to think of Druitt as a fellow soul in this repair shop for mental breakdowns.

The rest of them crowded against him, all talking at once. All but the gaunt doctor. He glared in silent anger. He plainly thought it outrageous of the dead man to be stirring up so much commotion. He paraded forward like an animated scarecrow, to investigate.

"Keep off those footprints!" Kane snapped.

The doctor looked down. He looked at Kane. "I had no intention," he muttered, "no intention whatever...." He let it go at that and backed away from the body.

C. Philip Cully pawed at Kane's sleeve, his face cod-belly gray. "T-those clothes!" he gasped. "T-they—t-they belong to *me!*" His chattering teeth transposed the bleat into code, but Kane caught the gist of it. "It's m-my suit he's wearing!"

Kane stared, scowling. "Your suit? You sure?"

"P-positive!"

Things began to make sense. "Don't any of you go near that body on pain of death," Kane warned. "Doc, you make sure they don't. Cully, you come with me. We'll call the police."

He led Cully back to the house, feeling sorrier for the man every minute as the ague increased and the tooth-chatter began to sound like a wood-pecker assaulting an empty tin can. Kane used the phone in the hall, hung up and guided Cully upstairs to the dead man's chamber.

"If that's your suit he has on, the rest of your stuff ought to be around here somewhere," he observed. "We'll take a look."

The room itself looked just as it had last night, when Kane had swayed out of it on his way to bed. The empty rum bottle on the table. Two empty glasses. Cigarette stubs. Smoke still clung to the ceiling and lay blue under the bed.

Kane opened the bureau drawers. In the top one, C. Philip Cully's missing pajamas were neatly stowed under some woolen underwear. In the middle one, under some shirts, lay Cully's flamingo necktie and his copy of *How to Win Friends*. In a suitcase in the closet, Cully's gold pen-knife lay hidden in a nest of soiled clothes.

Kane didn't touch these things. "Moroni," he said dourly, "will want this undisturbed. But it seems obvious our friend Druitt was a kleptomaniac. Had a passion for other people's possessions." He scowled, shoving the bureau drawers shut. "Seems obvious, too, he went out for a breath of air last night, wearing your suit, and was shot by someone who thought it was you. A stiff price to pay for such a mild mania, Cully. You should consider yourself lucky."

There was no humor in this. It was a statement of fact, glumly uttered. Kane was depressed. He'd liked the little guy. He'd been looking forward to more of him.

"We'll go downstairs," Kane said, "and wait for the Great Brain."

NOT SOLOMON in all his glory was resplendent as Moroni in pink-and-white striped shirt, well fed stomach and bulldog jowl. You sensed at once that Detective Lieutenant Moroni was of the significant few. You entirely overlooked Captain Moe Finch, Kane's bosom pal and Moroni's superior, for Moe was quiet and methodical. Moe was a lump of granite dimmed by Moroni's glitter.

"A hell of a bodyguard you are, Kane!" Moroni gloated. "A hell of a warden!"

"My client," Kane pointed out, "is still alive."

"By the grace of God and a kleptomaniac!"

"If this shapes up as it seems to," said Moe Finch, methodically surveying the scene, "your client's out of danger for a while, Kane, at least." He pointed to the dead man's footprints in the mud. "Seems certain Druitt was walking back toward the house when he was shot. That means he was shot from outside the fence. An outside job, Kane, and the guy will think he killed Cully unless we broadcast otherwise."

It was quite an investigation. A pair of Homicide men performed the bulk of the routine while Moroni swaggered hither and yon, like a bloodhound in an abattoir. Moe Finch calmly took notes with the stub of a well-chewed pencil. The Pulkey sisters and Mrs. Featherby trailed at a distance, agog with curiosity. Dr. Enderson stood in sullen hauteur on the veranda, and C. Philip Cully clung to Kane like a leech.

There was the body and there were the footprints in that patch of mud. Druitt's footprints, beyond a doubt. And Kane was saying: "He was a nice guy. He was drunk as a coot when I left him around two A.M. He must have changed clothes and wandered out here for some air. His shoes stink. He was sick over by the big maple tree."

Moroni marched over to the tree to investigate. "Plenty," he observed.

"You think I should post a guard around this place, Kane?" Moe Finch asked.

"Are you going to tell the papers about this?"

"Be better if we don't, I guess. We tell the papers, the guy will know he missed and may try again."

"Then a guard will be a waste of time. He won't come back until he knows he got the wrong man."

"It's a mess," Moe declared mournfully. "We worked like dogs on those letters and got nowhere. Now this. A guy murdered and not a clue. I'll check along the road to the village and see if anyone noticed a car, but who ever takes notice of cars?"

"You leave this to me," Moroni said. "I got an idea." He glared at the Pulkey sisters, who were edging closer. They retreated in consternation. "Not a blamed thing we can do just yet," Moroni continued importantly. "Let's go." He leered at C. Philip Cully. "You're safe enough now. But if I were you, friend, I'd get a bodyguard."

The Homicide men gathered up the corpse and Kane walked along with them to the gate, gazing intently at the dead man's soiled shoes and unsoiled trousers. Long after the departure of the law, Kane wore a meditative scowl. Then he walked over to the maple tree and looked at the ground. Little Mr. Druitt had been very sick there.

Kane went into the house, ignoring the questions of the Pulkey sisters and the frigid glare of Dr. Enderson. A disturbing idea went with him and Cully trailed them both. "I—I think," Cully said weakly, "I'll lie down for a while, Kane. You can imagine how I feel." He shuddered. "Will you—will you sit in my room?"

Kane shrugged. He was being paid to humor the guy. He sat and smoked cigarettes while Cully undressed and crawled into bed.

When the financier's throaty breathing indicated sleep, Kane went down the hall to Druitt's room.

Two bottles of rum had been delivered to Druitt through the fence. Only one stood empty on the table. Kane fished the other out of its hiding place in the bowl of the old-fashioned light fixture, where Moe Finch's men had overlooked it. He peered in the closet and opened bureau drawers. He opened the bottle and replaced the corkscrew on the table and tramped back to Cully's room.

In half an hour he felt much better. He even emptied his ashtray into the waste-basket and hung up the clothes Cully had dropped on the floor. And because there was a draft across the bed, or partly because of it, he closed the windows.

WHEN CULLY waked the room was hot, airless. Kane sat with his legs out-thrust on an end table, the rum bottle at his elbow, his eyes half shut. Cully had to shake him out of a partial stupor.

"It's almost time for lunch," Cully said. "Or do you want any lunch after guzzling nearly a pint of liquor?" His tone was petulant.

Kane sat up, inhaling deeply half a dozen times as he got to his feet. "You're awake, huh? Lunch? All right, I'll see you downstairs."

"And for heaven's sake, don't let Doctor Enderson know you've obtained liquor! He'll blame me! And don't," Cully added vehemently, "tell Mrs. Featherby. She's so dead set against the stuff she tried to kill a neighbor who drank too much. That's one of the reasons she's here."

"A good drink," Kane observed, "would make some of the people around here a heap more human." He went out. He had another drink in his own room and stood at the window, feeling very human indeed, until he heard Cully go downstairs. A bell tinkled imperatively in the dining room. Kane hid the bottle and shut his door behind him.

They were all at the table when he entered. They looked up because after crossing the threshold he stopped and stood scowling at them, with his fists jammed against his hips, his chin shoved out. Even in Dr. Enderson's home for hoop-rollers, that was not the customary way of entering for lunch.

They stared, bewildered, and Kane swept them with a gaze that spat sparks. "All right," he snarled then. "Which one of you took it?"

The silence was queer. Sophia Pulkey shattered it with a giggle. "Took what?" she inquired sweetly.

"My money! And don't act so chipper about it. All the thieving around this dump wasn't done by Druitt, that's plain! I had three hundred dollars in my bureau this morning, and now it's gone. And by God, I mean to get it back!"

"You're offensive," said the other Pulkey. "You swear too much."

Kane strode to the table, brandishing his arms. "If that three hundred isn't handed over to me in ten seconds, I'm going to rip this joint apart until I find it!" He glared from one to another. His glare struck Enderson just as that gaunt gentleman, redfaced and angry, was rising. Enderson sank down again.

Mrs. Featherby said to the spider in her mayonnaise jar: "Well, I'm sure *I* never took anyone's money. Did I, Leopold?"

The Pulkey sisters giggled.

Cully, on Kane's left, tugged at Kane's sleeve and said anxiously, in an undertone: "Kane, Kane, it's the rum. You've had too much!"

"So I've got to tear the joint apart!" Kane yelled. "All right, I'm willing!"

He stormed out of the dining-room, leaving the air behind him alive with static and rum fumes. Drunk? Well, anyhow, he staggered. He slammed up the stairs and at the top Dr. Enderson caught up to him.

"Mr. Kane! I won't have this!"

"Look," Kane said. "I'm out three hundred bucks. *I'm* running this." He placed a hand firmly over Enderson's cadaverous face and shoved. Had he pushed a mite harder, the gaunt man would have skidded all the way down the stairs instead of only half the way.

Then Kane went to work.

It was good and it was noisy, though most of the damage he did was superficial. He prowled from room to room, tearing into closets and bureaus, under beds and behind pillows. He was followed at a distance by the Pulkey sisters and Mrs. Featherby, who were at first horrified, then delighted. Toward the end they cheered him on like freshmen at a track meet.

Dr. Enderson frantically phoned the police and resigned himself to a nervous pacing of the veranda. C. Philip Cully gave up trying to remonstrate with Kane and ducked into his room, locking the door.

Kane prowled.

He quit after an hour of vain search. He thumped on Cully's door until Cully opened it. Then Kane trudged wearily into the room and sank onto a chair. He swabbed his sweaty face with a handkerchief, lit a cigarette, angrily snapped the match across the room. "Damn thieves," he said against his teeth. "But I'll get that money back, Cully! I'll get it!"

Cully sat on the bed and frowned at him. "Are you sure, Kane—are you sure you haven't just mislaid it? You were drinking heavily before lunch, you know. Isn't it possible—"

"Look," Kane said dourly. "Maybe you might mislay three hundred bucks, but I'm careful with my dough. I work for a living."

"Well, it was a suggest—"

"Thanks."

KANE SMOKED his cigarette and moodily lit another. He looked up after a while. "Nuts bury things, don't they?" he said abruptly.

"What?"

"I read that somewhere. People with a mental gear stripped—bugs like the Pulkey sisters and that dame Featherby—they have queer ideas. They're acquisitive. They hoard stuff. Bury it."

"I never heard of such a thing, Kane."

"Where would you bury something around this dump, Cully?"

"I? Good heavens, man, I—"

"No one's accusing you. But if you had to bury something, where would you do it? Out there by the fence? In the flower garden? By that old well, maybe?"

Cully entered into the spirit of the thing and looked thoughtful. "The well would be a good place, Kane. M'm, yes."

"Let's look around. You've got nothing much else to do."

"Well, no, I haven't." Cully got off the bed and reached for his shoes. Kane opened the door.

"Oh-oh," Kane said. "The law!"

Enderson's frantic phone call to the village had been answered. Behind Enderson now puffed a large edition of the local law, winded from hauling his two hundred fifty pounds up the stairs. He was short but fat. His face consisted of two round eyes, a lump of nose and a small mouth plastered to a scowl.

He looked at Kane and said to Enderson: "Is this the guy?"

Enderson took in breath to build a lecture. Kane said: "I'm the guy. Look, friend." He gave the fat man a solemn stare. "Where would you bury three hundred bucks?"

"Huh?"

"We got it figured out. The thief buried my dough. It isn't in the house, and these screw-brains wouldn't know enough to hide it in their bloomers. So it must have been buried. Nuts do that, you know." Kane pulled the constable closer and let his voice sink to a chummy whisper, cozily confidential. "Schizophrenics, that's what they are, friend. Acute victims of the contractional space-vacuums. Terrible condition. Even the Doc here shows signs of gradual disintegration. And they bury things. You own a divining rod?"

The fat man blinked his round little eyes. "What the hell," he said.

"Come with me," Kane commanded.

"Now you listen to me!" Enderson squared off. "You're trying to confuse the issue, Kane! Constable, arrest this man! I tell you he—"

"Come on," Kane ordered. "Got to dig a hole." He looped an arm around the fat man's shoulders and leered at him. "You're plenty husky, eh?"

"Me? Sure I'm husky!"

The constable's name was Keever and with a spade balanced over his shoulder he looked like a grave-digger, but capable. He and Cully and Kane made quite a trio. Cully theorized on where the money might be buried. Kane explored the selected locations. Keever did the digging.

This went on for three hours and used up most of the estate. Near the end, Cully showed signs of mental fatigue and Keever wheezed with every step. Kane was still fresh as a daisy.

"Well," Kane said finally, "we've done damn near every likely spot. We've done the well and the flower garden, the vegetables and the fence. How about under that back porch, Cully? Seems to me I saw that Featherby dame crawling under there a couple of days ago, after a garter snake. You think it's worth a look?"

"I hardly think—"

"O.K. We'll take a peek anyhow, just for luck. Come on." Kane smiled benignly at the constable. "You, too, Keever. Never leave a stone unturned." He headed for the back porch, Cully and Keever wearily at heel.

It was too much. Three hours in a hot sun had taken toll. Cully stumbled. He flung out his arms and dived into the backs of Kane's legs, voicing a yelp of surprise. He fell sprawling and Kane sat down on him.

Kane got up quickly. He reached for the financier and saw suddenly that Cully was hurt.

"M-my leg," Cully groaned. "Oh—my leg!"

Kane glanced at Keever, and the fat man laid down his spade. "His leg," Kane muttered. He got hold of Cully by the shoulders and Keever took the other end.

They carried him to the house and up to his room. While Kane fussed over him like a cat with kittens, Keever, looking worried and hot and weary, went after Enderson. The gaunt doctor was sulking in the parlor.

Enderson strode to the bed, his eyes blazing. "Mr. Kane, I shall hold you responsible for this! If anything has happened—"

"Nuts," Kane said.

Enderson looked at the leg. Kane looked, too. He didn't see any jagged bones protruding, or even discolorations, but you never could tell. He shrugged and walked out.

THE MORNING paper reached Dr. Enderson's woodland retreat between four and five in the afternoon. Hence it was five thirty the following day when Kane read the startling item in Kerry Conover's column, *Inside Out,* in the *Telegram.*

> ... We learn on unimpeachable authority that an attempt was made yesterday on the life of financier C. Philip Cully, who is in hiding while police endeavor to track down the writer of certain letters threatening his life.
>
> Someone shot Mr. Cully through the back of the head—cold-blooded murder. But the victim wasn't Cully. A case of mistaken identity. For Cully, a fortunate break. For the victim, a break of another kind. The police would like to move Cully to a new hideout, but we learn he is on the verge of a nervous breakdown following the incident, and cannot be moved at this time. More, perhaps, later.

About an hour after Kane read this, Lieutenant Detective Moroni arrived, with Moe Finch and a pair of large and husky Homicide men. And, significantly, the *Telegram's* Kerry Conover.

Moroni gave the orders. Moe Finch stood around looking tired and resigned to an unfair fate. The Homicide men lifted a large, blanket-wrapped object from the truck and toted it into Dr. Enderson's parlor.

Moroni unwrapped it. It was a store-window dummy with adjustable arms and legs. Moroni bent the legs into a sitting position and placed the dummy in a chair.

"The right size, hey?" he said, smugly self-satisfied. "I had a hell of a time getting it, let me tell you." He leered at Kane. "This is your client from now on, shamus. This is C. Philip Cully."

Kane sat on the piano bench and sucked a peach from the Enderson bowl of fruit. He peered at Kerry Conover. "So it was Moroni put you wise, was it?"

"Ha!" said Conover. He was a sallow man, thin as Dr. Enderson, tall as Kane almost, with a lumpy shank of neck and protruding ears.

Kane blinked at Moe Finch and the latter shrugged helplessly. Moroni finished fussing with the dummy. "All right, Kane," Moroni said. "Go get some of Cully's clothes. You're his nursemaid."

"His. Not yours."

"Suit yourself. All I say is—you keep your nose out of this. I'm running this show, Kane, and I'll brook no interference from an agency dick like you."

"So you're Moe's superior now, eh?"

Moroni grinned at Moe Finch. "Captain Finch and I," he declared unctuously, "are working hand in glove on this."

Kane saw through it and kept his mouth shut. He decided to hell with it and got off the piano bench and walked out. When he opened the door to the hall, there was a sudden scurrying of feet into the shadows back of the stairs, and he heard a giggle that could have come only from one of the Pulkey sisters, or both.

Kane went up to his room. He had a hunch Moe Finch would be up to see him, and was right. In less than ten minutes Moe entered and closed the door.

"Don't look at *me*," Moe said wearily. "It was the Great Brain's idea from start to finish." He sank into a chair and blew breath between his teeth. "But if it backfires, Kane, I take the rap."

"Maybe it will work, Moe."

"Like a Rube Goldberg cartoon," growled the Finch. "Anyhow, if it does work, Moroni reaps the profits. If it doesn't, your old pal Finch collects the whirlwind. It's always this way. Kane. That round black thing you see in front of me, big as the World's Fair perisphere, is known as an eight-ball." He spat. "I don't need to tell you. You know."

Kane knew. When a hot case cropped up, with headline possibilities, Moroni grabbed it by the tail. The Great Brain never missed an opportunity. He could climb over Moe Finch's head with pull that enabled him to reach the commissioner.

If his high-handed methods produced results, he saw to it that the papers played him up. If he missed, he was after all just Detective Lieutenant Moroni, taking orders from Captain Finch, his superior.

"If you don't mind," Moe said, "I'll just sit here and brood, Kane. I'd be in the way down there. The show's Moroni's, and he brought along that Conover squirt to cover the publicity angle."

The show was Moroni's. Through Kerry Conover's column he had already broadcast to the general public—more specifically, to the would-be assassin of C. Philip Cully—the fact that Cully was still alive. Also the important point that Cully was still at Dr. Enderson's rest home.

Moroni dressed the dummy in Cully's clothes. He placed it in a wheel-chair. When darkness lay velvet-soft over the house and grounds, he pushed the wheelchair out on the veranda and parked it just at the edge of a wan rectangle of light cast by one of the parlor windows.

Then Moroni and the two Homicide men—and columnist Kerry Conover—retired to strategic points of concealment and settled down to wait.

KANE WATCHED most of this from the window of his room, and with the window open, overheard snatches of conversation. The Great Brain was in finest fettle, issuing orders. "I want you, Doctor Enderson, to go to bed as usual, and make sure your patients do likewise. Got that? The man we're after knows your routine and we don't want to arouse his suspicions. He may not come tonight—no telling when he will come—but he won't wait too long, either, because Conover's column made it plain that we intend to move Cully from here as soon as possible.

Kane took it all in. He could look down through the trellis at the end of the veranda and see the dummy in the wheelchair. It looked real enough. To a killer lurking outside the fence it would look very real indeed. Nor would it be a difficult target.

"No matter what you see or hear," Moroni said, this time to the Homicide boys, "don't make a move until the guy actually takes a shot. Then blast him!

Kane went down the hall to Cully's room and found the financier in bed, quaking. He sat on the edge of the bed and grinned. "You need some of that rum I drank up," Kane observed. "Scared, huh?"

"It—it's gruesome!" gasped Cully through chattering teeth.

"It could be worse than that," Kane murmured, "if only Moroni knew all the angles. But don't worry, friend. At least he brought a dummy and didn't use C. Philip Cully in the flesh."

Cully put his face in the pillow and groaned.

"How's your leg?"

"I—I think it's b-better. But I'm not getting up, Kane. Not until this horrible business is over and done with!"

Kane went back up to his room, moodily sniffed at the empty rum bottle and pulled a chair up to the window. Moe Finch was despondently gazing into space.

An hour went by. The night had filled with waiting. A few stray stars shone wanly in a storm-weighted sky, there was no sign of a moon. The dummy sat in its wheel-chair. Out of the ground, out of the house, out of black sky flowed that mystic quality known as suspense.

Kane turned from the window. "All right," he said, "let's go."

Moe Finch looked up, blinking. "Huh? Where?"

"Why, hell—to nab your killer."

Moe Finch stared. He knew Kane. He knew Kane's methods, from way back in the old days when Kane had worked with him on Homicide.

"Lead on, shamus," Moe said softly. "You're not kidding!"

Kane opened the door and moved quietly into the hall, along the drab brown aisle of carpet to the stairs. Moe Finch took his cue from the big Beacon Agency dick and followed as soundlessly. The stairs creaked under them, but softly. At the end of the downstairs hall Kane opened the door to the kitchen.

It was dark there. Kane thrust a hand behind him to guide the Finch through a labyrinth of chairs, table, stove and refrigerator. He opened another door and the night air, damp and oppressive, closed over him like a tent as he stepped out onto the veranda. At the foot of the porch steps he paused.

"Well?" Moe Finch muttered. From where they stood, the front porch was hidden by the house. There was no faintest gleam of man-made light anywhere, nor whisper of sound other than the surflike sough of the wind in the trees.

"Stay here," Kane said. He dropped to his knees and went under the porch, and it was like crawling into a mine shaft. Weeds clammily caressed his face. Sharp stones gouged his hands and knees.

KANE HAD been here before. He crawled a dozen feet or so and slid a flashlight from his pocket, cupped the lens in his palm and aimed the glow around in a slow circle. That other time, he'd had to look hard. He'd had to push the stones and rubble aside with his fingers, baring the hard-packed ground.

Kane crawled to a bare space near the wall, where the earth was of a different color, freshly churned and slapped back into place. He began pawing at it.

At that moment Moe Finch let out a strangled yell of pain and surprise, and there were sounds of violent upheaval on the porch steps!

Kane flung himself around. His head banged the rotten boards above and for precious seconds a mist of colored lights blurred down to dim his vision. He cursed fluently, but the words were smothered by grunts and gasps and the turmoil of men thrashing about.

Kane stretched himself like a snake and won clear of the porch. He heaved to his knees, got no farther. A cyclone smashed into him. A hard and blunt bludgeon chopped at his head.

He whipped up his arms to protect his face and went over backward in a sprawling heap, with the cyclone raging on top of him. One thing he was reasonably sure of—his assailant had no gun. There'd been but one gun and that was buried under the porch.

But the animated hurricane had plenty else! Feet, fists and elbows, teeth and fingernails all were doing their damnedest to tear Kane's brains loose from his skull!

He doubled his legs and shot them out, out and up, with power enough to disembowel a horse.

The writhing creature dropped suddenly beside him, to be pinned instantly and effectively under Kane's big bulk. Once, twice he smacked out a fist, feeling his knuckles sink into squirming flesh. His assailant stopped wriggling. Kane fumbled for his flashlight and got up and stumbled over toward the porch steps, where lay the Finch.

A sorry sight, the Finch. The searching glow picked up his face through a glistening thread of blood that ran from his hair. He stirred as Kane bent over him. His hands went weakly to his head.

The Finch pushed up to his knees and leaned against Kane's legs, stopped groaning and began to swear. In a low, bitter voice, he plumbed the depths of a remarkable vocabulary.

"O.K.," Kane said. "You didn't know, Moe. I should have warned you, but I never dreamed.... Now look." He hauled the Finch erect and steered him around the porch. "Everything's under control and we've got the proof, mister. We've got every little thing—"

He was suddenly still, his gaze fixed on the fence at the far end of Dr. Enderson's property. For a fragment of a second the fence had leaped into gleaming relief, colored by the winking lights of a car creeping along the road beyond. The lights were out again. Their blink had been some sort of signal.

Kane stood rigid. He hadn't expected a car. He hadn't given a second's thought to the remote possibility that Kerry Conover's column might lure a killer into Moroni's theatrical trap. Now the thought occurred, icily, that he could have overlooked something.

He growled, "Wait here!" at Moe Finch and slipped soundlessly around the house-corner.

THE DUMMY sat in its wheel-chair on the front veranda, limned by the glow from the parlor window. Of Moroni and the Homicide men, nothing was visible. In low gear the car crept along the road and stopped. Someone got out of it and moved warily toward the fence. There was just light enough for Kane to follow the man's progress.

Kane prowled along the wall of the house, reached the veranda and stopped. He heard Moroni's voice whispering excitedly from a clump of Irish juniper less than ten feet away.

"That's him, Conover! You watch now. Get a load of this for that paper of yours. The minute he takes a shot at the dummy...."

That's right, Kane thought darkly. Get a load of it, Conover. Get a large load of Moroni, the Great Brain, so intent on his headline hunting that a guy named Peter Kane can prowl to within ten feet of him unawares. He heard Conover whisper something. Over across the yard, the man stood waiting at the fence, and suddenly winked a flashlight.

Moroni said hoarsely: "My God, he's got more than a gun! That thing under his arm, Conover! He used a bomb once before—or tried to—"

Kane plunged. A man's life hung on that plunge and it was an all-out effort. Head first, Kane crashed through the juniper and bowled Moroni over. Just in time. Just as Moroni's trigger finger tightened.

The shot went wild, but tore the night apart with its thunder. Kane yelled his lungs loose at the two Homicide men who came pouring out of hiding nearby.

"Hold it, you guys! Hold it!" The old ring of authority was in Kane's voice. "That man's no killer!"

The man at the fence made a dash for his car, and Kane's voice leaped out to snare him. "You! Wait! Wait, I tell you!"

The man stopped.

"Come in here," Kane yelled. "By the gate. No one'll hurt you, mister."

Moroni was up. His hand hit Kane's shoulder like a block of granite and spun Kane around. The face of the Great Brain was shapeless with fury. "By all that's holy, Kane, this time I'll—"

Kane stepped up to the man. "I'll take that, brother." He grabbed the package from under the fellow's arm. "Sit down now, until we're through. The lieutenant may want a word with you later." Gently he shoved the man toward the porch. "All right now, the rest of you guys come with me. Captain Finch wants you."

They trailed him around back. Moe Finch stood there, over the thing Kane had flattened. Kane handed his flashlight to one of the Homicide men. "You, Driscoll, crawl under the porch and bring out the clothes that are buried there. The clothes and the gun." He leered at Conover. "You getting all this, Conover? All the time Moroni's been chasing around with his dummy, Captain Finch has been quietly and efficiently doing his job. That would sound nice in print, friend. *Quietly and efficiently.*"

NO ONE said a word. The cop crawled out from under the porch with an armful of clothes and a revolver. He dropped the clothes and turned away, screwing up his nose. "Whew. This stuff stinks."

"Sure it stinks," Kane said. "That's why the killer had to bury it. Before Mr. Druitt died, he was sick. His shoes were a mess when we found him. His shoes, but not his pants. Maybe Lieutenant Moroni can be sick all over his shoes without getting his pants soiled, but most of us can't. So it was a cinch Druitt wasn't wearing those immaculate pants when he was shot. He was wearing other clothes— likely his own—and they were changed by the man who murdered him. Which meant he wasn't murdered by mistake, but on purpose. You getting this, Conover?"

The newsman dazedly nodded.

"It was an inside job, and the killer had to dispose of Druitt's clothes, which were none too sweet. I sniffed around the house and got nowhere. It was a cinch they'd been buried. Mr. Cully told me where."

Moroni said, "Huh?"

"We were looking for a mythical three hundred dollars," Kane murmured. "A short cut, friend, to save me the trouble of digging up the whole damned estate. Cully told me where to dig for the three hundred. Later I went to the one likely spot he hadn't suggested—here under the porch—and found what I wanted. And there," Kane said, pointing to the unconscious man at Moe Finch's feet, "is Cully."

Conover had begun to smell story and was trembling like a horse at the post.

"Here it is," Kane said. "Cully decides to kill Druitt. Writes himself letters and takes them to the cops. Plants a bomb in his apartment and pretends to find it in the nick of time. Acts scared, hires me to protect him, and comes here to hide. All this is build-up." He scowled at Conover. "You getting this?"

"Absolutely!"

"Right. The ground-work is laid. Cully's going to kill Druitt. It has to look like an accident. So Cully begins 'missing' things, insisting they're stolen. With that angle built up, he waits for the right moment. It comes when Druitt gets drunk and goes out for air. Cully slips out, gets between Druitt and the fence, fires the fatal shot when Druitt turns to go back to the house. It will look as though Druitt was shot from outside the fence.

"He takes off Druitt's clothes. He dresses the body in a suit of his own clothes. He plants the rest of his 'missing' things in Druitt's room. Why? So you birds will think exactly what you did think. But there were holes in it, as Captain Finch saw."

Kane paused. Conover had a pencil out now and was furiously scribbling notes by the light of a flash.

"First, there were no *other* stolen things in Druitt's room except the ones swiped from Cully. That was too pat. A kleptomaniac could run wild in this loony-lodge. He wouldn't be apt to steal solely from one room. Second, Cully should have removed those messy shoes from the corpse. That cooked him."

"So all right," Moroni growled. "So why does Cully murder the guy? You answer that one, you're so smart!"

"I wouldn't pretend to know," Kane said. "We could find out, maybe, by digging into a case history of the two of them, but there hasn't been time." He took a pail of water from Driscoll's hand and poured it over Cully's face. "Maybe he'll tell you. Personally I don't give a damn."

He turned away. Conover clutched at him. "That man in the car, Kane! That box under your arm...."

Kane smiled broadly for the first time in an hour. "Nectar," he murmured. "I was scared to death Moroni would blast the guy to bits and break the bottles." He patted the box lovingly. "Mr. Druitt's messenger didn't know Druitt was dead, of course."

He took Moe Finch's arm. They went upstairs to Kane's room. They were still there a couple of hours later when Kerry Conover knocked and entered.

"Well," Conover said, discreetly oblivious to the bottle and glasses, "well, Kane, he talked. Very ordinary motive, even if the method was superbly slick. He's in love with Druitt's wife. The wife sent Druitt here as part of the plan. Now about the credit for this job. I'd like to play up your work, Kane. I'd like—"

"Me?" said Kane, feigning amazement. "Me? Why, hell—Captain Finch did it all." He poured himself a generous potion of amber liquid and held it tenderly to his lips. "All I know," he murmured, "is what I'm going to read in the papers after the hangover."

KANE'S
OLD MAN

More than a good many gallons of high-powered whisky of one sort or another have gone down the hatch since that day last August when Peter Kane first saw the light and, with what was practically his first gesture, reached for the familiar square bottle. Up to now he has staggered his way through only four issues of Dime Detective *but already he has become a favorite character of you action-mystery fans. It's high time you got acquainted with the fond parent of this insatiable human tank.*

Meet Hugh B. Cave—the guilty party.

Here's what he's got to say for himself.

This is more painful than a book-length novel. A page to fill and mighty little to fill it with. You begin by being born and end by wondering why.

Began writing when I was fourteen or thereabouts. High School stuff and plenty terrible. Then college. Wrote godawful sonnets anent the Great Outdoors for a Boston newspaper… and got so doped with the idea that I went down Maine to see what the woods really looked like. Liked 'em so much I go back every Spring with a duffleful of fishing-tackle, home-made trout flies, and a bucket of fly-dope. Some day the black-flies will massacre me, to the huge delight of magazine readers everywhere.

Avocations: Photography in out-of-the-way places; fresh-water swimming with a partiality for Vermont's Lake St. Catherine; fishing of all kinds even to the goofiness of getting up at four A.M. on frosty mornings ; trying to worm the Chrysler through Maine lumber-roads and tote-roads intended for wild animals and garter-snakes. Also fire-fighting when drafted, Paul Whiteman, Edgar Arlington Robinson in small doses, and Popeye's pal Wimpy. Play a devastating game of ping-pong, can drink most anything except Martinis, and would drop work anytime to park in front of my electric phonograph and dig through the 500-odd recordings picked up over a space of ten years or so.

Have held down various odd jobs during a short lifetime. Bell-hop, dirty dish conveyor, showcard artist deluxe, blueprint salesman, editor of a string of trade journals now non-existent, and book-jacket designer. Some of the designs would give Frankenstein's monster the horrors. Also been a proof-reader, rewrite man, official slave in a book-publishing house, "literary editor," book reviewer, and a "Hey-why-don't-you-empty-this-wastebasket!" Mild life but dotted with high-spots, such as the day I tumbled off that log-boom into sixty-mile-an-hour white water on the Rip, all alone in a first-class wilderness. And the day of the thundersquall on Lake Harrington, when the Johnny with me was so plastered he tried to paddle the sinking canoe with a bait-bucket. And that day the drunk in the speakeasy took me for a State Copper because I was decked out in whipcord breeches and riding-boots. He was too soused to aim straight, but one of the two slugs from his thirty-eight reached the door before I did… and I can still see splinters flying.

They tell me I did a bit of traveling when a kid. Borneo, the South Seas, India and points adjacent. I wouldn't know for sure, but it may be true. Anyway, the pedal extremities do occasionally get restless even now.... And I go big for horse-back riding… and once in a while put a small so-so on some goat that looks "hot"… but if one of 'em ever came through I'd be too stunned to go collect.

Work best at night, and no complaints on that score because I'm still without wife. Began selling popular fiction in 1928 or thereabouts and have squeezed some hundreds of yarns past the editors since then… shorts, novelettes and complete novels. Kane's my favorite. I hope he lives long before he gets cirrhosis of the liver.

More power to Kane, say we, and may Cave never wean him from the bottle.

www.ingramcontent.com/pod-product-compliance
Lightning Source LLC
Chambersburg PA
CBHW020421030726
47495CB00006B/1606